THE DEBUT NOVELS

The Other Half

A highly promising debut. For anyone who has either been a wife or a mistress, *The Other Half* will certainly ring true. And for anyone who's been involved in a secret relationship or is considering an affair, this novel should be compulsory reading —**HEAT**

A wickedly funny ménage à trois —**Cosmopolitan**

British novelist Sarah Rayner has a talent for turning domestic tragedies (widowhood, infertility and, in this instance, adultery) into something quite special - amusing and astute studies in human resilience... An engaging, insightful portrait of infidelity, told with charm, Rayner plays it just right in the war zone of love —**Kirkus Reviews**

Getting Even

A MUST READ! —**The Sun**

Read this book! A bestseller without a doubt, this wickedly thrilling story will keep you amused and intrigued —**Bella Magazine**

If revenge is a dish best served cold, then this is surely the Nigella of cold-cuisine cookery books —**HEAT**

PRAISE FOR SARAH RAYNER'S NON-FICTION

Making Friends with Anxiety

Simple, lucid advice on how to accept your anxiety —**Matt Haig,**
Sunday Times bestselling author of *Reasons to Stay Alive*

Sarah's advice is very sage. Deeply personal, yet eminently practical, this accessible and engaging book should prove extremely helpful to anyone trying to cope with anxiety
—Dr Ian Williams, General Practitioner and author

Making Friends with Anxiety is a friend in itself. Reassuring, informative and written in a kind, inclusive tone that makes sense of everyday anxiety-provoking situations, I cannot recommend this book highly enough
—Josie Lloyd,
Sunday Times bestselling author of *The Cancer Women's Running Club*

Making Friends with the Menopause

★★★★★ Simply helpful! This book was really easy to read, no medical jargon to filter through, just condensed explanations. Really helpful for all women going through this transition, with lots of additional sources of support to access. —**Amazon Reviewer, 2022**

★★★★★ Great Book. This book has helped me understand that I am not alone and the symptoms I have are normal. There is light at the end of the tunnel. Highly recommend it, it gives you peace of mind
—Amazon Reviewer, 2022

Making Peace with Depression

★★★★★ A perfect book for people who feel controlled by depression: a superbly structured and well thought out guide to the issues involved – without the pages of dry theory or patronising dictates, or list of should-dos and unrealistic expectations to add to the overwhelm. *Making Friends with Depression* offers just the right amount of information to help you understand what's going on inside your brain and body, and ideas for how you can help yourself
—Leigh Forbes, author and publisher

BOOKS BY SARAH RAYNER

FICTION
One Moment, One Morning
The Two Week Wait
Another Night, Another day
The Other Half
Getting Even

NON-FICTION
Making Friends:
A series of warm, supportive guides to help you on life's journey

Making Friends with Anxiety
A warm, supportive little book to help ease worry and panic

Making Friends with the Menopause
A clear and comforting guide to support you as your body changes
With Dr Patrick Fitzgerald

Making Peace with Depression
A warm, supportive little book to lift low mood and ease despair
With Kate Harrison and Dr Patrick Fitzgerald

Making Friends with your Fertility
With Tracey Sainsbury

Making Peace with Divorce
With Pia Pasternack

MEMOIR
No More Tigers
A childhood memoir of a family who lived in colonial Burma,
and of what happened to them when World War II shattered their
lives Mary and Sarah Rayner

John Scott's Threads of Life
A unique collection of sewing advice, memories, mantras and more
from TV's favourite fashion guru

♩ ♫ ♪ ♩

Searching for Mr Yesterday

by

Sarah Rayner

2023
Creative Pumpkin Publishing

@Sarah Rayner 2023

Published by Creative Pumpkin Publishing 2023

An imprint of Creative Pumpkin Ltd

Sarah Rayner
Managing Director
Creative Pumpkin Ltd
5 Howard Terrace
Brighton BN1 3TR

Paperback ISBN: 978-1-7392132-3-7
eBook ISBN: 978-1-7392132-4-4
Audio ISBN: 978-1-7392132-5-1

Front cover image by: Engin Ayghurst @ Pexels CC0

Typeset in Gentium Plus 10.6pt/16pt by Blot Publishing
blot.co.uk

♩ ♫ ♪ ♩

About the Author

Sarah Rayner is the British author of five novels including the international bestseller, *One Moment, One Morning* and the *Making Friends* series of non-fiction books. She has sold over 750,000 books worldwide, and her works have been translated into 20 languages including Chinese, Japanese, Russian, German and Spanish.

Sarah was born in London, went to university in Yorkshire, and for the last twenty years has lived in Brighton, England, a seaside city known for its colourful past, sexually liberal attitudes and having the UK's only Green MP. She and her husband, Tom, a chef, helped care for Sarah's mother, Mary Rayner, a children's author and illustrator until she passed away in February 2023.

Sarah also has her own independent press,
www.creativepumpkinpublishing.com,
and her two most recent publications are this novel, and *John Scott's Threads of Life*, which can both be bought from her author website,
https://www.sarahrayner.com/shop/.
Sarah recently published her mother's memoir, NO MORE TIGERS, which can also be ordered through her author website,
https://www.sarahrayner.com/shop/
or via Amazon. Her website is for signed copies only. All her published books are listed on Amazon worldwide, and if you live outside the UK, you will probably find the best prices and fastest delivery via Amazon

♩ ♫ ♪ ♩

or another major online retailer.

You can hook up with Sarah via her author website,

www.sarahrayner.com

Through the website, you can sign up for her mailing list to receive her *Making Friends* magazine with a free short story and mood-boosting guide. You'll also find her on social media. She founded several online support groups including *Making Friends with Anxiety and Depression* and *Making Friends with the Menopause* on Facebook. Her latest updates can be found here:

Instagram @thecreativepumpkin
Facebook www.facebook.com/creativepumpkin
TicToc @thecreativepumpkin
YouTube @sarahrayner814

♩ ♫ ♪ ♩

1.

It lands on the doormat without fanfare.

Suzy is peering out of the kitchen window, checking for the hearse. She is aware of the squeak of the gate and the flap of the letterbox, but it's her son, Cameron, bounding down the stairs, two at a time, who picks up the letters from the hall.

'There's post,' he says.

Absent-mindedly, Suzy takes it from him, thinking how weird it is to see Cam in a suit, clean shaven and sandy curls dampened down in a vain attempt to look tidy. She is about to drop the letters onto the hall table when an envelope on the top of the pile catches her eye. *I recognise that handwriting*, she thinks, though where from she could not say.

Curious, she tears open the envelope. A clear plastic sleeve slips to the floor. She retrieves it, mystified. It's a disc. One side gleams silver like a mirror, and when she turns it, a spectrum of colours shines back at her, radiating green, violet, cerise, orange. The other side is plain white, matt. On it is written:

For Suze.

There is a note, but she has no hope of reading it without her glasses. Spidery writing dances before her, maddeningly out of focus.

The car is not even late, she reminds herself.

1

♩ ♫ ♪ ♩

At last, there is the deep throb of an engine. Cam opens the front door.

'Ready, Mum?'

Suzy smooths her skirt and checks around the cottage; teacups stacked high on the sideboard, sandwiches covered in clingfilm, biscuits and fairy-cakes made by her elderly neighbour, Doreen. Emotion rises in her throat. I mustn't cry, she tells herself. Not yet, or I'll smudge my make-up.

Somehow, she manages to sit for the car journey, a crawl at best, then walk up the aisle of the church, past a sea of faces, eyes brimming with sympathy, to the pew at the front by the coffin, lid splayed with lilies, a safe choice, traditional, respectful, perfectly suited to Joan. Strange to think that all that remains of her mother, for so many decades such a formidable physical presence, is encased in this box of polished wood with brass handles. The force of her personality, an entire lifespan of memories and moods, the body that housed her, is before them, small and silent and hidden from sight. Then she, Joan, will be buried deep in the ground, alongside her husband, Ken. Gone.

The organist strikes up *The Lord is My Shepherd* and many in the congregation hesitate, wondering if they are meant to stand. It's Doreen who rises and starts singing; belatedly others catch on, voices thin and reedy. It is only then Suzy realises she is still clutching the CD and note, knuckles white with tension. At least now she has time to rummage in her handbag and retrieve her glasses. Surreptitiously, she unfolds the piece of paper...

And all at once Suzy knows why she recognised the handwriting. Her fingers tremble as she tries to hold the letter steady, yet the paper flaps like a moth beating against a lampshade.

Dear Suze, she reads. There's only one person who ever called me that, she thinks. This can't be from him.

'I've just heard about your mum, and now seems a good opportunity to say I'm truly sorry, sorry about everything...'

It *is* from him. *Johnny.* Her first boyfriend, who she knew as a kid, who she learned to ride a bike with, played hide and seek with, grew up with. *Johnny*, who she fell in love with as a teenager, and who she loved so deeply, so passionately, it was as if he was part of her. *Johnny*, who she has not seen for nearly 25 years.

2.

During the wake, Suzy slips into the downstairs loo to read Johnny's letter for a second time.

This address came up as your studio on Google, and my mum is still friends with Rita from number 36, who told us. Your mother was a real character—she didn't mince her words. What she thought about your outfit when we went to Hammersmith Odeon to see Bowie. Remember?

As if I can ever forget, thinks Suzy.

I can't count how often I almost came to see you, how many notes I wrote and threw away, after what happened. Even all these years later, I'm struggling to find the words, but back then, I was at such a loss, I made you a tape of songs I knew you liked, only you left London before I got to give it to you.

I came across the cassette recently at Park Road. Dad's stereo with a tape deck is still going strong, so I played it and, God, it took me back. They're such great tracks, I burned them onto this CD. I thought you might like to give it a listen, so here it is, only about three decades late!!

Love, Johnny

She peers at the neatly written words in Johnny's familiar hand. Each letter distinct from the other, often not fully joined up, so utterly different from her own. He's put the titles in a circle on the back of the

♩ ♫ ♪ ♩   4

CD, and the years the songs were released, capturing a great chunk of her life in a succession of songs. He always loved music, she thinks. But to get this, now, she is awash with emotion.

David Bowie: Starman 1972
David Bowie: Rock 'n' Roll Suicide 1972
The Sex Pistols: God Save the Queen 1977
Blondie: Hanging on the Telephone 1979
The Beatles: Come Together 1969
Leonard Cohen: Suzanne 1967
Siouxsie & The Banshees: Spellbound 1981
The Shangri-Las: Leader of the Pack 1964
The New Order: Blue Monday 1983
Frankie Goes to Hollywood: Two Tribes 1984
Soul II Soul: Back to Life 1989
Sade: Your Love is King 1984

'Mum? You OK?' Cameron is knocking on the door, jolting her back to the present.

She raises her voice. 'Oh, er, yes, sorry. Her head is spinning. She can hear the songs in her head, without even playing the CD. '*Spellbound, spellbound... cracking through the walls, it sends me spinning, I have no choice...*' Or something like that, she was never exactly sure of the words. But my, how she loved her gothic namesake, Siouxsie, and this was her favourite Banshees song to dance to when she was out clubbing. '*Woah, Woah, Woah...*'

'You've been in there for ages.'

Suzy gets to her feet, splashes her face with water, unlocks the bathroom door. 'Sorry.'

Debs, her neighbour, is outside with him. 'You OK pet?'

'Mm,' says Suzy, not certain if she is.

'They've nearly all gone,' Cam reassures her, voice low.

As Suzy bids farewell to the last of the guests, Debs gathers up the dirty crockery and together they head to the kitchen.

'Are you sure the funeral was OK?' asks Suzy, trying to force Johnny from her mind by tipping dirty water from the washing-up bowl into the sink. Then she can start anew.

Debs picks up a tea towel. 'It's what your mam would have wanted.'

'Mm.' Any conversations Suzy overheard at the wake sounded stiff and polite, but then she pictures the church. 'There were *lots* of people. Whoever would have guessed? For my mum!'

Debs thwacks the side of her head. 'Er... Doh! I think most were there for you and Cam.'

'Oh?'

'It's hardly as if Joan knew anyone much round here.'

'True...' Suzy stops and swirls the water. Then, all at once, she is crying. Tears plop onto her blouse, her nose is running. She lifts an elbow and sobs into her sleeve to muffle the noise, but it seems she can't stop.

Initially the changes were imperceptible, diminishing her mother by degrees, like the sea eroding a cliff. Gradually the ground shifted. Gone were shades of grey. In their stead black moods, full of fury: 'GET OUT OF MY WAY!' and bursts of uncharacteristic appreciation, when her mum would smile and call Suzy her 'angel daughter'. In between were vast tracts of silence or confusion.

Presently she sees Debs is passing her a paper napkin. Suzy sniffs and wipes her eyes. 'Sorry.'

Debs smiles at her gently. 'No need to apologise. It's been awful for you.'

Doreen returns to the room and checks around. The jugs and mugs are hanging from their hooks on the dresser, the surfaces wiped, the tea towels draped over the steel rod of the aga to dry. She nods approvingly and zips up her tomato-coloured puffa. 'Looks as if you're almost done.'

Suzy dries her hands. 'Thanks ever so much.' She reaches for her elderly neighbour, yet Doreen remains rigid in her embrace, resisting intimacy.

'You sure you're alright dropping those back tonight?' Doreen jerks her chin at the mounting towers of white porcelain.

Suzy has been on her feet since dawn, so when Debs says, 'Rich has the car this evening, but I can whizz them back in the morning,' she wants to hug her. Moreover, she knows Debs is likely to hug her tightly back, going 'Ooh pet!' as she often does. Suzy knew from the moment she saw the removal men unloading a faux leopard skin chaise longue they would get on. Now *that*, she'd thought, admiring Debs' assertiveness as she barked orders in a strong Geordie accent, is exactly the antidote to Farrow & Ball this West Country village needs.

Doreen sucks in air through her teeth. 'The History Group will want them tonight...' Doreen can be a pain, but she means well.

Suzy struggles to mask a yawn. 'It's OK, I'll do it.'

Once Doreen has gone, Debs asks, 'I hope you're going to take it easy later?'

'I shall,' Suzy assures her. Although I'm not sure I remember how to, she thinks. I've been up every night for months, and it is eons since I dared leave Mum alone. Not since I came home from the supermarket to find downstairs full of smoke, a blackened saucepan on the gas ring, an empty can of minestrone beside it and Mum, oblivious, watching Bargain Hunt on the telly. She shudders at the memory.

'It's not every daughter who'd have their elderly mother come and live with them,' Debs continues, carefully placing the saucers into the box on the table.

'I had the room,' says Suzy.

'You didn't even *like* your mother!' observes Debs.

'That's a bit strong.'

Debs doesn't understand, thinks Suzy. I *owed* my mum. She and Dad looked after me when I was at my lowest, long after most children have left home. My parents were far from perfect, but without them... It doesn't bear thinking about.

Debs turns to fix her gaze on Suzy. "She's a narrow-minded, stubborn old cow." It's what you said when I met you. She moved in around the same time we did, the summer of the London Olympics.'

'2012... Was it really?'

'I can't believe you've coped for so long. Over five years! Promise me, you'll take some time for *you*?'

'Yes, yes.' Suzy turns to her friend. Debs' lipstick is long gone, her auburn hair in even more disarray than usual. 'You've helped more than enough though. Go home. I can manage the rest.'

It is still drizzling when Suzy loads the two boxes of crockery into the boot of the car. The smell of autumn is in the air: damp moss and rotting leaves and wood fires burning in homes nearby. She lets out a heavy breath, relieved the day is nearly done, and edges behind the wheel. She is about to start the ignition, when she has the strangest sense Johnny is beside her, long legs crammed into the well between the passenger seat and the dashboard of her ancient hatchback, unkempt brown hair brushing the roof.

'You did well today,' she imagines him saying, turning to squeeze her hand as she rests it on the gearstick. He is looking at her with those big brown eyes she found so beautiful, his smile tender.

She turns the key and there is a cough, as if her hatchback is clearing its throat before speaking, and the radio buzzes loud with static. With a pathetic splutter, the engine dies. She turns the key again. Nothing. She checks the switch by the steering wheel. Sure enough, it's on.

'ARGH!' She kicks the clutch. Bloody Cam! He must have forgotten to turn off the headlights after driving her car the night before. Rain is thundering on the windscreen, nonetheless, she hauls herself back outside.

The flat battery can wait until tomorrow, but the crockery can't. Nothing else for it, she decides. I'll have to carry the boxes. She picks one up and her back twinges in protest. She can't possibly manage both. It'll take two trips. She is only wearing a cardigan over her top and her suede pumps, whilst appropriate for a funeral, are not designed for heavy rain. Yet returning to the cottage for more practical clothing would be a faff, so she staggers down the drive, the contents of the box clinking against her midriff. Her hair and face are drenched in seconds. Soon her teeth are chattering from the wet and the cold.

I'll have a bath when I'm home, she tells herself. Listen to that CD. Relax, like Debs suggested.

The lane uphill to the church is narrow. There is no room for a pavement, but the streetlights glow red in the dusk, half guiding her way. After so many years in Wiltshire, Suzy knows every brick wall and beech hedge between her tiny, thatched cottage and the top of the village. The wide sweep of tarmac leading to the housing estate erected in the aftermath of the second world war where Doreen lives; the postcard-pretty homes which surround the village green with its duck pond and reed beds; the pub with its trampled lawn and rickety wooden tables where Cam likes to drink with his mates. As she approaches the T-junction by the vicarage, she takes care to keep on the verge, but the grass is sodden, the soles of her shoes slippery...

Suddenly, there is the SWOOSH of tyres through water and a dazzling beam of light. She feels herself slide and her heart lurches with the fear of falling in the dark and alone. It is as if her senses decelerate, and everything happens in slow motion. Instinctively she wants to lift her arm to protect against the glare but doesn't because she must NOT drop the teacups. They would smash and Doreen would never forgive her.

There is a screech of brakes...

The sound of skidding...

A crunch...

Pain shoots up her body.

Then she blacks out.

♩ ♫ ♪ ♩

3.

Slowly, Suzy opens her eyes. At once she closes them again. The strip light overhead is too bright. Her head is thumping, she feels sick.

'It's OK...' says a woman's voice. 'Suzy?'

The smells are unfamiliar—detergent mingled with disinfectant—and the sheets feel alien. Suzy senses a hand on hers.

'Hey... It's me...'

Suzy is being stroked, light fingertips on the back of her hand.

'She's coming round,' says another woman, voice brisk. 'Bound to be disorientated.' Suzy feels warm breath on her face, catches a whiff of stale coffee. 'Hello, Suzy, I'm Nurse Thomas.' Suzy tries to roll away. The nurse is speaking too loudly. 'It's good to see you awake. You're in hospital.'

Suzy struggles to respond but it is as if her larynx is clogged by glue.

'Thank goodness,' says a third person, younger, male. It is someone Suzy knows well, but who...? Her brain hurts as she tries to piece things together. 'Mu-um...' His voice cracks with distress.

Suzy forces her eyelids open against the glare and the familiar figure of her son comes into focus. *Cameron.* He is standing over her, beanpole tall, clothes crumpled and face in even more need of a shave than is customary.

'Hi,' she says weakly.

'Mum! You gave us a real scare.' His expression drawn and anxious.

'I'm sorry, love.' She can only raise a whisper.

He pauses, then says, 'Do you know what happened?'

'Er...' Suzy searches to make the connections. Then, in a rush, memories pile in. A crunch, a judder, louder than thunder, a splitting and shattering. Abruptly the music had stopped, the lights gone out... The world about her had turned on its axis and she had slipped, the grip of her shoes useless... There had been shouting, screaming, panic... And water, freezing water, colder than any ocean.

'You were in an accident last night,' interjects the nurse.

'Ah.' Suzy gives a brief nod. This explains it. She tries to get a better look at Nurse Thomas, but she is silhouetted against the window.

'Hit by a car,' says Cam.

The nurse pulls a curtain around Suzy's bed to shield her from the rest of the ward. 'I need to take your blood pressure. OK?'

The woman at her side stops stroking to allow the nurse to clip a device to Suzy's finger. Surely, I wouldn't forget her incredible hair, thinks Suzy. What's the word? It's not simply red, it's—? Try as she might, she cannot recollect. Her memory is full of holes. Johnny, she thinks, he was there... She can sense his presence, yet there is no sign of him. She raises her other hand to her face, keen to establish that she herself is real. My cheeks are wet, she notices. Have I been crying? She shakes her head, trying to jolt herself back to reality. It only makes the inside of her skull thump harder. None of this is making any sense.

'You were knocked down at the top of Bartholomew Lane,' adds her son. 'Near the village hall. Some arsehole in a SUV.'

The woman with the reddish hair turns to Cam. 'I don't think he was a *total* arsehole. He called 999 straight away.'

'Hmph,' says Cam. 'He was driving too fast, if you ask me. The T-junction is poorly lit and everyone in Amhurst knows it. He should have been more bloody careful.'

He sounds angry, thinks Suzy. His language is worse than usual. But I don't recall a car. Increasingly bewildered, she shifts her gaze to the woman at her bedside. 'What about the others?'

'There weren't any others.' The woman's profile is distinctive, yet

11 ♩ ♫ ♪ ♩

still Suzy cannot place her. She scours her memories. *I was with dozens of people. I'm sure of it. All shouting, terrified. Crying out for help.*

'There was a big group of us...' Suzy murmurs.

The woman frowns. 'You were taking the teacups back.'

'And I'm afraid your ankle is fractured,' interjects the nurse. Goodness, her voice is loud! Suzy longs to tell her to pipe down. Her head is throbbing.

'You've been badly concussed,' says Cam. 'You were out for hours.'

It's too much to take in. Her surroundings—the blue curtains, the beds full of other patients, the steamed-up windows, the grey vinyl floor—fold in like a giant envelope, and she cannot process any more.

When Suzy wakes again, it's dark outside. The fluorescent light is buzzing overhead and the TV on a nearby stand is on, volume low. The curvy woman with—aah—*auburn* hair has gone. So has the nurse. Only Cameron remains, slumbering in the vinyl-upholstered armchair beside her, snoring faintly. As Suzy edges herself more upright, the starched sheets rustle, and he jerks awake.

'I thought you were asleep,' he says, bleary. The tatty parka he has pulled up to his neck as a makeshift blanket, slides to the floor.

'You were snoring.'

'Sorry.' He grimaces.

'Could you... um... pass me a glass of water?' Suzy's throat is dry and sore.

She watches him pour, plastic jug to plastic tumbler, then she takes it and, with an effort, swallows. Her fingers tremble as she hands it back. It reminds her of her mother, being this shaky.

'Better?'

She nods, touched at Cam's concern.

'I've been thinking,' he says, voice low so as not to disturb others on the ward. 'The consultant said your ankle will be in plaster for six to seven weeks. You may well be on crutches for even longer.'

She checks the far end of the bed. So *that's* what's throbbing. Even through the cast, it's painful. Gradually she is piecing together what happened. Yet it seems no sooner is one element put in place, than another problem rises in its stead. Oh God, she panics, sobered by the implications. I was planning to do new paintings for that gallery in Bath... The light for my easel is best in the living room, but it's impossible with a hospital bed taking up half the space... She pictures herself in it, one invalid replacing another, and winces.

'You could stay with us for a bit, Mum,' Cam continues.

'NO!'

Her son looks shocked, then hurt.

'Sorry, darling. I didn't mean to snap.' But the idea of being stuck in a poky flat with Cam and his girlfriend is dreadful. Her son has a gift for looking after people—it's what makes him a good primary teacher —nonetheless, Suzy would feel horribly in the way. And she *hates* London. Especially where he is, close to the centre. Being trapped in a block shared with strangers—ugh. '*You can't see the edges,*' she'd wanted to say when he and Alice had settled in Battersea. '*How can you live in a place with building after building as far as the eye can see?*' Suzy has declined many invitations to visit, using her mother's dependency on her as an excuse. In truth, she couldn't bear to be anywhere she couldn't escape from. The sense of confinement, being locked in... She *had* to be able to rest her eyes on hills and woods and acres of green. In Wiltshire there are more sheep than people, and that's how Suzy likes it. She finds it hard to imagine she had lived nearby, in Clapham, when she was Cam's age and loved it. But there is a world of difference between being 55 and 25, she reminds herself. Cam needs to spread his wings and experience a life other than in a village in the countryside.

'I'll be fine at the cottage,' she assures him.

'Who'll look after you?' he persists.

'I'll look after myself. And I'm sure—' Darn it, the redhead's name is not forthcoming. It's as if Suzy's mind is a car boot sale full of junk;

13

most of its contents are of no use to her. With a Herculean effort, she yanks it free. '—*Debs* can give me a hand if need be.'

'I love Debs – she's a corker of a mate—pretty too, if you ask me.'

I didn't, thinks Suzy, smothering a smile. Her son knows how to charm women, myself included.

'But isn't that a heck of a lot to ask of a neighbour? If you came to us, Alice would be around in the day as she works odd hours, and I'd be home after school every evening. About four. Won't you at least think about it?'

'I shall,' says Suzy, knowing full well she won't. 'Thank you.'

It's pitch-black. Freezing. Suzy is being churned round and around underwater, powerless against the current and the waves, desperate for air. For a second, she gets her head above the surface and gasps, gulps in oxygen, but then another great, grey wave sucks her towards it and breaks across her like a sack of stones, bouncing her down so deep her ears pop. She swallows water, tries not to breathe it in but her ribs are about to burst. Then pain blooms at the top of her chest, spreading downwards and inwards. That's my lungs giving out, she thinks.

She wakes with a lurch, pouring sweat to find Debs at her side.

'You alright?'

Suzy is shaking from head to foot, teeth chattering, clack-clack-clack, like a wind-up toy.

'Here, pet. Let me help you. This should do it.' Debs picks up a remote, presses a button and slowly the mattress tilts until Suzy is sitting. 'Deep breaths...' Debs inhales and exhales to demonstrate. 'Trick I learned a while back.'

Suzy follows her example. Little by little, her shivering subsides. 'Thank you.' She gives Debs a wan smile.

'You poor thing.' Debs perches on the arm of the vinyl-upholstered chair. 'Nightmare?'

'I keep having them.' Suzy swallows. She is growing afraid of falling asleep.

♩ ♫ ♪ ♩   14

'It's probably an after-effect of the accident.' Debs' features crumple with concern.

It's not that, thinks Suzy. I've had flashbacks like this before.

There is a cough.

'Excuse me, Mrs Hope?' It's the orthopaedic specialist, Dr Schiller, clipboard in hand. 'I gather you're going home today?' Dr Schiller nods at Suzy. She appears around Suzy's age but there the similarity ends. Her face is heavily lined and pinched looking, her manner confident to the point of self-righteous.

'You're very quick to be discharging her,' says Debs.

'I'm afraid we need the bed.' Dr Schiller purses her lips, whether in embarrassment or irritation is unclear. 'And you must be...' She consults her notes. 'Deborah?'

'Call me Debs,' says Debs.

'Will someone be with Mrs Hope for the next 48 hours?'

'Me.'

'She mustn't be left alone.'

'I live next door and I work from home, so I can take my laptop to hers. OK?'

'Look out for any problems such as changes in Mrs Hope's behaviour or difficulty concentrating. Alright, um... Debs?'

'I should be able to manage that,' says Debs, voice laden with irony.

Suzy smothers a smile. *Underestimate Debs at your peril,* she thinks. But Dr Schiller merely nods. 'Remember, get plenty of rest, and you're not to put any weight on that foot.'

As if I'll be tempted to, thinks Suzy. *It's agony.*

'This is so good of you,' says Suzy, as they drive back to Amhurst in Debs' sleek silver BMW.

'PISH! Least I could do.' Debs turns her attention from the road to flash Suzy a smile. Debs' freckles are more visible in the sunlight, and her auburn hair gleams almost purple. The Pre-Raphaelites would have admired her, thinks Suzy. Or maybe *I* should paint her. It's been ages since I've done a portrait... Fleetingly, she recalls the aspirations she'd had as a young woman. I could have been an artist vying for space against Tracey Emin or Damien Hirst at Tate Modern, she thinks, then tells herself not to be so ridiculous. In comparison, the income she makes from her own artistic endeavours is pathetic.

She flips down the passenger visor and peers into the mirror.

'Ugh.'

Suzy's hair is fine and flyaway, but if she fluffs it up and uses the right products, it can look OK. She is lucky it is so fair that it masks any grey. Her skin is pale too, but blusher and lipstick can make up for what nature failed to provide and Suzy is a dab hand with both. Whilst she has only been called *beautiful* a handful of times, she has an individual style of which she remains proud. 'I told Alice you're a bit of a rock chick,' Cam had said prior to introducing the two of them, and Suzy had been flattered. Usually, she believes that she hasn't aged too badly, but today, with no make-up on and pallid from lack of sunshine, she feels far older than her 55 years.

Debs seems to read her mind. 'You look fine.'

'I do not.'

'No one appears their best after a fortnight in hospital.'

Gosh, was it that long? It is a relief to be out of the wretched place. And it *is* a lovely day.

She leans her head against the window, absorbing the gentle sweep of the chalk downs. Clouds skid across the sky creating shadows on the hills and, as they turn into the lane to the village, the sun blasts through the russet leaves of the avenue of chestnut trees, flickering bright then dark, bright then dark. Suzy closes her eyes against the strobe effect and at once she is back on a dance floor...

There is Tash, shimmying and swirling and twirling her fingers like a South London Mata Hari. Stef, pale limbs glistening with sweat, arms raised, pumping the ceiling in time to the track. And Nate, gorgeous golden boy that he was back then, cigarette bobbing in accompaniment to the disco lights, pupils wide with wonder at the beauty of the universe, grinning as if he is about to burst with E-induced bonhomie...

When she opens her eyes, Suzy is relieved to see the WELCOME TO AMHURST sign. It's only my mind playing tricks, she tells herself. Nonetheless, she can't shake the sense that she is straddling a timeline, where the past is pulling in one direction and the present in another, so she no longer knows what's real. I can't even put weight on both feet, she thinks. No wonder I feel so untethered. Her thoughts seem to have fractured along with her ankle, leaving her flailing like an autumn leaf caught in the breeze, whirling, fragile and ephemeral.

♩ ♫ ♪ ♩

4.

At the sound of the key in the lock, Suzy's little black cat comes running down the stairs to greet them.

'Patience Pushkin,' says Suzy, propping her crutches and edging with difficulty into a chair at the ancient pine table. 'We'll feed you in a sec.'

She falls silent, half watching as Debs makes her way around the kitchen, opening and shutting cupboard doors. But Suzy is thinking of the CD; for the life of her, she cannot recall where she left it.

Eventually Debs throws her hands in the air. 'I give up. Where *do* you keep the cat food?'

'In there.' Suzy points under the sink.

'Ah.' Debs squeezes the contents of a sachet into Pushkin's bowl. 'My, she was hungry!' she says, as Pushkin guzzles it down with such fervour that she propels the bowl along the stone tiled floor. 'I fed her this morning, I promise.'

Suzy smiles. 'She's a greedy girl, isn't she? My little barrel.' Pushkin responds to her voice and jumps up on the table, encouraging Suzy to stroke her.

'I'll make us some supper,' says Debs.

'Don't be daft. Just microwave something,' says Suzy.

'I'll do no such thing.'

An hour later Debs has made a large pan of soup from vegetables heading past their best in Suzy's fridge and it is bubbling gently on top of the stove, steaming up the windows.

'You OK if I nip home, say hi to Rich, check my work emails? I won't be long.'

'Of course!' replies Suzy. 'Don't rush, I'm fine.'

The moment she hears the front door close, Suzy reaches for her crutches. *'No weight on that ankle!'* Dr Schiller be damned. What a vile doctor she was. Now Suzy has taken Gabapentin, if she is careful, she can push herself to standing and manoeuvre around the ground floor. The pain she can manage, but the time leading leading up to her accident is a blur. She scans the kitchen, the living room, at a loss. It's only when she goes to the loo that she discovers the envelope, by the sink, with the CD and note still inside. If she can just find something to play it on...

Again, she is stymied. These days everything is digital; anyone can listen to anything, on any number of different devices. Suzy is hardly one for cutting edge technology, nonetheless she has all her playlists on Spotify; she listens to music on her phone, on the kitchen radio via Blue Tooth, and, in the living room, via a decent wireless speaker. The disc taunts her through its clear plastic sleeve. None of these are any help.

She is about to give up when her eyes land on her laptop. It's ancient, and, lo! It has a CD Rom drive. The computer takes forever to warm up. Finally, Suzy inserts the disc and holds her breath. For a few seconds she thinks it isn't working. The music at the start is so soft and gentle.

'Hey la-la
Oh, oh, oh...'

The sound is terrible; tinny and thin but doesn't matter.

The moment she hears Bowie's voice, her heart soars. Of course, Johnny would kick off with this track. *Starman* was their favourite song on *Ziggy Stardust and the Spiders from Mars*. It was so catchy, so uplifting, and its lyrics made her feel as if the whole universe was within her grasp. In a just a few chords she has rolled back time.

19

They are in her bedroom. Even indoors, it is hot, sticky.

'Ooh, look at him!' Johnny's older sister, Flo, is holding out *Jackie* magazine, so excited she is almost hyperventilating. 'Isn't he dreamy?'

'He looks like a girl.' Johnny wipes snot off his nose with the back of his hand, jabs the centrefold. 'He's wearing nail polish, see?'

'I know! Like mine!' Flo waggles silver-tipped fingers. 'I did them specially.' Flo might be fifteen, but she hasn't quite got the knack. The polish is blobby and smudged. Even so Suzy longs to paint her nails too. Or would, if they weren't bitten to the quick.

Johnny sniffs. '*And* he's wearing make-up.'

'I thought you liked him. You don't have to come if you don't want,' Flo threatens. 'I wouldn't 'v got you tickets otherwise. Keith and I had to queue for ages.'

'Dad said I could go 'cos I like his songs,' says Johnny. He thrusts out his chest and bellows: "There's a starman waiting in the sky..."'

'Ouch!' Flo puts her fingers in her ears.

Suzy is panicked. This is *David Bowie* they're talking about. 'We really want to see him, don't we Johnny?'

'Maybe you're both too young...' Flo flicks the pink paper tickets, enjoying winding them up.

'We are not!' Johnny glares at his sister. 'Mum said you'll look after us.' They have never been to a pop concert before and the prospect is so scary and exhilarating, all weekend Johnny and Suzy have been bouncing from one adrenalized game to another: bike racing, swingball, badminton, unable to settle.

'You need to change,' Flo declares.

Suzy glances at Johnny—his shirt is smeared with bright orange from the tinned spaghetti hoops he had for lunch. She looks down at herself—the knees of her jeans are mud stained. Flo, in her embroidered white waistcoat and flares, hair flicked and held with hairspray, appears far more grown-up. She has had her ears pierced and wears a bra. Plus, she has a *boyfriend*, Keith, who is seventeen. Johnny's parents are so cool, allowing Flo to take us, she thinks. My mum and dad are far too stuffy.

Johnny was in the same class at school, Suzy recalls, but he used to sit at the back, play the joker. Her dad nicknamed him *The Artful Dodger*, rather suited him. His dark hair stood up at odd angles had these big doleful eyes, a bit like the boy in the film, *Oliver*. Jack London, the actor was called. Johnny was permanently dishevelled; from dawn to dusk he looked in need of a hairbrush, clean clothes. Yet he was mischievous and used to get away with all sorts.

Right from when she was small, her father used to tease her. "Off to see your boyfriend?" and Suzy would get stroppy and say, "Johnny is not my boyfriend!" Back then she was far more interested in his *Rice Crispies* climbing frame, she recalls. So-called because it was advertised on the back of a cereal packet.

I was always at number 32, she thinks, and no wonder. When Suzy pictures her own childhood home it is brightly lit and dust-free. Every item in its place: tinned foods carefully stacked in cupboards, leftovers snapped into Tupperware boxes, clothes ironed and put away. As an only child, she was lonely, often bored. Whereas the Brown's house opposite was huge and chaotic, with nooks and crannies everywhere. They had holey carpets covered in Bohemian rugs and the hall and staircase were wallpapered in a William Morris design of peacocks and dragons right the way up to the attic, and the floor of Johnny's room was always covered in part-assembled Airfix models, bits of Lego and scattered dressing-up clothes. He never seemed to have to tidy anything up, but then neither did his parents. There were books and magazines and newspapers lying on every conceivable surface. It was the perfect place to make dens and play hide and seek with the other kids from their street. If she closes her eyes, Suzy can still hear the shrieking and laughter.

As a kid, Johnny seemed able to wind Mum round his little finger in a way I never could, reflects Suzy. She can almost hear Johnny saying, 'Chocolate is my *favourite*, Mrs Hope,' and sighing, '*My* mum never makes cakes,' as if he was on the verge of malnourishment. Joan would brush off his flattery, but Suzy could see she was delighted at outstripping Pat on the culinary front, and Johnny would plead with those puppy-dog eyes, 'Would you mind awfully if I had another slice?'

Whereas if *I'd* done that, Suzy thinks crossly, Mum would have told me I was greedy or getting fat. Her mother... Suzy lets out a long breath.

Remember what she thought of your outfit? Johnny had my mother sussed, thinks Suzy. Even then, Joan could be brutal.

Flo grins. 'See what I brought.' She shakes out a small item of clothing she has scrunched up in her hand.

At once Suzy recognises the faded pink denim. 'Can I really?'

Flo nods. 'Too small for me.'

Scarcely able to believe her good fortune, Suzy turns the hot pants, wide-eyed. They have brass buttons up the front and an appliqué rainbow stitched on the back pocket. 'Wow!' She holds them against herself before her bedroom mirror.

By the time they are ready, Flo has even shown Suzy how to use mascara and put blue eyeshadow on her lids using a sponge applicator.

In the hall, Suzy's mother takes one look and says, 'Suzanne, you are NOT going out like that! You've got make up on.'

'But Mrs H—we're going to see *David*,' Flo protests.

'And those are far too short!'

Suzy is crestfallen.

'They used to be Flo's.' Johnny points out with equanimity. 'Our mum lets her wear them.' He gives Joan his most persuasive smile.

Joan purses her lips. Suzy can tell she is weighing it up. Then she turns back to her daughter. 'Go upstairs and put your jeans on.'

'They're dirty,' Suzy mumbles.

'I don't care what state they're in. They're more decent than those. All that leg!' Then she leans forward and slaps Suzy's thigh, hard.

Suzy's eyes fill with tears. She glances at Flo and Johnny: their mouths are agape. *Their* mum would never be like this, Suzy is keenly aware. Pat differs completely; she smokes roll-up cigarettes and writes for a newspaper, exciting things like that. She can be distracted and more than once has forgotten to give Johnny his dinner money, but she allows lots of kids to treat their house as a second home and is kind.

I will *not* cry, Suzy tells herself, and runs upstairs to change.

Minutes later, when they are heading across the park to meet Keith, Flo says to Johnny, 'You wait here,' then beckons Suzy behind some bushes. She flashes a grin. 'Look what I sneaked.'

She wiggles something from her front pocket. A pair of silver nail scissors glint in the sun.

'Stand straight,' she orders.

'Why?'

Before Suzy has time to object, Flo folds a tiny pleat in Suzy's jeans, only inches below her crotch, and cuts across to make a hole. Then, with great concentration, she starts to snip, snip, snip. She continues right round one leg, then the other. The blades are tiny and blunted from use but eventually two columns of denim fall round Suzy ankles.

'Et voila!' says Flo, in what Suzy thinks might be French.

Suzy steps out of the fabric, bare skin exposed once more, buzzing with the daring and invention of it all. She has done nothing this naughty before, but her thigh remains pink and tender where her mother slapped her, and she still is smarting with defiance.

'Woo hoo!' Johnny laughs gleefully when they emerge.

'Cool huh?' says Flo.

He nods, clearly impressed by their nerve. The excitement is catching and the three of them race each other to the bus stop. When Suzy wins, she whoops with delight. Tonight, I'm going to see the *Jean Genie* himself, she thinks, and now I look the part.

5.

The moment they step off the bus, they can see the crowds.

'This way,' says Keith, striding with confidence towards the throng. He is wearing flared trousers which flap as he walks, his hair is orange and short on top, long at the back, like David's, but it is curly, so the effect is more poodle than fox-like. Johnny had said his sister's boyfriend was a bit full of himself, but Suzy decides he's OK. They had sat on the upper deck as the bus jerked through the stop-start traffic of Sheen High Street, Flo increasingly anxious they'd be late, but at Barnes Common the bus had picked up speed, swishing through overhanging branches, past the grand houses owned by rich people, and across the river as if the driver, too, had to get somewhere fast. Flo's attention had been on the road ahead, but Keith had swivelled round to chat, resting one plimsoled foot on his knee, setting them straight about David.

'I'm sure he's an alien,' Johnny had said, barely able to disguise his awe at the prospect.

Suzy had agreed, 'He's got really *weird* eyes.'

'Nah,' Keith had assured them, inhaling a drag of his cigarette. He had then exhaled a series of impressive smoke rings, eyes narrowed as he watched them disintegrate into the dusty sunlight. 'His real name is Davy Jones.' He'd paused, then added, with nonchalance, 'Of course, you know he's bisexual.'

This had caught Flo's attention, 'He's married!' she'd interjected. 'He just likes wearing dresses.'

'Hmph,' Keith had snorted. 'He's a poof.'

Suzy had been embarrassed to admit she didn't know what a bisexual was, though she would like to find out. Then Keith had asked them loads of questions, 'What are your favourite songs then?' 'What other popstars do you like?' and, best of all, admired Suzy's hot pants.

And now here they are, in Hammersmith, under the flyover with dozens of other fans, all older than she is. Many are dressed in eye-popping outfits; sequined waistcoats and lurex trousers, halter-neck tops and shorts that expose pink, sunburned limbs. They are so focused on each other that most don't notice when a dark limo glides into their midst. But Suzy does; it's the first time she's ever seen one and it's *huge*. Moreover, a man who looks like David Bowie is waving from the back. They're surrounded by boys and girls who resemble David, so it takes several seconds for other fans to cotton on, but when he gets out—wearing dungarees, no T-shirt, his chest and arms bare and white and skinny as Suzy's legs—Suzy cries, 'It's him! It's him!' and grabs Johnny's arm, they swarm round.

Bowie is puffing on a cigarette, inhaling deeply. He appears preoccupied, but then the limo pulls away and he turns to speak to some fans. He is so close Suzy can hear him thank them for coming.

'I hope you enjoy the show,' he says. He sounds almost posh, thinks Suzy, surprised. Like someone off the telly. Maybe he isn't an alien after all.

Still, he exudes a charisma which makes him seem as if he is from another planet and she remains spellbound for the entire performance. The whole concert is outside anything Suzy has experienced before. It's not merely most of the audience are adults whilst she's just a kid—as an only child, she's been the lone youngster amongst grownups countless times—it's far more. She has never been anywhere this thrilling, this hot and dark and crowded and noisy. For the first time she has a sense her own life doesn't have to be constrained. And throughout it all, Johnny is beside her, his expression equally rapt. It is as if they have grown wings and can fly, or have found a key to into another world, so altered is their perception.

The adulation of the crowd is palpable. All eyes are fixed on the stage, countless hands reach out in longing. If the audience are like something from a dream, Bowie is even more so: his outfits make even his most outrageous fans look tame, and he changes several times. One moment he's in a short cream kimono, spider legs encased in matching satin thigh boots, the next in a cape which falls into a half moon when he holds out his arms like a butterfly, and he keeps smiling in a way which seems to assume everyone is right to love him so much. Suzy can't imagine what it's like, being so confident—it's a million miles from Keith's cocksure braggadocio or Flo's older-sister one-upmanship. Bowie swaggers across the stage, every move delivered with a finesse which makes watching him electrifying.

'His singing's GREAT!' Johnny yells at her between songs, and they grin at each other in unspoken wonderment they've both been wily enough to get themselves here. They have already established no one else at their school was coming and tomorrow they can go in and hold court.

'The bassist, he had these crazy sideburns,' Johnny will say, gesturing to show how giant and fuzzy they were to the friends gathered round him in the playground. 'And Mick Ronson—he's the guitarist— was BRILLIANT.' Then he'll jump up, thrashing with his right hand and running his left arm along the neck of an air guitar, gurning to its deafening feedback.

But the shock happens after the second encore. There is a searing version of what Keith says afterwards was a Lou Reed song called *White Light/White Heat*. Everyone is going mad and there is a lot of screaming when Bowie, in a sheer-black top and glittery trousers, steps up to the microphone and signals he wants quiet.

'Everybody, this has been one of the greatest tours of our lives,' he says into the hush, adding, 'I'd like to thank the band, I'd like to thank our road crew and I'd like to thank our lighting people,' which prompts a cheer of appreciation. 'Of all the shows on this tour, this particular show will remain with us the longest,' he continues to an even louder cheer. 'Because not only is it the last show of the tour, but it's the last show we'll ever do. Thank you.'

Yelps of disbelief pierce the quiet. The opening chords of *Rock 'n' Roll Suicide* are beguilingly soft, but after two sombre verses, the third begins to build with drums and horns, there is a key change and the grandiose swell of strings and, as the significance of Bowie's words percolate, the crowd grows increasingly wild. By its climax Bowie isn't singing but shrieking, 'Gimme your hands!' and strutting to and fro, clasping random fingers reaching up to him. By the time it reaches its final chord of strings, the entire audience is in a state of hysteria.

'Thank you very much,' he says to the crowd, acknowledging a triumphant farewell. 'Bye-bye, we love you.'

Some of the audience begin shouting out, 'No, no, no!' and as the band leave the stage, beside Suzy, Johnny howls in disappointment. Surely, this can't be true?

Suzy turns to Flo and Keith to ask what they reckon, but they are kissing. She shudders, seeing their tongues moving, lips glistening with saliva, and looks instead to Johnny for reassurance, only to see his cheeks are wet with tears. She hasn't seen him cry since Infant School and she grasps it *must* be true. The realisation sets her off too. For several minutes, the four of them remain there, Flo and Keith snogging, Suzy and Johnny weeping, until the lights come on and they are forced to leave the auditorium.

6.

October 2017

Suzy has turned up the volume as loud as her laptop will allow. What *is* it about this song? The howl, *'Oh no love, you're not alone!'* Bowie's promise he would heal her pain? It still gets Suzy right in the gut, every time. Back then, she'd known it was at the end of the album, but that night at Hammersmith Odeon, she thought *Rock 'n' Roll Suicide* was the end of the band and the end of the world.

'COO-EY!'

Suzy is fumbling for the eject button when her friend breezes back into the kitchen, brandishing a bottle of red.

'Don't let me stop you,' says Debs, seeing the CD emerge from the laptop.

'No, no, it's fine,' says Suzy.

'What was it? I could hear it coming up the path.'

'Or, er, David Bowie. *Rock 'n' Roll Suicide*. The sound's crap on this, though.'

'Don't think I know that one.'

'You MUST! From Ziggy Stardust?'

'Nah,' Debs shakes her head. 'First I knew of Bowie, he was doing *Let's Dance*...'

Nowhere near as good, thinks Suzy. Perhaps there are some advantages to being a decade older, after all. She can't resist the temptation to add, 'I saw him play. As Ziggy, I mean.'

Debs is already uncorking the wine. 'Really?' She turns and looks at Suzy with raised eyebrows.

'Yup, his final concert. I was just a kid.'

'What year was that?' asks Debs, opening the cupboard to locate the glasses. 'Here.' She hands Suzy a wine without checking if she wants it.

''73.' Suzy calculates. 'We were ten.'

'We...?'

She fumbles for the right words. 'Yeah, I went with a friend.'

'Weren't you ever so young to be at a concert?'

Suzy nods. 'Possibly the only primary schoolkids there. Although at the start Bowie was a teenybop star. Lots of his fans were screaming girls. Bizarre in retrospect. He was so out there sexually.' Having started, Suzy can't contain herself. 'The boy I went with sent this to me,' she admits.

'You've lost me.'

'The CD.'

Debs picks up the item in question. 'For Suze,' she says aloud. 'What? This friend sent you the CD of the concert?'

'No,' says Suzy. 'It's a mix of tracks. A compilation. It came with this note, offering condolences.'

She is torn between the desire to keep the letter private and sharing the contents so they can dissect it. She is still making up her mind when Debs decides for her by grabbing the piece of paper, almost ripping it. Suzy winces.

'May I?'

'Sure.'

It takes Debs a couple of minutes for Debs to read it, then ask, 'Who's Johnny?'

Suzy keeps her voice light to conceal her consternation. 'I suppose he was my first proper boyfriend.'

'Ooh, exciting!' Debs claps her hands. 'I haven't heard you mention a Johnny before. When did you last hear from him?'

Suzy can feel her cheeks growing warm. 'I knew him when I was a kid. His family lived over the road. A bit weird, writing now, don't you think?'

Debs grins. 'Maybe he still holds a candle.'

'I doubt it. He's married.'

'Lots of people hold a candle even though they're married.' Debs nudges her shoulder. 'Anyway, how do you know he still is?'

Johnny doesn't seem the type to divorce, thinks Suzy. He was kind. Hard working. Loyal. 'The last time I saw him, he and his wife had toddlers,' she explains. 'Twins.'

'And how long ago was that?'

Suzy frowns, trying to piece together the timeline. 'Well... I'd just had Cam, so...'

'So that's over twenty-five years ago!' exclaims Debs. 'Anything could have happened in that time.'

Suzy wrinkles her nose. You didn't know Johnny, she thinks. He was fun, but he wasn't fickle.

'After all, you're divorced.' Debs states baldly.

Suzy winces. Ouch. Parting from Leo is not a memory she likes to linger over.

'Aren't you curious?'

'Not really.' Suzy is not sure what she thinks. She feels giddy again, sick.

Debs peers at her. 'What's this bit *"after what happened"* referring to? What did happen? Why did he feel he should write?'

Suzy gulps. 'Oh, er... It's something which... um... happened among my group of friends...' I can't talk about *that* now, she thinks. My head will explode. She imagines it shattering into thousands of tiny fragments, each piece a remnant of her past.

'Must have been serious.'

'Yeah... I guess, at the time, it was.' Guilt flares in Suzy's chest, a familiar sensation.

'Ooh, you've gone pink!' Debs is beaming at her, eager. 'Why don't we look him up? Google him. After all, he Googled you.'

Suzy considers. Maybe she *is* curious. Then she shakes her head. 'I don't think so.'

Debs edges forward towards Suzy, tilts her face upwards and flutters her eyelashes as if in a silent movie. 'We could always find out... online...' Her tone is cajoling.

Suzy laughs. 'You're as crafty as Johnny was.'

'I'm a bad influence.' Debs chuckles. 'Another?' She reaches for the bottle to top up Suzy's glass.

Suzy shakes her head. 'Wouldn't be wise on top of all those painkillers. Gabapentin is hard core.'

'Aw.'

'I'm only just out of hospital,' she reasons.

'So?'

'You're supposed to be looking after me, not egging me on!'

Debs tips the rest of the bottle into her own glass.

It's all very well for her, thinks Suzy. She wants the chance to live vicariously and perhaps, if I was still married, I'd feel same. But I've heard enough stories about couples who get together again after years apart. Someone always gets burned. Maybe not the couple themselves, but their partners, the children...

'Alright, alright,' Debs waves a dismissive hand. 'Maybe not tonight. Still...' She prods Johnny's note with a force again Suzy fears will tear the paper. He says he *thought of you all the time, Suzy!* You must want to find out more, surely?'

Part of Suzy longs to explain. *It's nowhere near so simple. If only you knew the full story...'* But this would mean telling Debs more than she bear to. The last thing she needs is to relive the memories she's kept hidden, events she has buried along with any keepsakes long, long ago. Big things, horrible things. Things which happened to Suzy she is too terrified to think about.

Stuff even Cam doesn't know.

7.

48 hours later and Debs is poised to leave, caring duty done. 'If you need anything, shout. And keep your feet up, remember!'

The moment she hears the click of the front door, Suzy flings back the blanket. *'Love* your work. Come and see us,' the well-dressed woman had said at a show in Amhurst village hall, fishing a card from her designer handbag. *Jennifer Blythe-Smith,* it had declared. Chances like this are rare so, first on the agenda: call Social Care to arrange collection of the bed.

'We'll pick it up Thursday.' The man at the council is gruff.

It's two days away.

'Can't you come sooner?' Merely looking at the headboard is enough to make Suzy queasy. She can see her mother propped up on pillows against it, hear Joan struggling to speak, the random shouts of distress and confusion, the rattle of her oxygen machine...

'Rota's already worked out,' says the man.

He is lying, thinks Suzy. Accidents and illnesses can't be diarised ahead. She tries her best to remain calm.

'Please. I'm a painter, and I really need the space to work. Is there no way—?'

The man cuts her off. 'Van's left for the day.'

Suzy feels herself flush with irritation. She scans the room. Everywhere she turns, her mother is still present. The walls are covered in insipid prints Suzy put up to help Joan feel at home, and the mantelpiece is given over to a collection of Royal Doulton figurines. There are women curtseying in flouncy skirts, girls doing up their dainty ballet shoes, children saying their prayers in floor-length nightshirts. Suzy had cleared space to put them in her mother's line of vision, hoping they would provide comfort when Joan became bedridden.

She gives it one last shot. 'Can't you call the driver?'

''Fraid not.' His tone declares he will not budge.

Cursing to herself, Suzy says, 'Fine,' and rings off, fingers trembling.

'On on,' she mutters. An hour later she has stripped the walls in the living room. I need to redecorate, she sighs, noticing paler rectangles in the spaces where they hung. She is packing the last of these in bubble wrap when it strikes her: she should offer them to Cam. Joan *was* his grandmother and, even if he doesn't want the pictures, maybe he could use the frames. Next, the figurines. They'd better go to charity. She reaches for the bubble wrap but—she flings down the sticky tape and scissors in exasperation—it's run out. Her mission to clear space is proving a major headache; she is ending up with more tasks, not fewer. Hopping across the room is taking its toll too, and her foot is throbbing badly.

'I'll never be able to stand at my easel and paint,' she thinks with a rush of panic.

Everything seems to be piling in like a tsunami, giant wave after wave, crushing her and all her mother's stuff. Suzy shuts her eyes, but she can't shake the image of debris left in its wake, the smashed bodies of figurines, their tiny limbs floating amongst broken bits of wood which were once picture frames...

Stop it! Suzy thumps her skull viciously with her fists. Then she props both crutches against the arm of the sofa and lowers herself onto it. *Take a break,* she tells herself.

As she relaxes back into the cushions, she catches sight of a something tucked into a narrow gap between the mantelpiece and the wall. She stretches to reach it.

I've not seen this photo in *years*, she thinks, heart softening. The edges are curling, and it's covered in dust, so she straightens it and carefully wipes the surface with her sleeve.

The picture is of Suzy cradling Cameron as a new-born; standing behind is her father, Ken. Both she and her dad are gazing down at the baby, their half smiles echoing one another. From birth Cam's hair was sandy, like her father's; here he is a mini mirror, as Ken's has yet to fully whiten. Suzy is struck by her father's posture—he appears sturdy and upright, middle-aged, rather than hunched and old.

Oh Dad, she thinks, with a rush of longing, what I wouldn't give to hear your voice once more! Not for the first time, she considers how much easier it would have been had Ken not died so many years before Joan. He was a good man, a loving father, and endlessly patient with her mum. Shy socially, and the way he tiptoed around her mother's sniping and temper often exasperated Suzy, but Ken was of the war generation and imbued with a sense of duty; he would never have left his wife. If only he had cared for himself more and Joan less, Suzy used to think, then her mother might not have wielded such power.

July 1973

The house is in darkness when Flo and Johnny see Suzy to her front door after the concert.

'If you're quiet, I reckon you can slip upstairs to bed unnoticed,' says Flo.

'Do you want us to wait?' offers Johnny.

'It's alright,' whispers Suzy.

The moment she steps into the hall, a light comes on, dazzling in its brightness. It takes Suzy a second to realise her mother is standing before her.

'Suzanne, what *are* you wearing?' snaps Joan without preamble. 'Are those your jeans?' Then she spins Suzy round, sharp nails digging into her flesh. 'YOU CUT THEM UP!' She stands back and is raising a hand, ready, as Ken comes hurrying from the lounge.

'What's the matter?' he asks, stepping between them, but Suzy is still devastated by Bowie's farewell, and now she is frightened, too. She races upstairs to her room where she falls on the bed, sobbing, awaiting her mother's fury.

Yet it is her dad who taps on the door a few minutes later and whispers, 'Little bear?' He tiptoes over and sits down on the edge of her mattress, which sinks under his weight and strokes Suzy's hair until she calms. Then he asks, 'How was the concert?' and listens patiently as, swallowing tears, she tells him. When she has finished, he says, 'That sounds quite something. I'll have to listen to one of this David Bowie's records. We often like the same music, don't we?' They are quiet for a while, before he says softly, 'Well, now... I've persuaded Mum to leave be for tonight. You've school tomorrow so you should get some sleep. But first thing, you had better apologise to her.'

I doubt Mum will accept an apology, thinks Suzy. Nonetheless she is grateful to her father for intervening.

In the event, her mother had nodded briskly and said, 'Apology accepted,' the following morning.

Yet the punishment proved worse, much worse, than being thwacked. Suzy was forbidden to see Johnny or his family, ever again.

'*Never?*' Ken had protested. 'Joan, darling, that's very harsh. How about we ground her for a month, something like that?'

But Joan was intractable. And if she knew that every night her daughter's pillow was damp with tears and every morning Suzy woke with a heavy heart, unable to see how life would ever be fun again, she never said so. As far as Joan was concerned, the Browns were off-limits, and that was the end of the matter.

8.

June 1977

Queen Elizabeth has been on the throne for 25 years, and across the nation, Britain is celebrating.

'Hmph,' says Ken, when Joan announces she is helping to co-ordinate a street party to mark the occasion. 'Country's on the verge of bankruptcy. I can think of no better distraction.'

But gosh, what a chance it is for Joan to shine! Directing the occupants of their Victorian terrace, she is in her element: up and dressed and outside early, barking orders. Soon Park Road is full of men huffing and puffing as they blow up balloons and string bunting in zigzags from one house to another, then groaning and sighing as they heave kitchen and dining tables outside and lay them end to end in the middle of the street. Indoors, women butter dozens of slices of bread, seal them with fish paste or sandwich spread or strawberry jam and cut them into triangles. There are plates of Bourbon biscuits laid into flowers and squares of Battenberg cake, and by noon paper tablecloths are pegged into place, ready to catch spills from jugs of squash and pots of tea.

Joan looks askance at the plate of sandwiches Flo slips quietly onto the table in the No-Man's-Land between their two houses. 'Trust Pat not to cut off the crusts,' she mutters to Ken, but otherwise lets it go. She is in a good mood, Suzy notices. The rain which was forecast is holding off and everyone is doing as she bids.

♩ ♫ ♪♩

Several hours later, her parents are flushed with beer and wine and smiling with bonhomie.

'Come and have a bop!' Ken grabs Joan's hand. Suzy winces, sure he'll be rebuffed, then pauses to watch, agog, as her mother allows herself to be led through the sea of union jacks towards the sound system blasting out the Bee Gees further up the street.

The small children parading in fancy dress, the group of men playing dominoes, Pat rolling cigarettes for both herself and Rita, Flo draped round her latest flame — it begs to be caught on paper. Suzy's art teacher, Miss Ellis, has been urging them to 'capture the magic of every day'—advice Suzy's classmates have ignored. Not Suzy. Drawing is something she can do alone and unchallenged, entering a world where she need rely on no one for hours at a stretch.

Suzy is head down, concentrating, when a 'Psst!' interrupts her thoughts. 'Here!' There is a tug on her skirt. 'Suze!' She lifts the tablecloth and there, on all fours like a dog hoping to catch titbits, is Johnny.

'Hark at you, Vincent.' He nods at her pad.

She whispers loudly, 'We're not supposed to talk!'

In four years, Suzy has not gone against her mother's wishes. Inevitably, she has *seen* Johnny—how could she not when he lives so nearby? They have exchanged the odd word and, more recently, shy glances. She has watched him grow nearly a foot, fill out and cut his hair. The mullet is gone, replaced by short spikes, and she has heard his voice deepen. She knows he has a Saturday job in a boat hire place on the river and he plays football for the school. More impressive still, he is in a band, *The Gloop Dragons*, who are rumoured to be good, and Johnny writes most of their songs. Nonetheless, ever since Joan marched across the street to issue her edict, Suzy has only ever seen him in class or on the bus.

'Let's have a look.' Johnny jerks his head at the space next to him. He is still a chancer, evidently.

Suzy leans back to appraise her drawing. There are hastily drawn thick black lines and more hesitant thin ones, and lots of smudges. Her fingers are covered in charcoal. She wavers, anxious. 'They mustn't see us!'

'Why do think I'm under here?'

She checks one way, then the other. In the distance she can make out her parents waving their arms in time to *Boogie Nights*.

I'm sick of Mum telling me what I can and can't do, she reasons. I'm nearly fifteen. Then, stifling a burst of nervous laughter, she slips along the seat of her chair and lowers herself beside Johnny, still clutching her sketchpad.

'Show me then.'

Reluctantly she holds out her drawing.

'Blimey.' His brown eyes widen. 'That's ever so good.'

Suzy is about to protest but false modesty irritates her. Some of the girls in her class are like that about the very things they're best at, and drawing is Suzy's thing; she works hard at it. 'Thanks.'

'You've captured Flo and Steve,' he nods. 'Though there's one thing you missed out.'

'Oh?'

'*The Great Smell of Brut*. He reeks of it.'

Suzy laughs. 'I hate when boys wear aftershave.' She isn't sure if this is true, but it sounds sophisticated.

It feels very daring, their being so close, and Suzy is conscious of yet more ways Johnny is different. She has noticed before how fit he is, but here it is just the two of them, she can see his jaw is more defined, his brows have thickened, the hair on his upper lip has grown darker and he smells weird; but grown up, male, not smelly or sweaty, like some boys.

'I've been listening to everyone's conversations,' says Johnny. 'Come on. It's a laugh.'

He leads the way, crawling along the tunnel of tables and draped paper, away from the music and the dancing. She follows, wishing she had worn trousers not a skirt, trying not to scrape her knees on the tarmac. Directly beneath his mother and Rita, they halt.

♩ ♫ ♪ ♩   38

'Why don't you put some of this in?' Rita is saying. An arm reaches beneath her chair and she fumbles around. For a dreadful moment Suzy fears Rita is going to peer down and see them, but—'Ah!'—she locates her handbag and hoists it onto the table.

There is a rustling then Pat snorts with laughter. 'You can't be serious!'

'No one's watching,' says Rita. 'Go on.'

'What are they doing?' whispers Suzy.

'Shh,' Johnny puts a finger to his lips and mouths, 'It's pot.'

'What?'

Johnny leans right in. She can feel his breath on her ear. 'They're rolling a joint.'

Suzy's mouth drops into an 'O'.

'People will smell it,' says Pat.

'No, they won't,' says Rita. 'And if they do, they're all too pissed to care.'

Suzy and Johnny hurry to the end of the tunnel and they dart into Rita's front garden, where they collapse into hoots of laughter on the lawn by the hedge.

'I can't believe your mum!'

'Rita grows it,' says Johnny.

Suzy gasps. 'Where?'

'In her attic.'

'How do you know?'

He shrugs, as if to indicate it's common knowledge. 'Flo buys it off her sometimes.' There is a pause then he adds, 'Not everyone is like your mum.'

Suzy looks at him, unsure whether he means this as a dig, but his expression holds no malice. Quite the opposite: he is smiling. She had forgotten how his face lights up when he grins. 'It's nice to see you.'

'And you,' she replies.

'No one will catch us here,' Johnny assures her. They fall silent. Suzy watches a Red Admiral, its wings opening patterned and closing

39

brown, land on a nearby Buddleia. It reminds her of Bowie's cape that magical night, when she thought she could fly, before it all went wrong. Then, just as she sneaks another look at him, Johnny glances at her.

'Your mum...' He shakes his head.

'I know.' Suzy sighs. 'She's such a pain.'

'I've wanted to talk to you for ages,' says Johnny.

Suzy's can feel herself reddening, so plucks at the grass, hoping he won't see. 'Really?'

'Yeah. It was awful. I... um... missed you.' His voice is low.

'I couldn't, I just couldn't.' She is mortified. He must think her cowardly, not standing up to her mother. She has tried to be more assertive, but her dad always seems to want to soften everything, smooth any tension.

'It must be tricky when it's only you,' says Johnny.

Suzy can hear her mother say, 'I was sent away at half your age,' as if her daughter is lacking resilience in comparison. 'Evacuated. Five years old and labelled like a piece of luggage.' Suzy pictures dozens of children lined up at Paddington station. Being torn from her family sounds awful, but does it justify treating Suzy's friendships as equally expendable? Suzy bites her lip, unsure whether to share this.

When she glances up again, Johnny is gazing at her, and this time he doesn't look away. His big brown eyes are at once tender and hopeful, and there is a spark, like electricity, which passes between them; Suzy can almost hear it fizzle. She feels a faint stirring between her legs and her heart starts to thump.

Johnny leans forward and brushes her blond fringe aside. 'I like your new hair style.' Suzy is not used to hearing him speak so intimately. 'It suits you.'

'Thanks,' she mumbles. Secretly she is thrilled. She had it cut into layers a few weeks earlier and has received almost enough compliments to believe he might be right.

Then he edges even closer.

Help, thinks Suzy, alarmed. Is he going to kiss me? I wasn't expecting this... Not remotely. Her thoughts race. Will he think I'm a terrible kisser? How much tongue should I use? The prospect is exciting, but she has no idea what to do.

'Suzanne?' A sing-song voice pierces the air.

Suzy pulls away and sits bolt upright. 'That's my mum!'

'SU-ZANNE!' The call is louder this time.

Johnny remains calm. 'Go back the way you came. Under the tables. Say you dropped your pad. We must have left it there.' He gets to his feet and brushes down his trousers. 'Go on,' he urges.

Suzy has no time to come up with anything better. She ducks down and scuttles along beneath the tables. Sure enough, her sketch pad is lying on the tarmac. She scoops it up and—'Hi Mum,' emerges like a jack-in-a-box into her chair.

'There you are!' cries Joan, collapsing onto the seat next to Suzy and fanning herself.

Moments later Suzy hears the familiar opening chords of The Sex Pistols' *God Save the Queen* blasting from the sound system.

Joan scrunches up her face in distaste, but there's a 'whoop!' from Flo and Steve, who get to their feet, and soon a large teenage contingent has piled into the middle of the street and is bouncing up and down in unison to the rhythm. Over her mother's shoulder Suzy sees Johnny give her a double thumbs up. Then he grins, tosses his head and dives into the throng.

October 2017

I'm still a punk at heart, thinks Suzy. Galvanised, she squirts yellow ochre onto her palette so she can mix a lurid shade in homage, and adds several brushstrokes with gay abandon. So what if Sid Vicious couldn't really play? That riff, the thrashing guitars — between the

41

four of them, those lads made an iconic single, full of anger and energy, and no one could sneer like Johnny Rotten. She pictures him on stage, an evil orange-haired sprite in a ripped jacket held together with chains and safety pins, yelling into the mike. The lyrics were unforgettable and are still provocative now; comparing the monarchy to a '*fascist regime... She ain't no human being...*' The melody wasn't half bad, either. That so many adults found *The Sex Pistols* repugnant — they got right up her mother's nose — only made them more appealing.

Suzy stands back from her painting. The extra colour works well.

What she wouldn't give to be 15 again, diving into the mosh pit. Being on the short side, pushiness was her only option if she wanted to see properly at a gig. A murmured, 'Excuse me...' 'Sorry but would you mind...?' would work to a point, but inevitably there were numbskulls who needed a sharp elbow to the ribs. Looking back, she is surprised how brazen she was. By the end of the night, she would be wet from sweat and spittle, her clothes torn from the rough and tumble, but the rush of those gigs was unparalleled. They saw some great bands: *The Clash* at the Lyceum Ballroom, *Buzzcocks* at The Rainbow in Camden, *The Stranglers* in Battersea Park, all without her parents knowing.

For Johnny to choose this track makes her smile, because she suspects he was remembering that street party too, and their near-kiss, and the other Johnny, all those decades ago, sticking two fingers up at the world.

9.

'You'd best get it, Mum.' Cameron jerks his chin towards the bell. His arms are full of bubble-wrapped canvases.

As they wait to be granted entry, Suzy leans on her crutches and looks up. Every window ledge boasts a perfectly manicured trough of ivy and cyclamen; there is not a brown leaf or dead bloom in sight. The windows are freshly glossed, and the door fixtures polished so thoroughly Suzy can see herself reflected in the brass. The place is so smart, their mark-up will be astronomic. But Jennifer Blythe-Smith approached *me*, Suzy reminds herself, and being exhibited in a gallery in Bath, I'd reach a whole new market.

The handle turns and Suzy is disarmed to see, not Jennifer, as she'd expected, but a man on the threshold. He is very dapper, with a beard that's carefully trimmed as topiary in a National Trust garden. His navy suit is trendy; close fitting and edged with scarlet stitching.

'Mrs Hope, good to see you. Glad you found us OK.' His accent is a mix of well-to-do Brit and East Coast American.

'Please call me Suzy. This is my son, Cam.' She stretches out a hand and her scarf tumbles to the floor.

He waits while she picks it up then says, 'Julian Atkinson.'

She senses him look her up and down, then Cam. Her coat is unbuttoned, and she is wearing leggings which are fraying where she has had to cut off the bottom to pull over her plaster cast. Cam's jeans are faded, his parka far too casual, and his trainers are covered in mud. His blond hair looks greasy and he could do with a shave. Normally Suzy wouldn't think twice about such trivialities—they are just Cam being Cam and she loves every inch of him regardless. But today they make her wince. We should have taken more trouble, she thinks, as they step inside.

The floor is pale parquet, the lighting so discrete as to be invisible. Each painting has ample room, so visitors have no choice but to focus on the works, but it does little to ease her discomfort. Suzy needs the loo, but Julian is walking at such speed even Cam is finding it hard to keep up. At the far end of the gallery, they pause, waiting for her to limp and join them.

Julian opens a door, and they are in a meeting room, bare but for a long oak table and spindly stools with seats far smaller than Suzy's bottom.

'If you'd like to lay out the work here,' says Julian, 'I'll let you know if anything is suitable.'

'Oh!' says Suzy, unable to conceal her surprise. 'Is Jennifer not going to look?'

'Who?'

'Your—' Suzy stops. She can see Julian's mouth contorting, a line forming between his brows. Hesitantly, she asks, 'Partner?'

'Jennifer is not my partner,' he states. 'She's my *scout*.'

'Ah.' Oh no, thinks Suzy, trying to mask her consternation. Beside her, Cam gently lowers the stack of paintings onto the table and begins to remove the packaging. She can tell he is trying to undo the Sellotape as quietly he can, but the lack of soft furnishings makes it echo horribly. Eventually the oils are ready to view.

Spread out across the table it seems a very hotchpotch collection. One of the canvases it hasn't had time to dry and has smudged but Julian is radiating impatience. Hurriedly she sorts the paintings into groups of a similar hue and stands back.

Immediately she spots how she could have matched them better, but Julian nods and says, 'Thank you. Perhaps you'd both like a look around the gallery.' It is more a command than a suggestion.

She and Cam do as they are bid, wary of speaking. The only sound is the squeak of Cam's trainers, and the tap and click of Suzy's shoe and crutches.

As she takes in the exhibits, Suzy's heart sinks further. There are eerie abstracts, bold portraits and urban landscapes, metal sculptures and light installations. All seem to radiate creative confidence, and every item on display is HUGE. The last vestiges of hope drain when Julian beckons them back, unsmiling.

'I'll level with you. These are very good, but I was hoping for something, um, braver,' he opens, not unkindly.

Suzy is aware of colour rising in her cheeks. 'They aren't as large as I usually paint. I had to do them seated.'

'Yes, I see.' He glances at her foot and grimaces, although whether at his own pain or Suzy's is unclear. 'The problem isn't the size... It's that here we show artists with a more *singular* vision. One of the first things we look for is a distinct point of view. We like to see a substantial and consistent body of work.' Julian magics a slender computer from a shelf beneath the table and slips it in front of them. 'Have you looked at our current artists on Instagram?'

I haven't, thinks Suzy, sense of inadequacy mounting. 'I've seen the gallery website...' Her voice trails off.

'Permit me.' Julian flicks through a series of open web pages until he finds what he's after. 'Take these watercolours, by Theodora Koning. She's exhibiting here in the spring. Notice how, even as thumbnails, her work sits together well? The wonderful sense of light and space...'

'Mm.'

'If you look at your work in comparison...' He gestures at her abstracts. 'See how doesn't quite hold together as a single entity? This painting works well.' He gestures at the one with yellow splodges. 'But it's got a different feel from the rest.'

Suzy feels tears prick behind her eyes. She has worked so hard over the last few weeks, fighting pain. Producing her canvases has left her so exhausted she can barely see straight. Under the table, Cam presses his shoe lightly on Suzy's good foot. She gives him a small smile, grateful for his support.

'William Settle is another example,' continues Julian, oblivious to the effect he is having. 'He doesn't only get a wonderful likeness; he captures the personality of his subject.'

'The portraits next door? I'm not sure you'll ever get Mum painting anything like those.' Suzy can tell from his tone Cam is irked.

'Obviously not. Though you get my drift? This is an artist who has edited and refined his artistic imagination. He has a strong, consistent message.'

'Like Picasso, you mean?' says Cam drily.

Julian ignores the remark. 'I always say to up-and-coming artists, if you're most passionate about portraits, don't include landscapes—even if you paint them occasionally—in your presentation to a gallery or on your website.'

'What if someone should be browsing the internet who likes landscapes?' interjects Cam. 'If you don't show them, they won't know you paint them.'

Suzy is touched by her son's loyalty. It's no use, though, she knows. 'It's OK. I understand what you're saying.'

'Don't give up.' Julian surprises her by smiling. 'We hold a competition, annually. Why don't you submit? Were you to win, you'd get a prime spot in the gallery in the run up to Christmas next year.'

'It's a thought,' Suzy mutters, as she and Cam gather up the pictures.

'I'm so sorry!' she wails as they head back to her son's car. She looks around at the crescent of houses, their Doric columns glow gold in the afternoon winter light. Each classically proportioned frontage is an echo of its neighbour, every railing is black, every door and window frame white. The whole of Bath seems to deliver a strong and consistent message, thinks Suzy, and berates herself for believing she deserved to be on show here.

♩ ♫ ♪ ♩   46

'What have you got to be sorry for?' Cam's eyes spark with indignation.

'I've wasted your time, dragging you up from London.'

'*You* didn't waste my time.' Cam scowls. 'He did. What a jerk. Imagine telling Van Gogh to limit his colour palette so his paintings work as a single body.'

Suzy laughs.

Even so, once he has dropped her home and disappeared off down the M4, Suzy is sorely tempted to go to bed and hibernate for the remainder of the day. I don't know how many knockbacks I can take, she thinks, sitting sorrowfully the kitchen table. And what made the encounter worse is Julian was right. My work *used* to be brave. At school, I loved to experiment, push boundaries. Whilst others were focused on neat pencil drawings, she was mixing media and combining collage with emulsion and papier mache. She recalls Miss Ellis observing, 'Your creations might not always come off, Suzy, but it's great you're so willing to try everything.' And at art school she was considered radical.

It's not only with my paintings, Suzy realises. I used to be braver socially, willing to meet new people. She casts her mind back. At uni, I was out all the time. We'd go to parties and have such a laugh, and later, much later, when Cameron was small, I loved spending time with him... *And* I used to have sex, yet I haven't had done that in... She is embarrassed to admit to herself how long it has been. I used to be the daring one, she thinks. I took risks to be with Johnny, we were the first to be into Bowie and punk, and now look at me! I can't even drive myself from A to B.

Well, enough is enough.

I might not be able to get behind the wheel, I might not be able to stand and paint, but I'm no longer tied by caring for Mum. I want to laugh more, play more, have sex again, be free.

I want to find the girl I used to be.

10.

May 1979

It's here at last: the night of Suzy's sixteenth birthday. All day she has been giddy at the prospect, and the only thing left is to finish getting herself ready. She is wearing a top with a wide neckline which she found in a jumble-sale, and pedal pushers, which she made herself. She has washed and backcombed her hair, and she has *Blondie's* first album propped by her mirror for inspiration: along with just about every girl in her class, Suzy wants to look like Debbie Harry. She has the right colouring and is good at using brushes thanks to being artistic, so does a reasonable job of recreating Debbie's mussed-up hair and cat's eye make-up, but nothing can give her that rosebud pout. She'd like bigger breasts too, but she can hardly stuff her bra with tissues tonight.

Anticipation mounting, Suzy listens for the familiar sounds of her parents retiring: her father bolting the front door, her mother's bathwater emptying down the drain. She waits a few minutes then pulls on her plimsoles, and carefully tucks her pillows beneath the cover so it appears as if she is in bed. Then, softly, softly, she edges open the bedroom window and gingerly climbs out onto the garage roof. From there she hurries along the garden wall and jumps onto the drive. She checks her parents' window, nervous she has landed with a thud, but the curtains remain closed. Phew.

As planned, Johnny is waiting, ready to let her into number 32 via the side passage. 'Juliet!'

'Romeo!'

'You made it.' He grins. She follows him through the wooden gate and into the back garden. 'I'll check the coast is clear.'

He disappears into the house and Suzy waits outside, nerves mounting. Will it hurt? Will there be blood? It could be awkward, though Johnny has said it won't matter. She knows it probably won't be amazing, not the first time, though she'd like it to be. In the bodice rippers she devours almost solely for the seduction scenes involving men rippling with muscles, it seems sex is always amazing, especially if the man is commanding, almost brutal. Not that Johnny has ever been commanding or brutal, far from it. He's no pushover, but he makes her laugh too much to be menacing.

I like him *so* much, thinks Suzy. What if I make a mess of things? He might go off me. We've been together over a year, longer than anyone else our age. I couldn't bear it.

'They're watching the news,' he says, re-emerging.

They tiptoe up to his attic bedroom.

'You're still in your uniform,' she says, taking in his white shirt and black trousers.

Johnny pauses in his attempt to drag a chest of drawers against the door to stop anyone barging in. 'Sorry. I thought it could be a giveaway if I changed. I had a shower though.' He smiles, but she can tell he is anxious. She is surprised; he is normally so confident, or compared to her, anyway. He's prepared to get up *on stage*, for goodness' sake; he's played lots of gigs with his band, and he takes them all in his stride. Fleetingly she wonders whether this would have been better with someone who wasn't a virgin too.

She looks around his room. There are no rose petals on the bed and Johnny's navy sheets are bobbly with age. 'It's a bit bright,' she observes.

'We could turn the lights out if you want.' He sounds reluctant.

'Be weirder.' She would rather be able to see him. She likes his body.

She hasn't much to compare it to, but nonetheless she has told her friend Sal, 'It's because he's into football,' because she knows footballers have good legs, and Johnny's are gratifyingly muscular, rock solid compared to her own. She likes his chest, too, which is growing broader almost as noticeably as her own breasts are rounding out. But what she finds most appealing is he is tall and these days he must bend when he is standing and kisses her. As kids, she and Johnny were the same height. This having changed is thrilling.

'Hang on...' She opens one of the drawers, rummages, then yanks out a *Clash* T-shirt and drapes it over his bedside light to create a seductive red glow.

He lies down on the bed. 'Why don't you go on top?' he suggests. 'At least to start.'

She doesn't argue. Now they've got this far, she wants it over with. She straddles him and, fingers trembling, unbuttons his shirt. He wriggles his hips and helps her ease him out of his trousers.

'I like this,' he says about her top. 'You look gorgeous. So sexy.'

Inside, Suzy purrs with pleasure. My effort paid off, she thinks.

By the time he is unclipping her bra, Johnny is so hard the fabric of his underpants is pulled taut into a pyramid, like a pole in the centre of a tent.

'I got some of these.' He reaches into the drawer of his bedside table to retrieve a packet. She watches half repelled, half awestruck, as he opens it and removes a plasticky, bright pink condom. She is glad of the soft lighting.

'I've been practising this,' he admits as he rolls it on, and she laughs. 'I did wonder.'

Then, at last, she feels the electric prickle of his hot skin against her own. She leans in and despite the shower, he still smells of Johnny; a scent that is at once arousing and reassuring. He looks at her with those liquid, brown eyes—*bedroom eyes*, she thinks, recalling the phrase from one of her bonkbusters. They kiss, at first tenderly, then more urgently—how she loves kissing him! Then he pulls back, glances at her again—presumably to check she's OK—and leans in, kisses her some more. This time she relaxes a little. Mm, she thinks, this is nice. Really nice. He smells all yummy. They fumble awkwardly, and finally, he is inside her. He doesn't grab her wrists and pin her back as he thrusts himself into her like men do in some of the films she's seen. He lets her continue to sit astride him, which is altogether far less uncomfortable and frantic than she expected, and together they move slowly and gently, until she tells him she is sure it isn't hurting.

The rest has blurred into the haze of the countless occasions they made love. She can't even remember if she came. Realistically, I didn't, thinks Suzy, although I shall never regret losing my virginity to Johnny. He was so much a part of me, the 'me' I wanted to be, who was nothing like my parents. He hadn't even said he loved me; not yet. Nonetheless, it was beautiful.

November 2017

'That is such a *lovely* story.' Turning off the ignition, Debs brings *Hanging on the Telephone* to an abrupt halt a few bars in.

'Can you leave that on?' asks Suzy.

''Course I can.' Debs puts the key in and turns it. 'Back in a sec.' She jumps out, opens the boot of her car, grabs the box of china figurines.

Suzy remains in the passenger seat, watching rain batter the windscreen. She hums along, then starts to sing. Nearly 40 years on, she still knows all the words! WhatsApp, Twitter, Messenger, email — these days the sheer volume of communications is overwhelming. Yet in 1979 getting hold of people could be tricky. There were red phone boxes on street corners, and landline telephones in many homes, but *that was it*. Not answering a call could make or break a relationship— and by the end of the track, Debbie Harry is growling with fury. That she was not a woman to messed with was one of the reasons Suzy liked

51

the band. And, according to the timer on the dashboard, the song is all of two minutes forty seconds. An entire relationship summed up in less than three minutes—what a perfect pop song.

Yet Johnny never kept *me* waiting, Suzy recalls, wistfully. Not everyone's first boyfriend is as good to them as Johnny was to me. Come to that, not all *my* boyfriends were as good to me as he was...

Debs bounces back into the car. 'Where next?'

'The tip.' Suzy nods. At the recycling centre, she watches as Debs hurls more of her mother's possessions into the skip. An electric bar heater, a clapped-out hairdryer, a food mixer—the clank of metal landing on metal is grimly satisfying.

'Thanks so much for that,' she says, as they drive back to Amhurst in the drizzle.

'Do carry on,' Debs urges.

Suzy feels duty bound to entertain her friend in return for her help, yet she is wary of revealing too much.

'Enough about me. Tell me about you and Rich. How did you get together?'

As Debs launches into her own narrative, Suzy is relieved that her friend doesn't push her further. I know what it's like to have had my private life exposed without my permission, she recalls. It made a horrific experience a hundred times worse, feeling I had nowhere to hide. Being doorstepped by newspaper journalists and TV cameras was hideous. That level of intrusion...

It's not something I want to repeat, or force on someone else.

Ever.

11.

'This is ridiculous,' says Pat, as her rumpled son and Suzy come into the kitchen for breakfast. Suzy props her portfolio against the fridge and drops her schoolbag next to it. Johnny's mother is already at the table with a mug of Nescafe, smoking a roll-up. 'You stay here such a lot, Suzy. Doesn't your mum ever ask where you are?'

'She thinks I'm at Sal's,' says Suzy, reaching for the sliced bread and putting two pieces in the toaster.

'What, *three* nights a week?' scoffs Flo. She's been back at number 32 since splitting with Keith in the summer. Only now it's December and despite a new beau, Flo seems reluctant to leave. Not sure I'd want to either, thinks Suzy. She *loves* being at the Browns' house. Not only are Pat and Colin cool about Suzy staying; they are funny and interesting. Colin, a local Labour councillor, casts judgement on almost everything, especially privatisation and the sale of social housing, and he hates Margaret Thatcher almost as much as Suzy's mother reveres her. And whilst she used to find Pat's questions mortifying, Suzy has got used to them and these days she can talk Johnny's mum in a way she never can her own.

'I bet she knows really,' says Pat.

Johnny tips a mountain of *Shreddies* into a bowl. 'That's what I've said, eh Suze?'

'Mm.' Suzy gulps.

'All the fuss about those shorts was *years* ago,' says Pat, creating a space to squash out her cigarette in the overflowing ashtray.

'It's not as if Johnny's dealing drugs or lounging about on the dole,' says Flo.

'Most people on the dole *want* a job,' says Pat as Flo leans across her to grab the *Golden Shred*. 'I don't want to be rude about your mum,' her tone becomes serious. 'You know you're always welcome here.'

It isn't concern for *me* that makes Mum uncompromising, Suzy wants to explain. My mother hates admitting she's wrong. Most people can be swayed by others, alter with changing circumstances, see nuance. But Joan is utterly rigid. It's another contrast between the two families; when Flo and Johnny and their parents argue around the dinner table, they *debate*. Whereas Suzy's mother dictates like an army major and she and her dad fall into line.

'Give it a rest, Pat love,' says Colin, easing himself into a chair. A heavily built Scouser with beard and gruff manner, he is a bassoon to Pat's piccolo. 'What's with the giant folder?' he asks Suzy, reaching to turn on the radio on top of the fridge.

'You should show them.' Johnny looks round at his family. 'She's really good.'

'Go on,' urges Pat. 'I'd love to see.'

Johnny raises his brows at Suzy encouragingly, so she fetches her portfolio and lifts it onto a chair. Trepidatious, she undoes the ties, and it falls open, revealing her latest artwork.

'Wow!' says Flo.

Pat gets to her feet to get a better view. As she tilts her head one way, then the other, appraising, Suzy waits with bated breath. Finally, Pat nods in approval.

'It's great,' says Colin.

'Be a brilliant album cover,' says Flo.

Before them is a brightly coloured image of a punk with a Mohican, a studded dog collar round his neck, clothes held together by straps and chains. He is standing against a bombed-out building and graffitied behind him are the words *No Future*.

Johnny beams at Suzy. 'Told you.'

'What technique did you use?' asks Pat.

'It's a lino cut,' says Suzy. She explains how she has chiselled the lino then printed each colour layer by layer, building the picture in stages.

'I like the social commentary,' says Colin.

Suzy is more chuffed than she can say.

'Of course, all art is political,' interjects Pat.

'How do you mean?' asks Flo. Suzy is relieved Flo has asked; she isn't clear either.

'Whenever an artist chooses a subject, they make a choice,' explains Pat. 'By focusing on a punk, say, like this, Suzy is showing disaffected Britain. Whereas—'

'SHHH!' snaps Colin. He tips back his seat and stretches an arm to turn up the volume of the radio. 'Listen.'

'John Lennon was coming home about four hours ago with his wife, Yoko Ono, to their apartment building, the Dakota on New York's Upper West Side... He got out of the taxi in which he was travelling when he was approached by a man. This man apparently wanted an autograph, there was an altercation and then Lennon was shot several times...'

The blood drains from Flo's face. 'Is he dead?'

Colin flicks a hand to show they should continue to be silent.

'It's believed the first shot was fatal... He was pronounced dead upon arrival at the nearby Roosevelt Hospital...'

'Our lad,' says Colin, choked. 'Our John.'

Of course, Colin is from Liverpool. More than once he has told Suzy how he got to know The Beatles before they were famous, swanking he was a regular at The Cavern. 'Often shared a bevvy with the band before the show.'

As the news programme segues into a compilation of Lennon's

singles, Colin's face crumples. Suzy is shocked. She has not seen a man cry before. Pat reaches for his hand.

'I was named after him,' Johnny reminds Suzy.

'The Beatles had their first number one the week you were born.' Pat's voice catches.

The rest of breakfast passes in silence. Slices of toast remain with mouth-shaped crescents bitten out of them, growing cold; Johnny's *Shreddies* linger half eaten in his cereal bowl, floating like miniature rafts on a sea of milk. Pat sits there squeezing Colin's palm so tight her knuckles turn white, while he gently weeps, body curled in on itself like a wounded animal.

'He was only forty,' says Ken when he returns from work. Suzy can tell from the heavy sigh as he takes off his coat her father has also been affected by the news.

'It's awful,' she says. At her school, there was talk of little else.

Ken drops onto the sofa and turns on the TV. Aerial footage of Central Park fills the screen. Swathes of mourners have gathered, some are weeping, others are waving flags and banners. *WHY?* asks a hand-scripted placard. *Goodbye Nowhere Man*, says another. *John Lennon's words will live forever*, declares a third.

'I don't understand why everyone's so upset,' says Joan, wiping her hands on a tea towel as she comes into the room.

Suzy is taken aback. 'He was in the biggest band in the world.' Surely, he is a bridge between our generations, she thinks. We all listened to The Beatles.

'He was younger than both of us,' says Ken.

'He's not the first popstar to die young,' says Joan.

'He was shot!' says Suzy, hackles rising.

'He took drugs and was married to that dreadful Chinese woman,' says Joan.

'Japanese,' corrects Suzy.

'He wrote some great songs,' says Ken.

'Exactly,' says Suzy. 'Whatever you thought about him as a person, Mum, you must agree there.'

'You love those old Beatles tracks,' adds her father.

Joan harrumphs. 'I prefer McCartney.'

Suzy grits her teeth. Her mother's obstinacy jars, today of all days. At least her father gets it.

'Shall we play one of your records, Dad?' She goes to the side cabinet and begins riffling through Ken's LP collection. It is arranged alphabetically so doesn't take long. 'How about this?' she pulls out *Abbey Road,* not caring that the choice may provoke her mother more than one of the early albums. She tips it from the sleeve, blows off the dust and lays it on the turntable. There is a crackle as the needle hits the vinyl. Then the distinctive muffled tom toms, muted guitars, and deep, resonant bass of *Come Together* fill the room.

Ken starts to tap his foot.

This is *so* original, thinks Suzy.

'"Joo joo eyeballs!"' Joan sneers. 'What on earth does that mean?'

At this, Suzy snaps. 'Who cares what it means? It's music!'

'Otherwise, it's just nonsense.'

Suzy has been holding back resentment for so long, her rage rises in a giant, unstoppable wave. 'You wouldn't know great art if it smacked you in the face,' she blurts.

'Now Suzy...' Her father sits forward on the sofa.

She turns to him. 'No. I will *not* shut up, Dad!'

Ken looks winded. Suzy yearns to shake him, to make him feel just a touch of her fury. How can he be so unresponsive, so passive? Doesn't he care? She pictures Johnny's father that morning. Colin was *crying,* he was so upset, and Pat was so tender, she held her husband's hand. Why can't her parents be that open and feeling? Why can't they comfort one another like that? She stares at her mother and father. They seem so uptight, so narrow-minded, so dull. Then the dam inside her gives way and out it all pours.

'You don't understand me, either of you.' Her words swill around them in a tide. She glares at her mother. 'Can't you hear yourself, getting worked up about The Beatles? It's *embarrassing* how old fashioned you are.'

'I am *not* worked up!'

Joan's face is puce, her arms are rigid. For the first time Suzy sees her mother through adult eyes. I don't just disagree with her views, she thinks. *I don't like her.* She is a bully. That Johnny was named after Lennon makes her heartlessness seem personal. 'Why must you hate everything I like?'

'Sorry?'

Suzy pictures the *Rice Crispies'* climbing frame, the bike races round the lawn, the days of making dens and secret hideaways. She recalls the years she was forced to watch from the side lines whilst chains of other children ran in the front door of number 32, out the back and round the garden. My mother denied me all that, she thinks. No wonder I escaped into my art. 'You aren't interested in anything which interests me. You don't care about me or what I'm good at. You just want to make me into a mini you. But there's no way I'd want to be you. *Not in a million years.*' Suzy is channelling the rebelliousness of John and Yoko. Their *Bed-Ins for Peace* have been on the news repeatedly all day.

'Little Bear—' Ken reaches out a hand.

Suzy turns to her father. 'Don't "Little Bear" me! I'm not six! Why do you always let Mum walk all over you?'

Ken flushes. 'When you're older you'll understand,' he mutters.

'No, I won't! The older I get, the more pathetic you seem.'

Her father falls silent. For a split second Suzy regrets hurting him, but she is fuelled by anger. 'You think you know it all, don't you?' she says to her mother. 'But you blind yourself to everything that doesn't fit your world view.' Suzy gives a bitter laugh. 'Though now I think about it, you're so blind, you don't have a clue what *my* views are. If you ever bothered to look at my paintings, you might understand more.'

'Pah!' Joan's contempt is palpable.

'For a start, I hate Margaret Thatcher.'

Joan snorts and gives Suzy a small, patronising smile.

'Oh, *FUCK OFF*, Mum.' It is first time Suzy has ever sworn at her mother. Joan and Ken are dumbstruck.

Suzy does not wait to be lectured. She races straight upstairs, footsteps thundering despite the shagpile carpet. Hurriedly, she grabs her toothbrush, make-up and some fresh underwear, wedges the whole lot into her school bag alongside her books and returns to the living room. Her parents are still seated on the sofa.

'I suppose you're off to Sally's again,' says Joan.

Suzy shakes her head. 'No, I'm not.'

'Oh?'

Suzy is angrier than she has ever been. 'All this time, you think I've been going to Sal's, I haven't.'

Her mother's eyes narrow. 'Where have you been going?'

'Over the road.'

Joan's face clouds with confusion.

'To the Browns.'

Silence.

'For God's sake, Mum, don't you get what I'm telling you?' Suzy thumps the side of her head to indicate Joan is being thick. 'I'm going out with Johnny. You know. *That boy.*'

It's as if she's dropped a grenade, and neither parent knows how to react.

'And before you say I'm forbidden to see him; can't you see how ludicrous it is? It was *years ago*. All over a pair of jeans. It wasn't even Johnny who cut them up—it was Flo! Johnny is not a criminal. He's clever and he's popular and he's in a great band.'

Her mother's jaw is open.

Suzy turns to her father. 'Dad...?' She searches his face for a sign that he is prepared to intervene. 'I've been seeing him for ages. He's nice to me, Dad. He's kind and funny. He wants to go to university. Isn't it a good thing?' Suzy is tempted to yell, *I love him! And it's not a teenage crush, but proper, grown-up love. We connect. We fit. We understand each other. We like each other. It's amazing, given we're only 17.* But she does not say this. It is too precious a declaration. Her parents don't deserve to know how deeply she feels.

'Of course...' says Ken, but he glances at his wife rather than Suzy.

His prevarication seals it. He can be such a wet blanket! Her parents can get their heads round this in due course.

Suzy turns on her heel and strides down the hall, slamming the front door behind her.

She'd gone straight to over the road, she can remember as if it were yesterday. Johnny had come hurtling down the stairs to greet her and sensing something very wrong, had wrapped her in his arms, while she'd explained through gasps for breath what had happened.

'I'll go and talk to them,' he'd said, but she was convinced it wouldn't help. 'You know there's always a place for you here,' he'd assured her. 'Mum and Dad love you.' They were like a second a family, thinks Suzy. So many of the gaps left by my parents were filled by the Browns.

Gradually, her resolve about getting in touch with Johnny begins to soften. What's the worst can happen if she thanks him for the compilation? He was the one who made the first move, and it wasn't 'a move' anyway. He simply offered condolences. She'll be very diplomatic, and she would like to know how the Browns are doing. Not just Johnny but Flo, and his parents too.

Before she has time to change her mind, she reaches across the table for her laptop, switches it on and while it warms up, gets herself a glass of wine to steel her nerves.

She opens Safari, and there it is, just as Debs suggested.

Google.

12.

He's more likely to be John online, not Johnny, Suzy calculates. When he left school, he'd dropped the diminutive, although she and his family stuck with Johnny.

John Brown, she types, with a shiver of excitement.

'*John Brown advocated the use of armed insurrection to overthrow the institution of slavery,*' says Wikipedia helpfully. She scans down; site after site is dedicated to an American abolitionist Suzy has never heard of. Adding *UK* only brings up the *John Brown* who was a favourite of Queen Victoria. There is *John Brown Publishing, John Brown,* buddy of Bramwell Bronte and *John Brown* who makes bespoke shutters, but no one who could be her Johnny. Perhaps I would recognise him, she thinks, heart quickening at the thought of seeing how he looks now. She watched him turn from boy to man; arguably, there's no one, other than Cam, whose face she knows so well. She switches to searching through images.

John Brown in owl glasses, *John Brown,* a beefcake in a lumberjack shirt, and *John Brown,* a bald and angry football manager, stare back at her. I like the lithe limbs of *John Brown Yoga Instructor,* she thinks, but he looks about Cam's age.

She tries *John Brown Park Road* where they used to live. Nothing. *John Brown* with the postcode: another blank. She repeats it all with *Johnny Brown.* No joy.

Silently, Suzy curses Colin and Pat. She gets the Lennon thing, but *Brown* has to be up there with *Smith* and *Jones.* There must be thousands of John Browns across the country. How frustrating!

♩ ♫ ♪ ♩

She hops over to the fridge, tops up her glass. As she lowers herself back into her chair, an ad flashes at the top of her screen: **FIND JOHN BROWN ON FACEBOOK,** it declares.

Blast. She has forgotten her password. After three attempts she gains access to the site which chides her for her absence like an over-needy friend. Acquaintances chivvy her to sign petitions she has no interest in, advertisers coax her to buy menopause supplements and incontinence pads. Her feed is full of people sharing pictures of their Christmas trees and Debs has tagged Suzy in some photos taken months ago where she looks heinous. It takes a while to work out how to search for someone, but finally she manages and although Facebook encourages her to add dozens of *John Browns* to her friends, not one of them has the warm, expressive face and distinctive big brown eyes of her Johnny.

'Fat lot of use,' she tells Pushkin, as the cat jumps up and marches— fhapsjf [tj qpj poia—across her keyboard.

Suzy is about to give up when she sees she has two *Friend Requests*. One is from Cam's girlfriend, Alice, so she approves it at once, flattered; the other from someone called *Asin Fitzgerald*. It's hard to see what *Asin* looks like from the thumbnail, so Suzy clicks to glean more. The cover picture is a beach shot with the sea at a skewed angle. As an artist, she's intolerant of those can't get a horizontal line straight. This doesn't bode well, and Suzy is tempted to decline the request, but zooms in on the face to be sure.

'ZELDA!' cries Suzy. Pushkin jumps off her lap in alarm. Gone is the cropped peroxide hair and scarlet lipstick, but even with a salt and pepper bob, glasses and faint traces of a jowl, there is no mistaking HER friend Zelda Shaw. She and Suzy lived together as students. I get the *Fitzgerald*, thinks Suzy, but *Asin*? Ah! *Zelda as in Fitzgerald.*

Whilst many found her sardonic humour, baldly stated opinions and unrestrained swearing scary and intimidating, Suzy had liked Zelda from the off. Within a week of their arrival in Manchester, they had bonded over a love of Bowie and the Banshees and a mutual disdain for Bananarama.

'Don't tell everyone but my actual name is Tracy,' Zelda had admitted, one drunken evening. 'But there were three fookin' Tracys in my school year, so the teacher asked if any of us had a middle name we could be known by. I dreamt up the most outlandish one I could think of. What's a girl to do?'

Zelda's background was working class, and she'd told Suzy hers most certainly wasn't, yet it turned out they both had nightmare mothers who had precipitated their escape to university. Far more outré, Zelda had declared she was bisexual—'Don't worry, I don't fancy you.'

In return, the best Suzy could muster was she had a boyfriend back home. When Zelda had opined, 'Yeah, yeah. Anyone who starts Poly with a boyfriend or girlfriend at home dumps them in the first year— you'll see,' Suzy had been shocked.

'But I love him,' she had protested.

Curiosity piqued, Suzy accepts the request and at once Zelda's life unfurls before her, startling and colourful as a pop-up book.

Zelda is still very politically active, she notes. Suzy can still picture the CND and *Reclaim the Night* posters Blu-tacked to her bedroom wall. Thirty years on and she is declaring her allegiance to Extinction Rebellion.

'Glad to see you're still keen to save the planet,' says the top comment. Then there is an emoji wink. At once Suzy's heart starts to race. *Glenn Pemberton,* it says by the tiny photograph. There can't be many men with that name, who know Zelda too. Zelda she's not seen for over a decade, but *Glenn?* It must be over thirty years.

Suzy clicks, and yes, of course, it's him.

Bloody hell.

She sits back, winded. Glenn was so hard drinking, so reckless, so prone to burning the candle; she wouldn't have been surprised to learn he was dead.

Yet here he is. Moreover, he is still really good looking! Perhaps his profile picture is merely an excellent shot, but no. Predictably, Glenn hasn't revealed much about himself, but he has not been cautious about the privacy settings on his photos; other pictures reveal his skin is weather-beaten and his once jet-black hair is threaded with grey. Nonetheless, he's still got it. God, those intense hazel eyes! Even now they make Suzy's stomach flip. Or maybe it's the wine...

It seems he continues to ride a motorbike—in one picture he's leaning against a gleaming silver machine. She is keen to establish whether he is hooked up with anyone, but although she has a thorough snoop around, there's nothing to indicate either way. To find out more, she'll have to send a *Friend Request*.

Finger hovering over the mouse, Suzy frets about her pale midwinter skin and her less-than-toned body. But it's my profile picture he'll see, not me in my slippers and leggings, guzzling wine, she reasons. 'I told Alice you're a bit of a rock chick,' she recalls Cam saying. She zooms in on her own profile photo. She is laughing. There is no hint of her jowl, and her chubbier midriff is nowhere to be seen. It is high summer, and her hair is blowing in the breeze and appears its fairest and most flattering, and she has a glow to her skin sorely lacking now. Perhaps she has not lost her mojo entirely, after all.

To hell with it. She catches a whiff of her younger, wilder self, and presses *Add Friend*.

Hey, she notices. This is fun! Why stop here? There are lots of people she is intrigued to learn more about. Although she's most curious about her exes; they're the ones who for periods of time she was closer to than anyone and who then dropped out of her life completely, as if the world were flat and they've fallen off the edge. She's not unique in this, she knows, but it has left her wondering and occasionally mournful, with only memories to contemplate alone.

Of course, I know all about *Leo*, she reminds herself. Cameron keeps her updated; he still sees Leo regularly. It is such a cliché, resenting wife number two, and it is not as if Suzy was without fault when it came to their marriage. Far from it. Still, Jili is beyond annoying. She is into crystal healing and is currently studying online for a diploma in Reiki massage. Privately, Suzy finds her a bit of a joke.

Leo was always a good networker, she thinks. He is bound to be on here.

Suzy types his full name, *Leo De Luca,* into Search, and sure enough, in mere seconds, she has tracked him down. In his profile picture he appears gallingly well. Still bald, of course, but tanned and slimmer. Her eyes widen at the sight of his cover picture. This must their home in Northern Italy. With its tumbling bougainvillea and white shuttered frontage, it makes Suzy ache with longing, not for him especially, but for the wealthy world they inhabited as a couple, full of people with homes so beautiful they'd be featured in Interiors, Elle Deco or Grand Designs. *He* liked my paintings, she reminds herself. Then she worries what he'd think of her work now. Maybe she has lost the knack...

Don't be so down on yourself, she thinks. It's not as if you're asking for financial help, and we're on reasonable terms considering.

Before she can restrain herself, she pings him a *Friend Request* too.

The list of Suzy's old flames does not stop there. Because, of course, there was Nate.

Nate, Suzy thinks, with the lurch of sorrow which accompanies every thought of him. Merely his name chokes her up with emotion. To imagine him in the context of her other lovers—the pain is so excruciating that she has to has dig her fingernails into her thighs to stop herself from howling.

Whenever she pictures Nate in her mind's eye, the sun is shining. His limbs are tanned, his corkscrew curls turned the colour of straw by the sun, and he's smoking, eye half-closed so he can hold a cigarette in his lips whilst he continues talking. Funny. He was a social smoker, no more, but he was such a party animal that she thinks of it as one of the trademarks of the years they were together.

Soon Suzy is weeping too intensely to see the screen. There is no point in continuing, so she closes her laptop and makes her way up the narrow staircase to bed.

As she drifts off, she thinks of Nate. Suzy loves it when he joins her again in slumber like this. She can't help it. She should be over it, but she isn't, and she never will be, so the only option is to be glad when she dreams of him as he was, laughing and chatting and dancing and smoking, eternally young and sparking with energy and light.

13.

December 2017

She wakes with a jolt, head pounding, throat dry. She must have drunk more than she realised.

Tea, thinks Suzy. I need tea. She gets up, pads downstairs to the kitchen. While she waits for the water to boil, she tidies away the washing up, wipes the draining board then sits down at her ancient laptop. The engine burrs into life, painfully slow. She taps in her password and one by one the windows open. Top of the pile is Facebook. She has received a message. She knows it isn't wise, she ought to head back to bed. Yet she is intrigued, so clicks to see who it's from.

'Oh my God, no way!' says Debs, when Suzy tells her.

There wasn't a hope of getting back to sleep after *that* response. At 9am Suzy is on her neighbour's doorstep, in the drizzle. Debs' hair is damp, and she appears halfway through a piece of toast.

'You sure it's not a bad time?'

'I've got to leave for a meeting at round half ten but won't take me long to get ready,' she says, mouth full. Debs is dressed for work but for her footwear, a pair of furry slippers. *Foxy* it says on one foot, *Lady*, on the other. Surely a present from Rich, thinks Suzy and, as she follows her friend into the kitchen-come-living room, feels a small stab of envy. She doesn't even *like* the slippers, but it's such years since a lover gave her a present.

♩ ♫ ♪ ♩

She is being ridiculous, of course. Debs and Rich's home—indeed almost everything they own—could hardly be further from her own taste. A vast, open-plan space with floor to ceiling windows looks out over a wide lawn with shrubs surrounded by bark chip. There are no quirks and few personal touches, and the place is so modern, it lacks a sense of history to Suzy's mind. Neither Debs nor Rich is particularly creative, and they would rather pay for professionals to design for them. They have both said as much to Suzy—or more likely it was Rich; he is keen on splashing his cash with grandiose gestures. The counter-tops are white marble and streamlined, the cupboards open with a magic push and 'click', not handles. Upstairs the master bedroom houses the famous leopard-print chaise longue and large photos from Debs and Rich's lavish wedding. Yet despite their differences, Suzy admires their chutzpah and the fact they aren't cowed by the country set. The village is full of properties which are hundreds of years old—her tiny thatched cottage included. And when it comes to displaying art, their clean white walls and high ceilings are undoubtedly a super-ior backdrop to her own mildewed wallpaper and peeling plaster. At right angles to the windows is one of Suzy's abstracts. Suzy could not have wished for a better setting to show it off.

Debs sees her eyeing it. 'I still love it.'

She needn't be so kind, thinks Suzy. It was generous enough to com-mission me.

Yet Debs continues, 'Especially on days like today when it's so miserable outside. It gives the room such a lift.'

I suppose the touches of cadmium yellow stand out well in the low light, Suzy concedes.

'Coffee or tea?' asks Debs, swallowing the last of her toast, and maybe it's because her friend is being so kind and seeing her painting has reminded Suzy of Julian's rejection, but all at once Suzy is fighting back tears.

'Hey,' says Debs at once. 'Hey Suze—'

The use of Johnny's name for her tips Suzy over the edge. She is overwhelmed by waves of emotion and then she is gone, down a hole to the past, back to the darkness and panic.

There is a deafening crunch, the sound of splitting wood and ripping metal and once more Suzy is fighting for breath. Dimly she recalls death by drowning is supposed to be euphoric: instead, she feels helpless, overwhelmed, her bones brittle as dry twigs, about to snap. She can't last much longer, scrabbling to kick against the current and the freezing cold. Her lungs are burning like lava. *I have to survive,* she thinks, trying to slow the cacophony of her brain. *I have to reach the surface. I don't want to this to be it.*

At long last she feels air, *air,* on her skin. She gulps it in, swallows water, inhales again.

It is then she hears the screaming. It is the screams, most of all, she can never forget.

Suzy has no idea of how long she is away but, gradually, she comes back to herself. First, she is aware she is gasping, gulping as she hyperventilates, clawing her legs... Then she can sense Debs' home again, although she is still not herself, not at all: she is in a sweat, pulse racing, head whirling. She is vaguely aware she is rocking in her chair, backwards and forwards, backwards and forwards. She can hear herself repeating, 'Please, let them be safe... Please let them be safe...'

It isn't real, she tells herself, although the flashback was so vivid, she can't shake the sense it is happening right now. *I'm here.* She fixes her gaze on the rain lashing at the window, but her heart is still thumping so fast it's scaring her.

Presently she hears Debs saying, 'It's OK, it's OK...' and she realises her friend is stroking her hand, exactly as she did in the hospital, and wonders if she has been doing this a while and it's only now that she can feel Debs' touch.

She grabs Debs' palm, squeezes it tight. *I'm here, I'm safe.*

Yet no sooner does she begin to calm when, in a rush, it comes again, another wave, this time from her stomach. She heaves—BLEAURGH!—and pale brown liquid pours from her mouth in a repugnant fountain. It splatters the plaster cast and pools onto the polished concrete floor.

She is mortified, but her whole body is juddering so hard she can't control it. Again, her stomach contracts, again she retches, and another stream of liquid adds to the first. Then she heaves and heaves and heaves, but no matter how hard her stomach contracts, nothing more comes up.

Presently the urge to vomit fades, the shivering subsides. Suzy wipes her lips with the back of her hand. She can taste bile. Hideous.

'You poor love!' exclaims Debs, shifting to rub Suzy's back.

And now she is crying and sniffing with shock at what she's done, all the vomit, but at least she is here, in the present.

'Better?'

'I'm so sorry. What a mess I've made!' Humiliation makes Suzy weep harder.

'Don't be daft. It's only your last cuppa, by the look of it.'

Suzy smiles through her tears. I love this woman, she thinks, grateful. 'Can I use your bathroom?'

'Of course. I'll fetch you a towel.' Debs slips away and returns with a pair of tracksuit bottoms too. 'Here pet, borrow these. Reckon we're roughly the same size.'

They are so soft they are clearly expensive. 'Are you sure?'

''Course!'

By the time Suzy has washed her face, gargled with mouthwash, and changed, she feels much better, as if she has unburdened herself of something far bigger pressing on her insides.

'I'm so sorry,' she repeats, returning to the kitchen.

'No need to apologise.' Debs is sitting at the table, bag of cosmetics before her, applying her make-up, but Suzy sees that the floor has been mopped beneath where she was sitting and there is the smell of bleach.

'Maybe it was something I ate.'

'Could be.' Debs nods, and although she adds, 'You've had a lot going on,' which suggests she doesn't think is the reason.

'I reckon I'll be OK now,' says Suzy.

'Great.' Debs tautens her mouth to apply her lipstick.

'I don't know what got into me.'

'That seemed awful. Was it a panic attack? You had something a bit similar in the hospital. Maybe we ought to get you back to the doctor?'

'NO!'

Debs stops. Then she holds up her hands. 'No pressure. It's your call.'

'I hate doctors.' Her mother, her broken leg, Suzy has had more than her fill.

'Understood.' Debs nods and rummages for her mascara.

It's over, Suzy thinks. I'd prefer not to talk about it. There is an awkward silence and for a few dreadful moments she fears that Debs is going to head down a therapeutic route and ask her to delve into her past. Lord knows what that would bring up. More than vomit, she is certain.

'Sorry if I bit your head off,' Suzy says after a while. It's that I don't want Debs treating me like one of her clients, she reasons to herself. Debs is a consultant, specialising in conflict management. People don't end up with huge homes by chance, and she feels beholden already.

Thankfully, Debs laughs. 'You're not the first.' Then she comes to stand at Suzy's shoulder. 'You want to show us this message?'

'Sure.' Suzy, relieved to be moving on, reaches for her phone.

While she hunts through her correspondence, Debs asks, 'Where does he fit into the grand scheme of things then, this ex of yours?'

'Er—'

'Stop!' Debs grabs the phone. She taps the screen then expands the space between her two fingers. 'This him?' She turns it. Glenn's profile picture grins out at Suzy.

'Yes.'

'He's totally lush!'

Suzy laughs.

'Is he single?'

'No idea.'

'Excuse me, may I?' Debs taps the screen a couple more times. 'Yes, he is!' She hands the phone back, smiling broadly.

'Blimey. You were quick. How did you establish that?'

'Says here.' Debs points. 'Under RELATIONSHIP. See?'

'Hark at you, Mrs Marple. I didn't know it had that option.'

'I'm on Facebook all the time. Much more than I should be. Comes in handy though, eh?' They both laugh. Suzy is beginning to feel more herself again.

Debs leans in. 'Wey hey, he's written back fast.'

'That's what I thought.'

They both pause to read.

Hi Suzy, long time no hear! So, what have you been up to all this time? I see you have a studio in Amhurst. I like the abstracts you've got online—

'He's checked you out, see?' Debs elbows her. 'You're in there, lass.'

Do you live in Amhurst or just work there? After Manchester, I assumed you'd go back to London. Can't imagine you living in the country, though you're looking good on it. If you fancy getting together some time, let me know. Amhurst isn't far from me—I'm near Marlborough. We could go for a ride—I promise to bring a spare helmet this time!

'Very forward,' says Debs. 'What's this about the helmet?'

'He's referring to the first time we went out,' says Suzy.

♩ ♫ ♪ ♩   72

'Which was when you were how old?'

Oh dear, thinks Suzy. This is what I feared, dredging up my past. Though I can hardly backpedal, not when I came round specially to talk.

'Nineteen, twenty? I'm not sure exactly.'

'Hold up,' says Debs. 'You need to fill me in. What happened to Johnny? I liked the sound of him.'

Suzy shifts in her seat. The memories make her uncomfortable. 'I didn't behave very well. Regarding Glenn I mean.'

'You heartbreaker!' Debs is gleeful. 'Hell lass, if you had this lad coming on to you, can't say as I blame you.'

'It was more complicated than that. Johnny went to uni a year ahead of me. I did an art foundation and stayed local. There was another girl—' Suzy checks her watch. 'Oughtn't you go?'

'Long as I leave by half ten, I'll be fine, like I said. Go on, shoot.'

♩ ♫ ♪ ♩

14.

November 1981

All the way back to Johnny's flat on the campus, Suzy has felt something isn't quite right. Now she is perched on the edge of his bed, with him beside her. It's been drizzling but she is still wearing her coat. Although the room is stuffy, she has an urge to keep it on, as if a sixth sense is telling her she needs extra protection.

It's Suzy's first visit since Johnny left for university a fortnight earlier, and she has missed him dreadfully. Time and again she has fingered the passport photo she carries of him in her purse, smiling at the sight of the face she knows so well; those big cow eyes, his flop of brown hair, which he currently wears spikey in a style reminiscent of the lead singer in one of their favourite bands. He's posing for the camera, collar of his coat up, face turned to emphasise the slant of his cheekbones, and she recalls he was on the verge of laughter.

Johnny had embraced her when he met her from the train and held her hand when they walked through the rain to get here, yet his answers to her questions about how he is finding university are short and staccato, and when she enquires if he's made any friends during Freshers' Week, he avoids a direct answer. He mutters something about meeting a couple of guys interested in forming a band. Suzy has to push to get him to say even this much. She is used to him being open and affectionate, but he hasn't properly hugged or kissed her. Maybe he has been waiting until they are alone. Now it is only the two of them, seems the right moment. Yet when she leans to kiss him, she can sense he is rigid with tension. Eventually he pulls away.

'I'm sorry, Suze...' He stares at the floor.

She recoils. 'What?'

'I—I—er...' It's as if time slows to an almost stop. She hears him mutter, 'I can't lie to you... We've always been honest with each other...' Then she hears him say something about getting very drunk on the second night he was here, that there had been a gathering in the girls block nearby. Yet it seems as though he is far, far away, only just audible.

'I don't understand,' says Suzy.

'It was just a kiss...' he says tentatively. Five words. Each is like the slice of a razor blade. 'I didn't sleep with her or anything.' He tells Suzy it was an awful mistake, that it will never happen again.

'What's her name?' Suzy's voice is so quiet she can barely hear herself speaking.

'Does it matter?' He looks at her, brown eyes filled with guilt and sorrow.

'Yes'

'Alison.'

Suzy's gaze falls to the duvet. Johnny has brought his bedding from home; it is the same forest green checked cover he had on his bed there. Suzy has fallen asleep curled up in Johnny's arms beneath it, cuddled him countless times wrapped in it. She has had sex with him on top of it, under it, with it discarded on the floor. A tear rolls down her cheek, then another, and drops onto the polyester cotton.

She wraps her arms tight round herself, circling the bobbly tweed of her second hand coat, but she remains cold, shivery with shock. She glances again around the nondescript room, with its utilitarian furniture and white breezeblock walls. CRASS declares the poster opposite, white out of black. They are a band Johnny likes, and Suzy doesn't. He hasn't even put it up straight, she thinks. Normally she would straighten it for him—she has a better eye. But the thought of Johnny with another girl here, where she, Suzy, is sitting, is so repugnant, everything about the space seems hateful. She wants to leave but cannot tear herself away.

'You didn't... get off with her here, did you?' Her voice is a whisper.

He exclaims, 'No! I'd never have brought her here.' He promises, *swears* that this other girl has never been to this small inhospitable bedroom. 'I love *you*, Suze. I realised it was wrong, so I stopped.' She glances up at him and he begs, 'Please don't finish with me.'

Suzy doesn't want to end it, but she is horribly shaken. Pat kept telling us we were young, she recalls. She made a point of saying that life holds 'lots of opportunities' for us both. This was probably what she was alluding to. For a moment she resents Johnny's mother for foreseeing what she didn't, and then she remembers Sal saying, 'Someone's bound to try and get off with Johnny, he's so nice looking,' and redirects her anger at her friend. Although she is not truly angry with either of them, she knows this is not their fault.

She is used to other girls looking at Johnny. He plays lead guitar in a band, for goodness' sake, women were always ogling him. Sometimes when he was gigging with *The Soup Dragons*, she'd watch the girls watching him, and get irked. But she only ever had to show up backstage and he'd make it so obvious that Suzy was his girlfriend—he'd throw an arm around her, pull her to him, kiss her—she had not been hugely threatened. Never, in her wildest imaginings, had she thought Johnny would get off with another girl so soon after starting his studies.

Suzy is hurt, dreadfully hurt, and at that moment, she cannot imagine that the agony will ever ease. Her trust has been violated and she feels a fool, an utter fool. She is also angry with Johnny for his lack of willpower, and with herself for being so naïve.

As if from nowhere, she snaps, 'I've decided to go to Manchester Art School.' The statement is as much of a surprise to herself as it is to Johnny.

♩ ♫ ♪ ♩

Good, thinks Suzy, watching his expression crumple. It is gratifying to hurt him, too. He deserves to suffer.

'Sorry?'

'I want to get away from my parents. And your Mum told me Sylvia Pankhurst went to Manchester, so I checked it out and it looks great.' That Pat has recommended it will deepen his distress. Suzy is being vindictive, but she is reacting out of instinct, fighting back using the best means at her disposal.

'I thought you were going to stay in London.'

'I'm not.' On this score, she has ammunition. 'I wouldn't get a grant. I have to be living away from home for that. Like you. Remember?

'Oh.' He swallows hard. She can see his eyes glistening with tears.

She loves Johnny, of course she does, so then she feels bad for upsetting him. Perhaps I shouldn't have said that. Maybe I should come here, do Fine Art at Brighton Poly?

'Of course, you must go wherever feels right,' he says magnanimously.

I don't want to split up with him. I can't imagine my life without him in it, thinks Suzy. As she unstiffens, stance relaxing, she leans into him, and he puts one arm around her.

'I heard this song the other day,' he says, gently brushing her fringe from her eyes with his free hand. 'The guy down the corridor was playing it. It made me think of you.'

'Oh?'

'I recorded his album. Hang on...'

Johnny fumbles with his cassette player; there is a click as he presses *play*.

A guitar begins strumming a spare, hypnotic melody and is joined by a male voice so deep and melancholy, it is as if he is speaking from beneath the concrete floor.

'*Suzanne takes you down...*'

Suzy starts at the sound of her name.

77 ♩ ♫ ♪ ♩

'Hush, listen.' Johnny whispers.

The song tells of a beautiful woman who lures the singer to her place by the river where she feeds him '*tea and oranges all the way from China*'. In the background, a lilting female chorus keeps rising and falling with each verse. The lyrics are haunting and enigmatic, and at one point Suzanne is described as wearing '*rags and feathers from Salvation Army counters*', and here Johnny momentarily leans in even closer to whisper 'See? Like you!' and Suzy feels that yes, the Suzanne in this song from the 1960s might be her; for she too has a knack for finding and styling second-hand clothes and making them somehow her own. The words are full of romantic and spiritual longing, each verse ends with a similar refrain: '*And you want to travel with her/And you want to travel blind/For you've touched her perfect body/With your mind*'. It ends as tenderly as it began.

'Who is it singing?'

'Leonard Cohen,' Johnny says. 'Isn't it beautiful?'

'I'm not sure I understood it,' admits Suzy.

'I don't think it matters,' says Johnny. 'I'd give my right arm to write a song like that. It's only four chords.'

'Really?'

'You can see why I had to share it with you.'

And then they kiss, and although she still senses the pain of betrayal lurking beneath the surface, Johnny smells so lovely and his mouth is so soft, that she allows him gently, carefully, to help her out of her coat. Having relinquished its warmth, other layers follow; she strokes his back and eases off his jumper then T-shirt, undoes his belt, unbuttons his flies. It's a dance at which they are practised, within seconds his fingers are under the elastic band of her skirt, yanking it down her thighs with an increased sense of urgency, both of their breath coming in shorter, keener gasps. And then with a flutter of dexterity off come her woollen tights, her knickers, top and bra, his jeans, his underpants.

'It's cold,' she says, and Johnny has goosebumps too, so they swivel themselves up and under his duvet, with its familiar cover, all cosy and reassuring, and at last they are together, skin touching skin. Their lovemaking is prolonged, poignant. Afterwards he plays the song again for her, and this time Suzy weeps, and Johnny comforts her as best he can, but he's all choked up too. And when they are lying in one another's arms after the song has finished for the second time, Johnny asks, voice full of apprehension, if they are OK.

'Yes,' says Suzy because she cannot bear to think otherwise. Thus, with this tacit agreement, they put Johnny's aberration behind them.

Nevertheless, that Freshers Week something has got into their relationship, some impurity, another influence, and the dynamic has shifted so that not even Leonard Cohen's exquisite song can repair it. The next morning Suzy can sense it, and for the rest of that term, that year, there are moments when she is reminded of that feeling, however hard she tries not to dwell upon it. The resentment, the sense of broken trust, of hurt and humiliation remains buried deep within her and it is still quietly, invisibly festering when she goes to Manchester Poly the following September. It needs igniting, a flame to bring it forth, but one day it'll happen, and then she'll feel better, properly better, and on a par with Johnny again.

15.

February 1983

'Fookin' 'ell!'

Zelda strides across the concrete floor in her DMs, appraising the vast, cathedral-like space. The heavy-duty steel columns and yellow-and-black-striped bollards that rise from the dancefloor are more reminiscent of a factory, where hazard lines might warn of oncoming forklift trucks, than a nightclub.

'It's a bit empty,' observes Suzy, raising her voice over the thudding bass of the Human League.

'I like it,' Zelda declares. 'Very industrial.' She looks right at home with her peroxide flat-top haircut held rigid with gel, granddad shirt and chunky cardigan, but Suzy is less sure.

'I'm freezing.' She rubs her arms.

'It's February, what did you expect?'

Somewhere warm, thinks Suzy. Compared to London clubs like *The Camden Palace* where she has been with Johnny, with its rich brocades and plush velvet sofas, the seating looks hard and uninviting, the colour scheme gloomy and grey.

Zelda seems to read her mind. 'Don't be such a soft Southerner. Put another jumper on next time. Drink?' She doesn't wait for an answer and heads straight to the bar, sliding to the front as if she has oiled herself specially. Moments later Suzy struggles in beside her, feeling awfully plump and short.

♩ ♫ ♪ ♩

'The acoustics are terrible.' The guy next to them raises his voice as the DJ segues effortlessly into the kickdrum opening of *Blue Monday*. As the bass guitar and sequencer fade in, he nods towards the stage. 'It's better up there, but the rest of the place, it's shit.'

'Who's next?' asks the barman.

'Me.' It's not true, but Zelda never has qualms about using her height to get attention. 'Bottle of Newkie brown. And a lager and lime for her.'

The barman says to Suzy, 'Half?'

'Pint.' Suzy bellows to make herself heard.

Before he turns to get their drinks, the barman holds Suzy's gaze for a second too long. Suzy watches, mesmerised, as he slips a glass beneath the tap, leaving it to fill while he fetches Zelda's bottle of ale. He not as tall as Johnny, but he is lithe, and his hair is dark and unfashionably dishevelled. She notices he moves in time with the syncopated rhythm of *Blue Monday* as he works. How he could not? Those drums, that swooshing keyboard and finally, after an intro the length of some singles, those robotic vocals. Suzy is pulled in two directions: she can't wait to hit the dance floor, yet he holds her, mesmerised.

'Oi! Put your tongue back in.' Zelda drops her voice and elbows her. Suzy laughs. Zelda can't mean it; she is hardly one to lecture. Men, women, young, old, after a few beers, she's not picky. 'Making up for lost time,' she'd reasoned. 'There's not much talent in Skeggy, trust me.'

All evening Suzy is conscious of the man behind the bar. The way he's dressed—in worn leather trousers and a Motorhead T-shirt—suggests he needs no one else's approval; they are hardly a fashionable band. On the far side of the club Suzy sees another girl sneaking glances in his direction. The girl is icy cool and slim, and her make-up is perfect. Even the way she is smoking, holding a cigarette in the tips of her fingers and taking tiny drags, seems chic. If he fancies either of us, it's bound to be her, Suzy decides, but the girl seems to consider her a threat anyway as she stares straight at Suzy, hard, declaring, *Don't you dare. He's mine.* For a while it seems the barman hasn't noticed either of them, but when he comes around collecting glasses, stacking them into a tower that curves over his shoulder with casual confidence, Suzy catches him looking at her. At once she is hyper aware of her breasts in her bra beneath the strings of her necklaces and vintage lace top. Her toes curl. Imagine if he could read her mind! I mustn't think like this, she scolds herself. I love Johnny.

At the end of the night, after the last track has finished, the barman comes up to Suzy and murmurs, 'How are you getting home?' He is more well-spoken than she'd expected, and for a moment she thinks she hasn't heard him right, then she realises he is standing there waiting.

She gulps. 'Um, I'm catching the bus.' She tips her head towards Zelda. 'With my friend.'

She hopes he'll say he'll go with them, but he replies, 'Shame. I was going to offer you a lift,' and slips back to the bar to wash the last of the glasses.

He fancies me, thinks Suzy, as she and Zelda head to the cloakroom, but there is no way she'll leave her friend to get the bus alone; none of the female students ever do. The streets are poorly lit, and the Ripper is an-all-too-recent memory. She's about to write the barman off as too brazenly only interested in one thing, when she sees him nip in at the front of the queue.

'Ah, Glenn.' The guy handing over coats acknowledges him.

Glenn leans over, reaches an arm round behind the door, and retrieves a leather jacket and motorbike helmet. Suzy's pulse quickens as she registers her mistake and, doing up her coat, she finds she is brushing elbows with him.

'Hello again,' he says.

'Hi.' She feels peculiarly giddy.

'What's your name?'

'Suzy.'

'Hi Suzy.' He flashes her a smile. 'I'm Glenn. What are you doing at the weekend?'

Zelda gives her a kick. Suzy ignores it. 'I'm not sure.'

'How about I pick you up Sunday and we go for a ride?'

'Oh, er....'

'Where do you live?'

She reaches into her handbag and finds a pen but nothing to write on.

'Here.' He grabs the book of cloakroom tickets and tears one out.

Hurriedly, conscious they are holding up the queue, she scribbles the address on the tiny space on the reverse.

Zelda leans in close and whispers. 'Thought you were spoken for.'

I'm jeopardising something incredibly special, thinks Suzy, but carries on writing. I can always change my mind, she reasons.

He takes it and reads, 'Rusholme. Ah, you're a student, are you?'

'Yes,' she says.

'About midday, OK?'

She nods and in seconds he is gone, leaving Suzy wondering if he is toying with her, or will turn up on her doorstep.

'I can't get on that,' she says, eyeing the motorbike on the pavement outside their red brick terrace. *750* it says on the side; the mere rev of the engine is daunting.

'I've got a helmet,' says Glenn, undoing the clip beneath his chin.

'But where's yours?'

'I'll do without,' he says.

'Isn't it against the law?'

He shrugs. 'No one will see.' As he helps her put it on, she can feel his breath against her cheeks, the tickle of his hands against her chin. She can tell he is concentrating and doesn't know where to look. 'Is this jacket all you've got to wear?' he asks, checking out her vintage wool blazer. 'It's cold on the back of a bike. You'll freeze.'

Suzy blushes, feeling naïve. 'Should I get something warmer?'

'You'll thank me for it,' he tells her, so she hurries back for her anorak to layer on top, and gloves and a scarf. 'S'pose it'll do.' He appears dubious. 'You'll need to get on first.' She hoists a leg over and edges back into the seat. 'Rest your feet here,' he indicates, 'and you'll have to hold on my waist.' She slips a hand round his midriff, conscious of the closeness of their bodies, the tautness of his torso, the smell of petrol, his leather jacket; him. Fleetingly she thinks of Johnny, his familiarity, how different he is from Glenn. The only other time she has ridden pillion was on the back of Johnny's pushbike as a kid. Then she would sit on the carrier, legs out like sticks on either side, while he pedalled them both round and round the garden, showing off. Eventually they might tumble onto the grass, but no harm ever came to either of them. Whereas Glenn makes her wary, something about him frightens her, and when he turns and says, 'Make sure you lean with the bike, OK?' she dares not to look back at the house; she is sure Zelda will be watching from her bedroom window and smirking as, with a roar of the throttle, they sweep off down the road.

So what if Zelda took the mickey because she was up for this? 'Call yourself a feminist? I can't believe you're succumbing to such awful sexual stereotypes, being seduced by an outlaw biker,' she'd jibed. 'The man must think he's Marlon bloody Brando.'

The feel of the cold wind beating against the sleeves of her anorak, the road only inches below her feet—Zelda would love it if she tried it, thinks Suzy. The rush of adrenaline, the sense of danger: it's like a fairground ride, only far more intense.

'Wow, this is brilliant!' she shouts as they pick up speed on the dual carriageway, her voice lost to the air in their wake.

She might be hanging onto Glenn for dear life, but that she has no choice but to rely entirely upon him is part of the magic. All at once she starts caring about everything which might affect them: potholes, bumps in the tarmac, puddles. She is hyper-conscious of their surroundings: the chill wind, buffeting them side on, the air rushing by, filling her nostrils with smells that change every second: exhaust fumes, pollution, grass, trees, a river. She can sense every nuance of cold weather, too: temperature, moisture, sun, shade. We're at the mercy of the elements, she thinks, keenly aware of her own mortality.

Soon they are beyond the south-city suburbs which Suzy knows from various student pubs and parties and in the outskirts of Manchester. They pass the airport and within minutes are on a country road. Moving through a tree-lined avenue, she can feel the temperature drop, and then, with a clear stretch of road ahead, Glenn accelerates again. We must be breaking the 60mph limit, she frets. Our lives could be snuffed out as quickly as the flip of a switch. Yet perversely she finds it utterly liberating. Never has she felt so free. All thoughts of Johnny and the trips he's made up north to see her vanish in a trail of exhaust.

A few miles on, Glenn slows the bike and turns into a large estate. *Lyme Park* declares the sign. It's owned by the National Trust, apparently. Absurdly, Suzy is reassured. Presently Glenn pulls into a car park and turns off the engine.

'How was it?'

'Great!' She is at a loss for adequate words.

'You OK walking?'

'Sure,' says Suzy, and they dismount. Her legs are wobbly, and her cheeks and fingers are freezing, but she doesn't say so.

'I'll take that,' he offers, referring to the helmet.

'You're alright. I can manage.' He's from a different planet, she thinks; the idea I might feel patronised doesn't seem to occur to him. She keeps the helmet clutched tight to her chest. Even so, she allows him to lead the way through a gate then along a stony track beside a meadow and into a wood. Their boots crunch in the frosty leaves as they walk.

'What sort of music do you like?' she asks, hoping to find common ground.

'Oh... Frank Sinatra, The Carpenters. You know?'

'The *Carpenters*?' Given the Motorhead T-shirt, this is not the answer she expected.

'She has such a beautiful voice,' says Glenn.

Yes, thinks Suzy, but aren't they a bit... cheesy? She can't fathom him. She can't work out why he doesn't reach to kiss her, he doesn't even touch her. And so what if I do kiss him? she reasons. Didn't Johnny snog Alison? All the time they walk, Glenn keeps a distance between them, but she can sense the space charged with energy and when he looks at her the intensity of his gaze is disarming. His eyes seem eerily green, or maybe it's the surrounding trees which make them appear that colour...

They sit side by side on a fallen branch, breath steaming in the cold.

'See that?' He points a leather-gloved hand.

On the top of a hill, a dark stone building is silhouetted squarely against the thundery sky. 'Is it a castle?'

'Apparently, it was built as a hunting lodge so ladies could admire the riding skills of their menfolk,' he says. The irony does not escape her. Then he adds, 'It's called *The Cage*.'

'Sounds sinister.'

'Some say it was named after *The Tower of London*. The man who built it was imprisoned for treason there.' It does look similar, thinks Suzy. 'Others say it's because they used to lock poachers inside.' He grins at her, but Suzy is unnerved. She has a sudden vision of herself trapped within its walls, screaming.

They fall silent. Don't be silly, she thinks, he's an ordinary bloke; he works behind the bar in *The Hacienda*. It's only he seems so different from any of the boys Suzy knows, not just Johnny, but her student friends too, who tend to be carefully coiffed trendy types; people she earmarked soon after she arrived in Manchester as likely kindred spirits. Glenn seems older somehow, and he's dressed more like a rocker from the '50s or '60s than someone her age. His patched jeans are tatty and grubby, his T-shirt splattered in oil from his bike. And she knows so little about him; where he is from, where he lives now, if he does any kind of work other than being a barman.

He removes his gloves, picks up a twig, starts scraping lichen from the bark.

'So, what do you like doing?' she ventures, hoping to draw him out.

He pauses, then shrugs. 'I like making bombs.'

She starts. Again, this is unexpected, but this time it is so outside her comfort zone, she has no idea how to reply. She must appear horrified, for he adds, 'Only small ones... More like fireworks really. I like chemistry and stuff.'

He's a nutter, she thinks. Images of the Yorkshire Ripper flash into her mind. What an idiot she is to have come out with him here, all alone. Or maybe he's in the IRA. Whatever, she should have told Zelda where they were going. 'You haven't hurt anyone?'

'No!' He looks startled she would countenance such a thing.

'Where do you set them off?' she asks, wary, yet fascinated.

'Round here,' he says. 'Sometimes. Or else further out, Edale, Castleton. I don't like to scare people.' He flicks a bit of lichen.

Could have fooled me, thinks Suzy. She has a crazed urge to laugh. Just wait until she tells this to Zelda. 'Doesn't anyone ever stop you?'

'Never get caught.' He scowls and brushes a dark strand of hair away from his eyes.

When they are leaving the park, they don't see the policeman walking up the hill towards them until it's too late. He flags the bike down and Glenn slows to a stop at his side.

'A Triumph Bonneville.' The policeman stands back, impressed. 'That must have cost a pretty penny.'

He is older and is a sporting a thick moustache. Maybe he thinks he is *Magnum P.I.*, thinks Suzy, but what works in Hawaii looks naff in Cheshire. Suzy doesn't trust coppers. He seems to be implying Glenn has stolen it which riles her.

Yet to her surprise Glenn smiles and replies, 'I did it up myself, sir. It was in a bit of a state when I got it.'

'I see,' says the constable. 'Nice job. Anyways, someone reported a bike going into the woods. You shouldn't be riding up there, not off road.'

'I'm terribly sorry, sir,' says Glenn. Suzy is struck by how polite he is being. That he should choose to turn on the charm is another surprise.

'Can you freewheel it down the hill, so you won't make any more engine noise?' asks the policeman.

'Yes, of course,' says Glenn.

'I see you've only got one helmet between two,' the policeman continues.

'I'm afraid I only have the one, sir,' says Glenn.

'Very gentlemanly, I'm sure. But you, young lady... You shouldn't be on the back of the bike when he's without a helmet.'

'No, sir,' says Suzy. She is vaguely aware Johnny would disapprove of her cow towing to someone in authority, but she doesn't want Glenn to get into trouble, so follows his example.

'Don't let me catch you doing it again.'

'No, sir.'

Back in Rusholme, Suzy dismounts and hands back the helmet. Glenn looks at her with that intense stare again, then mutters, 'I... um... that was nice.'

They're only inches apart. She senses he is about to kiss her. Suzy would like to kiss him too but instead, she blurts, 'I've got a boyfriend.' And for a split second it's as if Johnny is standing right there between them, eyes narrowed with suspicion.

Glenn pulls away, shocked. 'Oh. I'm sorry.'

'No, um, don't be.' She has no idea why she told him. Maybe it was fear or guilt? In any event, it's too late: it's out there. They stand for a few seconds, the air between them thick with tension once more. Despite her gloves and boots, her fingers and toes are freezing from the cold. She yearns to ask him in so they can warm up and have a cup of tea, but Glenn is so embarrassed and self-conscious it flusters her, too, and before the atmosphere can get any more awkward, he picks up his foot, kicks the starter and speeds off down the road.

December 2017

'Guess it's what folk mean when they talk of "the appeal of the bad boy,"' says Debs. 'Never gone for the type, myself, maybe 'cos of my da'. Never showed his feelings or said he loved any of us. Still, yeah, I can imagine how, with that 'un—' again she jerks her head towards Suzy's mobile '—it must have been alluring.'

'It was,' says Suzy. 'He turned my insides to jelly.' Then she sighs. 'Though he could also be hard work.'

'You never know,' says Debs brightly. 'Maybe he's changed.'

'Hmm.' Suzy thinks of all the people she hoped might change over the years; her mother and father, her ex-husband... Even Zelda, whose political stance she might have expected to soften over the decades, seems the same old Zelda if her Facebook posts are any indication. 'I'm not sure people ever change much.'

'Don't you think? I reckon people are more dynamic.' Debs gets to her feet and collects up their mugs. Then she laughs. 'I mean, Glenn's certainly making his *feelings* clear in his message.' She winks.

'Do you reckon?'

'For God's sake!' Debs casts her eyes skywards. 'Could a man be any more obvious?'

'I suppose...' Suzy hesitates. Maybe Glenn was trying to flatter me, she reasons. After all, he doesn't know if *I'm* single. She glances at the time— that Debs wiping the table is a hint she should go. 'I'd better get home.'

'You don't escape so easily. Not without telling me.'

'Oh?'

Debs pauses midway to the sink, cloth in hand. 'You going to meet up with Glenn, you daft cow, or what?'

16.

'What do you think?' Suzy is perched on the edge of Zelda's bed. It's Tuesday, but neither of them has lectures till noon, so both are still in their pyjamas. 'Brrr! It's chilly.'

'Get under here.' Zelda edges over to make room and lifts the duvet. Suzy slips beneath the covers and remains silent so Zelda can finish reading. Scanning the words over her shoulder, they seem hopelessly inadequate.

'Don't know why you're asking me,' says Zelda eventually.

'I don't know who else to ask,' says Suzy.

Zelda runs a hand through her flattop and a pouf of dust from yesterday's gel catches in the light streaming through the dormer window. 'You want my honest opinion?'

'Go on.' Suzy braces herself.

Zelda taps the letter. 'This stuff about wanting to be friends. What planet you on?'

'Hmph.' Suzy had spent ages working out what to say. 'Why?'

'You can't be friends with someone you've been out with.'

'Surely you can if you both want it badly enough?'

'What makes you think he'll be keen?'

'We were friends a long time before we became girlfriend and boyfriend.' I can't bear to lose Johnny completely, thinks Suzy. For years he's been my world. Park Road will be awful without him. Who else can

I talk to back home who gets me like he does? Where would I go to listen to decent music and watch my favourite programmes on telly? Mum and Dad might stomach *Top of the Pops* but there is no way they'll stand *The Tube*. "I wish the presenter would stop mumbling into his collar," Joan declared about Jools Holland. "And why does that silly girl titter all the time?" Suzy shudders at the prospect of wall-to-wall quiz shows like *Blankety Blank* and *Bullseye*. And what about when she and Joan argue, who will unerringly see her point of view?

'S'pose there's no harm in asking,' Zelda concedes. 'But... you're not going to like this.'

'Oh?'

Zelda drops the piece of paper. 'I don't think you should write to him at all.'

Suzy flushes. 'Why?'

'It's a bit shabby, finishing with Johnny in a letter.'

Suzy squirms. Of course, Zelda is right. When she'd drafted the words in the small hours, Suzy had managed to persuade herself she could get away with it because Johnny had got off with someone first, and she hasn't done anything yet with Glenn. The fact she hasn't been able to stop thinking about him is by the by. That she owes Johnny more than a few hastily written lines after all their time together is not something she can face. Truth is, she doesn't want to see how upset he will be, or give him the chance to dissuade her. This is what happened when he got off with Alison in Freshers' Week; when confronted by Johnny and everything she loves about him in the flesh, he always tugs at her heartstrings. It could become horribly protracted and she would lose Glenn in the process. The fact Johnny is 300 miles away is probably why her attraction to Glenn has happened at all.

'I don't want to wait two more weeks,' she reasons, which is when she and Johnny have arranged that she will next visit. She could go and see Johnny before this, but to traipse to Brighton to have what is bound to be an agonising conversation is not a prospect she relishes.

'You're bound to find it tough, being so many miles apart,' Pat had warned them. Seems she was right all along.

Nonetheless, Zelda is steadfast. 'Ring him then.'

Suzy is no more comfortable with this suggestion. Even from the phone box at the end of the street, I'll still be able to hear his voice, she thinks. I know the effect he has on me. Plus, I'll have to contend with at least one other person stamping their feet outside, impatient to use the pay phone after me, and the beeps on the line when my money is about to run out. It's hardly conducive to an easy conversation at the best of times.

'You did ask.'

'I know.' Suzy avoids Zelda's gaze. It's a long way from the endorsement of her missive she was after. She was hoping Zelda would help her see clearly. Instead, her friend is muddling her more.

'Feel free to ignore me,' says Zelda. 'I'm hardly one to moralise. Why don't you wait a bit?'

I'm no good at waiting, thinks Suzy. If Glenn turned up here, I'd drag him to my room and rip his clothes off this minute.

'Nothing might happen with Glenn,' Zelda adds.

Suzy is surprised. Zelda is usually black and white in her judgments and disdainful of any kind of woolly thinking. 'Isn't it worse stringing Johnny along?'

'One night isn't going to make any difference. Send it tomorrow.' Is Zelda saying what Suzy thinks she is? Before she can ask, Zelda holds up a hand. 'Yeah. Yeah. No need to wet yourself. I'll go.'

Suzy's guilt fades as excitement surges through her. The suggestion doesn't have to be made twice. Tuesday is cheap night for students and, 12 hours later, they are back at *The Hacienda* and, sure enough, Glenn is behind the bar. This time Zelda doesn't even wait for him to serve them. She elbows her way to the front, leans forward and grabs his shirt sleeve.

'OI!'

♩ ♫ ♪ ♩   92

Glenn whips his head around and glares, his face softening when he sees Suzy at Zelda's side.

'She's dumped him, mate,' says Zelda, relinquishing the shirt sleeve.

Glenn turns to Suzy, bewildered. At once, Suzy goes beetroot.

'Is that so?'

'Er...'

Zelda kicks Suzy so hard she is forced to stifle a yelp and interjects, 'Do I look like someone who would lie to you?' Before he can retort, she says, 'Good, glad we've got that sorted. We'll have our usual please.'

'I can't believe he remembered what we drink!' says Suzy as they make their way to find somewhere to sit.

'I can.' Zelda raises an eyebrow.

And later, when he and Suzy are lying on her single bed enjoying a moment's pause for breath between kisses, Glenn chuckles. 'As if a six-foot woman with hair like Woody Woodpecker is easy to forget. Especially when her mate has the best tits in Manchester.'

'Cheeky!' Suzy gives his bottom a playful slap.

'Maybe I'd best take a look at them to be sure.' He starts to ease open the buttons of her top.

Suzy laughs. 'If you must.'

'It's an essential fact-finding mission,' he says, slipping a hand into the cup of her bra.

Turns out the bounce in Glenn's walk was no accident. He is physically fit, toned in a way not a million miles from Johnny, who is into football and cycling, but in someone who works behind the bar of a nightclub is an unexpected boon. The stubble on his face is darker and more noticeable, he has more hair on his chest, and he is a fair bit older—24, not 20—so his manliness is unchartered territory, exciting.

The next morning, Suzy posts her letter to Johnny. *We promised to be honest with each other,* she reminds herself. It would be awful to two-time him. I couldn't live with myself if I did that.

17.

December 2017

Suzy peers at the CD, bemused. *The Leader of the Pack* by The Shangri-Las. Seems an unlikely choice for Johnny. Yet she bought the single long before Glenn was on the scene—dimly, she recalls it being used in an ad, it must have been then, because she clearly remembers she would sing for Johnny, 'They told me he was bad, but I knew he was sad', hamming up the vocals and laughing, because what it captured so adeptly was the heartbreak of going out with the guy your parents didn't want you to date. 'My folks were always putting him down'; that's her and Johnny. Yet again, it seems, he has got the measure of her.

The realisation spurs her into action. Before she can backtrack, she opens Messenger:

Hi Glenn. So glad you like my pictures! OK. You're on. Maybe not a bike ride as my foot is in plaster (long story), but let's meet up. Be good to see you. Suggestions welcome! Suzy

Next, Johnny's mother. She frets Pat might think ill of her, then reminds herself Johnny doesn't seem to bear a grudge so it's unlikely his mother will. All it needs is a cover note. Suzy has had a few of her paintings printed on postcards. Perfect.

♩ ♫ ♪ ♩   94

Dear Pat,

I hope this finds you well. It's been many years since we were in touch, but I still think of you and Colin so fondly. Right from when I was a small, you always made me welcome in your home, then later, when Johnny and I went out together, I felt part of the family. I owe my choice of art school to you, too—I recall you suggested Manchester and I loved my years there, despite the endless rain! My mother died a few weeks ago and Johnny was kind enough to drop me a line. I would like to thank him but don't have an address. From his card I gather you're still at number 32. If you could forward this on, I'd be very grateful.

Love, Suzy xx

Writing to Johnny is the hardest. For a few minutes Suzy is paralysed, unsure where to start, but on second thoughts, a postcard will work for him, too. She can save detail for future correspondence, and this way, she can include it in an envelope and send both cards to Pat.

Dear Johnny

You're right, my mother didn't mince her words! How kind of you to send a card and the CD—what a lovely thing to do. I wanted to thank you, but I haven't been able to find you online, so I'm sending this to Park Road and hope it reaches you via your mum.

Anyway, there's no need to apologise for anything.

'I was a coward,' she could admit, although in some ways she was brave, moving away as she did. Things are so rarely clearcut. And from the tone of his card, it seems Johnny is capable of a more nuanced understanding. If not then, he seems able to be magnanimous now...

I said to your mum I think of her and Colin fondly, they were so generous to me.

It wasn't just them who were kind, she thinks. Johnny was—is—cut from similar cloth. The realisation brings tears to her eyes; briskly she wipes them away. FFS, Suzy! She is running out of space, so reduces the size of her handwriting.

I've no idea what you're up to these days. I spent several years caring for my mum (she had dementia) so I feel—

What *does* she feel? Suzy can't tell. One minute she's overwhelmed by panic, the next planning to take off on the back of Glenn's motorbike. Yet Johnny is the one who set all this in motion. On a whim she adds her mobile number, then finishes:

— ready to expand my horizons.
Love, Suze x

Any more would be weird, given Johnny is happily married and everything.

♩ ♫ ♪ ♩   96

18.

'Here we go then,' says Zelda, as the CGI titles flash across the TV screen. She and Suzy are sitting in the kitchen in Rusholme with their housemates, Scally and Jez.

'Chuck us a beer, will you?' asks Jez.

Scally removes a can from the plastic hoops and throws it over. Other than Suzy, they're all in the middle of exams. Regardless, none are planning to head to bed any time soon.

'From now until 4 in the morning we'll be bringing you the fastest service of results,' announces the TV presenter. 'Elections are a struggle for power and this one was at a time of Prime Minister Margaret Thatcher's choosing.'

'I'm not sure I can bear to watch,' says Zelda.

'Is this the best signal we can get?' asks Jez. The figures on screen are ghosted and the picture keeps rolling.

'Hang on.' Suzy gets to her feet. The black-and-white portable telly on the sideboard is hers and she is familiar with its quirks. She gives it a thump to cure the horizontal hold, then perches the aerial on top of the gas grill. 'Better?'

Jez grunts in appreciation. The kitchen is spacious enough to house a large, if ancient, sofa, on which the four of them are squashed. When they moved in, Suzy tried to camouflage the unappetizing brown walls with a few of her sketches, but she's been fighting a losing battle against condensation and the corners of paper are continually coming unstuck and curling. The vinyl-covered floor, on the other hand, is always sticky—they keep arguing about who is going to wash it, yet no one ever does—and the fluorescent strip light makes them all look tired and ill even when they're feeling chipper.

'You know Michael Foot was in Manchester last week?' says Scally, hooking a dining chair with a crepe-soled shoe and pulling it over to stretch out his wiry legs. 'He was

trying to drum up support in seats Labour is likely to lose.'

'It's a sad state-of-affairs if the opposition can't rely on the vote in *this* part of the country,' says Suzy.

'Exactly.' Scally counts, one bony a finger at a time. 'Three million unemployed, riots in London and Liverpool, spending cuts, strikes...' He grimaces. 'Should'a been shooting fish in a barrel.'

Suzy isn't sure she agrees with his analysis but is cautious about disputing it. She can sense Scally, a politics student, is squirming with tension already and Zelda's fuse has been short all day. Both are so quick and confident of their opinions Suzy often feels shy and unworldly beside them, floundering to keep pace.

'But the press are *so* biased,' counters Zelda. 'All the uproar about Foot's coat. What's so bad about a donkey jacket?'

Suzy is tempted to suggest it might help if Michael Foot got a decent haircut as then he'd look more statesmanlike, but fears she'll get shot down.

Zelda reaches for one of Scally's cigarettes. 'Do you mind?'

'Go ahead.' Scally nods, and as he leans to light it for her with his Zippo, Zelda's crest of hair falls alarmingly close the flame.

Zelda gives Scally's brothel creepers a gentle kick with her DMs. 'Budge up. I want to put my feet up too.'

With a sigh, Scally creates space.

'How can people vote for Thatcher with so many out of work?' says Zelda.

Jez yawns. 'Labour don't help themselves with their in-fighting.'

Suzy imagines what her mother would say, and ventures, 'A lot of people like a leader who sticks to their guns. I'm not saying I do, but *This lady's not for turning*, all that. I understand the appeal of it.' She waits for Scally and Zelda's reaction, wary she has spoken out of turn, but they are interrupted by a sharp knock on the back door.

'Expecting anyone?' asks Scally.

They all shake their heads.

'It's open!' bellows Zelda, and to Suzy's surprise, Glenn steps inside. His eyes meet Suzy's and again, he holds her gaze for a second too long. At once her heart begins to thump with excitement. I hope I look OK, she frets. It's hours since I applied my makeup, and I haven't back-combed my hair since this morning. It must be horribly flat. How she wishes she could check in a mirror!

'I got off early,' he says. 'Place was empty.'

''Cos everyone is watching this,' says Zelda.

'Get an ale in yer mate,' says Scally.

Glenn reaches for a can. 'Cheers.'

Despite her consternation, Suzy is thrilled. Glenn rocking up on the spur of the moment is further evidence he is keen, surely. Since they have been seeing each other, he has proved a strange mix; taciturn one day, animated the next, getting drunk one night, the following morning heading off on a punishing cross-country run before Suzy has even surfaced. She often senses he is holding back, yet no sooner has she convinced herself his reticence is a sure sign she likes him more than he likes her, than he will surprise her with a wildly romantic gesture. A month earlier he had whisked her to Edinburgh for the weekend; 'My aunt's away, we can stay there,' was all he'd let on. 'Zelda, it was a frigging *palace*,' Suzy had rhapsodised on her return. Plus, the sex is great. Not that it wasn't good with Johnny. Nonetheless Glenn is older and more experienced and knows a thing or three she and Johnny didn't.

For all these reasons, Suzy would dearly like Glenn to be able to sit next to her on the sofa, but she knows better than to expect one of her housemates to relinquish their space. Glenn picks up the vibe, pulls out a chair from the table and sits down, stretching out his legs in a fashion conveying he is not dependent on anyone else's generosity to make himself comfortable. I hope they all like him, thinks Suzy. He's *so* attractive, I fancy him *soo* much. However, both boys, like Zelda, had warmed to Johnny when he visited. Especially Scally—the Liverpool connection, the shared political outlook—the two of them ended up yacking into the small hours. In contrast, Glenn is not the matey type. Thus far, she's not met one of his friends, and he lives alone in a studio.

'Who's supposed to declare first?' he asks.

'Guildford, Torbay or Cheltenham apparently,' says Suzy, relieved to have remembered.

'No prizes for guessing which way *those* seats will go,' says Scally.

Glenn laughs. 'What time they due in?'

'Just after 11.' Suzy is rapidly reappraising how long she might stay up. With Glenn so near yet out of touching distance, she senses her bedroom pulling like a magnet.

They turn their attention back to the TV.

'I'm going to ask our computer to tell us party by party just how we think the new parliament will look,' the commentator is saying. 'And there it goes...' A line of blue and another of red shoot across the TV screen but the blue keeps going. 'The Conservatives 398, Labour 208.'

'Shit,' says Zelda.

They all fall silent, taking it in.

A few moments later Zelda jumps up. 'It's the fucking war,' she declares, stubbing out her cigarette with force and pacing the room. 'It's what this is *really* about. We all know Thatcher had dreadful poll ratings until the Falklands conflict.'

'She's a war monger,' says Scally. 'All this cosying up to Reagan.' 'I never understood why we risked lives retaking the damn place anyway. Only a few bloody sheep farmers.' Zelda helps herself to another Marlboro from his packet without asking.

Scally leans forward to light it. 'You're welcome.'

'Because you can't just roll over and let a dictator invade your territory,' says Glenn. His voice is measured but Suzy can tell he is needled from the set of his jaw.

'I'd question why we considered some islands 8000 miles away were ours in the first place,' continues Zelda regardless. She exhales and a plume of smoke heads up towards the fluorescent light. 'It's colonialism gone mad.'

'Actually, it's turned out better for the Argentinians,' says Glenn quietly. Until this evening Suzy and Glenn haven't talked much about current affairs. Unlike Johnny, she had assumed he wasn't interested, but it sounds as if he is. Moreover, he seems to have a different perspective from the rest of them.

'Really?' she prompts, curious.

'Galtieri had his own reasons for invading the Falklands,' Glenn points out. 'He hoped it would take people's minds off everything going wrong in his own country. Only it didn't.'

'Yes, I know.' Zelda rolls her eyes theatrically.

'You think it would be better if we'd lost?' asks Glenn.

Suzy is impressed: it takes a brave person to challenge Zelda. Scally is usually the only one who dares.

Zelda turns to face him. 'Better not to have gone at all.'

'Seriously? You'd like us to have sat back and done nothing?' Glenn shifts his legs, tucking his feet beneath his chair. He looks about to pounce.

'I hate all the triumphalism,' says Zelda. 'GOTCHA! STICK IT UP YOUR JUNTA and stuff.'

'It's *The Sun* being *The Sun*,' says Glenn.

'But people believe it,' says Zelda.

'You reckon even though Galtieri had to resign, and it looks likely civilian rule will be restored over there, it would have been better if we'd stayed at home?' Glenn laughs, yet Suzy can tell he is not remotely amused.

This is the man who makes bombs as a hobby, she recalls, wishing her housemates would pipe down.

Yet Zelda remains defiant. 'If it had brought Thatcherism to a grinding halt a year ago, then yes, I certainly do.'

Glenn exhales, shaking his head. 'None of you have the faintest idea what you're talking about.' His tone is ice cold. Oh dear, thinks Suzy. This isn't going how I hoped.

Scally leans forward, defensive. 'Oi, watch your mouth. You're out of order.'

'Sitting round drinking beer. You're just a bunch of students.'

All four housemates are blindsided. There is long silence. Suzy feels her cheeks flame.

'And what are you exactly?' says Zelda, face hardening. 'Last time I noticed you were a barman at *The Hacienda*.'

'I served in the Falklands,' says Glenn.

'Eh?' Scally frowns, uncomprehending.

'You heard me,' says Glenn. 'I was in the Falklands task force.'

'And the first results are in,' announces Dimbleby. Only they seem less important.

'You're a *squaddy*?' Scally, normally so fast to pick up information, is only able to process gradually.

'I was in the navy,' says Glenn.

'You went to Sandhurst and that shit?'

'No,' says Glenn. 'Sandhurst is where army officers train. Though I'm still not sure I'd call it *"that shit"*. I went to Dartmouth.'

'Stone me,' says Scally. He turns to Suzy. 'Did you know?'

Suzy shakes her head. She wishes the sticky vinyl floor would swallow her up whole.

'I don't get it,' says Zelda. 'What are you doing working in *The Hacienda*?'

Glenn gives her a sideways look. 'What's it to you?'

'Doesn't add up.'

'It's obvious,' says Scally.

'Oh?' says Zelda.

'He's done a runner.'

'Is he right?' asks Zelda.

Suzy is too taken aback to speak.

'I chose to leave,' says Glenn slowly. Suzy notices his fists are clenched; his arms taut with tension. All at once his startling muscularity makes sense.

'Wadid I tell ya?' scoffs Scally.

Suzy fears Glenn is going to punch him.

'I don't owe any of you any explanation,' he growls. Abruptly, he pushes back his chair and drains his can. 'Thanks for this.' He crumples the metal as if it were a tissue. 'I'm off.'

He yanks open the back door which swings back with such force the handle dents the wall, and is gone.

19.

January 2018

Hair up? Suzy turns to check in the mirror. No. Emphasises her jaw is not as sharp as it was. She takes out the clips and reappraises her reflection. It's better down, although this is how she always styles it. Zipping up the dress she'd planned to wear, it looks all wrong. Too staid. 'Nothing ages a woman more than moving to the country,' Zelda warned years ago. And when Suzy turns to check her rear view—yikes! She can't get the dress off fast enough.

OK. So tried and trusted it is. Suzy pulls on her most forgiving trousers and tries to quash the fear they make her appear mumsy by adding a sequined top. All this chopping and changing is making her hot. If she is not careful, she'll smudge her makeup. Stomach churning, she squirts on perfume, grabs her coat, and hurries out of the door.

Inside the pub, three lads are playing pool—Suzy believes one might be a child she taught when she was working at Amhurst Primary. I liked it there, she thinks with regret. If only caring for Mum had not meant giving up teaching art. I didn't foresee her living so long when I took on the caring role. If I had, who knows what decision I'd have made?

She starts as a gust of cold air from the door behind her announces another customer, but it's only a group of builders, covered in dust and trailing white powder.

'Boots off, boys!' bellows the woman behind the counter. Suzy

♩ ♫ ♪ ♩

knows the landlady, Martha. She and her husband have run the village local pub for years. The men glance at each other, nod in agreement, and stomp out.

Suzy casts around, but Glenn doesn't appear to have arrived. Eager to kill time, she heads to the women's lavatory. She touches up her lipstick and fluffs her hair, yet when she emerges, there is still no sign of him. She had deliberately been late herself, so now it's twenty minutes after their scheduled meeting. I knew this was an awful idea, she says to herself. I should never have allowed myself to be persuaded. It merely proves people don't change. Glenn's behaviour was always erratic.

Martha sees Suzy from across the room and gives her quick smile, and Suzy realises she needs to sit down. The village pub is the furthest she has walked without crutches since her plaster was removed, and the consultant advised her to take it slow. But she hates drinking alone in a pub. Maybe a younger woman might do it more readily. Then again, maybe not. Some things never alter, or if they do, the pace is slow. Being pestered by unwelcome strangers remains a hazard. On other occasions, events shift at breakneck speed. She shudders, recalling how her world was shattered in a few nightmare minutes...Then she pushes the thought away. She is being haunted by the past enough already. Suzy is about to leave, when she notices a man on a stool down the far end of the bar. His back is turned, and his clothes are dark; he was easy to miss. Yet no, she decides. This man is broad across the shoulders and thickset; his upper arms fill his shirt sleeves. It is not Glenn.

These days Suzy's paintings are invariably abstract, yet she often used to sketch her friends. It was often a struggle getting Glenn to sit still, so most of her attempts had failed to capture him. However, once, when he was asleep, she had got an excellent likeness. Also, Glenn was her lover. Not only had she watched him move around her room, getting dressed; she'd also followed the curve of his cheek with her fingertips, run a hand from his shoulder along his inner arm to his wrist, traced the line of hair on his belly. Glenn was lean. Toned, yes, but athletic, wiry. She would be sure to recognise him.

However, as she turns to the door, something in the way the man at the bar reaches for his pint makes her stop. Is it the way he takes hold of the glass? The angle of his head? She moves to get a closer look. It's as if he senses her eyes on him and turns and sees her.

'Suzy?' He seems to pick up her uncertainty. 'Hi. It's Glenn.'

His hair is greyer than in the photos on Facebook, but it's not this that disconcerts her. It's that he doesn't fit the mental image she has of him. He is stockier, his hair is different, much shorter, his face is not merely lined, but marked by age spots. Yet when he looks at her directly, holding her gaze, he has those same remarkable green eyes, that intense stare. For a few seconds, he looks serious, almost grave, and then he grins.

'You haven't changed a bit.'

Of course, I have, she thinks. She's torn between feeling flattered and suspicious: is she being played? Though maybe I haven't changed that much, she permits herself to consider. Zelda had said as much on seeing Suzy's recent photos on Facebook.

'Good to see you,' he continues, folding up his paper before she can see which it is. Shame. That could have revealed a lot. 'Can I get you a drink?'

'Yes, please.' Suzy needs one to steady her nerves. She is disconcerted, already, by what this is stirring up in her. 'White wine, please.'

'Large or small?' Then he laughs. 'Forget I asked.' He nods at Martha and Suzy cringes in the knowledge Martha will be wondering who Glenn is. Such are the perils of living in a village. Compared to London, or Manchester, say, most residents of Amhurst know each other and curiosity abounds. 'Large white wine,' he tells Martha.

Is that *large* because he wants me to relax, because he wants to seduce me, or because that's how he remembers me, as a hedonistic, to-hell-with-it girl? From the empty bottle beside him, it appears he has opted for low alcohol beer. Maybe he has stopped drinking, thinks Suzy. Although if he came on his bike, that would explain it. All this whilst she is struggling to absorb his physical presence, the fact he is here, beside her. 'I used to shoot rats when I was a kid,' he'd told her once. 'What with?' she'd asked, appalled. 'My dad's airgun,' he'd replied blithely, as if every family had one. Suzy has met no one who courted disaster like Glenn before or since. Yet here he is, not just very much alive, but still *so* handsome. Suzy even likes his clothes: jeans and an olive-green sweater and, flung on the stool next to him, a leather jacket, naturally. Yet the quality is better, gone is the reek of oil and the torn T-shirt. His hair is combed, he is freshly shaven, and he smells clean, of shampoo and soap. Yes, he has fleshed out, but he appears to have built muscle rather than fat, which is unusual in a man his age.

'Let's move,' he says, slipping off the bar stool once Martha has brought over Suzy's wine. 'Where would you like to sit?'

Help, thinks Suzy. Instinctively she'd rather they were somewhere they won't be overheard, but if she opts for a dark and secluded corner, it could imply she is interested romantically, and it is way too soon know. He waits for her to answer. He is still polite, she notices. 'Gentlemanly,' her mother would say; 'posh,' according to Zelda.

'Here.' She opts for a table close by and with relief, lowers herself into a chair.

He takes a seat opposite and leans forward, looking at her with those intense green eyes. God damn it, his gaze can still affect her. His face is serious, almost pained. 'I'm glad we met up again,' he murmurs.

'Me too,' she replies, frankly. The prospect has been thrilling, but she isn't about to let him know that. She wants to safeguard herself, her heart. 'I hoped you'd be fat and bald.' She laughs, the relief of not being stood up emboldening her.

'Oh?'

'As punishment.'

107

He winces. 'I guess... when I was younger... I treated you and other women like shit.'

'Other women?' She sounds biting. Suzy doesn't enjoy being made to feel like one bead on a necklace strung with many conquests.

'I found it hard to settle.'

She snorts.

He looks down, embarrassed, then glances up. 'I did know you were special.'

'Funny way of showing it.'

'I know,' he shrugs, and she is thrust back to the way he used to shrug all those years ago, when he couldn't articulate himself fully, leaving her to fill in the gaps and wonder what was going on, what he felt, beneath the evasion and bravado.

November 1983

'I think I'm falling in love with you,' Glenn says, eventually, and Suzy wants to fling back the duvet, jump up and dance around her sunlit attic bedroom with delight. It's been a long wait, this declaration. He is so emotionally cautious that getting Glenn to express himself has been like trying to harness water. Even Jez had observed, 'Doesn't say much, does he?' Quite something coming from the quietest member of their household. And yet the way Glenn looks at her is so hypnotic, Suzy feels he is boring into her soul. It has led her to believe he has feelings for her, despite his inability to articulate them.

'Really?' she asks, keen to have him say it categorically. They are lying together, naked. It's midday, a Sunday. They were out late the night before and have no need to get up early.

'Mm,' he mutters, which leaves her uncertain whether to say, 'I love you,' back. Instead, she leads him down a different avenue, one she's been burning to ask about since election night, but which he seems to have cordoned off, declaring without directly stating that it's a no-go area.

♩ ♫ ♪ ♩

'Can I ask you something?' She strokes the inside of his arm with her fingertips, hoping it'll help him relax.

'Maybe. Depends what.'

Argh, he can be maddening!

'You know you said you'd served in the Falklands...?'

At once she feels his body stiffen. 'What of it?'

'I was wondering, I dunno...' She tries to avoid wheedling. But she has left the subject for weeks and fears if they don't speak of it soon, they will avoid it forever. And it must be significant. She cuts to it. 'Why did you leave?'

His mouth twists. Then, abruptly, he moves his arm so she can no longer stroke it and tucks it behind his head. She fears he is annoyed and holds her breath.

'It wasn't for me,' he offers after a while, pulling himself to a seated position.

'The navy?'

'Yup.'

Ah, she thinks, that's what I suspected. She can't imagine him following commands. 'Why?' She sits up too.

'I should never have gone into it,' he says.

It seems she is getting somewhere. 'Why did you?'

He shrugs. 'It's what we did, we Pembertons. My brother, me. It's what our parents expected.' The bitterness in his voice is unmistakable. 'My father, Captain Pemberton, especially.'

'So, er...' Suzy tries to keep her tone light. 'When you left—'

'Actually,' he interrupts. 'Can we do this another time?'

Suzy is thrown. She swallows her hurt and nods. 'Sure.'

Glenn stays sitting rigid against the pillows, saying nothing, staring straight ahead, scowling. The atmosphere is horribly uncomfortable, but if she changes the subject, it will sound phony, might irritate him more.

'I need to go to the bathroom,' is the best she can do. She pulls on a dressing gown and heads to the loo but though she tries to pee, she fails because she is so tense. Glenn is so different from Johnny, who was as open and easy to read as Glenn is closed and tricky. She is at a loss.

When she returns to her bedroom, Glenn is pulling on his clothes. Instinctively she fears he will leave, but then he says, 'I'll make you breakfast.'

She is pleasantly surprised. 'I've not got much in.'

'I'll go to the shop,' he offers.

Moments later, as she watches him from her dormer window, walking down the road with that distinctive bounce in his step, her emotions jangle. It's like trying to open a clam; no sooner has she prised his shell apart, just a millimetre than—whoops—she makes a mistake, and he snaps again, tight shut. Yet he said he *loves* me, she thinks. That's a huge breakthrough, surely?

20.

'Glad we got that out of the way.' Glenn laughs, a touch nervously, and takes a slurp of his beer. 'Tell me. What have you been up to?'

Wow... Where to start? *So* much has happened in the intervening decades. 'How long have you got?'

'I'm in no rush.' He leans back and stretches, evidently settling in.

'I presume you don't want a day-by-day account.'

'Update me, I dunno, however you want. Major life events... Marriage? Kids? Have you been divorced long? You've said a bit in your messages, but not much, and your profile on Facebook is scant, considering.'

'Considering?' Suzy's breath catches. He must mean *considering what happened.* At once she is afraid that he is attempting to coax her down a path she prefers to steer away from. She gives an involuntary shudder. But he wouldn't expect me to share any of *that* on my profile. No one would, let alone someone as intensely private as Glenn.

'OK, you've got me.' He holds up his palms in admission of defeat. 'I guess I meant considering you're a woman. You must admit women tend to reveal more about themselves.'

Suzy exhales. She is relieved. 'Almost *everyone* reveals more than you do.'

He splutters on his beer. 'Touché.'

Already she is liking this new, older Glenn. OK, he's making sweeping statements about women, but Suzy is not guiltless of generalising, and he seems more able to laugh at himself. Maybe he has loosened up. Yet whilst they need to learn about one another—it's why she is here, too—she is keen to avoid focusing on the past. An idea comes to her.

'How about we work backwards?' Glenn appears baffled, so Suzy explains, 'Starting now. Then maybe you can do the same.' He's not getting away without a turn in the spotlight, she avows.

'Hmm...' He edges back, narrowing his eyes, a hint of a smile on lips. 'I can see what you're playing at.'

He's flirting, thinks Suzy, with a flutter of excitement. *Take it slow,* she says to herself. She gulps, then offers up neutrally, 'I guess the biggest thing that has happened recently is this.' She raises her left foot. 'You remember I messaged that I broke my ankle?'

'I do. Ah, you've had the plaster removed?'

'That's right. Ew, it felt weird! You ever been a casualty of something like that?'

In an instant Glenn's expression clouds. He blinks, then says, 'Er... Not exactly, no,' and looks away. Has she stumbled on something? She swiftly moves on.

'These days, they do it with an angle grinder.' She shakes her head in disbelief. 'It's specially set up to cut through the cast but not the padding. *Apparently.* But I could feel the blade judder down my calf, and when it went round my ankle,' she scrunches up her face. 'It was hard to keep my nerve.'

'I can imagine,' says Glenn. 'How did you break it?' She tells him about the accident and her mother's funeral. 'You had your mum living here, in this village, with you?'

Suzy has a sip of wine. 'I did.'

'For how long?'

'Oh, ages. Sounds mad, doesn't it?' Suzy laughs, keen to make light of it.

'Not *mad,*' Glenn corrects. 'Though I'm surprised because I remember you didn't get on. You used to avoid going home.'

♩ ♫ ♪ ♩   112

'You're right,' says Suzy.

'What changed?'

She pauses, unsure how to explain her motives. 'It was partly money,' she confides. 'She didn't have enough to pay for a home.'

'Doesn't the council have to chip in?' He coughs, awkward. 'Sorry, I don't mean to pry into your family's finances. It's just we've been through all this recently with my father.'

'We?' Suzy's stomach turns over.

'Me and my brother,' says Glenn.

'Ah.' Of course. Suzy had forgotten. She is so attuned to being an only child, especially having only one herself. 'Inevitably it affected her mind as well as her body. She had not been herself over the last few years.' It's not as if my mother became any *nicer* though, she reminds herself. She can still hear Joan shouting, 'I will NOT go into a home!' For a long while it became her mother's stock response when guests asked how she was, a constant reminder of her truculence and talent for emotional blackmail. No matter what I did, it was never enough, Suzy recalls. It was like pouring my energy into a black hole.

'That's a heck of a lot to take on,' says Glenn.

'There was a time when she did a huge amount for me,' Suzy admits, increasingly eager to change the subject. Talking about her mother will hardly make for an uplifting evening. 'But you're right: I probably didn't think it through properly. Cameron—my son—had just gone to university, so I had space.'

'You were on your own by then?'

'Mm,' Suzy reaches for her wine and takes a generous mouthful. I must sound a right saddo, she frets. And we haven't even touched on the worst of it. 'Leo and I split up in 1999,' she clarifies.

'Sounds like you've had more than your fair share of difficulties,' Glenn looks at her and holds her gaze. She recalls how disconcerting it is, as if he can see past her sidestepping and cut straight through the vulnerable woman beneath. Panic rises in her chest, as for a few horrible moments she is sure he will ask her directly about *that* summer; after all, Johnny had touched upon the incident in his card. However, Glenn says, 'Divorce, dealing with dying parents, guess we've got a fair bit in common,' and pushes back his chair. 'Can I get you another?'

'Oh, um...' Suzy is flummoxed by the rapid changes to their topics of conversation. Though Glenn had always liked to duck and dive. 'Er, yes, please. That would be nice.'

She watches his back as he heads to the bar. *Glenn doesn't know*, she realises. Either that, or he's decided not to mention it. Somehow, she doesn't believe it's the latter. For all his discomfort talking about himself, he would never ignore the fact she had been through something so traumatic. He is considerate in that regard. As she allows this understanding to permeate, she senses her shoulders relax. We don't need to go there, she assures herself. I don't need to relive events; I don't have to cope with his reactions. With Glenn, I can be the Suzy I was before that happened. Maybe we can even pick up where we left off. Imagine the thrill of riding pillion again, all that sex. What I wouldn't give to be twenty again...

21.

December 1983

There is a tap on Suzy's attic bedroom door.

'Oi! You two, stop shagging,' comes Zelda's voice from the landing.

Drowsily, Suzy gets up, grabs her dressing gown, and undoes the bolt. 'We're not.' She slides back into the bed, Glenn still slumbering beside her.

'Good.' Zelda strides in and drops onto the bottom of the mattress.

'Those are my feet.' Suzy winces.

'Didn't realise you stretched that far.' Zelda grins.

'Shhh.' Suzy puts a forefinger to her lips and jerks her head towards Glenn.

Zelda drops her voice. 'You know you said you didn't want to go home?'

Suzy yawns. 'Ye-es...'

It is nearly the end of term, but the prospect of returning to Park Road for Christmas is hanging over Suzy like pollution over a city, poisoning her mood. Similarly, Zelda is keen to minimise her time in Skegness. Nevertheless, they both expect grief from their parents should they opt to remain in Manchester.

'I've had an idea.' Zelda waves an orange flyer. 'Why don't we go to this?'

Suzy hoists herself to a seated position and leans to take a better look. The headline reads:

**Thousands of WOMEN will reclaim
GREENHAM COMMON
on Sunday 11th Dec '83**

There is a graphic of a chain-link fence with light streaming through it and a mother and child superimposed on top. Below, it says:

**Bring mirrors—to turn the base inside out,
trees to plant, candles for silent vigil
and instruments for songs.**

'You serious?'

'Yes!' Zelda thumps the duvet.

'But it's this weekend!' Next to her, Glenn stirs.

'So?'

'It's *December*,' Suzy reminds her. 'It'll be fucking freezing.'

'Don't be such a wuss!'

'How are you suggesting we get there?'

'A bus is going from the student union,' says Zelda.

'What, there and back in a day?' Newbury must be about two hundred miles from Manchester.

'It's going on Saturday, coming back Sunday.'

'We'd stay overnight?'

Zelda looks uncertain. Then her eyes light up. 'I've got a tent!'

'Yeah, ri-ight. Here?'

Her face falls. 'Oh shit, it's in Skeggy. Though I'm sure we can borrow one. C'mon Suzy, you know you want to. It's important. The first missiles arrived two weeks ago. This is a chance for women to protest before it's too late.'

'Let me think about it?'

'Think about what?' mumbles Glen.

'Nothing,' Suzy says lightly.

♩ ♫ ♪ ♩   116

Too late, his curiosity is piqued: sleepily, he reaches over, and before Suzy works out what he is doing, grabs the flyer. He holds it up, squinting. '*Bring pictures to peg up—banners, posters, photos, women and children's clothes, nappies etc.*' He reads the words on the reverse out loud. He sits up sharply. '*Anything related to "real" life as opposed to the unreal world that the military base represents.*' He flips over the flyer. 'You're not going, are you?' His tone is scathing.

'We are,' says Zelda, defiantly. 'Well, I am.'

Oh shit, thinks Suzy. I'm not ready for this. I haven't even had a cup of tea.

Too late. Glenn thrusts the leaflet at Zelda. 'What exactly is *unreal* about a military base?'

'It's not just any old military base,' retorts Zelda. 'It's a US one. Housing their cruise missiles.'

'If you believe a load of women tying teddies to a fence will make an iota of difference, you're living in cloud-cuckoo land,' says Glenn.

'I'd rather do that than sit around on my big fat arse while Reagan uses our country as a launch pad.'

'It's pathetic,' spits Glen.

This is too much. Suzy won't have Glenn attacking her friend. 'It is *not* pathetic! Maybe a nuclear missile feels more real to you than teddy bears and babies' bottles.' She enunciates every word with staccato precision. 'But it doesn't to me. They're things that are precious to a lot of women.' She remembers a further argument. 'If nothing else, doesn't it worry you how easy it's been for the women to get inside the base? Whatever you think of them, if they can do it, so can anyone. Isn't *that* a point worth making?'

'You've no idea what a risk you're taking.' Glenn's voice hardens. She is surprised how flushed his face is; she has never seen him so angry. 'The American military will be ruthless if pushed much further, trust me.'

How patronising, thinks Suzy, frustration mounting. He is making it sound as though I can't look after myself. And if he is privy to a per-

♩ ♫ ♪ ♩

spective on these issues from his time in the navy, I wish he would talk about it. She feels a gap widen between them, as if a fault line has created a yawning gulf down the mattress.

'Bunch of hippy weirdos,' he mutters.

Suzy is aghast. It sounds like something her mother would say. This is a genuine movement begun by women with genuine feelings. How can Glenn not see that? Women with the courage to take risks and disrupt their lives. Suddenly Zelda's suggestion sounds *exactly* what she wants to do.

'You're on,' she says to her friend. 'Let's experience some action.'

'Brilliant!' Zelda slaps her thighs. 'You could bring your sketchbook, capture it all, like a war artist.'

'That's a great idea,' says Suzy, abuzz at the suggestion. If art is a tool to make a statement about the world, she speculates, what a powerful declaration those drawings could be.

Zelda leans closer and murmurs into her ear. 'And if we come running back with our tail between our legs, it won't be any less than Glenn's already done, anyway.'

'WHAT DID YOU SAY?' Glenn bellows.

'Nothing,' say Zelda and Suzy sweetly in unison.

Zelda jumps up from the end of the bed looking pleased with herself. 'Hope I didn't disturb you too much.' With that, she hastens from the room.

22.

December 1983

'We're going to put that bastard behind us,' says Zelda, wedging herself into the seat next to Suzy.

Suzy is staring out of the window at the squat redbrick building, home to the Poly student union, but she is not focusing on it: she is focused on Glenn. *He's not a bastard,* she protests to herself. Zelda hasn't seen the way he looks at me, hasn't talked to him late into the night, hasn't slept with him. There is an intensity to him, *us.* That is—was—special. Didn't he say only days ago that he was falling in love with me?

As the coach pulls out onto Oxford Road, Suzy blinks back tears. If she is right, why did Glenn finish with her so abruptly? They'd clashed before and always reached a truce of sorts, albeit a taciturn *we'll agree to disagree.* Suzy would have preferred to iron out their differences like she used to with Johnny, yet Glenn did not operate that way. When he is riled, sometimes he would sit there, silent and smouldering, until he would abruptly change the subject. More often, he would roar off on his bike heading Lord-knows-where for several hours, but he always came back, eventually.

I can't do it. Sorry. Glenn.

That was all the note said. She had gone to the bathroom the morning before and washed her hair. This took a while—it was clogged by hairspray, as usual. When she had returned to her room, Glenn was

119 ♩ ♫ ♪♩

gone. It had been several minutes before she had seen the piece of paper. It had been torn from one of her notepads on the bedside table and from the scrawl, seemed written in a hurry.

The coach weaves its way down the littered thoroughfare of Curry Mile, past endless tatty terraces and out onto the M56. Suzy wonders, is this is how Johnny felt? As if his heart had been yanked out, sand-papered red raw, then replaced? It was awful to receive a missive that left so many questions unanswered. She had phoned Glenn's flat, been round and banged on his door, to no avail. It had only been 24 hours ago, yet every moment since had been torture, full of anguish and self-blame. '*WHY?*' she wanted to scream. I must have caused Johnny similar hurt, she realises. Zelda was right, I owed him so much more. She gulps back tears. Now she's feeling terrible about Johnny *and* Glenn, and what an awful person she is. The pain is almost too much to bear.

'C'mon,' Zelda, sensitive to her heartbreak, elbows her. 'Have one of these.' She passes Suzy an iced bun.

Suzy gives her friend a weak smile. She knows me so well, she thinks, biting into the soft, gooey dough appreciatively, and, as Zelda reaches for her thermos flask, the white icing melts on her tongue.

'Hold the cup,' Zelda orders, and Suzy struggles to keep it level while her friend pours the chestnut-coloured liquid. Zelda wrinkles her nose. 'Bit stewed.'

'It's fine,' says Suzy. And it is fine; tea helps.

'I bought you a present,' Zelda says next. 'In fact, I bought one for each of us.'

'Oh?'

Zelda puts a carrier bag into Suzy's lap. Whatever is inside feels hard and heavy, but Suzy's hands are already full, so she swallows the last mouthful of bun and hands Zelda back the cup before opening the bag. Inside is a pair of bolt cutters, huge and unwieldy.

As she turns them over, examining them, the women at the front of the bus start singing:

♩ ♫ ♪ ♩

'Well, have you seen pictures of bodies all burnt?
Imagine it's you and your family so hurt
We can stop the madness, but we must do it now
So come down to Greenham, take a fence down at Greenham.
We won't move from Greenham, for time's running out.

Suzy leans her head on Zelda's shoulder.

'I'll look after you.' Zelda strokes her hair with unusual tenderness. 'It'll be alright, you'll see.'

'I'm Yoshi,' says the young woman, in heavily accented English, and thrusts out a hand, which Suzy and Zelda shake in turn. She is slight and pretty, yet her grip is so firm that instinctively they put their trust in her. She is one of a group of women who greeted their coach on arrival at the camp; she marched straight up to Suzy and Zelda while they were still yawning and stiff from the journey. 'Do you have a tent?'

Zelda delves into her rucksack and pulls out a thick plastic sheet. 'This is the best we could find.'

'OK.' Yoshi does not seem phased. 'I'll show you how to make a bender. You can leave those here.' She gestures at their bags. 'Bring the sheet. Now come. Follow me.'

She moves rapidly and with purpose, forcing Zelda and Suzy to hurry in her wake, out of the camp and onto the common. 'The best branches went already,' she explains without breaking her stride to check that they are keeping up. 'We have to walk more now.' She continues, heedless of mud and brambles, until she finally stops at a group of saplings. 'This looks good.' Yoshi yanks a knife from her back pocket, flips it open and hacks away at a slender trunk. 'I'll do this,' she says, seeing Zelda and Suzy looking on, helpless. 'You can collect bracken.'

'What for?' asks Zelda.

'Sleeping on,' states Yoshi baldly.

'I thought the plastic sheeting was for that,' murmurs Suzy. Alongside Yoshi, who is dressed in a torn anorak and waterproof trousers, she feels inadequately attired. Suzy's lumberjack shirt was purchased from a stall in Afflex Palace—she has never cut a tree in her life. The dirt on her workman's dungarees is paint from art school and her tangled hair the result of painstaking back combing, not exposure to the elements. Already she is regretting her lack of foresight; her boots lack grip and she has forgotten her gloves. And why, oh why didn't she bring a thick jumper and woolly hat like Zelda?

'You need the plastic to keep out the wind and the rain,' Yoshi clarifies.

Already Suzy is getting cold. 'Of course,' she mutters, picturing her little attic with its electric heater. And to think she moans it takes ages to warm up that room!

'You been here long?' asks Zelda a while later, as they head back to camp.

'18 months,' says Yoshi,

'What brought you here?'

Yoshi is dragging several branches behind her like a post-apocalyptic wedding train. She stops to catch her breath. 'My father is a hibakusha.'

'Why don't you put some of your branches in here?' Suzy interjects, realising that the plastic sheet full of bracken that she and Zelda are carrying between them must weigh much less.

'OK,' says Yoshi, dropping her load so they can divvy it up.

'What's a hi...' Zelda stumbles over the word.

'Hibakusha,' Yoshi repeats. 'In Japan, it is what we call survivors of the bombs.'

'I didn't know there were many survivors,' says Zelda.

'My father was a child. Very small.' Yoshi gestures to her thigh. 'Only three years old.'

'Oh gosh.' Suzy is shocked. 'Does he remember it?'

Yoshi's deep brown eyes fill with sadness. 'Not much. He told me that the surroundings turned blindingly white, like a thousand camera flashes all at once. Then, pitch black.' She picks up her reduced load of saplings and resumes walking. 'He was buried alive under my grandparent's house. When my aunt found him, she was certain my father was dead. Thankfully, he revived. But he lost his hearing in one ear because of the blast.'

'How terrifying,' says Suzy.

'People say it will not happen again. They do not believe it possible. They say the bombs are a deterrent and that no one would dare. But my father says people did not believe Hitler would kill six million Jews, yet he did.'

Yoshi nods in the direction of the camp. 'Soon, there will be 96 missiles in there. You know each one has four times the power of the Hiroshima bomb?'

'I heard,' says Zelda gravely.

'My father says the heat burned the shadows of victims onto the walls and pavements in the city. You can still see a few of them. It is as if they are frozen forever, going about their daily lives.'

Suzy and Zelda fall silent, uncertain how to respond.

'Are they here in England, your parents?' asks Suzy after a while.

'No,' says Yoshi. 'They are in Tokyo. But I came here for my family and our future. The tragedy of Hiroshima and Nagasaki is not only Japan's. It is the world's. It is our responsibility to prevent another nuclear disaster.'

Suzy is humbled. Suddenly the journey from Manchester to Greenham seems awfully short and easy.

It is so cold under the bender that Suzy finds it impossible to get to sleep. She thinks of Hiroshima, all those victims whose shadows still haunt the city. She is unable to stop ruminating about Glenn, too, and her tears slip onto the anorak she has rolled up as a makeshift pillow. When, in the

123

small hours, she hears the patter of rain on the plastic sheeting above, she stops trying to mask her weeping and sniffs and gulps until Zelda stirs in the sleeping bag beside her and whispers, 'You OK?'

'I'm freezing,' says Suzy, teeth chattering.

'Southern wuss,' Zelda teases, not unkindly. 'Why don't we see if our bags will zip together? We'd both be warmer that way.' She fumbles for the one torch they have brought between them and clicks it on. Suzy's fingers are so numb that Zelda takes over matching up the fasteners, but in due course they succeed. For a while they shift about, bracken snapping beneath their weight, trying to get comfortable and uneasy at the intimacy. Their knees knock when they face each other; back-to-back is not as snug. Eventually Zelda huffs, 'For fuck's sake, stop wriggling. I'll spoon you.' Suzy is surprised how comforting it is having Zelda's arms around her, and within a few minutes her breathing slows, and she drifts off.

They wake to the sound of chatter and clanking saucepans close by, hurriedly pull on their clothes and clamber outside. Yoshi has managed to light a fire, impressive given how damp it is.

'Tea?' she offers, and they both nod, eagerly. 'I'm afraid there's no milk.'

They huddle under the arch of the bender, sipping from plastic mugs and watching, wide-eyed, as more and more women arrive at the camp. A battered estate stalls close by and several young children in rainbow-coloured clothes pile from the back squealing with excitement, able to release their pent-up energy at last. Before the harassed-looking mother behind the wheel can herd them up again, a large minivan is forced to stop in its wake. Eventually its rear double doors open and out spill several older women in wellington boots and anoraks, huffing about being kept waiting. Soon there is a logjam of vehicles, including two coachloads of women with banners declaring they are members of *The Transport and General Workers' Union*, united by a desire to ban the bomb.

♩ ♫ ♪ ♩   124

'I wasn't sure how many would turn up,' says Yoshi to a middle-aged woman in a mud splattered pink poncho who introduces herself as Val.

'Looks like even more than last year.' Val smiles with satisfaction. Her weather-beaten skin suggests a life spent outdoors, and the two of them squat down alongside Zelda and Suzy, who are still in awe at the sheer scale of it all. Never have they seen so many women in one place. Some stand in pairs, facing each other with both hands linked, staring deep into each other's eyes, their bodies swaying. A few openly kiss and cuddle.

Val waits until Suzy and Zelda have finished their tea, then stands and stretches.

'Well, my lovelies, you ready?'

She takes the lead and gradually, with a mixture of sobriety and excitement, the four of them pick their way through the mud and puddles towards the base. There are tents and make-shift awnings everywhere, and more than once Val bellows, 'Watch your feet!' lest they trip over a guide rope or folded pushchair. It is hard not to be overwhelmed by the jostling crowd and large police presence, especially with so many officers mounted high above them, horses whinnying and stomping and straining at their reins. The natural dips and rises of the terrain make it impossible to see the entire perimeter and the women surrounding it. Nonetheless it is invigorating being part of such a large mass, and when they all fall silent and begin to link arms to form a human chain, Suzy's heart swells with pride. One moment it feels like a dance, the next she fears the chain will break, but the sense of solidarity strengthens her resolve. At one point, Val squeezes her hand and tells her to pass it on, so Suzy squeezes Zelda's next to her. When the hand squeeze comes back the other way a while later, it's a sign that finally they are all linked around the nine-mile perimeter. Then, as they stand in sombre and silent vigil, Suzy senses she is part of something momentous and beautiful and believes that she and these other women really can change the world.

Then, abruptly, the mood shifts, and Suzy sees a group of U.S. soldiers coming to line up on the opposite side of the fence, in what seems to be an act of open hostility. It's at this point the women who have brought mirrors drop their hands and hold them up. The mounting tension finally causes the silence to break.

'See this mirror?' Val urges a young man who comes to stand, bolt upright, gun over his shoulder, before her. 'That's *you* reflected there, guarding these weapons of mass destruction.'

Suzy looks from one to the other, struck by the profound contrast in their values. On his side is the military base, cold and grey and steely. Its grim architecture is echoed by his uniform and behaviour, a world which operates according to strict rules and conventions. Across the divide is the encampment with its anarchic array of tents and caravans and makeshift awnings, full of brightly dressed women, not one of them the same as the next, who refuse to conform to ready stereotypes.

Beside Suzy, Yoshi yells at him. 'NUCLEAR WEAPONS REPRESENT EVERYTHING THAT IS EVIL IN THE WORLD. THEY ARE A COMPLETE DEGENERATION OF HUMANITY!'

The young man casts his gaze somewhere into the distance, his face immobile.

'WE REFUSE TO GIVE UP!' shouts Zelda and, all around, others echo her defiant cry.

Another woman warns of the Defence Secretary's declaration. 'Heseltine says if we trespass, we risk being shot!'

'The American military will be ruthless if pushed,' Suzy recalls Glenn saying, and for a moment she is scared the soldier might turn his gun on them. But then she sees Zelda striding forward, waving her bolt cutters as if she were Bouddica, and remembers that she has a pair too. Anger takes over and with a roar of rage, she and Val and Yoshi surge forward against the fence, its barbed wire woven with poems, ribbons, photos, flowers and embroidery, determined to bring it down.

23.

'You got time for one more?' asks Glenn.

Suzy checks her watch. Goodness, she realises, we've been in the pub two hours. It has been months, *years*, since I had a night out with anyone this attractive. She can sense her resolve weakening. Another glass of wine and she might do something she regrets. 'I'd better not.'

'How were you getting home?'

'Walking.'

'I could give you a lift?'

'On your bike?' She is tempted, then imagines how awkward it would be, getting on and off with her foot still so sore. 'I'll be fine. It's not far.'

'I'll walk with you,' Glenn offers.

I'm not ready to say goodbye yet, thinks Suzy. And it would be reassuring to have someone beside me given her accident. 'OK.'

'It's a nice village,' says Glenn, as they step slowly along the road. There are snowdrops on the kerbside, frost on the grass.

'If I had more money, that's the place I'd choose.' Suzy points at the Georgian house opposite. The same elderly couple have been living in it for decades, and they clearly struggle to look after it, so during the day the peeling paint and moss-covered roof are hard to miss, but in the moonlight its elegant proportions and grand frontage hold their own.

'Can see why,' says Glenn.

'You can almost imagine the coaches and horses pulling up outside, can't you?'

They fall quiet. Suzy would like to take his arm to help steady herself but doesn't, worried it would give the wrong—or would it be right? —signal. She is acutely conscious of the tension between them.

'This is me,' she says breezily when they get to her small wrought-iron gate. 'I would ask you in, but...' Her voice trails off.

'I understand,' says Glenn. He looks down at his feet, then directly at her. 'Though before you go—I... er... wanted to say something.'

'Oh?'

There is a lengthy pause. Then he blurts, 'I wanted to say sorry, to apologise, properly. That's what I meant earlier, but... um... it didn't come out how I meant it to.' He appears sheepish. 'I behaved badly towards you. I look back and realise you probably thought I was a complete bastard.'

Well, I never, Suzy says to herself. Maybe he is a reformed character. All evening she has been getting an increasing sense he might have changed—he's seemed so consumed by regret and mournful. Then she would consider the fact he had left his wife and didn't seem to see his kids that often. Although they were grown-up, so maybe that was why? In the end, she wasn't so sure.

'Ye-es...' she says slowly. 'I guess I did. It was that you completely disappeared.'

'I did love you.' His voice is choked.

Suzy tries—and fails—to mask a gasp. 'I thought so,' she says gently. Then adds silently: *me too.*

'I... er... suppose I couldn't cope with it.'

'What, my going to Greenham?'

He shakes his head, unable to articulate.

Then, starting small, it rises inside her; a feeling that has been gathering force ever since Glenn said, 'I did know you were special,' earlier. She remembers, vividly, how distraught she had been at the way they had finished. That terse note and the way he looked at her, how they didn't add up. How he'd avoided facing her and bolted.

I was right, she thinks. He *did* care. Deeply. It's only taken 34 years but, at last, she is vindicated.

Suzy is lifting the latch of her gate when she recollects.

'Don't go,' she says, catching Glenn's arm.

'Oh?'

She flushes, he could so easily misinterpret her intention. 'I've just remembered something,' she explains, in a rush. 'I got it for you, back then. Do you mind... er... waiting here?'

He nods in assent, and she hurries up the path as best she can, ignoring the pain in her ankle and up the stairs to her bedroom. Ah, yes! There it is, in top her drawer of her dressing table, exactly as she hoped, along with her ticket to the Ziggy Stardust concert, the battered Greenham flyer and other precious mementoes from her youth. She limps back out and down the path where Glenn is still waiting.

'You have owls,' he observes.

'Tawny ones.' Suzy tilts her head, listening. Presently, there is a distinct 'to-wit' followed by a 'to-woo'.

'A male and a female.' His voice is soft.

'I hear them a lot. Apparently, they do it to mark the boundary of their territory.'

'And to keep in contact with one another.'

Their eyes meet. It takes all Suzy's willpower not to reach for him. 'Anyway, here.' She holds out her hand.

In her palm is a piece of thick steel wire. He picks it up, turns it over, peers at it. 'What is it?'

'It's from the fence,' she replies. 'You know, at Greenham.'

He shakes his head. 'You're kidding!' He examines it carefully and his face cracks into a smile.

'I brought it back for you, but, well...' She doesn't need to say it. They never saw one another again.

He gives a brief snort; it seems more an acknowledgement of '*Yeah, you got me,*' than derisive. 'You know the stupid thing?'

'What?'

'All that stuff I said about Greenham, not wanting you to go. I remember being so rigid about it. I was being a jerk.'

'Oh. What makes you say that?'

'Because deep down I agreed with you. Cruise missiles weren't a weapon of defence. I never thought they were. They flew under a radar and gave the west an advantage.' He looks at her, eyebrows raised. 'Can I keep this?'

'Yes.' She smiles at him. 'I got it for you.'

'Thank you.' He seems genuinely chuffed.

'Tell me.' She cajoles. 'Why *did* you disagree so vehemently?'

He exhales slowly, runs a hand through his hair. 'It's too long to go into now. Not unless you're going to invite me in.'

The brief shake of her head and he picks up that she won't. Nevertheless, she is flattered that he has tried.

'I'm afraid I'm not. My foot is really hurting.' It isn't a lie: pain is shooting up from her ankle and she badly needs to put her leg up to rest it horizontal. Then, on impulse, she adds, 'Though we can meet again. If you'd like?'

He nods and folds his fingers round the piece of wire. 'I'd like that.'

'Me too,' she says. And then, because it is 2018 not 1983, she leans in, gives him a kiss on the cheek, and says, 'I'll call you,' before heading back up the path and into her cottage.

Suzy wakes at three, bewildered to find herself on the sofa; she must have drifted off as she lay resting her foot. She goes to the front door, but before she performs her evening ritual of pulling the chain across and locking the bolts, she steps outside, looks up. It's astonishingly clear: the sky is awash with stars. For the first time she can pick out spring constellations: Ursa Major, Leo, Cancer, a sign that perhaps warmer weather will soon be on its way.

The owls are calling to each other again.

'To-wit...'

'To woo...'

Perhaps it's not such a strange thing that she's doing, calling out to her lovers, seeing who will respond. She imagines the postman wheeling his trolley along Park Road, her letter landing on the doormat of number 32...

Of course, there is one letter she longs to send which she knows will never be answered. Although maybe that's what the stars are for; to remind her that Nate's light still shines in her memory, and in the memory of the others who also loved him. And the longer she gazes up at the firmament, the more stars she sees, and the more it seems as if each star is an envoy for a soul.

It is an intoxicating notion; that there are stars not yet born, and stars that have died but whose light still shines across the universe because those viewing from earth have yet to catch up with their timescale. And if there are rare moments when two souls pass close to one another and make contact, only to part for years and make contact again, Suzy has only to think of Johnny, Glenn and Zelda to appreciate the miracle of that occurring. And for this she suddenly feels more grateful than words can express, so she puckers her lips and blows a kiss, stretching out her arm to send it on its way to the heavens above.

24.

January 2018

Rich returns from work as Debs and Suzy are chatting in the open-plan kitchen over tea and biscuits.

'Suzy was telling me about Greenham,' Debs explains, as her husband empties his pockets of sleek electronic devices and flings his coat over a chair. In truth they have been dissecting Suzy's meeting with Glenn the previous evening, but Suzy appreciates her friend's discretion. It is far too soon to let anyone else know she has met up with an old flame, let alone Rich. She is certain he would relish teasing her.

'Greenham as in the peace camp?'

'She was there in the Eighties,' says Debs.

'Really?' Rich takes a seat and leans forward, eager to hear.

Suzy hesitates. Not everyone is as passionate about nuclear disarmament as she is—or rather *was*—and she is aware the protestors were an easy target at the time. The right-wing press usually portrayed them as 'looney lefties', and whilst she isn't sure exactly where Rich sits on the political spectrum, she braces herself for an attack.

'Yes,' she admits.

'Well, well.' Rich grins, loosens his tie and undoes the collar of his shirt. Then strokes his chin and says, 'You *are* a dark horse.'

'Am I?' Suzy counters. 'Why?'

'Wouldn't have had you down as a militant feminist,' says Rich.

Debs gets to her feet and, with a pointed sigh, picks up Rich's coat and goes to hang it in the hallway. Before she can sit back down, he catches her waist, pulls her to him and looks up at her beguilingly.

'Fetch us a drink, will you, babe?'

'All right.' Debs extricates herself to get him a whisky on the rocks.

Suzy fights the urge to say, *Why don't you get your own? Debs has had a long day, too.* 'Perhaps you don't know me as well as you think you do,' she retorts.

'Perhaps not.' Rich nods.

Rich seems to enjoy prodding people to get a reaction purely for entertainment, the way a lion tamer might. His technique may work well in business, but she finds it tiresome.

'I guess you've only ever known me as a country mouse,' she says, with a hint of sarcasm.

'I'd hardly call you that!' interjects Debs.

'Tell me, did you camp there?' Rich goads. 'Wasn't it horribly filthy and smelly?'

Suzy snorts. It is no surprise this is what he focuses on.

'The camp smelt of wood smoke. That was pleasant. The tanks that we used as loos were deep in the woods, a long way from all the makeshift shelters.'

'What about washing?' asks Rich. 'Didn't you stink to high heaven?'

'They banned us from the launderettes in Newbury,' Suzy admits. 'But the Quakers were a godsend. They installed a coin meter for hot showers and a washing machine for us in their central meeting house, and they let us cook in their kitchen.'

'That was kind,' says Debs.

'It was,' Suzy agrees.

'Bet *you* were in a caravan with all mod cons or something though, weren't you?'

Suzy is determined not to let him rile her. 'I'm not that precious.'

Debs reaches for Suzy's hand over the table. 'This is *fascinating*,' she says, clutching it. She beams at her husband. 'I told you Suzy's got some amazing stories.' Then she turns back to Suzy. 'Why don't you stay for dinner? I'd love to hear more. Wouldn't you, Rich?'

'Sure.'

'I reckon it's wine o'clock then, says Debs to Suzy. Fancy some?' Then she jerks her head at Rich. 'He's already drinking.'

'Yes please. We made our own shelter,' she tells Rich.

'Made of what?' asks Rich, so Suzy tells him about the bender. When she finishes, he says, 'You slept on a bed of bracken?'

'Originally we only planned to stay one night,' Suzy explains. 'Though the police put paid to that.'

'What happened?' asks Debs, carefully placing three coasters on the table, followed by three crystal wine glasses and *Sancerre* in a cooler.

'I got arrested,' says Suzy.

December 1983

The bolt cutters slice the wire with ease and by working together it doesn't take long for Suzy and Zelda to make a hole big enough to scramble through. Yoshi, being small and agile, slips into the base first, with Zelda and Suzy only seconds behind. Suzy is not sure where Yoshi is going or what she is intending to do, but in the heat of the moment, it doesn't matter. The chief thing is to wreak havoc, and Suzy is pumped with adrenaline, driven by fury with Thatcher and Reagan, Heseltine, the police, the military, even with Glenn. The young soldier reaches out to grab her, but she darts from his grasp. She notices a police constable running after Zelda, but his riot shield slows him, and Zelda makes good headway.

'FOLLOW ME!' yells Yoshi and, with a speed and agility that appear to defy the law of gravity, she zigzags between two mounted police and an army truck. Zelda and Suzy thunder behind her. In that moment, they are like a trio of racehorses who've escaped their riders and are galloping for the sheer hell of it to the finish line. Before she is clear what Yoshi's aim is, Suzy finds herself scrambling hand over hand up a steep incline. She is running out of breath and energy, but she makes it and, with a 'WHOOP!' joins Zelda and Yoshi on the flat grass at the top.

'We made it!' Yoshi laughs and punches the air. 'You know what this is?'

'It's one of the silos.' Zelda bends over, hands on her knees, panting for breath.

'YESSS!' Yoshi jumps up and down, triumphant. Directly below them, inside the grassy hillock and protected by tons of sand and soil, steel plating and reinforced concrete, is what they are campaigning to remove: a Trident missile.

'YE-HAH!' shouts Suzy. From this prime vantage point, she can see everything: the crowds have brought a substantial length of fence down and are running amok; the police with their batons and riot shields are trying—and failing—to herd them up; the human chain on the far side of the base is still holding tight.

Suzy beats the flat of her palm against her mouth to make a 'WA! WA! WA!' noise; a technique she used when she and Johnny played *Cowboys and Indians* as kids. She knows the war cry is provocative, but at that moment she is so charged up by the recollection this missile has four times the strength of those used in World War II, nothing can rattle her.

Moments later there is a deep bellow, 'HERE'S ONE!' and Suzy turns to see a policeman has clambered up the silo in her wake. He throws himself at her headlong, grasps her ankles and fells her like a tree. Before she can reach out to break her fall, she crashes to the ground. Next second another policeman grabs her arms and—WOAH!—they are skidding back down the slope with her body stretched between them, so fast she has no time to call out to her friends. Then 'ONE, TWO, THREE!' they hurl her as if she were a sack of potatoes headed for market into the back of a police transit and—BOOM!—slam the doors.

'Oh my God!' says Debs. 'Were you OK?'

'We cut swathes of the fence down that day,' says Suzy, recollecting how heedless they were. 'My hands were slashed by barbed wire and brambles. The police even set dogs on us.'

Debs shudders. 'How awful.'

Suzy shakes her head. 'It wasn't. I'd been on marches before, but Greenham was different. The energy of the demonstration that day was incredible. Before I went, part of me was afraid of what might happen. But when I got there, it was the first time I'd experienced the power of direct action.'

'I remember it being on the news,' says Debs.

Rich and Debs are a decade younger than I am, Suzy reminds herself. They'll have been kids when she was at Art School. 'When I was a student, many of us were vehemently opposed to the arms race. It was the height of the cold war and we really believed nuclear missiles were a threat, and that we had to stop them.'

'What happened next?' asks Debs.

'In the back of the van I admit I was wary, 'cos I'd heard that the police were being increasingly heavy handed. They took us to the station in Newbury. A lot of the locals hated us and gathered around the entrance yelling things like, '*If your children are so important to you, why aren't you at home with them?*' I remember one woman grabbed me and yelled, 'YOU'RE A PIECE OF HUMAN EXCREMENT!' She spat in my face.'

'No!' Debs mouth falls open.

'That wasn't very lovely.' Suzy laughs ruefully. 'Afterwards, I heard other women say they were threatened with rape and being gassed like animals.'

Rich reaches for the bottle to top up her wine.

'Just a half glass, thanks,' says Suzy. It would be easy to drink more than she means to as she recounts such stirring events.

'Did the police charge you?' he asks.

'No.'

'That must have been a relief,' says Debs.

'It was. Though I had to spend the night in a police cell. You ever done that, Rich?'

'*Rich* in a police cell? He'd never survive.' Debs chuckles.

Suzy pictures the cell with its tiny, barred window and hard, narrow mattress, recalling the indignity of being forced to use a stainless-steel toilet in the same space and silently agrees. 'It's not an experience I'd recommend.'

'Didn't get you anywhere though, did it?' Rich retorts.

'Depends on your perspective,' says Suzy. 'I'm proud of what we did. Several years back, Mikhail Gorbachev came over, spoke at a conference. Bunch of scientists against armed conflict. It was on the news.'

'Oh yeah?' Rich is swivelling the ice in his whisky glass, his tone seems deliberately mocking, but Suzy is determined to make her point.

'Gorbechov was surprisingly frank. Said he only felt able to risk meeting the President in '86 because he trusted the European peace movement would hold the US to account. So you could say that without the Greenham women, he might not have proposed nuclear disarmament.'

'I never realised all that,' says Debs. She turns to her husband. 'Did you?'

'Lots of people don't,' says Suzy.

Rich grunts. 'Sounds like you're reading a lot into it.'

In stark contrast to his nonchalance, Debs is on the edge of her chair. 'What happened next? To you, I mean. When did they release you?'

'The next morning, they told a few of us we were being allowed to go, but instead of taking us to the camp, they drove us in the back of the van and dumped us in the middle of nowhere.'

'The bastards!' Debs is agog. 'What did you do?'

'There weren't mobile phones in those days. We had no choice: we walked 10 miles, or whatever it was, back to Greenham. I didn't have any gloves and my feet were freezing. I've never been so grateful to see Zelda in my life.'

Grateful. Suzy cringes at the paucity of the word. That's an understatement. But further revelations are not necessary or appropriate, and at least she seems to have finally wiped the smug grin off Rich's face.

25.

Yoshi is the first to notice Suzy stumbling through the mud and puddles and into the camp. She flings down her tin plate of baked beans and rice and runs to greet her, with Zelda not far behind.

'Oh, thank God!' Zelda pulls Suzy to her bosom, and before Suzy can say a word, she is being hugged so tight she fears Zelda might damage her spine. Her legs are so shaky she can barely stand, but she manages to give the women she has been walking with a wave of thanks over Zelda's shoulder. Then she allows herself to be propelled to the campfire, where she collapses into a chair.

'I was so worried!' Zelda crouches at Suzy's feet, looking up at her, face fraught with concern. 'Can I get you anything? Tea? Something to eat?'

'I'll sort it,' says Yoshi.

'I didn't know where you'd gone.' Zelda's voice is choked; she seems close to tears. Suzy has never seen her friend this upset before; she always seems so resilient. 'One minute we were together, the next you'd disappeared. Val said she had seen the police arrest you and when you didn't come back last night, I imagined all sorts. The police didn't beat you up or anything?'

'No.' Suzy is keen to reassure her. 'I wasn't even charged.'

Zelda's shoulders slump with relief, yet Suzy cannot stop shivering. 'You're freezing!' Zelda takes hold of Suzy's hands and rubs her fingers.

Gradually they warm up, but Suzy's teeth continue to chatter. 'Here, have this.' Zelda yanks her oversized jumper over her head.

'Won't you get cold?'

'I'll be fine,' says Zelda. 'Used to it, remember?'

Relieved and thankful, Suzy pulls it on. It smells of Zelda and wood smoke and provides the warmth she has been craving. Eventually she thaws out enough to fill Zelda in on what happened.

'I barely had a wink of sleep,' she finishes.

At Zelda's insistence, Suzy goes to bed straight after she has eaten. A while later, she is woken by the sound of rummaging close by in the bender. There is a *click* and the sudden glare of torchlight.

'You awake?' whispers Zelda.

'I am now,' says Suzy.

'I... er... wondered... shall we zip the bags together again?'

Suzy agrees and soon they settle with the torch propped between them, gazing up at the circle of light on the plastic sheeting above.

'Are you *sure* you're OK?' asks Zelda.

'Yes.' Suzy yawns.

'I'm so sorry.'

'Why are *you* sorry?'

'It's all my fault.'

It is unusual for Zelda to be this rattled, thinks Suzy. 'How do you work that out?'

'I persuaded you to come.'

'You hardly forced me.'

'If I hadn't suggested it, you wouldn't have had that row with Glenn. You might still be together.'

Suzy considers. Everything has happened so fast, already Glenn's note seems weeks, not days, ago. Zelda is being unnecessarily harsh on herself. She sighs. 'If he couldn't cope with things I feel strongly about, we'd have split up anyway, in the end.'

'I promised to look after you and they arrested you. I feel dreadful.'

'*You* didn't dump me on the other side of Aldermaston.'

Zelda turns to look at her. 'You're not angry with me?'

Suzy rolls to face her. In the dim light she can see a different Zelda, one with no lipstick and whose peroxide spikes no longer defy gravity. She seems younger somehow, more vulnerable. 'Don't be daft! It's been great, in some ways.'

'Really?'

'Yeah. I'm glad we came.'

Zelda exhales. 'Phew.' There is a lengthy silence. Then Zelda laughs. 'I swear, I'll never call you a wuss again.'

Suzy gives her a playful kick. 'I'll remind you of that.' She chuckles. 'And it's certainly taken my mind off Glenn.'

'Good. Bit of a drastic solution, though.'

'Come here.' Suzy reaches out her arms and the sleeping bag rustles as Zelda moves close. By now their faces are almost touching, and Suzy can sense Zelda's breath, warm against her cheeks. She notices how sweet her friend smells, like honey; the same scent she noticed on her jumper. Zelda adjusts so she can rest her head on Suzy's shoulder, snug in Suzy's embrace. Suzy has long known that Zelda is nowhere near as tough as she pretends to be, but this is unprecedented. It is as though her hair is not the only thing softened by the rain.

'He didn't deserve you,' Zelda murmurs.

'Who?' says Suzy, though she knows exactly who Zelda means.

Zelda doesn't answer, however, and she begins to snore, ever so faintly. Gently, Suzy moves her friend onto her side, a trick she learned with Johnny when he was breathing too heavily. *Would he have been as snarky as Glenn about my coming to Greenham?* Of course not, she decides. He'd probably have encouraged her. Fleetingly, she wonders if she made the right call to split up with him. *He'd never take me back though*, she thinks. For a while she lies staring up at the full moon of light created by the torch, wondering if she'll ever get relationships right. Then her eyelids begin to droop, so she reaches with her free

♩ ♫ ♪ ♩

arm and turns off the torch. It is much darker under the bender than it is in her room in Manchester, where streetlights filter through the gaps in her curtains, but she can still hear the crackle of the fire and murmur of women chatting. Comforted, she falls back into a deep sleep, not stirring until she hears Val asking, 'Has anyone has seen the tea bags?' late the next morning.

January 2018

The few days after her supper with Debs and Rich, Suzy receives two officious-looking brown envelopes. Apparently, she has received several weeks' Carer's Allowance from the Department of Work and Pensions that she is no longer entitled to. The second is worse news. The DWP has failed to stop her mother's state pension payments, even though Suzy informed them of Joan's death *weeks* ago. She is expected to pay the overpayments back without delay. The total is over £1200. Money she simply does not have.

I thought I was due an insurance pay-out after the accident, she thinks, confused. The nurse in charge of the ward at the hospital had put her in touch with a solicitor who specialises in personal injury, Victoria, she is called, and she's both efficient and pleasant. It has been agreed the driver was at fault and going dangerously fast, the first responders at the scene have told her this, but it's been months and still Suzy has had nothing tangible come through. In the meantime, what is she supposed to live off? Air?

Since Suzy gave up her teaching post to look after her mother, she has been struggling to make ends meet. Her divorce settlement made it possible to buy her tiny cottage outright. A combination of frugality, careful management of her mother's pensions and the occasional painting commission mean she has remained solvent—but only just. She hasn't been abroad in ten years; her car is so ancient it is barely roadworthy and she only ever buys clothes second hand. Her lack of income has been a major concern since the accident, but she had told herself until she was back on her feet, there was nothing to be done. Now something needs doing, swiftly, or she'll end up in debt, big time.

She feeds Pushkin on autopilot, trying to curtail a mounting sense of dread. I can't ask Debs, thinks Suzy. I am already so indebted to her, and I would rather declare myself bankrupt than prostrate myself in front of Rich. I could talk to Cam; he is level-headed and practical. But I'm his *mum*. I should be responsible for him and not the other way round.

She tries to distract herself with long-overdue household chores. She puts Johnny's CD on shuffle, turns up the volume and gets down on her hands and knees to scrub the oven. When it launches straight into a grandiose intro, she recalls from her nights clubbing as a student, there is no mistaking the track. In seconds it goes up several gears, then Holly Johnson starts to sing: '*When two tribes go to war, one is all that you can score...*' Suzy never was that sure of the words. The pumping beat, that was the main event. '*Working for the bad guys...*' *We got two tribes... We got the bomb, Yeah...*' She can picture the video of Ronald Reagan and Konstantin Chernenko in a wrestling ring as if it were only last week. Two ancient fat boxers, each taking a swing for each other. Frankie Goes to Hollywood burst onto the scene like a social hand grenade, she thinks, as she gets to her feet to find a wire pad. They had the whole country eating out of their hands. You couldn't go to the shops without seeing a FRANKIE t-shirt.

All at once it comes to her: *Zelda*. From the handful of messages which they have exchanged through Facebook, Suzy has established Zelda works in social care on the far side of London. Her salary will be low in social work, and the cost-of-living is so high in the capital, it is most unlikely she will be able to bail Suzy out. And a loan might help short term, it won't solve the situation long term anyway. Yes, she decides, I'll ask Zelda for advice, and I can trust her to tell it how it is.

The moment she stops to consider, Suzy has a longing not to message

Zelda, but to call her. To her surprise, Zelda answers her mobile at once. Suzy wasn't even sure she'd have the same number, but she does.

'Oh! Hello,' she exclaims, winded. 'It's Suzy.'

'I know who it is,' says Zelda. She sounds gruff, thinks Suzy. Perhaps this was a bad idea.

'Sorry. I didn't expect you to answer.'

'Isn't that what people usually do, when someone rings their phone?'

Suzy gulps. She had forgotten how abrasive Zelda can be. Then she laughs. 'Not all that often. These days I find it impossible to get an answer straight away. More and more it seems we all have to book in times for phone calls, don't you agree?'

'S'pose you're right,' Zelda concedes.

'Is this a bad time?'

'I'm on my lunch break—what I get of one. At the Post Office. The queue is insane. Go on then, tell me. I thought you'd fallen off the planet. What prompted you to ring? And before you say that you've messaged me on Facebook, I'll say *bollocks*. That's hardly intimate. I heard neither hide nor hair from you about a decade before that. Fucking hell, I didn't even realise your dad had died, never mind your mum.'

'Sorry,' says Suzy.

'I'm not having a go at you,' says Zelda, and Suzy realises she isn't. This is just how Zelda talks. If Zelda is going to be blunt, she might as give it to her straight.

'I'd like to see you.'

There is a pause. Suzy is fearful Zelda will say no. 'Really?' she retorts eventually.

'Yes.'

'Why? You managed without me for long enough.'

Suzy flinches. Any criticism is fair; Suzy is the one who let the friendship drift. She cuts to it.

'I miss you.'

'Oh!' Zelda sounds winded.

'A lot has happened,' Suzy adds.

'A lot always happens to you,' observes Zelda drily.

Hmm, thinks Suzy. A lot has happened recently, and a lot happened when I was younger, but the years I spent caring for Mum nothing much happened at all.

'Gotta go,' says Zelda. 'I'm about to get to the front of the queue. About bloody time.'

'Ah.' Suzy is disappointed; she doesn't want to leave it like this.

'Tell you what,' Zelda says hurriedly, 'You're still in Amhurst, aren't you?' She doesn't wait for the reply. Suzy had forgotten the speed at which Zelda's mind works. 'I'm going to Birmingham, there's a conference at the NEC in about three weeks. I'd need to check the dates, but I could stop off and see you on the way. You're just off the M4, aren't you?'

'That would be brilliant!' Suzy's heart lifts.

'I'd normally go via the M1 so it's longer if I come via you—'

'You could stay if you like,' Suzy interjects before she can stop herself.

'I'll check the dates,' says Zelda. 'That's the buzzer and I'm next. I'll message about timings.'

And before Suzy can bid her farewell, she cuts her off.

Suzy gives a little skip of excitement. Does it matter if she seemed keen? She is going to see Zelda, and it has been *way* too long since she last clapped eyes on her.

26.

December 1983

The night before they leave Greenham, Zelda and Suzy kiss. It seems inevitable; they've experienced events that have brought out their vulnerabilities and strengths and for all the cold and damp and discomfort, being under the bender where they can't escape the elements makes them more aware of their bodies, their physicality. Then, as they are heading to bed, it snows. They watch the flakes swirl and land softly on the tents and awnings and cars and clutter about them.

'I hope it settles,' says Zelda. 'It will keep us warm.'

Suzy is doubtful anything can help on that score. Nevertheless, it is romantic. Maybe there will be a white Christmas.

They undress, and once cosy inside their joint sleeping bag, Zelda is stroking Suzy's arm when she whispers, 'Suzy?'

'Mm?'

'Would you mind if I kissed you?'

Suzy shifts onto her side to look at her. Even in the strange shadows cast by torchlight, Zelda's face is so familiar, her emotions—a mix of trepidation and tenderness—are easy to read. All the same, Suzy is surprised by the directness of the question.

'I thought you didn't fancy me.' As she utters the words, she knows this isn't true. Zelda's antipathy towards Glenn, her concern for Suzy's welfare, the suggestion they zip their sleeping bags together like this— on some level, Suzy has known for a while.

♩ ♫ ♪ ♩   146

'I'm not sure I'm a lesbian,' she explains. *Although,* she wants to add, *I have been wondering what it might be like.* She is scared. This is unknown territory. She might never come back.

'I know.' Zelda gives a hoot of laughter. 'I'm a *terrible* lesbian. I sleep with men!'

Suzy laughs with her. And yet the women at the camp seem to have assumed we are a couple from the off, she thinks, and it hasn't appeared to bother anyone; that some relationships are sexual is another bond between us all.

Zelda resumes caressing Suzy's arm, edging closer to Suzy's clavicle. '*Lesbian* is just a label. Something people assign it to women to help make sense of the world.' Her fingers flutter lower. 'Sexuality is more fluid than that...'

'Mm.' Suzy closes her eyes. Her mind goes back to the Bowie concert she went to with Johnny, all those rumours he was bisexual. Did it really matter what he was? Not to her it didn't. He was beautiful and talented and his music changed the world.

Sensing she has been given permission, Zelda lifts her head, and Suzy feels her breath on her face and leans forward, and their mouths meet. Zelda's lips are full and soft, her face is smooth, not bristly. And her cheeks, mmm, they are like pillowed velvet. Briefly, Suzy is reminded that barely a week ago she and Glenn were similarly entwined, and she wonders if she is on the rebound, but she can't analyse it; her brain is so full already, her heart too raw. Earlier that evening, she had got tearful about Glenn as she sat sketching the other women around the fire, seeing a recent drawing of him in her pad. Despite this, over the last few days, Suzy has become more convinced that her relationship with Glenn will never work out. Not when she is so passionate about the issues he dismisses.

In contrast, as she alters and re-forms herself, it seems only natural that she and Zelda are drawn closer, and when Zelda reaches under Suzy's top and runs a hand over her breast, it doesn't feel as if she is ricocheting. I am not the Suzy I was before, she thinks. I can be whoever I want to be. Thus, she lets go a little more, and her fingers reach out and brush Zelda's stomach. Soon they are kissing again, more intensely, and for several hours they go where pleasure takes them.

'I've no expectations,' says Zelda next morning, as they stand on the concourse at Newbury station, waiting to head in opposite directions. 'I don't expect us to carry on... er... you know...'

'No,' says Suzy. 'Though it was nice.' They both stand there, tongue-tied and self-conscious. All at once Suzy remembers what Zelda said about her letter to Johnny, when Suzy had written that wanted to stay friends and Zelda had warned her it would be impossible. Suzy pictures the first time she'd glimpsed Johnny after their break-up, the hurt in his eyes, the way his cheeks had flushed crimson. Then he'd hurried away, clearly keen to avoid her. Suzy had seen him several times that summer coming and going from number 32, but each time he ignored her, dropping his head to avoid eye contact. Once had she caught him staring up at her bedroom window; because it was dark inside, he couldn't see her. He looks broken, she'd thought, and for the rest of that day she'd been tempted to go over and try to make amends. But in the end, she'd been too much of a coward.

Zelda was right, thinks Suzy. Johnny and I have not spoken a word since I sent that letter. I was selfish. I owed him more. Before she can stop herself, she bursts out, 'It won't affect our friendship, will it?'

'Not unless we let it,' says Zelda.

'I'd hate it if it did.' The prospect of things being awkward with Zelda when they are so close is awful.

'Me too.'

Suzy checks her watch. Her train is due any minute. 'I'd better go.'

'Good luck with your mum and dad.'

'Hmph.' Suzy is dreading seeing her parents; more than ever she fears being forced into a version of herself she is not. 'Merry Christmas,' she says, swinging her rucksack over her shoulder to give Zelda a hug. 'See you in the New Year.'

♩ ♫ ♪ ♩   148

Over time, Suzy comes to see that Greenham gave her two gifts that winter: a different version not only of herself, but also of her friend. Zelda is no longer as biting or brazen, and when she is, Suzy gets it. Suzy tells no one about their nights under the bender. It is no one's business but their own. And although there are dozens of occasions when they crash out in the same bed—after a party if they drink too much, when they've been clubbing and it's too late to catch a tube— they are not intimate sexually again.

One day, Suzy hears the expression *friends with benefits*, and wonders if this is what they were to each other for that brief period. And yet, she decides, the phrase belittles them both. For many more years, Zelda remains Suzy's best friend. She understands Suzy, in some ways better than Johnny did, because she is a woman too, and they are changing and meta morphing together. Certainly Zelda gets her better than Glenn. And even when they meet new partners after leaving university, it is not until events several years later rip Suzy from her world with horrifying force that she and Zelda stop being as open with one another. But that's when Suzy stops being as open with everyone.

To be otherwise is too painful.

27.

February 2018

Now what?

Suzy scours the cottage. The living room looks more her own again, but the paler rectangles where her mother's paintings used to hang remain. She heads upstairs and, reluctantly, lifts the latch of the second bedroom. She is looking forward to putting Zelda up for the night, but inside it smells awful, a mix of mustiness and her mother's perfume—a scent Suzy never liked. The furniture is Joan's too; she slept here until she could no longer manage the stairs. The oak dressing table and matching tallboy might have been the height of post-war fashion, but the dark wood is dingy and depressing. Similar is true of the single divan with its upholstered headboard. The only item not decades old is the mattress. Suzy had replaced it when her mother shifted downstairs as Cam had complained it smelt of urine. Since he was the only person who ever offered to stay and help, Suzy decided this was the least she could do.

Painting the furniture a paler colour would help, she thinks. I could do the living room walls while I'm at it. Some pictures might brighten the space, too. But she is loath to hang the oils rejected by Julian. That would remind her of an encounter she is keen to forget, and she isn't keen on turning her home into a gallery of her recent work. Putting up some of her older paintings would feel less self-aggrandising, but where has she stored them?

♩ ♫ ♪ ♩

There is only one possibility. Suzy opens the hatch to the loft and pulls down the rickety wooden ladder. I must install a proper light, she thinks, plugging in her bedside lamp nearby and mounting the steps with it clutched in one hand. She ignores the inner voice scolding her that all this is most unwise given her ankle and, at the top of the ladder, turns on the light. Propped close by are her mother's pastel watercolour prints, left in easy reach for Cam to take his pick. There is no room to stand, so Suzy edges her way into the space, shuffling on her hands and knees.

Lord, so many boxes, and so few with labels! What a hopeless organiser she is. Eventually she finds the one she is looking for. Hauling the box back down the ladder, her luck runs out; it breaks under the weight of its contents and Suzy watches, powerless, as her sketchbooks tumble down the stairs to the hall. Several loose pages fly from their binding and float in slow motion to the carpet. Immediately Pushkin dashes from the kitchen. *Birds!* Suzy imagines the little cat thinking gleefully as she pounces and catches one, two, three pieces of paper, crumpling and tearing them. Suzy hurries down the steps in their wake, distracts Pushkin with a bonus helping of dried food and gathers up the drawings. One is a painting of Park Road and, from the childish signature, it looks to have been done whilst she was still in primary school. The exuberant colours make her smile.

I don't remember filling so many books, she thinks, stacking them in rough date order on the kitchen table. She stops to leaf through one labelled 1983 and sure enough, there is the sketch of Glenn asleep. She wonders if she should show him next time that she sees him, or if he would be embarrassed. Because yes, he *was* slimmer—weren't they all? —but what strikes her is the tenderness of the drawing. He is lying on his front in bed, naked, his face partly hidden by a pillow, yet there is enough detail for him to be instantly recognisable. His lips are parted and the lashes against his cheek are so carefully delineated that it's obvious how attractive she found him, and she is consumed by a desire to be that intimate with someone again. It has been so long.

Several pages later are her sketches of Greenham. A great many, she observes, considering we were at the base less than a week. The loose lines suggest there was no time for colour or detail and, as she reflects, she remembers her fingers being so cold that drawing at speed was the only option. All the same, she recognises Yoshi, her slight frame swamped by a torn anorak and baggy trousers, and Val, with her straggly hair and poncho. Oh, my word, that poncho! Suzy can still envisage its texture, matted from the rain, and its lurid bubble-gum hue. Particularly evocative is a series of charcoal sketches of the women around the fire at night, where Suzy has smudged black over much of the paper then used a rubber to pick out the figures and flames.

These aren't bad, she thinks, pleased to have laid hands on them. She flicks through pads from subsequent years, and the sketches alter after 1985, which is when she graduated. Thereafter the drawings continue to be experimental, and brave. Now I consider myself an abstract artist, she thinks, yet for all those years I was enraptured by figurative drawing. Strange I'd forgotten. She makes space to open the biggest sketchpad. *1988-,* it says on the cover. The lack of an end date pulls her up short, but, curious, she opens it.

First up is a coloured pencil drawing of her London flatmates, Tash and Stef, watching telly. With hindsight, the style is a homage to the Viennese painter, Egon Schiele. With elements of David Hockney thrown in. Still, she thinks, I was good at getting a likeness. I would know both these people at once. Stef, the pallid lanky German, Tash, his big-hearted, big-bosomed Brixton-born girlfriend. Her throat catches at the memory. She stops, fearful of what she might find next, before turning the page.

Her heart falters. She has used the same set of pencils and it is an even better likeness than the previous drawing. That curly golden hair, that expressive face, that easy smile. Can it truly be nearly thirty years since she last saw him in the flesh? Yet beside her signature in the bottom right corner, it says *1988,* so it must be.

She feels tears prick behind her eyes and is about to slam the pad shut when she stops. To close this door on her past, when she has laid bare so much of her youth again, seems wrong. But what else can she do? She can hardly frame this particular drawing. Could she cope with seeing Nate every day? Of course, she couldn't.

28.

February 2018

'Things are always happening to you,' Zelda had said.

Maybe she has a point, thinks Suzy, slowing the car to turn off the A4. Her old friend is due in three days and now, on the spur of the moment, Glenn has invited her over.

'You fit to drive?' he had asked.

'The question is whether my *car* is fit to drive.'

Suzy had not been joking, but after 35 miles, the clipped voice on her phone app declares, 'You have arrived at your destination.' She pulls up on the verge to check her surroundings. She is several miles from the nearest town, on the edge of a large wood. There is only one dwelling. Is this the right place? She isn't sure where she expected Glenn to live, but it wasn't in a large caravan. Or maybe *mobile home* is the term, although it is so firmly wedged in by long grass and nettles, evidence suggests it hasn't been moved in a long while. It's only when she spies a motorbike chained up close by that she is certain that the satnav has not failed her. There is a space next to his bike that is off the road completely and perfect for her hatchback, so she parks her vehicle there. As she is getting out, the door of the caravan swings open and Glenn comes down the steps to greet her.

'Thought that must be you.' He grins, wiping his hands on a dish-cloth and throwing it over a shoulder. 'Sorry, I must stink of garlic. Been cooking. Good to see you.'

'And you.' Unsure whether to give him a hug or a kiss or neither, Suzy remains where she is and turns, slowly taking it all in. Spring is coming, she notices. The earth is beginning to smell of burgeoning life. On the other side of the road, the Wiltshire downs sweep gently to the horizon, but Glenn's home is sheltered by trees which have yet to awaken from their winter slumber: beech, by the shape of the fallen leaves. 'When you said, "Come to my neck of the woods," I didn't realise you meant it so literally.'

He laughs. 'I thought I told you what I did for a living.'

'Yeah, but you told me you were a *Woodland Manager* and I guess I absorbed the word *manager* and ignored the word *wood*.'

He shakes his head, still chuckling. 'You pictured *me* behind a desk somewhere?'

'I did.' She grimaces at her own stupidity. Suzy notices the oily rags and toolbox by the bike, the dirt-spattered boots on the caravan steps. It had been hard to imagine Glenn in an admin job but, having no interest in desk jobs herself, she had let it slide. The appeal of this remote spot makes much more sense.

'It's so quiet.'

'That's why I like it.' He glances up at the cloudless sky. 'It's well known for bluebells so in a month or two it'll be swamped, but for much of the year I can go a whole day without seeing a soul. No planes, no busy roads, just the sounds of nature.'

Suzy cocks her head. Right on cue she hears a rich, flute-like call. 'Blackbird?'

He nods. It's followed by a *ru-hoo ru ru-hoo*. 'And that?'

'Woodpigeon.'

'Easy that one.' Next is a loud series of piping notes, like an alarm.

'Ooh, bit harder.' Suzy closes her eyes in order to focus. 'I'd say it was a woodpecker, but they're not as high pitched.'

'Nope. Nuthatch. Still, not bad.' He turns back to the caravan. 'I'd better switch off this casserole. Come in. Fancy a tea, or a stroll?'

Suzy stops to listen before following him inside. The wind is rustling in the trees. Again, she is struck by how much he seems to have mellowed. Though many people soften as they age, she tells herself. Perhaps it would be more unusual—and certainly less appealing—if he hadn't. To be a tearaway at 24 is one thing, to be that reckless pushing 60 would be sad, like a rock star who insists on keeping his hair long despite being bald on top.

What I can't work out is where the wife and the children fit in, thinks Suzy. A middle-aged man escaping from the rat race makes sense, but his kids? Where do they sleep in a mobile home? She steps inside. The main living space is quirkier than she would have expected given the plain exterior and looks largely handcrafted—the pale wood cupboards have black wrought iron hinges, and the skylight is surrounded by stained glass. The worn Turkish kilim is something she might even have chosen herself. There are two doors off the primary living space suggesting it has a bedroom and a bathroom, That must make it hard for his offspring to stay. It's a problem she recognises, having had to cater for Cam and her mother at the same time.

'Have you been living here a while?' She probes him.

'On second thoughts, the light will go soon.' She wonders if he is being deliberately evasive. 'If we're going on a walk, perhaps we'd ought to do that first. Would you like to?'

'Sure.'

'How about we take our tea with us?'

'Good idea.'

As she watches him set about the task, she is reminded of their first encounter at the Hacienda bar. He seems unfazed by the confines of a tiny kitchen, deftly moving to fill the kettle and locate two travel mugs. He crouches to retrieve milk from the fridge in a fashion she has not been able to do for months because of her ankle. He still has an air of nonchalance that suggests a man at ease with his physical being, she observes. She recalls edging down the loft ladder, unable to keep hold of a cardboard box and feels cack-handed in contrast. Glenn turns back to the counter, and she appraises his rear view. Hell, even his bottom seems toned. Sure, we are both heavier than we used to be, Suzy says to herself, but who am I kidding? Everything points to Glenn having put on muscle. I am merely chubbier.

When he says, 'Shall we go?' and adds, 'To answer your question, must be six years,' she is thrown.

'Did you move here when you and um...' Damn, she has forgotten his ex-wife's name.

'Pippa?'

'Pippa.' She nods, following him outside and onto a narrow path into the wood.

'When we split up? God, no.' He holds open a gate, and she steps through. Bare branches reach high above them, interrupted by an occasional flash of evergreen. 'Pippa and I divorced long before that.'

Interesting, thinks Suzy. I wonder if he has had other relationships in the interim. She is pondering that this is a long time for someone as attractive as Glenn to spend without a partner when she reminds herself that she has not been naked with anyone in *years*. She is so out of practice. Hopefully kissing is like riding a bicycle—something one never forgets—but the rest of her body has changed so much. She has heard that after the menopause the vagina can become as fragile as tissue paper but has never had cause to test this out. The prospect of sex being painful, perhaps not even possible, casts dating in a whole new light. What if nothing functions down there in the way it did? Imagine if her insides have dried up like a prune and she can't accommodate his cock! It could be hideously embarrassing. Suddenly she feels dreadfully old. 'Rock chick,' she mutters to herself, thankful Glenn is striding ahead and cannot see her blush. Who am I kidding?

Her thoughts are interrupted when the path intersects a bridleway and Glenn asks, 'How long would you like to walk for?'

Suzy is tempted to say, *Hours, because so long as we are walking there's*

157

no danger of anything else happening. But she still can't manage to put weight on her ankle for that long. *I can't possibly tell Debs I scarpered before dinner,* she rebukes herself. *And who's saying Glenn is desperate to have sex with me, anyway? It's not like I've committed to sleeping with him tonight. We'll walk, we'll talk, we'll eat, and then I'll drive home.*

'Half an hour all right?' Glenn chivvies. 'Or we can make it shorter? Please, just say. I don't want to push you too hard, what with your ankle.'

'Oh, er, yes. Perfect.' *Glenn is being very considerate,* she notices.

'Great.' He smiles, pausing so they can walk together. Then he turns onto the bridleway and, to Suzy's consternation, reaches for her hand. His grip is firm though not tight and the longer their fingers are entwined, the more powerful the connection seems to become. All around them are signs of spring: buds are beginning to brighten the stark tree branches; wild primroses add a splash of colour to the woodland floor; an elder is bursting into life with a glorious display of white flowers, the catkins on the hazel trees have turned golden with pollen. To be strolling with someone so at ease with his surroundings is seductive and by the time they break apart to go through the gate once more, Suzy feels it as momentarily painful, like ripping off a plaster.

Next morning, she wakes with her head full of a dream she is reluctant to leave. She had been with Glenn somewhere dark, sweaty, illicit... She reaches down between her legs. *She suspected as much; she is damp, swollen. I needn't worry,* she tells herself, *my body is obviously capable of arousal.* It was the previous evening when we kissed farewell.

She rolls over, hugging her knees in tight, turned on again at the memory. *Mm, delicious...*

'You're welcome to stay,' he'd said, and knowing she was desired as well as desirous tempted her to say *Yes, I'd like that.* Yet a small voice had urged her to wait, whispered that her appetite, and his, might grow, so she gradually prised herself away, insisting, 'I must get home.'

Now she is glad she held off. It gives her the chance to check herself out, make sure she is in good working order. Like taking a car on a test drive, she smiles to herself, and throws back the duvet.

Suzy finds the toy wedged deep in her top drawer amongst her knickers and bras, just as she hoped, and hurries back to bed, flinging off her nightdress as she goes. She lies back, expectant. She'll start slow, as she used to. Tentatively, not wanting to overwhelm herself with anything too sudden, she presses the switch.

Nothing.

She looks down at the vibrator. Aside from buzzing, isn't a light supposed to come on? She presses the switch again.

Still nothing.

It can't be broken, surely? Exasperated, she gives it a shake. There is a faint tickle in her hands then, again, zilch.

The batteries must have gone, she realises, with mounting frustration. Still naked, she hastens downstairs to the kitchen, yanks open the door of the cupboard under the counter where she keeps the cat food, pulls out the plastic box where she stores spares and peers inside. Great! There are plenty of triple and double As. Then she unscrews the base of the vibrator. Four batteries, slim and flat as two-penny pieces, fall into her palm. For goodness sake! She knows at once she has none like this and hurries back up the stairs. On the way, she catches sight of herself in the hall mirror and notices how she wobbles when she moves. Her skin is grey and blotchy, too.

She dives back bed and under the duvet, breathless and chilly. Her fingers will suffice. She closes her eyes and reaches down between her legs. She circles around, first one way, then the other.

Mm...

Touching herself is beginning to have an effect when, purring, Pushkin pushes a wet nose into her face. Oh dear. She needs feeding, thinks Suzy.

'Wait,' she says firmly, moving her fingers more urgently back and forth, yet Pushkin starts paddy-pawing her chest, her claws little pin-pricks of discomfort. Soon Suzy's head is full of other issues: *I need a cup of tea, I wonder if the paint has dried on Mum's old furniture, I've got to find a way of earning money...*

After a while, she stops. It is to no avail. The moment has passed.

29.

Suzy is taking out the rubbish when the toot of a horn makes her start.

She hears a familiar voice shout, 'Why the hurry?' and sees Zelda leaning out of her car window, scowling at the motorist behind. He beeps again and Suzy realises that it is Rich in his Merc, wanting Zelda to move her vehicle forward so he can turn into his drive. Zelda finishes parking outside Suzy's cottage, and he accelerates past her and up the slope.

'TOSSER!' yells Zelda.

Suzy heaves the binbags to the pavement and waits for Zelda to gather her things.

'That your neighbour?' says Zelda, opening the car door.

'Yes.'

'Twat.'

Suzy laughs. 'He is a bit.'

'A *bit*?' Zelda still has the brass neck to use her height to her advantage. She goes to the hedge and peers over, making little attempt to conceal herself. 'Like that's "a bit" Grand Designs?'

'His wife's lovely,' says Suzy.

Zelda harrumphs.

'Can I take anything?'

'You're OK.' Zelda opens the boot and grabs a hold-all. As Suzy leads her up the path, she raises her voice. 'MUCH PREFER YOUR PLACE.'

'Hush! I have to live with these people!'

Inside, Zelda drops her luggage on the kitchen floor. 'Cum'on short-arse. G'is a hug.' She flings her skinny arms wide, and they embrace. Then they stand back and hold each other at arms' length, appraising.

'You're looking good,' says Zelda.

I'm hardly at my best, thinks Suzy. I must have looked dreadful last time she saw me. She takes in the woman before her. 'Bob suits you.'

'I know.' Zelda grins, tosses her head and over one shoulder gives a theatrical pout.

Again, Suzy laughs. 'It's great to see you.' And it really *is* a pleasure. She feels a rush of regret. Why did she leave it so long? She and Zelda have missed out on so much time.

'Likewise. Have to admit, I wasn't sure I'd ever see you again. You've become such a hermit.'

Scarcely an accolade, thinks Suzy.

'So, your mum died.' Zelda unzips her hold-all, rummages through her clothes and yanks a bottle of wine from the depths. 'That must have been a relief.' She thrusts the bottle at Suzy. 'Hope red's OK. They didn't have any white in the fridge and I can't be fagged to wait for something to chill. Can we open it now?'

'Sure.' Suzy smiles. It is reassuring Zelda doesn't seem to have changed a jot, and they can slip back into their intimacy with ease. I wouldn't want her to, she realises. I used to enjoy our banter.

'OK, so explain to me,' says Zelda, dragging a kitchen chair across the floor so she can put her feet up. 'Why *did* you decide to look after her? Don't think of you as the martyr type.'

Why did she? It's a question she seems to keep being asked, yet which she feels less and less sure of how to answer.

'It's not as if you liked her.'

'That's what Glenn said.' The words are out before Suzy can edit herself.

Quick as a farmyard cat, Zelda pounces. *'Glenn?'*

'Yeah.' Suzy tries to sound nonchalant but a blush betrays her. It will be impossible to backpedal now.

'Seriously?'

'Mm. I saw you two were friends on Facebook.' Suzy gets up on the pretence of fetching some crisps then recalls she has bought none.

'I wouldn't call Glenn anything more than a Facebook friend,' says Zelda. 'You and he were an item.'

'You know what I mean.'

Zelda's eyes narrow.

Suzy continues searching through her cupboards for something to serve, to no avail. She is forced to return to her seat. 'He commented on one of your posts,' she flounders.

Zelda raises her eyebrows.

'All right, all right.' Suzy throws up her hands. 'I befriended him.'

'As long as you're only friends on Facebook, I don't have a problem with that.'

Suzy rotates the stem of her wineglass, curious. Why would it bother Zelda if she is in close contact with Glenn again? It is true that when she met Zelda, Suzy had been going out with Johnny who had been miles away, so Zelda had had Suzy mainly to herself. Then Suzy had met Glenn, and she had wondered if Zelda was jealous of their intimacy at the time. But that was *decades* ago, Suzy reasons. Right now, it is more important to avoid a grilling. Zelda has only just arrived, and they have bridges to build.

Zelda seems to read her mind. 'It's you I care about. He treated you badly, remember?'

'Mm.' Suzy resists the urge to point out that people change but cannot argue without risk of being drawn further. Damn Zelda for being so savvy!

'Just don't do anything stupid. I've seen too many people get together with their exes and come a cropper. Trust me, I speak from experience.' Zelda leans back in her chair and Suzy tries not to worry her ancient furniture might not be up to it. 'Anyway, my life is dull these days. Daisy and I are rub along well enough, all things considered. Notwithstanding her Buddhism—' Zelda rolls her eyes '—and all the hippy shit she's into, we've got a lot in common. You must meet her. Tell me, you started dating, given you're free of the maternal shackles? I'm dying for the chance to live vicariously.' Her grilling echoes Debs' thinks Suzy.

'How about I show you your room?' Suzy sidesteps.

'It'll wait.' Zelda waves an arm. 'I want to hear what you've been up to.'

'I've put up some pictures I thought you'd like to see.'

'Ooh!' Zelda jumps to her feet. 'Not old photos of me I hope?'

Suzy laughs and leads her up the stairs. 'No.'

'Oh my gosh, *these!*' Zelda rushes to look and scans the wall. 'Wow, they take me back.' Then she tucks her bob behind her ears and, one by one, examines each more closely. 'There's Yoshi! And Val! Weren't those women great?'

It was worth removing Mum's insipid watercolours from their frames for this response, thinks Suzy.

'I'll never forget Yoshi telling us about her dad.' Zelda's expression turns serious, and she moves to stand before the charcoal drawing of women around the campfire, lets out a long breath and eyes Suzy. 'You're bloody good, you know.'

'Was bloody good,' Suzy mumbles.

'Don't be daft. You're still talented.'

I don't *feel* talented, thinks Suzy. I feel like a has-been.

'Remind me,' Zelda has stepped to the much larger drawing on the adjacent wall. 'Stef and...?' She points at the dark-skinned girl wedged up against him.

'Tash,' says Suzy.

'That's it! She was a laugh. This is a *great* drawing, Suzy.'

'Thanks.'

'I'm serious. It captures them so well. You shared a flat, didn't you?'

'We did, yeah.'

'Don't tell me...' Zelda clicks her fingers. 'Clapham. It was near the common. I remember hanging out there. Bit of a shithole, but enormous space on the ground floor...' She scrunches her face, then stomps with pleasure. 'To watch the football! The Hand of God game. That was it.'

30.

June 1986

It is a balmy midsummer evening in England.

'I bet it's blistering in Mexico City.' Stef sizes up the packed Azteca stadium on the tiny TV screen. 'Look at the state of that pitch.' The grass is brown and goal area worn bare.

'Rather them than me,' says Tash, as the teams emerge from the tunnel. The crowd roar with excitement.

'Get set for Falklands II,' says Zelda, cracking open a can.

'No, look!' Tash protests. 'The Argentinians are giving each England player a present.'

'*Pennant.*' Stef corrects. 'The word is pennant.' From his mastery of English, it's hard to believe Stef is not a native speaker. The only tell-tale sign is a slight German accent. Nonetheless, Suzy feels indignant on Tash's behalf. Stef can be so patronising.

'I don't think they will forget the Belgrano that fast,' says Zelda. 'They lost more than double the men in that war than we did.'

The back door opens and a slender young man with a mane of golden hair steps into the living room from the garden. He is wearing red shorts and flip flops and is so tanned the whites of his blue eyes appear almost luminous.

'Didn't hear the doorbell.' Stef jerks his head in welcome but doesn't shift his gaze from the screen.

'Side gate was open,' says the young man.

He must be a friend of Stef's, thinks Suzy, awaiting an introduction. But Stef merely gestures towards the stash of beers. 'Help yourself.'

Suzy casts about, wondering where Stef's friend can sit.

'I'll sit on Stef's knee,' offers Tash. That won't be comfortable, thinks Suzy. Stef is so bony!

'Careful!' Stef winces and shifts her weight. 'Don't get in the way, OK?' He splutters as her halo of frizzy hair catches in his mouth.

'Cheers.' The young man takes Tash's space and checks round. 'I presume you're all supporting England?'

'Stef's backing the Argies,' says Zelda.

'Goes without saying,' says his friend.

Surely, he should support West Germany? Suzy is confused. Aren't they in the quarter finals too? From atop Stef's lap beside her, Tash shrugs, also flummoxed.

'It's a Red Letter Day for Stef every time England gets beaten,' quips his friend.

'UNLUCKY!' bellows Zelda as an effort by Beardsley, against an unguarded goal, billows against the side-netting.

A cluster of photographers on the edge of the pitch appear to be making it hard for Maradona to take a corner.

'They should move,' says Suzy.

'Whose side are you on?' Zelda jibes her. 'It's good they're making it difficult.'

Maradona removes the pole to attack the ball from another angle.

'What is that linesman on about?' asks Stef's friend.

'He wants Maradona to put the pole back,' says Zelda.

'But it's holding up play,' says Tash.

'Jobsworth,' says Stef's friend.

Finally, the linesman gives Maradona the nod. With grim inevitability, the shot sails straight into the goalkeeper's hands. When the whistle goes after 45 minutes, the score remains nil-nil.

'Good. I'm going to the loo,' says Tash, getting up from Stef's lap.

'Not up to much, that first half,' says Stef.

We weren't up to much, thinks Suzy, but keeps schtum. 'Perhaps now you could introduce your friend?'

'Oh. Yes. Sorry.' Stef rubs his thighs and winces in relief. 'Everyone, this is Nate.'

Nate leans forward on the sofa so he can see Suzy and Zelda beyond Stef.

'Hi.' He lifts a hand.

'Hi.' Suzy smiles. He's incredibly brown given it is only June, she thinks. Maybe he's been somewhere exotic. He reminds her a *bit* of Michael Hutchence from INXS, except he's not as good looking – few men are - and his hair is far blonder.

'She's Suzy, and I'm Zelda.' Zelda gets up from the arm of the sofa and stretches.

Barely five minutes into the second half, Steve Hodge slices a high, looping ball into the middle of his own area. It falls just in front of the penalty spot and is met by Maradona in mid-air. Somehow, he elevates the ball over the goalkeeper's head and into the empty net. It all happens so fast Suzy fails to see how it got there.

'He punched it!' Zelda jumps up from the arm of the sofa. 'He pushed it into the net with his fist. HANDBALL!' She charges over to the tiny TV. 'You useless Tunisian, didn't you see?' She thwacks the side of her head in dismay at the ref's failure to disallow the goal.

'OUT OF THE WAY!' shouts Stef.

Maradona runs off on his own to celebrate, but virtually everyone else on the pitch stops: Stephen Hodges, the referee, the linesmen.

'They're appealing for offside,' says the commentator, Barry Davies.

'ARE YOU BLIND?' yells Zelda. 'He touched it with left hand!' By this point, they are all jostling shoulder to shoulder to view the screen up close.

'The linesman should have spotted it,' says Nate.

♩ ♫ ♪♩   168

The action is replayed twice. They fall silent and slope back to the sofa. Zelda is right.

They are still fuming when, four minutes later, the ball is shuttled upfield to Maradona again. He speeds down the right side of the pitch, nips by Butcher and gathers pace, seeing off Beardsley and Reid as if they were troublesome toddlers. The ball scarcely seems to leave his foot, until, with a force that defies belief, it hits the back of the net.

'You have to say that's magnificent! There is no debate about that goal. Pure football genius,' opines Barry Davies.

'That's it then.' Nate slumps back. He looks personally beaten, and reaches into his shorts, fishes out a pack of cigarettes and lights a fag.

'Bring it on!' Stef claps gleefully, takes off his glasses and throws them in the air then re-catches them at the final whistle. 'The final! Argentina are sure to beat Belgium.'

'You've got to beat France yet,' Nate reminds him.

'We'll do that no problem.' Stef grins, tips Tash off his lap and gets to his feet.

'You're on your own celebrating,' says Nate.

'Oh, come on,' Stef looks round to chivvy them. 'You've got to admit that was a great match.'

Four stony faces fail to reflect his buoyancy.

He continues. 'But that second goal was—'

Zelda cuts him off. 'Go crow somewhere else. We were robbed.'

February 2018

Zelda taps the glass in front of Suzy's drawing again. 'Stef and Tash, they were with you and Nate... weren't they?'

Suzy stops dead, bracing herself for what is coming.

'You know, when...' Zelda stumbles, then falls silent. For once, she cannot find the words.

Suzy so needs this. To be held tight, after so many years of holding others. To let go and allow herself to fall into his arms. To give in to the smell, the sense, and the taste of another human being.

'Hi,' she says, pulling away eventually.

'Hello.' Glenn brushes her fringe from her eyes. 'That's better. I want to see your face.'

'My hair needs cutting,' she says.

'Looks fine to me. I like your hair.'

A memory ignites. 'That's not what you used to like best about me.'

He laughs; it has a deep, seductive ring to it. 'Didn't expect to see you back here so soon.'

'Didn't expect to be passing.' She smiles, a naughty smile.

'I don't generally get many people passing these woods.'

'I should hope not.' She steps back, spins, dress catching in the breeze, and skips up the steps of the caravan, calling over her shoulder, 'I was in Marlborough. Five miles is virtually passing.'

He hurries in her wake. 'I'm afraid I haven't tidied up.'

'I don't care.' She dives inside, giddy, giggling. To text, on a whim, as she has done; Suzy is *never* that impulsive. Not nowadays. Perhaps it was the pleasure of being with her dearest friend, who'd urged Suzy to keep pressing about the injury claim. 'You'll get it in the end, I'm certain of it. If the police are prosecuting, it's certain he was at fault. Be insistent, and you could get back thousands.' After so many months of worry, to hear Zelda's utter conviction made Suzy's spirits lift.

And then there was the sunshine, the birds singing, the smell of leaves opening and daffodils' scent, soil softening. She felt she could move more freely again at last. Whatever, Suzy had become increasingly turned on by the thought of Glenn that morning. She had put on lipstick, a scarlet gloss that she's not worn in ages which smells of peach and makes her want to kiss the world. And she'd riffled through her wardrobe and a floaty turquoise dress she'd forgotten all about had seemed to tumble from its hanger, calling out, *You can dance in me! I am made for flirting, for seduction, for taking off and letting drop to the floor...* And then, feeling pretty—yes, *pretty* for once—Suzy had driven to Marlborough; Zelda had a mate who ran a gastro pub there. 'You should show him your pictures,' Zelda had urged when they'd finally got round to discussing Suzy's finances. 'He often displays local artists' work. It's got to be worth a shot.' Normally Suzy would have emailed, opted for facelessness, but the clear sky, the dress and the lipstick had emboldened her to get in her car with her pictures in the boot. Not bubble-wrapped, but loose, bumping together all the way there. It was reckless, the oils could so easily have got damaged, but none did. And Zelda's mate, Paddy—*what* a nice man—had been very enthusiastic. 'I like them,' he'd beamed. 'What would you think about naming them? If you call this *Pewsey Vale*, say, people will see the local landscape in it.' It was so obvious this would make them much easier to sell, but he was so quick to smile, that Suzy had come away feeling boosted, rather than dumb for not thinking of it before. He'd asked her what price she had in mind and when she'd told him, Paddy had told her they were worth double. *The Marlborough Arms* might not be a Bath gallery, but still it was classy pub in the middle of a historic market town, and he'd promised to hang them right away. What a result! Was it any wonder that she had texted Glenn?

So here they are, in Glenn's immobile home and, before she can turn to face him, he has his arms around her waist and is kissing the back of her neck and she is tingling with goose bumps across her shoulders and down her spine. Again, she feels those lips that first kissed her so long ago, and she is at once in the present and the past, her younger self and herself as she is today, reawakening. And he is leading her—or is she leading him?—into the bedroom. It turns out it is ever so small, scarcely more than the bed, with space to shut the door at its foot. Which means there are walls right round to put her feet on, bare against the panelling, to support herself should she want to (and she does) and for him to brace his hands against. It turns out having him inside her is fine—more than fine—as he goes down on her for ages first, licking and gently tugging. For a while she loses herself so completely that she doesn't know which way is up which makes it all more surprising and fun.

That is what I needed, she thinks afterwards, when they are flaked out, dizzy, sheets rumpled, mattress askew, her dress on the floor, lipstick gone. Maybe I needed to see someone else turned on, to be truly turned on myself.

Later, he asks if she's hungry and she says, 'Yes, starving,' and he says he could cook something or he's got a pizza and she says, 'That'll do, let's share it,' and so he heats it up and cuts it into wedges and brings it to her in bed. They sit propped up by pillows in a way they both agree is reminiscent of their times in Rusholme, except this room is warmed by a wood burner and reminds her of a sea cabin.

'In Manchester your room was always freezing,' he says, and she says that's how she remembers it too. And then she remembers something much more recent that piqued her interest.

'You were going to tell me something,' she says, mouth full of Quattro Formaggi.

'That I still think you've great tits? Yes, you have.'

'Not that!' Laughing, she hits his arm with her fork. 'When we met up before, you said you'd tell me why you were so dead set against my going to Greenham.'

'I believe I said it wasn't your going to Greenham that bothered me.'

'You said it was too long to go into unless I invited you in.' She reaches for the pizza. Why does sex always make her hungry? She picks up another wedge but pauses with it, bending and gloopy, in midair. 'Why don't you tell me now?' She folds the pizza and takes a big bite.

'Oh God.' He pales. 'Are you sure?'

'Only if you want.' She shrugs, not because she isn't curious, but because she doesn't want to coerce him.

'I haven't even had a drink,' he says.

'Don't let me stop you.' Oops. This is a bigger deal than she appreciated.

'Haven't got any.' He scowls. It reminds her he used to scowl a lot, and she decides he doesn't seem to do it as much, these days, which is a good thing, surely. He lays down the piece of pizza he is eating. 'I guess now is a good a time as any.'

Excellent. She settles back on the pillows, expectant.

'It was to do with the Falklands,' he opens. 'That's why I behaved kind of weird back then.'

At once, Suzy is apprehensive. She didn't intend to dredge up anything that difficult. Not when they are having such a great time.

'You know I was in the forces.' This is a statement, not a question. 'I told you I left, didn't I?'

'Yeah. Though I'm pretty sure you never told me why.'

'I didn't tell anyone. I couldn't.'

Gosh, she thinks, could he have been discharged? Did he do something shameful? She can see a muscle twitch in his cheek. His entire body, so relaxed only moments ago, has stiffened. His eyes drift towards the window. He gazes into the distance but without focusing, as if he isn't seeing what's out there.

'You remember *The Belgrano*?' he asks.

'Of course.'

'Everyone remembers *The Belgrano*.' He sounds a touch aggrieved. 'I don't suppose you remember *HMS Sheffield*.'

Oh dear, thinks Suzy. I probably should. A snippet of information, the flash of an old newspaper headline, comes to her. 'Was that the ship which was hit?'

'Mm. She was a Guided Missile Destroyer.' His voice wavers. 'I was on board.'

'Oh God!' The exclamation is out before she can stop herself. She goes hot and cold.

His eyes flick to her face, and away. 'It was...' He stops. His mouth opens, then shuts.

'Tell me,' she urges, being careful to keep her voice low. 'I won't mind what you did or didn't do. I only care that you're OK.'

'I'm not very good at this... I find it hard to talk about.' He pulls his knees up and hugs them close to his chest.

'I'm sure.'

'I was pretty caught up in it...' His voice trails off. Then he snorts. 'You know afterwards, my parents didn't ever say they were glad that I'd survived? That was so typical of them.'

He still seems angry, thinks Suzy, even all these years later. Sounds as if Glenn's parents were stiff-upper-lip types; back then it was common at officer level in the armed forces. It makes her think that however cold her mother was and however weak her father, they were never that bad. When she *really* needed them, they were there for her.

'Well, *I'm* glad.' She strokes his back, hoping to comfort him.

'Thanks.' He gives her a faint, sad smile. 'Perhaps it'll be easiest if I tell it all at once.' He closes his eyes. His eyelids flicker, as if he is seeing events from the past projected onto them. 'The ship was pitching and rolling, the sea was very rough. We had just had lunch, so it was about half one...'

'You were in the South Atlantic?'

He opens his eyes and glances at her.

Oh dear. She has interrupted. She meant not to.

'Yes,' says Glenn. 'The islands are near Antarctica, most people don't realise. Anyway...' He closes his eyes again and shivers. 'It was freezing, and the boss asked if I'd go down and make tea and coffee for everyone. Because I knew most of the chefs on board, I was happy to. Plus it gave me the chance to be in the warm for a bit.' His voice is eerily flat. 'When I got to the galley, the hot water had run out, so I had to refill the urn and wait for it to boil. I stayed down there chatting, must have been for about twenty minutes. Then I came back on deck with a tray and handed round the tea, and I was talking to the pilot on our starboard ridge wing...' His hands are trembling, and Suzy resists the urge to grasp the one nearest her. Instinct tells her it is better to wait. 'At approximately two o'clock, we looked slightly to our right, and we saw this fireball coming towards us. The pilot shouted "EXOCET!" and there was an announcement to take cover. I only had time to duck behind an ammunition box before the missile came in.' At this Glenn opens his eyes wide, as if he is seeing the horror of it before him right there, in the bedroom. His shivering grows more intense.

Suzy's heart goes out to him. Yet she remains silent.

He continues, 'After a few seconds we were called to open fire with what we'd got, but we couldn't see what we were shooting at because of the smoke. Then we were told it was one of our own helicopters. Meanwhile, the fire was getting worse. The Exocet had severed the ship's water main, so we had to use buckets—imagine, sinking them on rope into the water and pulling them up?' He glances at her, so Suzy nods. Although she doesn't understand every detail, she can get the gist. 'There was this burning propellant that ignited diesel oil in the engine room... and the blaze got worse. No sooner had we thrown one lot of water on the ship's side than it dried at once. *HMS Yarmouth* came down our starboard side, *HMS Portsmouth* down our port side and they used their hoses, but it was so hot, the heat was coming in my boots through to my feet, and it was hard to breathe because of the smoke. Soon it was impossible to stay on the deck.' By now Glenn is scarcely audible; his voice is so quiet.

'After four or five hours, Captain Salt gave the order to abandon ship. No captain ever wants to do that, but he had no choice. The last I remember seeing of *The Sheffield* was from aboard *HMS Portsmouth*. She was billowing smoke, but when it cleared for a few moments, I saw this enormous hole in her side.' He glances from one wall of the bedroom to the other. 'It was about two, three times the length of this room.' He pauses, and when he next speaks his voice is high, like a boy's, such is the intensity of his distress. 'That's when I knew all the lads I'd been talking to in the galley were dead.'

Glenn starts to cry. Suzy has never seen him like this; face crumpled in pain, lips trembling. She senses she should pull him in close and comfort him, but something stops her. She feels at a loss, paralysed.

'Every day for the last thirty years, I've thought about the incident, and I've said, *Why should I be happy? Why should I survive when twenty men lost their lives? Why should I live?*'

The more Glenn weeps, the more removed Suzy feels. Even though she wants to listen, his voice seems to be going in and out of range like a radio losing and re-finding a signal. When he clumsily wipes away his tears, his quivering hands are horribly reminiscent of her own in the wake of her accident. The memory is jarring. Then, suddenly, Glenn hits his forehead with his knuckles. The hard, cracking noise, bone on bone, jolts Suzy back to what he is saying.

'I often believed everyone would be better off without me. The amount of grief I've caused... My family... My dad... My kids... Pippa... And to you... I couldn't... I can't... I'm not that good at... getting close to people.'

Faintly, ever so faintly, Suzy glimpses the possibility that Glenn's guardedness might mirror her own resistance in some way. *'You've become such a hermit,'* Zelda had said. But then, like a ship in the fog that is only briefly visible, the realisation slips away and disappears into the mist once more.

32.

Suzy wakes with a lurch, confused. She must have drifted off. Her surroundings are unfamiliar, and although the lights are low, everything seems eerily bright. She senses someone next to her, under the bedcover, struggles to remember, then relaxes. It is Nate. They are in a wood-panelled cabin—she can see with her own eyes—so presumably they are on a boat. Her thoughts seem to slide from her grasp, as if her mind is in a tug of war, pulling her between reality and uncertainty.

I'm lying on a mattress, she says firmly to herself, but her senses refuse to confirm it; her body feels to be floating in space, the room appears to be changing shape and colour, and when she holds out her hands, her fingers morph from elongated bony talons into stumps, with short, wide nails, like toes.

Beside her, Nate exhales, and Suzy reaches out for the soothing warmth of his flesh. But as she shifts the duvet, she recoils in horror. Whoever is next to her has short, dark hair, and she has no idea who he is. It is happening again; her memory is full of holes. It's vile, this feeling. She can't waste time fathoming it out. She has to go home, feel safe, so she slips from the bed, quiet as she can, swiftly gathers her things. There isn't space to dress, so she tiptoes out of the bedroom to pull on her clothes.

Outside, the air is chilly, the ground covered in frost. She tries to hurry, but it's as if she's moving on a bouncy castle, unable to balance and make her limbs obey. Inside her car, the smell is familiar, her position behind the wheel one she knows well, and she breathes a sigh of relief, but then she hears a door bang and sees the man with dark hair running towards her, fast. He thumps on the car window beside her, startling her further.

'SUZY! WHERE ARE YOU GOING?'

She fumbles to turn on the ignition, but she is so shaky, she cannot find the slot for the key, let alone speak.

'ARE YOU FUCKING DEAF?' The man opens the car door beside her before she can think to lock it. His voice is terrifying in its volume.

She flinches and, fearing he is going to pull her from the vehicle, leans forward against the wheel to tighten the seatbelt around herself.

'ANSWER ME!' he bellows.

Almost simultaneously, she finds the hole for the key and manages to start the car. She thrusts the gearstick into reverse and releases the handbrake. She needs to turn on the headlights but dare not relax her grip on the steering wheel to flick the stick control. It's on the right side, and if the man grabs her hand driving will be impossible.

'IS THIS SOME KIND OF SICK JOKE?'

Suzy glances sideways at him. She thinks she recognises him, but he is so angry that his nostrils are flaring, and his eyes are hard and flinty, plus it is dark, so she cannot be sure. She hears his breath coming hard and fast. To get away, she may send him flying, but what choice does she have? It is her or him. She takes her foot off the clutch and the car begins to roll backwards. In a split second, it seems he feels the bump of the door against the side of his body and realises what is about to happen, so jumps back, narrowly missing a nearby motorcycle. Still furious, he reaches and slams the car door and kicks it as Suzy lunges the hatchback into first gear.

'Go-Suzy-Go-Suzy-Go-Suzy,' she murmurs to herself like a mantra, knuckles white as she grips the steering wheel. The car is ancient, what if it fails her now? But thank God, it doesn't, and some intuitive part of her brain tells her which way to turn onto the road, so she swings left and then she's in third gear and fourth and then at last can turn on the headlights and put her foot down fully, able to see where she is going. In the rear-view mirror she sees the man getting smaller and smaller. He is still shouting when he fades from earshot.

As she drives, the hedges, high on either side, seem to press in on her little hatchback; she fears the country lane will soon be too narrow to navigate. But then she comes to a T-junction, sees a sign that reads *Marlborough* and soon is on a road she recognises. Nonetheless, steering through the town centre is terrifying; the pubs are emptying, and people dart from nowhere, not looking as they run across the high street, jangling her nerves and causing her hands to slip from the wheel. There is a jam at the end of the road. It feels as if it takes forever to get home but eventually, she is back at the cottage, bewildered as to how she made it without having an accident. Once inside the house, she locks the front door and checks all the windows. It's only when she sees the clock and reads it is only 10.30 that she gradually begins to calm.

After a while, recent events begin come back to her, though bits are still missing, as if the evening has broken into shards of glass. She checks her mobile in a bid to piece it together; *Glenn* it reveals, has called several times. She isn't sure if she should respond—yes, she left with no explanation, yet his anger had scared her. It seems she can only stare at the screen, mystified as to what to say and after a while she realises she simply hasn't the strength, and so she turns off her phone, tugs off her clothes and climbs into bed, hoping here, at last, she will feel safe. But she cannot sleep. She lies there, heart racing and body rigid, believing whilst knowing it is irrational, that if she were to let go and fall into slumber, she might never wake again.

33.

February 1987

Suzy is leaning against the wall at the gallery entrance, gazing into space, when there is a cough behind her.

'Excuse me?' A young man is holding out his ticket. 'Do you need to see this?'

'Thanks,' she says, tearing it in two and handing one half back to him. She expects him to move off to look around the exhibition, but he hesitates.

'Er... Haven't we...?'

'Yes!' she exclaims. 'Sorry. I didn't expect to see you here. You're Stef's friend.' Oh dear, thinks Suzy. I can't remember his name. Summer is long gone; it must be six months since we met. He is no longer tanned, but his hair is still streaked with gold and curls into corkscrews. It puts her in mind of a merman.

He smiles. 'Hi. I'm Nate.' Then he grimaces. 'I'm sorry, I've forgotten your name.'

'Nice to see you again, Nate. I'm Suzy.' Again, she expects him to move away, but he lingers. There is an awkward pause, so she fills it. 'I guess you've come to have a look around?'

'Yeah. This is it then?' He swivels, appraising, then his shoulders slump. 'I was told to come.'

Suzy smiles to herself: he couldn't make it sound more like school-work if he tried. 'Who by?'

'My Creative Director. I work for Saatchis. For my sins.' He glances at her to gauge her reaction.

'That makes two of us.' She taps her name badge. 'Though I presume you're in advertising?'

'Yup. I'm a copywriter.' He brightens, and she detects a touch of pride in his voice. 'Though before you ask, no, I didn't come up with the *Labour Isn't Working* headline.'

'Glad to hear it.'

'I work for a much smaller agency, the other side of Regent's Park. Saatchi's has just bought us out and we're doing up the office. I didn't have much on today, so the CD suggested I see if I can get some posters or something.'

'I get it. To look the part.'

He steps into the gallery, then reverses back to Suzy's side. 'Bit of a naff idea, isn't it?'

'Yes,' she says bluntly.

He's very skinny, Suzy observes. His suit is well worn, and so loose it looks the wrong size. Perhaps it's a family cast off, or from a charity shop. In any event, the effect is more Charlie Chaplin than Master of the Universe.

Whereas from the moment she got this job, Suzy has made an effort. She is front of house and Nate isn't, and at the interview, the woman who runs the gallery good as commanded her backcombed hair would have to go. Now she has a choppy bob with a long fringe, and today she is wearing a Rifak Ozbek box jacket—a sample Tash blagged at London Fashion Week which she allows Suzy to borrow—and a dogtooth-check pencil skirt. Never mind that her stilettos will be killing her by 6pm.

'Truthfully?' she asks, and he nods. 'Most of the exhibits are 3d so don't reproduce that well. Though why don't you have a walk round, anyway? It's interesting.'

He scans the gallery. Save some angled windows in the roof, it's devoid of adornment. 'Looks drab to me.'

'Ah, but that's deliberate,' she says. 'Somewhere like the Royal Academy, the building can get in the way. It's all so grandiose, has so much history. Here there are no outside distractions, so the focus is on the work.'

'Have to admit I've never been the Royal Academy,' Nate mutters. He heads over to the nearest exhibit. Jutting out of the plain white wall is a plain white sink. 'Is this it?' There is no one else about, so he can talk freely.

Suzy steps to join him.

'Feel like I'm in the Men's toilet.' He sounds more perplexed than dismissive. His lack of pretension is refreshing, thinks Suzy. He seems nowhere near as arrogant as his friend, Stef. Not that it is surprising; Stef doesn't tolerate competition.

'Hold on...' Suzy hotfoots it to the door, checks up and down the street. 'My boss has gone for lunch. I can show you round if you like. Though if she comes back, I must leave you to it.'

'That'd be great.' He gives her a broad smile.

'There are nine artists in the show,' she tells him as they move into the next room. 'Most of them wish to overthrow what they call "*the primacy of the unique object.*" This is the Jeff Koons on your ticket.'

'So, if I got a poster...?'

'It'd be of this.'

'Right.' He thrusts his hands in his jacket pockets, walks around a large shiny silver rabbit. 'Is it made of balloons?'

'It's stainless steel.'

'Looks like the something you'd get a guy in to make at a kids' party.'

'That's supposed to be the point. Whereas traditionally the aim of art is to make something unique that hasn't existed before, these new artists are more inclined to downplay that ambition in favour of appropriating existing idioms from the recent past.' Suzy stops, conscious she is parroting the exhibition brochure.

'Seriously?' He tilts his head, peers at the rabbit again, then gives her a quizzical look.

They both burst out laughing.

'What a load of wank!' he says.

'I know!' Suzy wipes a tear from her eye. 'I hate it.'

Next is a series of graphic optical illusions. The patterns seem to dance before their eyes.

Nate nods, more appreciative. 'Trippy.'

'Bridget Riley does this sort of thing better,' says Suzy, and again they laugh.

Nate straightens his face. 'Sorry. I shouldn't take the mick. My Art Director would be first to tell you I'm better with words than pictures.'

'No need to apologise,' says Suzy.

He steps back, eyes her. 'What led you into this?'

At once Suzy is self-conscious. 'Er... This is my day job.'

'And at night?' There's a touch of innuendo in his tone.

She retorts, po-faced. 'I'm a painter.'

'Impressive you have the discipline. I'm trying to write a novel but it's the last thing I feel like after writing ads all day.'

'Ah, but this job isn't creative in the same way as yours,' says Suzy. She hopes it sounds as if she knows what his job entails; in truth, she isn't certain.

'What stuff do you do?'

'Nothing like this.' She wonders how to describe her recent work. Then an idea comes to her. 'You know what you should suggest to your agency board directors?'

'What?'

'That they buy some original art. That'd be more of a statement than endorsing stuff Saatchi is already into. Much braver. You never know. It could prove a good investment.'

'You mean buy one of yours?'

'Maybe...' Suzy blushes. He has seen straight through her. It would thrill her to sell a painting to people in the Saatchi empire and have it on display in an agency, even if it is a small offshoot. But she is also wary of coming across as too pushy. 'Needn't be mine. There are lots of young British artists here in London.'

'Hmm.' He drums his fingers on his cheek in a hammy display of deliberation. 'You know, I reckon they might like your thinking. I'll put it to them.' He reaches into his inside breast pocket. 'Here, let me give you a card.'

Nathan Quinn, she reads. *Junior Copywriter*. She turns it over in her palm. 'Impressive.'

'Smart, eh?' Again, she detects pride in his voice. 'We've just had had them printed.' Then he admits, 'You're the first person I've given one to.'

Two days later, Suzy arrives at work to find a plain white envelope has been hand-delivered for her. *Susie*, it says on the outside; so someone unaware how she spells her name has sent it, clearly. It's mid February. Could it be...? Excitement mounting, she tears open the envelope. Inside is a small card, about two inches square. On the front is a tiny hand-drawn red heart, inside is an equally tiny line drawing. She recognises it at once as Jeff Koons' rabbit. There is no signature, only a question mark.

A Valentine's!

Suzy is thrilled. She tells Stef, who cannot resist deriding the gesture as paltry compared to his own. Suzy resists retorting that a dozen red roses is a cliché. Luckily, Tash argues for her. 'It's hardly the same,' she rolls her eyes at her boyfriend. 'We're already going out.' Privately, she says to Suzy, '*I* think it's romantic. Do you?' Suzy says, 'Yes, I do.' 'From what I know of him, Nate's a nice guy. I'll see if I can get Stef to invite him over,' says Tash. She is good as her word, and the following weekend Nate and a few other single friends come for dinner. 'The others are a smokescreen,' says Tash. 'Don't want it to look like a double date, do we?' and, again, Suzy agrees.

'I got my art director to do it,' Nate admits, embarrassed. The other guests have departed, and Stef and Tash have diplomatically retired to bed. 'I can't draw that well.' But Suzy doesn't mind. Not remotely. It's the thought that counts.

When she looks back, she finds it hard to express exactly what made Nate so appealing. They don't share years of history like she and Johnny did, nor is he good looking like Glenn, or forthright like Zelda. He does not make her legs turn to jelly or fill her with zeal to change the world. That he is only a junior, yet so proud of his job; that he's creative, like Suzy, but in a different way; that he's not embarrassed to admit he knows little about art yet is curious to learn more; that his clothes don't fit but his hair puts her in mind of Michael Hutchence... It is no one thing, yet the mix is beguiling. Plus, there is the timing.

Spring 1987 and gone are the ship builders, steel workers and miners. The public sector is being privatised and in London, the doors have been thrown open to people on the make: estate agents, mortgage lenders and share dealers, celebrity chefs and supermodels. Even everyday folk are eating microwave meals and buying shiny new cars and home computers, swapping small family-run shops for supermarkets the size of football pitches and putting all their purchases on plastic.

Within a week of that dinner party Nate and Suzy sleep together and soon they are an item, each one half of a golden couple, brought together by their creativity and way they are both part of this new world order yet stand apart from it. Nate's work in advertising means he can enjoy the high life—the fine dining over business lunches, the banter with bright colleagues, the thrill of billboards boasting his catch phrases on display the length and breadth of the city. Suzy sells several of her paintings—including one to Nate's agency—cuts back her hours at the Saatchi Gallery and for six glorious months she only works two days a week, more to network and 'keep her eye in' than because she needs the money. The rest of the time she focuses on her own art, and her reputation grows.

'He's so funny,' she tells Zelda. 'He's no pushover, but he's really affectionate when it's only the two of us.'

That Nate grew up in Camden means he knows the inner-city streets of the capital like the back of his hand. They share candlelit dinners in tiny restaurants in Soho that only those who work locally are aware of; he takes her to Janet Reger's Bond Street store to buy silk lingerie and they are both turned on by how luxurious it feels. Within six months, they have moved in together. It makes total sense; Suzy's room is huge, and Nate is friends with her flatmates. If Steff and Tash are cool with it, they agree, why look for somewhere new?

Then, in the early hours of 16 October, hurricane-force winds batter the south of England in the worst storm in 300 years. Suzy is woken by the sound of tiles being dislodged from the roof and crashing onto the pavement, but it is not until they leave for work that she and Nate realise the extent of the damage. The wooden fence in their neighbour's garden has been flattened and bus shelter on the corner has buckled under the weight of some fallen scaffolding from a nearby construction site, splintering glass across the road.

'I can't believe you didn't even stir,' says Suzy as they walk to the station, increasingly agog at the wreckage. Across Clapham Common dozens of trees have been torn up by their roots, and there are crushed cars, bits of building and debris everywhere.

'You could have woken me,' Nate grumbles. 'I've missed the excitement.'

They are home, chastened, by 8:30am: the tubes are not running.

Three days later, the stock market crashes. Nate has managed to catch a tube to work on Monday morning, but by lunchtime rumours are spreading and soon the agency is aflame with panic. 'Listen to the news,' he urges, ringing Suzy on the landline at the studio she rents in Elephant and Castle. Within an hour she is surrounded by the group of fellow artists who are in that day, clustered around her paint-spattered radio, trying to fathom what's happened and why. 'It's because of excessive risk taking,' Suzy tries to explain. 'And foreign trade agreements or something,' but she has never fully grasped how the stock market works and fears she will sound a fool, so leaves the analysis to others and focuses on trying to keep pace with events. Within hours investor panic has set in and by the time she and Nate are at home watching the nine o'clock news, the Dow Jones has shed 23 percent of its value.

'The gods are having a laugh,' says Nate and it seems he is not wrong—only weeks later their landlord puts the rent up.

'At least we haven't bought it and got trapped with negative equity,' Nate observes in glass-half-full mode, but his optimistic temperament is tested when Saatchi's start cutting back staff in swathes. *Last in, first out* logic leaves him constantly afraid he's going to be laid off yet, somehow, he survives several rounds of redundancies. 'It's because I'm cheap,' he says glumly. 'It's because you're *good*,' Suzy counters. And although their wages freeze and they work longer hours, the edges are softened because around this time MDMA starts being manufactured in bulk in labs in Holland and consumed by clubbers in Ibiza, where DJs discover a rhythm of 120 beats per minute turns crowds into a sweaty mass of pulsing bodies who can dance all night. Soon after, Ecstasy arrives on the shores of Britain, and once 1987 has rolled into 1988, Acid House and the Rave Scene are where it's at, and Nate and Suzy and Stef and Tash are often to be found hugging and smiling along with hundreds of others at covertly organised illegal gatherings in empty industrial warehouses, living for the weekends.

34.

August 1988

'Anne?'

Oh no, it is her mother. Taking personal calls at work is frowned upon, but Joan has repeatedly ignored requests to ring in the evenings.

'I think it's time your father and I met this new boyfriend.'

Suzy is aghast. What has brought this on? She and Nate have been together for over a year, so their relationship is hardly 'new' but, fearing her mother's judgment, initially Suzy kept it from her parents. When she finally told them, she was deliberately low key, saying, 'It's nothing serious' and avoiding mention of their cohabitation.

'Your father and I are coming into the West End this afternoon and... er... we wondered if you like to join us for dinner?'

'Mum, that would be very nice,' Suzy lies, wincing at the prospect of repeating the awful rows they had over Johnny. 'But the thing is, we've been invited to a show later. You know, some up-and-coming artists?'

'Maybe we could all go!' Joan interjects.

Lordy, thinks Suzy. My mother at a contemporary art exhibition? I don't think so.

'I'm afraid this do is at the Surrey Docks,' says Suzy, very much hoping the fact this is miles from Mortlake will put her mother off.

'That's alright. We can find our way there,' says Joan. 'We're perfectly capable of looking at a map.'

'I don't think you'd like it, Mum. It's a rough area.'

'Clearly *you* think it's safe, so I'm sure we'll be fine. Would you be able to get us tickets? With your job at the gallery, I would have thought that would be easy.'

What a nightmare, thinks Suzy. It is true she can get her parents into the show—the organisers are admirers of the Saatchi collection and have been vocal in saying they wish to emulate its scale and ambition. A guy from Leeds—she recognises the Yorkshire accent—has been into the gallery a few times. He's confident to the point of pushy and on one occasion Suzy gave him pointers about producing a quality brochure. 'I can see it'll be tricky,' agreed Suzy, when he said the press 'won't be shagged to shlep to Surrey Docks'. 'Send me a few invites,' she'd offered, 'and I'll spread the word.' Nonetheless, the idea of introducing her parents to her boyfriend at an exhibition of artists roughly her own age is beyond toe-curling.

'Let me see what I can do about getting you on the guest list,' she says to her mother to buy time. Hurriedly, she calls Nate.

'I'm not bothered,' he tells her, typically easy-going about it. 'Could be a laugh.'

'You're no help at all!'

'We've got to face it some time. If nothing else, it'll be fodder for my novel.'

I cannot believe this is happening, thinks Suzy, when a couple of hours later she glimpses Joan's bouffant helmet of hair across the crowded warehouse. Getting closer, she sees that her mother is wearing a floral blouse with pussy-bow tie and matching fuchsia skirt; bang goes any possibility of whisking her at speed round the show without other guests noticing. Thank heavens Dad is less flamboyant, thinks Suzy, gratefully taking two glasses of wine from the guy at the nearby drinks table and requesting Nate do the same.

Only when she and Nate draw up directly before them does Suzy appreciate that behind her parents there is a gigantic photo installation featuring a glistening, fleshy vagina-like wound radiating from parted hair. Foreseeing her mother's reaction, she tries to move them away.

Fat chance, however: as she is introducing Nate and he proffers their drinks, a suavely dressed gentleman with long grey hair swept back into a ponytail says admiringly, 'Wonderful reflection of urban reality,' and stands back to absorb the piece.

'Gloriously grim,' says his female companion and bends to read the label. 'Mat Colishaw, *Bullet Hole.*' The comments cause Joan and Ken to turn. The image is so unbearably magnified, Suzy cannot conceal a shudder. There is a moment's silence, during which Suzy knocks back her wine in one gulp, bracing herself.

'HOW DISGUSTING!' says Joan, voice cutting through the hubbub like a machete.

At once Suzy is thrust back to her own final show, when Joan had pronounced, 'Any child could do this!' at maximum volume before a fellow graduate's work. 'These are my *friends*, Mum, can't you keep your voice down?' Suzy had pleaded. If these fine artists from Gold-smiths are anything like she and her peers, they will have laid their souls bare on the surrounding walls.

'I can't say I like it especially, but it's important younger artists are taken seriously,' says Suzy's father. Took us less than five minutes to end up here, thinks Suzy, noting he has opted for the middle ground. Our dynamics never change. Still, at least Nate has been forewarned.

Joan ignores her husband and moves on to the next exhibit.

'Are all these dots supposed to be part of the show?' she asks.

'I think so,' says Nate.

'Why on earth are they painted straight onto the wall?'

'Does look a bit rough around the edges,' says Ken, then adds, 'Though I think they're rather beautiful.'

She has a rush of affection for her dad. He's always been more into the same things I am, thinks Suzy. Compared to Mum, he is much more sophisticated in his understanding of popular culture and art.

'And these flashing lights!' Joan comes to a halt in front of another installation. 'Can you explain to me, darling, what they're all about?'

Suzy pauses, surprised for a moment by the term *darling,* before realising it must be for Nate's benefit. 'I guess all of us are dealing with what it means to inherit postmodernism...'

'It's a shitty fate,' agrees a young man, overhearing. 'This is mine, by the way.' He gestures towards an abstract oil painting, then eyes Suzy's name badge. 'You're from the Saatchi gallery?'

'Yes,' she says. 'I was wondering, why is the exhibition called *Freeze*?'

'I've no idea.' The young man shrugs.

'She's an artist, too,' says her father.

Suzy just manages to pick up the touch of pride in his voice before her mother interjects. 'Very weird name, you ask me. Reminds me of that funny lettuce.'

'This is my mum,' adds Suzy, hoping to stop the young man giving her mother the response she deserves.

'Frisée?' The young man laughs. 'Fair point...?' and raises his eyebrows to communicate he would like to know her name.

'Joan,' says Joan. 'And this is my husband, Ken.'

'Shall I get us another drink?' suggests Ken.

'Good idea,' says Suzy. But as she raises a hand to point him in the right direction, Suzy sees the guy who served their wine earlier collapse behind the table, drunk, onto the floor. Beneath the chatter, it is possible to make out the sound of vomiting. Fortunately, this sight is hidden by the drapes of a white tablecloth.

Nate clocks the situation. 'I'll go,' he says, bending his lean frame to nip past Ken.

Linen tablecloths and fresh flowers, Suzy observes. Plus, bottles of Perrier and white wine in ice buckets. Compared to my student show, this is all very slick. The young man we are chatting to is wearing trousers with *braces*, for goodness sake. She can hear Zelda scoffing what yuppies they all are.

'I'd have thought you'd approve of these artists' entrepreneurship,' she says to her mother.

'I'm sorry?'

'Isn't that one of the basic tenets of Thatcherism? "Every man a capitalist" and all that?'

'Yes...' Joan pinches the bridge of her nose, squeezes her eyes tight shut.

I'm making Mum uncomfortable, Suzy observes. Yet she is increasingly irritated. Every jibe, every sneer, every incredulous remark is really directed at *me*, she observes. It's about time Mum understood that not all artists are scroungers living on the breadline.

'Self-starting helps boost the economy,' she continues, reflecting her mother's catch phrases back at her.

'Of course.' Joan nods. She glances to see if the young man is still listening.

Suzy senses her back stiffening, her throat become tight. 'Well then, perhaps you shouldn't be so dismissive of these artists' work.'

'I wasn't being dismissive!'

'Ah. I must have misunderstood.'

'She was only expressing her opinion,' says Suzy's dad. 'Weren't you Joan?'

'Yes,' says Joan.

'A negative one,' says Suzy.

At that moment, Nate returns, carefully balancing four more glasses of wine. 'What opinion?' he asks cheerfully.

'About the art,' says Suzy, snatching one of the glasses from him and thrusting it at her mother. 'Mum hates it.'

Joan takes the glass, blinking rapidly. Suzy snatches another for herself and takes large gulp.

Then Nate calmly hands Ken his and interposes. 'You know, Joan, Suzy and I first met at her gallery?'

'No, I didn't,' says Joan. Suzy notices that beneath her foundation, her cheeks are pink. Fancy Mum blushing, she thinks.

'I'll be honest with you.' Nate leans into Joan conspiratorially. 'A lot of it I can't stand either.'

'Oh!' Joan exclaims. She takes a nervous sip of wine and glances up at him.

At this precise moment, everything that is attractive about Nate seems to come together. His long blond curls catch in a shaft of light. It's late July, the magic hour just before sunset, when daylight is redder and softer than when the sun is higher in the sky. His skin appears golden. His eyes, which often look grey, a piercing blue. And that morning, Suzy had persuaded him to ditch a vintage suit in favour of a navy T-shirt and stonewashed jeans. The mix of blues suit his colouring.

'Really?' asks Joan.

'Really.' Nate nods, expression sober. '*Conceptual art?* I don't understand what that means. Do you?'

'No,' admits Joan.

'I'll let you into a secret.' He drops his voice theatrically, so he is still clearly audible. 'I don't even think Suzy likes a lot of it.'

Ouch, thinks Suzy. Over Joan's head, Nate gives her a surreptitious wink.

'Is that true?' Her mother turns to her.

'I guess so,' mutters Suzy. For a split second she is annoyed, but then Joan titters. Oh my god, Mum *fancies* him, Suzy realises. How hilarious!

'That was *genius*,' she says to Nate as they stand propped by the doors of the tube home. 'You had her eating out of your hand!'

He grins. 'You know me, good with words.'

Suzy raises herself on tiptoe to kiss him. 'And nightmare mothers,' she says, and runs her hands through his gorgeous curls, and they laugh.

35.

August 1989

It has been a good summer, the hottest in several years, but it is nearing its end. Stef's friend, Oliver, a banker, has told him a party is in the offing. It's a colleague's birthday and, apparently, he's loaded and easy going, so won't mind extra guests. 'Oliver says his parties are always brilliant,' says Stef. 'But he's not sure what time it's due to start, so someone's going to call Oliver once they know.'

'Why don't we go to the park near Oliver's for a bit? We can chill,' Tash suggests as evening approaches. It is warm, almost balmy. If this party is anything like the impromptu raves the four of them have been to before, it won't kick off till late.

'I think we should go straight to Oliver's,' says Stef.

'I don't want to spend all evening stuck indoors in some flat,' says Suzy. She has a new turquoise satin dress—it is barely more than a slip, there is so little of it. Nonetheless it will crumple if she spends all evening sitting; she'd imagined herself floating around the party in it, standing chatting and dancing. It suits her, she knows. The colour offsets her blonde hair and she feels sexy in it.

'Oliver's place is totally cool,' says Stef. 'It overlooks the river.'

'We don't know how many more nights there will be like this,' says Nate. September is approaching so it's a reasonable argument, but what he doesn't say is that whilst he and Suzy are keen to go along to a rich guy's party, they aren't eager to spend all evening with Oliver.

'What a Hooray Henry!' Nate had observed on meeting him. 'That voice, Jeez.' Oliver isn't merely posh: he speaks at an embarrassing volume and doesn't so much as laugh as guffaw. 'And the shirt—ew!' Suzy had grimaced. 'Promise me you won't *ever* wear candy stripes.'

'Let's compromise,' suggests Tash. 'The park shuts at half ten. How about we go to Oliver's then?'

Which is how they end up sitting on the steps of the Peace Pagoda in Battersea Park, drinking wine from plastic cups and eating crisps, watched over by a vast golden statue of the Buddha.

'I knew it was a good idea to come here,' Tash congratulates herself. The sun is setting behind Albert Bridge, turning the pink structure a peachier hue. 'You should paint it, Suzy.'

'Yeah,' says Suzy. Yet the suggestion doesn't fire her. I would end up producing the sort of painting my mum likes, she thinks. An idyllic scene which communicates nothing new or exciting. 'I'd prefer to sell one of my portraits,' she admits.

'That one you did of us is brilliant,' says Tash. 'Isn't it, Stef?'

Stef grunts.

'I prefer the one of me,' says Nate. He catches Suzy's eye and bites back a smile. It's a game they play: winding up Stef.

'Of course, you do,' Stef retorts. 'It is of you.'

Suzy nearly spits out her wine; so strong is her urge to laugh. If anyone is the narcissist round here, it is not Nate. Stef is the one who likes to outshine everyone else. Nonetheless, I love these people, she thinks, looking round at them, and it's not even as if I've had an *E*. There is Tash, flaunting her fabulous bosom in a scarlet bodycon dress—nothing understated about her, as ever; Nate, cigarette bobbing between his lips as he focuses on re-lacing his deck shoes, and Stef, scoffing Doritos without offering anyone else any. It always amazes Suzy that he's so skinny. Not many couples who share a flat get on as well as they do.

'If you're so keen to sell paintings, you should start working on

Oliver,' says Stef, removing his glasses to clean them on his t-shirt. 'He's got loads of wall space.'

'I can hardly do that tonight,' says Suzy. 'How's he going to see my work?'

'It's all about who you know though, isn't it? And he earns more in a year than any of us will earn in a lifetime.'

'No need to rub it in,' says Nate. That week he has been told his salary will be frozen for another year. He leans to stroke Suzy's arm. 'I know you want to sell more pictures, sweetheart.'

'I do.' She nods, thankful he is taking her seriously. 'It's been weeks.'

'Weeks!' Stef laughs. 'Van Gogh didn't sell anything his whole life.'

'We hardly want Suzy to put a bullet through her head,' says Nate.

'It's bollocks, that story,' says Suzy, laughing. 'Van Gogh's uncle bought lots of his paintings. Plus he traded his work with other artists in exchange for food and art supplies. It's just an urban myth.' She refills her plastic cup with wine.

Stef opens and shuts his mouth as if he can't think how to respond. He appears wounded, but if he can't handle the odd jibe, he shouldn't dish it out so much.

'I know what you need.' Nate grins at Suzy and she assumes he is being lewd, but then he jumps up and hurries down the steps of the Pagoda. 'I'll be no more than half an hour,' he calls, disappearing behind some nearby shrubbery.

'What's he doing?' asks Tash.

'No idea,' says Suzy.

A while later, Nate comes skipping back.

'Voila!' He crouches down and holds out his palm. The three others hunch over it to get a closer look. Whatever he is proffering is small and delicate in appearance and, in the fading light, it takes a moment to see clearly what it is.

'Oh my gosh!' Suzy exclaims, delighted. 'You're kidding! Is that real?'

'It is.' Nate beams with pride.

'I wasn't sure they actually existed,' says Suzy.

'Aah, but they do,' says Nate.

'I bet it's a fake,' Stef scoffs. 'You probably had it in your pocket already.'

'Can I?' Suzy is keen to pick it up but does not want to damage it.

'Of course,' says Nate. 'I got it for you.'

She lifts it from his palm and gently rotates it in her fingers. It is so fragile that it trembles in the faintest breeze. 'It's real alright,' she tells Stef.

'Sure is,' says Nate.

Tash scoops back her abundant hair so she too can peer more closely. 'That is so cool.'

'You just need to know how to find them,' says Nate. 'It's takes patience and focus, that's all.'

'You were only gone a few minutes,' says Tash. 'Your eyesight must be awesome.'

'I guess it's OK,' says Nate. 'Nothing unusual, far as I know. There was a streetlight close by, which helped.'

There is a beat of silence and Suzy is aware of Nate's eyes upon her, gauging her reaction. Her heart swells. It is such a touching gesture. Suzy doesn't think she has ever loved Nate as much as she does in that moment.

'Thank you.' She longs to kiss him, but if she moves, his little gift might blow away.

'I bet the odds of finding one are more than you think,' says Stef.

Tash scowls at him. 'Don't spoil it!'

'I believe you'll find they're about one in ten thousand,' says Nate.

'Yeah, right.' Stef sounds unconvinced.

'Can you hold it a sec?' Suzy asks Nate. He takes it from her while she rummages in her handbag for something to use as makeshift protection. She finds a used train ticket and folds it in half, places the tiny good luck charm in the centre, then carefully slots it between the credit cards in her purse.

Now she can kiss him.

After all, it is not every day that she is given a four-leafed clover.

Later that evening, Tash tells Oliver about Nate's find and Oliver asks to see. Suzy holds her breath as she watches him turn the fragile leaf this way and that with his plump pink fingers, scared he will harm it in some way.

'That's bloody clever of you to find it.' Oliver's voice is deep and plummy, his tone admiring. Suzy finds herself warming to him more but Stef rolls his eyes.

'Isn't it?' Suzy beams. A four-leafed clover is something not even your money can buy that easily, she thinks. And who knows? Maybe Stef is right, Oliver might invest in a painting. *This is a sign some luck is headed my way.*

To Stef's credit, Oliver's flat *is* incredible. It is vast and modern, like something from a movie, with an entire wall of glass that overlooks the river. A pale L-shaped suede sofa and marble coffee table takes up half the living space; the other half has tiled steps leading to a hot-tub. It is the swankiest apartment that I've ever seen, thinks Suzy, by quite some measure. She narrows her eyes, picturing one of her paintings on display. Given the dimensions and style, something abstract would work best, she decides. Just a hint of pastel pink would mirror the hue of Albert Bridge. It would have to be very subtle, mind...

The shrill ring of a telephone cuts in on her musing. Oliver grabs the receiver, talks for all of a few seconds, then says, 'We're on! Antonio's arranged everything.'

'Excellent.' Suzy had been beginning to doubt his plan would come together. They are used to party venues being kept secret until the last minute, but it has gone midnight. Most raves would be kicking off by now.

'We've got to be at Embankment pier within an hour,' Oliver announces.

Tash uncurls herself from the sofa. 'Better get a shifty on.'

'We'll hail a cab,' says Oliver, and hurriedly they gather their things.

The change of gear makes Suzy flustered. 'Do we need to take booze?'

'There will be a bar.' Oliver is confident.

It is not until they are squashed into the back of a cab that Suzy remembers.

'Oh no! I've left the four-leafed clover at your flat.' She looks worriedly at Nate, not wanting to upset him. 'I think it's on the table. Damn!'

'It's OK, I'll keep it safe,' says Oliver. 'Perhaps it is better you left it. Might get squashed otherwise.'

'Thanks,' says Suzy. It's true her handbag is tiny. She wants to be able to dance. Nonetheless, she is cross with herself for being so remiss.

Nate squeezes her knee, leans in and murmurs, 'It's a good excuse to see Oliver again.'

'Mm.' Suzy leans her head on Nate's shoulder, grateful. That he is so supportive of her artistic endeavours is a quality she treasures in him. It's because he is creative too, she muses. He knows how fragile we painters can be.

34.

March 2018

After the night in Glenn's caravan, time continues to toy with Suzy, expanding and contracting and twisting back onto itself. Seconds turn into hours, whole days seem to vanish in a haze, and Suzy finds it hard to recall a single thing that happens—does she eat, drink, go to the loo? Feed Pushkin? Shower? More and more she loses track. Chronically hyper alert, she sleeps two to three hours at most, and her daytime is filled with flashbacks. Every crunch of noise, every judder, makes her jump. The bin men coming: the thrum of the lorry's engine, the shouts from one man to another. Even laughter from her neighbours strolling down the lane makes her want to scream. Again and again, she relives the trauma.

That the sun shines and daffodils dance in the breeze outside her window only makes her want to retreat further and, despite being surrounded by villagers she has known for years, her world shrinks to the tiny sphere of her home. On the rare occasions she ventures beyond her threshold, she obsessively checks that people she knows are nowhere in sight. She stops reading messages and emails and lets her phone run out of juice. Letters remain unopened on the doormat. Her food supplies diminish. Yet because she is barely eating, it doesn't seem urgent that she heads out to get more. Only when Pushkin's supplies are gone does she bother.

Her fear is closing in, her panic attacks escalating. Soon the pull to yesteryear is so strong, it is as if she has been physically transported back to that evening permanently; she is dwelling almost entirely in the dark side. Sometimes she thrashes about on the sofa, jerking and shaking. She seems to be having some kind of fit. On other days, she sits with the curtains drawn, rocking back and forth on her haunches like detritus afloat on choppy waters, occasionally calling Pushkin to her, 'Push, Push, Push,' in the vain hope the little cat might throw her a life raft.

Most of the time, however, she doesn't think about anything sensibly or straight at all. She simply wishes she could end what is happening, that she was dead.

April 2018

'HELLO?'

There is a loud banging on the front door of the cottage. A man is yelling through the letterbox.

Suzy ignores him.

'She's in there!' It's a woman's voice, closer by.

Suzy looks up, and, terrified, sees a face peering through a gap in the living room curtains.

'Mum! Are you OK?'

'Let us in, why don't you?' orders first voice.

She continues to sit on the sofa.

A moment later he bellows, 'SUZY! Open the bloody door!'

Suzy curls into a ball, hands over her ears to block out the shouting.

'No, no, NO! Go away! GO AWAY!'

'There's need for that,' says the woman. She sounds to have moved back to the front door. Her Geordie accent is familiar, her voice far more gentle. 'We've got a key.'

They are coming in anyway, thinks Suzy, teeth chattering in fear.

Next moment, three people rush into the room. Startled by the

♩ ♫ ♪ ♩

commotion, Pushkin jumps from the sofa and shoots up the stairs. Suzy wishes she could run away too, but she is rigid with terror.

'At least the cat's alright,' says the man.

'Suzy...' The woman crouches down by the sofa. 'Oh my god, Suzy.'

'How long have you been here, Mum?' says Cam. His voice is high pitched. He sounds scared too, thinks Suzy. 'We've been trying to get hold of you for ages.'

'I don't know.' She can only manage a whisper.

'What happened?' The woman's hair is a beautiful colour, thinks Suzy. She crouches down in front of Suzy and reaches for her hand. 'You look terrible, pet.'

'Er...'

'We thought you'd gone away,' says the woman.

'She reckoned you were with some bloke,' says the man.

'I didn't put it like that,' the woman snaps, then drops her voice and addresses Suzy. 'You didn't answer your phone. I thought you might have been with Glenn.'

Through a haze of mixed-up memories, Suzy begins to recall the odd, fleeting moment. 'I was...'

'He didn't attack you or something, did he?'

'Mum!' Immediately Cam crouches down close by, too.

Little by little Suzy pieces together some sense of what is happening; this is her neighbour, Debs, and Rich, Debs' husband. Ugh, Rich, she thinks. I wish he'd bugger off. He's so in your face, so full of himself.

'Please, explain. You can tell us,' Debs urges.

'No,' she whispers, hoping Debs will understand. 'No, he didn't...'

'Thank God for that.'

'He shouted at me though.'

'Did that scare you?' asks Debs.

'Not exactly...'

'What happened?' asks Cam, searching Suzy's face for answers.

♩ ♫ ♪ ♩   202

'I can't...' Suzy whispers.

'You can't what?' asks Cam.

She has never told him. She has never told any of them.

'I can't,' she repeats. 'I'm sorry.'

Tears are streaming down her face. Even though so many years have passed since, she finds it impossible to talk about that evening. She starts to shiver again, teeth chattering.

When merely thinking about it is makes her so frightened she can't breathe, how can she possibly speak about it to anyone?

37.

August 1989

'Keep the change,' Oliver thrusts a note in the taxi driver's hand through the open cab window.

Tash is already taking the lead. 'That must be it!' she cries, pointing at a mass of twinkling lights. Bobbing on the Thames's dark waters, moored to the pier, is a pleasure boat, roughly the size of a double-decker bus.

'Oh how pretty!' says Suzy, skipping in her wake down to the river's edge.

Getting aboard is as easy as walking through a door; there are no tickets to present, nobody waiting with a list of names.

Almost all the boat is divided into wide-windowed cabins, but at the prow is a small deck left open to the elements. It's here the host welcomes Oliver with a backslap and a smile. 'Good to see you, buddy!'

'Happy birthday, old chap.' Oliver is opening his mouth to introduce the four of them, when an Amazonian blonde slides a hand through Antonio's arm. 'Darling, there's someone you must meet...' And they are off, weaving their way between guests.

Close by, a young black guy with a beautiful, almond-shaped eyes is waving at some friends headed his way along the narrow gangplank. A couple of women with glossy manes of dark hair are chatting in Italian. Their voices clash with a loud American who is trying—and failing—to impress a group with his knowledge of maritime affairs who are gathered to watch the captain in the wheelhouse.

'Let's look round,' Tash urges Suzy. 'Boys, you get the drinks in, OK?' She doesn't wait for an answer, grabbing Suzy's hand and marching straight through the double doors into the upper cabin. She continues down to the lower level saloon which is already thronging with people.

'Blimey, someone's got a few quid,' she jerks her head as a waiter edges through with two ice buckets, each containing a magnum of champagne. Suzy notices a couple of middle-aged men ogle Tash's cleavage and whisper to each other in a lascivious fashion, so she jabs the one nearest to her with an elbow as she squeezes past.

The boat is narrow and soon guests are jostling to get from one space to another, looking for the host to wish him a happy birthday, for friends who have become separated, or for someone with a spare cigarette or snort of something stronger...

I'm OK for a bit, thinks Suzy. They each had a line of Charlie at Oliver's.

The vessel is small, and it doesn't take long before Suzy and Tash have worked their way back with a polite but forceful, 'Excuse me, excuse me,' to their boyfriends, who are waiting with their drinks at the bar. It is excellent timing; at this very moment, the engine splutters into life and the boat starts to edge slowly away from its berth.

Suzy and Tash clap their hands in glee. To be here, at this amazing party, with all these glamorous people, aboard this magical little boat...

It is so exciting; it's what life is about.

'Come on.' Nate, energised by Charlie, is impatient to hit the dance floor, so they deposit their drinks on the ledge by one of the open windows and step to the centre of the room.

We might not be as wealthy as this lot, thinks Suzy, yet I reckon we can show them a few moves. And as she picks up the rhythm of the track and starts to sway her hips, she is conscious of the satin of her dress against her skin, the flow of its fabric, fluid and sensual. She watches Tash shimmying and swirling and twirling her fingers; Stef, pale skin glistening with sweat, arms raised and pumping in time to the track, and Nate, cigarette bobbing in accompaniment to the disco

lights, she can't stop herself from smiling. She is used to their idiosyn-
crasies, loves each of them for their individual styles, but she has not
seen Oliver dance before, and beside the others he is slow and lumber-
ing, uncoordinated. She sees Nate notice and he grimaces, more in
sympathy than judgement.

The boat is very crowded however, and the dance floor rapidly
becomes so full that Suzy can no longer feel the breeze from the open
windows. Soon she is so hot, she is keen to get some air.

'Shall we go out onto the deck?' she asks Nate, raising her voice so
he can hear her, but at that moment the DJ segues into the shuffling
beats of *Back to Life*.

"Stay and dance!' Tash tugs his sleeve.

The vocals are hypnotising, and Suzy likes *Soul II Soul* too, but the
view beckons more. She is finding it hard to breathe. It's stifling inside.

'I'll join you in a sec,' Nate yells into her ear, so she heads to the
prow alone.

Out front, she leans back against the rail, letting her thoughts drift.
London is magical at night, she observes. The full moon reflected on
the water lends it a fairy tale quality. From this distant vantage point,
familiar landmarks appear different; not just smaller but less fixed in
place, like the playthings of children creating a fantasy world. Portside
are the broccoli-like trees of the gardens on the embankment, and if
she cranes her neck, she can see the silhouette of the Houses of Parliament and Big Ben disappearing behind a bend in the river. Starboard
are the stark concrete boxes of the South Bank lit up in orange, and
directly ahead, spanning the river with an almost lazy elegance, are
the low arches of Waterloo Bridge.

Yet if she looks directly down, the water is dark as coal and doubt-
less freezing with it. She can just make out the tide rushing westwards
as they head east.

The volume of the disco seems to increase as the little boat draws
parallel to the grand grey frontage of Somerset House. On past the

♩ ♫ ♪ ♩   206

derelict Oxo Tower and the great dome of St Paul's cathedral, the people inside start singing along.

'*Rock the boat, don't rock the boat baby...*'

It sounds fun, and by now Suzy, refreshed, is ready to head back inside. But as the captain manoeuvres into the middle of the river so he can navigate through the central arch of Southwark Bridge, she sees a vast wall of blackness coming towards her. It is huge. Almost as tall as the bridge itself.

Another boat?

No way, thinks Suzy. That's the size of a seafaring ship, we're on the Thames. It must be my imagination.

Then she hears someone yelling, 'Get out of the way!' and jerks her head upwards. Two lookouts on the prow of the larger vessel are gesturing frantically; the boats are veering wildly close to one another. The sheer cliff-face of metal towers over their little boat, and is moving much faster, too. Most terrifying of all, it seems to be headed for the same arch of Southwark Bridge.

Suzy can tell there isn't room for them both. Nor is there a hope in hell of their little boat steering away in such a short time. Even if there were, it seems that whoever is at the helm of each vessel is unaware of how their paths are converging. Seconds before it happens, she sees what is coming.

They are about to crash.

Everything appears to slow down for a moment, and then the huge vessel collides with theirs. There is a crunch, a judder and Suzy hears the record skip.

Inside she hears someone shriek, '*Whoa, that was fun!*'

But this is no game, she is certain. She has seen how monstrous the other vessel is. Those inside have not.

She is seized by panic.

'**NATE!**' She lunges, desperate to return to the dance floor, but then the little boat is hit again by the starboard prow of the larger vessel.

This time the impact is harder. She reads the name **BOWBELLE** in white against black as it smashes past and watches, unable to move for fear, as the goliath boat grinds onwards, slicing through the top cabin where Nate and Tash and Stef and Oliver are dancing.

This is a living nightmare. It can't be happening.

There is a splintering of wood, a sharp crackling sound, and a deafening shattering of glass. People are screaming. Immediately the boat begins to tip, the passengers who are on the opposite side of the prow begin to slide across the deck, and one, two, three and land on top of Suzy, heavy as bags of sand. She scrambles out from beneath them to avoid being trapped.

Yet there is no time to gather herself.

In the next instant, she sees that the force of the collision has caused the boat to rotate completely. The windows of both cabins are open or broken, and water is gushing through to the interior.

Nate, Tash, Stef, Oliver. Where are they?

But it all happens too fast. In less than 30 seconds, the hull disappears beneath the surface.

Beside her a young man shouts, 'We have to go in!' and grabs his girlfriend; it is then Suzy grasps they are about to go under too. If she tries to swim, *The Bowbelle* will surely crush her. But if she waits, she will be dragged under. For a split second she hesitates. Then, before she can reconsider, she leaps into the water.

At once she is sucked into the bowels of the river. Even here, in the ice-cold water, it is chaos. She can hear *The Bowbelle* above; the thundering of its giant propeller blades slicing through the river. It is almost pitch black, yet she feels people grabbing onto her, limbs, heads, torsos colliding. At one point she thinks she sees Nate, face right up close to hers under the water, his eyes wide in horror, blonde hair swirling about him like the merman she has always felt him to be.

Yet in a nanosecond, he is whipped away as the engines of both vessels fight the pull of the tide. Suzy is tossed and turned like a piece of litter; every time she senses she is about to surface, she is yanked back down. Something hard and hefty smashes against her right arm—a piece of loose furniture, perhaps, or a speaker from the disco. She feels herself getting heavier and heavier as unconsciousness approaches. Her chest tightens and as the desire to breathe becomes overwhelming, she is filled a profound loneliness, the fear that she is going to die, here, without Nate, without anyone.

Then, miraculously, she surfaces again, battered and winded, still out of her depth. Finally, *finally*, she can gulp in air, frantic. She can hear the screams of men and women, desperate and panicked, but shouting from closer by too.

People are calling, 'Over here, over here,' and it is then she sees another boat, much like the one they have been aboard, but bigger. It too is strung with fairy lights; these people are at another party.

I must be hallucinating, thinks Suzy. Have I died? She tries to signal, but she cannot lift her arm. The pain is excruciating. The next wave offers further reprieve, carrying her towards the lights. Hands reach out and grab her and she cries in agony as they haul her up under her shoulders and onto the deck.

And then she is coughing and coughing, throwing up water from the river, silk dress torn to shreds, barefoot, feet finding purchase on something solid at last.

38.

April 2018

'I can't... speak... about it,' Suzy repeats. She looks around at them. Her son's expression is so distraught, instinctively she yearns to comfort him.

But Rich... At that moment, Suzy hates Rich. She wishes he would go away. He is bound to poke fun at her. She stares up at him, blinking.

Debs reads the situation. 'I think, maybe... How about making us all some tea, eh?'

'Oh.' Rich rubs his forehead, then says. 'Yeah, sure.' He leaves the room and presently there is the sound of the kettle being filled with water.

'Better?' Debs shifts from a crouched position to cross-legged, putting her face on a level with Suzy's. Cam follows her lead. Their three heads are almost touching, nonetheless it feels less intimidating.

'Thanks,' Suzy murmurs. Yet her thoughts are still a muddle, her body is continuing to shake. However hard she tries, she cannot gain control. 'Maybe...' She makes a gesture with her hand to indicate. Fuck, fuck, fuck, what is going on? Why can't she make herself speak? Why can't she find the words?

'You could write it down?' asks Debs.

Suzy nods. Thank God for her friend. She is so incredible.

'Let's get you some paper,' Debs leaps up again, hurries to the kitchen. In seconds she is back with an envelope and a pen. Before she folds herself to seated once more, she grabs a book to lean on from the coffee table. 'Here.'

Suzy's fingers are trembling so violently she can barely hold the biro. She is weak from days of panic and lack of food. It seems to take an age, but eventually, she forms the words. It is easier if she uses capitals. Finally, she swivels the envelope round so Debs and Cam can read it. The script is so shaky it's almost illegible.

I WAS ON THE MARCHIONESS, it says.

Debs' fingers fly to her mouth.

'Oh my God!' Then she reaches for Suzy's hand and clutches it, hard. 'I am so, so sorry. I had no idea.'

'No...' Suzy's lips tremble, and she starts to cry. Soon she is weeping hysterically. Her breath comes in short bursts. She feels about four years old.

'I don't understand.' Cam rubs his forehead and looks to Debs for an explanation.

Get a grip, Suzy tells herself, desperate to ease Cam's confusion. And yet she cannot stop bawling.

'Tissues,' Debs mouths at Cam, and he hurries from the room. 'Are you OK if I explain to him?' she asks while he is gone. 'He won't have clue what that was, will he?'

'I guess not...'

'I can get Rich to, if you prefer.'

Suzy sniffs, wipes her nose with the back of her hand. 'You do it,' she says between gulps. Despite the scramble of her brain, intuitively she trusts Debs to tell her story.

'Sure.' Debs gives her hand another squeeze. 'You must say if you want me to stop. OK?'

Suzy gives a single nod. *Though I don't know what I want from one second to the next,* she thinks.

''Fraid this is all I could find,' says Cam, handing Suzy a loo roll and sitting back down.

'*The Marchioness* was a boat,' Debs tells him, dropping her voice. 'A pleasure boat, on the Thames. There was a party. I can't remember when it was, exactly—'

'1989,' says Suzy. She lets out a wail.

'It OK,' says Debs. She rubs Suzy's knee, calming her.

Debs swallows. 'Right. I remember I was a teenager when it happened.' She glances at Suzy. 'You must have been a fair bit older.'

'Twenty-six.' Suzy blows her nose.

Cam looks stunned. It is exactly the age that he is. 'What happened?'

'There was an accident,' Debs continues. 'One summer night. Correct me if I get any of this wrong, Suzy.'

'Not so far,' says Suzy. The tears are still falling, but at least her shaking seems to have stopped. That Debs is holding her hands is really helping.

They are interrupted by Rich coming back in with a pot of tea and some mugs chinking on a tray.

'Thanks,' says Debs. She gives him a small smile.

'I wasn't sure how you take it,' Rich says to Suzy.

'Milk no sugar,' says Cam. 'Mum and I have it the same.'

'Put it down here, love, OK?' Debs indicates that he should lower the tray onto the carpet beside them. 'You alright to pour, Cam?'

'Mm.'

The sound of tea being poured from a pot is so comforting.

'I think we're fine for now.' Debs stares pointedly at Rich to communicate he should leave them alone. Suzy slumps in relief when she hears him let himself out of the front door. She is also thankful when Cam hands her a mug of tea.

'*The Marchioness* was heaving with dozens of guests.' Debs raises her eyebrows at Suzy, who nods.

'More than 130.' It seems her voice is coming back.

'And there was another boat, it was much bigger, some sort of industrial vessel...?' Debs glances at Suzy again.

'*The Bowbelle.*' Suzy convulses at the name. 'It—it was designed to dredge tons of sand and gravel from the seabed beyond the Thames Estuary...' She turns away. Their horrified faces are making it hard to gather her thoughts. 'Then take its load back upriver to its berth at Nine Elms.'

'That's near our place in Battersea,' says Cam.

'Yes, love. I know.' It's why I can't visit, she thinks. 'Debs is right, *The Bowbelle* was huge. It—she—was over 250 feet long and weighed nearly 2000 tons.' It seems to take her forever to say this. 'In comparison, *The Marchioness* was tiny.'

'How tiny?' asks Cam.

'She only weighed 46 tons... In the collision that made all the difference...'

I could never have told you any of this before the accident, thinks Suzy. Just as I had no clue that *The Marchioness* was over sixty years old, or that there were no EXIT signs on board. There is no way I can forget now. The facts are seared into my brain.

'Am I right in remembering the boats didn't see each other?' asks Debs.

'Yes... The views on *The Bowbelle* were obstructed by dredging gear.' Suzy closes her eyes. At once she sees the wall of iron looming high above her. She opens her eyes again before the darkness sucks her in.

'When the vessels collided,' Debs continues, '*The Bowbelle* was pretty much OK, but *The Marchioness* was so much smaller, she capsized, and she sank really fast.'

'Shit, Mum,' says Cam. 'I can't believe you went through that and didn't tell me.'

'I was one of the lucky ones,' she says, then thinks, *how trite that sounds.* As if anyone that night was lucky.

'Lots of people weren't.' Debs stares down at the carpet. 'I'm sorry, I can't remember how many people died.'

Suzy rubs her upper arms to comfort herself. 'More than fifty...' Her voice trails off. She could explain that the disco deck had the two forward doors hooked open and some people managed to escape through those, but everything was terribly difficult because the boat was at 90 degrees. She could add that others tried to break windows and found they weren't glass, but Perspex, which swelled and jammed, keeping them trapped inside. Yet none of this was apparent that night, she recalls. I didn't even know the name of the boat which rescued me.

'How awful.' He has gone very pale.

'They were all so young,' says Debs, choking up. 'That's what I remember.'

'Who were you with?' asks Cam. He has gone very pale.

Then Suzy feels it coming, a wave of panic, hysteria.

'Were they OK?'

But she has disappeared down a black hole.

Again.

39.

August 1989

Suzy is surrounded by people on the deck of the boat asking if she's OK. It's very surreal; music is blaring, they are dressed in party clothes too. But Suzy feels no connection to any of them. She can still hear screaming from the other side of the river, and soon the sound of beating helicopter blades and ambulance sirens add to the pandemonium.

A couple from the party help Suzy to the shore, where a paramedic says he needs to check her over.

Suzy edges away, saying, 'My boyfriend. I've got to find him...' Yet she stumbles after a couple of steps.

The paramedic catches her, causing her to yelp out in pain. 'Woah! Steady. I wouldn't go anywhere right now.' He tries to mobilise her arm and says her shoulder is dislocated, and soon Suzy is being whisked to St. Thomas's Hospital in an ambulance, blue lights flashing.

A doctor in A&E gives her a sedative and shifts the joint back into place. In mere minutes, she is sent away with her arm in a sling and some painkillers. No one asks if she was with anyone, or if there is a family member who might come to fetch her.

Outside the hospital, Suzy sees a woman with rivers of make-up streaked down her face and still-wet hair, a man in a badly torn suit, a young lad without his shoes. Still wobbly and barefoot, she staggers over, searching for her friends. As word of the accident begins to spread, a crowd begins to gather. Some were aboard *The Marchioness*, others the second boat, she hears it called *The Hurlingham*. Nowhere is there anyone from *The Bowbelle*. It seems incredible that the huge vessel continued up the river, oblivious to the destruction left in its wake yet it seems the only explanation.

Suzy lurches from stranger to stranger, pleading. 'Have you seen a tall bloke with blond curly hair? He was on the dance floor...' but the responses are, in essence, the same: a shake of the head, a 'No, I'm sorry', a look of sympathy, a shrug of 'I hope you find him.' 'My friend, Tash,' she babbles. 'She's black, she was wearing a skin-tight red dress...' Surely *someone* will remember Tash? Yet no one seems to know anything, there is only confusion and distress. Everywhere people are in shock, unable to process events, terrified their loved ones are amongst the dead or injured. Questions fly, some yell in anger at the lack of answers, others weep. Most are silent, stunned.

Eventually, a policeman says that he believes not all the survivors are being brought here, to the hospital.

'Yeah, there were some people who reached the riverbank and were OK,' agrees the man in a torn suit. 'I overheard one lot say they were going to walk home.'

Hope surges. 'How many were there?'

'Three, four?'

That must be them, Suzy decides. They will be back at the flat waiting for me.

She asks if anyone knows where to find the nearest taxi rank.

'It's over there,' says a nurse. She points. 'But I'd go round that way. There are reporters waiting out the front.'

Suzy can hardly believe it when she sees a face that she recognises waiting inline.

'Oliver!' His rosy cheeks are so pale, he looks grey. 'Thank God you're alright!'

'Good to see you, too.' Gone is the cheery boom from his voice. He sounds flattened, lost.

'Have you seen the others?'

He shakes his head. 'I thought they were behind me.'

Suzy tries to get him to say more—'When?' 'Which way did you go?'—but she after a while she works out that however frantic she is for him to recall those vital seconds, he can barely speak and her pushing him is only making him withdraw further.

When a black taxi pulls up, diesel engine purring, Oliver suggests they share it.

Only then does Suzy put two and two together: she has lost her little beaded bag along with her shoes. The strap must have broken when she was underwater. 'I haven't got any money,' she says dumbly.

'It's OK, I have an account,' says Oliver, and presents the cabbie with his card. They drive back along the Embankment sitting on the back seat as far apart from one another as they can get, in silence. Suzy leans against the window, not really seeing the lights of other vehicles flashing by. It is remarkably quick to get back to where their evening started, on the south side of Battersea Bridge.

'You can pull in at the bus stop,' says Oliver. As he gets out, he insists that the driver takes Suzy on to Clapham. 'Charge the whole lot to me,' he declares, in those few instants sounding his usual self. Yet the last she sees of him, he is stumbling down Battersea Bridge Road, headed away from the river and his flat, disorientated.

Once he has dropped her off, the taxi driver is so eager to return to a more lucrative part of the city that he accelerates away without checking that Suzy makes it safely inside.

The main door of the Victorian building is on the latch as usual, so it is only once she is in the hall and reaching for her handbag that she remembers, of course, it is gone. Which also means she doesn't have keys. How could she be so stupid?

She rings on the doorbell, pressing her finger on the white button for ages. She flaps the letterbox, then holds it open and calls inside. Then she leans against the door of their flat, and it's this that confirms there is no one in. If someone were home, it would not be double locked, and there would be more space between the door and the frame, whereas they are tightly wedged, she is the only one here.

Bizarrely, laughter rises in her throat. She cackles wildly. Everything feels so unreal, perhaps this is a massive, horrible joke.

Though maybe, she thinks, hope rising again, I am ahead of them. I was in a taxi, after all, and Southwark Bridge, where the accident happened, is miles away. Yes, she decides, they are bound to be back shortly. I'll wait here, on the doorstep, till they arrive.

♩ ♫ ♪ ♩

40.

April 2018

'I think you should come and stay with us mum,' Cam is saying. They are still in the living room, drinking tea.

'NO!' Panic surges. Suzy's breath grows short.

Suzy hears Debs say, 'I don't think that's a good idea,' and they mutter, voices so low she can only catch the odd snippet. '...had no idea...' '...so frightening...' '...Battersea.' Hearing that name, Suzy judders as if she has been given an electrical shock.

Debs tries to soothe her. 'It's OK...'

'D-d-don't make me go there!'

'Where?' says Debs gently.

'B-B-Batt...ersea...'

Suzy sees Cam's face, confused and hurt. A tiny part of her knows she is not being rational, but the has no idea how to make her brain work like it used to. Time and again it seems she is being caught under water, gasping for air.

Debs leans in close, looks Suzy straight in the eye. 'Suzy. Listen to me. You're OK. It's me, Debs, see?' Suzy struggles to focus on the face in front her. Pale skin... Grey eyes... Auburn Hair... Freckles... *Join the dots,* she thinks.

'You're at home,' Debs continues firmly. 'In Amhurst. Look—there's Pushkin—yes?'

Oh yes. There, across the room, the little black puss is washing her hind quarters, back leg hoisted up like a chicken drumstick.

'No one is going to make you go anywhere.' Debs flicks a glance at Cam. 'Are they?'

'No,' says Cam. 'I'll stay with you here, Mum, that's fine.'

'No one is going to hurt you.'

Gradually the tidal wave recedes.

'Sorry,' says Suzy. 'I'm so sorry. You're both being so lovely to me, so kind...'

After a while, Cam says, 'I'm going to call the doctor, Mum. I've found the number of the surgery. Debs and I think it's a good idea,' and he is gone from the room before Suzy can object, leaving only her and Debs, floating somewhere between Amhurst and Battersea.

'Let's breathe for a bit, together, like we did before,' Debs urges. 'Remember how helpful it was?'

They sit there, inhaling and exhaling slowly together. Eventually, it pulls Suzy back to her surroundings.

'Thank you.' Suzy gives a wry laugh. 'When the feelings go, I think I might be OK, but when I'm caught in them, I can't seem to stop the panic...'

'I understand,' says Debs. 'Lots of people get anxiety attacks. I've seen friends and people at work have them before.'

'Do they ever get better?'

Debs smiles at her. 'Yes, pet. They do. And one of the first things I always suggest is they try to reduce their stress levels.'

Easier said than done, thinks Suzy. Everywhere she turns it seems responsibilities are piling up. Then a random thought comes to her. 'Can you get hold of Glenn for me? Ring or text him or something and say I'm sorry. I can't manage seeing him right now.'

'Are you sure?'

'Yes,' says Suzy.

'Seems a shame, you could have done with something positive.'

'Who's Glenn?' asks Cam, returning to the room.

'A friend of your mum's,' says Debs. 'How did you get on?'

Cam takes a seat on the end of the sofa. 'There's a cancellation at 3,' he says to Suzy.

'This afternoon?' Suzy had not imagined he would get an appointment so soon.

'I'll come with you if you like.'

'That would be great.' Her attention slips. 'What have you got there?' He is clutching a pile of papers to his chest.

'Your post. Seems you've not opened anything for a while, and a few seem to be bills. I thought perhaps we could go through them together.'

Suzy closes her eyes. Why, oh why, can't someone simply spirit this awful stuff away? But she cannot avoid the bills forever, and maybe she could deal with just one or two of them, with Cam to help her.

'If you're having difficulty, you can probably pay in instalments,' he says.

He is good at helping me, she reminds herself. He is so level-headed. Whatever would she do without these people to prop her up? Is she always going to struggle this hard? It seems that way. The dark side of my life is bleaker than most people's, she thinks. I must dwell there from time to time. It's the price I pay for being here, when others didn't get the chance. Nearly thirty years, I've had. Three decades more than my friends. And all because I needed fresh air, and I didn't stay and dance to one more song.

39.

August 1989

Next thing Suzy is aware of, her face is being licked. First her eyelids, then her cheeks, then her lips. Ugh. She jerks her head away.

'Barney!'

She opens her eyes, a crack. She can just make out a pair of broad dark knees, strong calves and feet in mint-coloured sling-back sandals.

'Jesum! You OK?'

Suzy tries to open her eyes fully, but the inside of her lids are so gritty they graze her eyeballs. Tash's mum, Cynthia, is crouched beside her, and with her is a dog. Suzy can sense his long ears brushing her ankles as he licks her feet. She's met them both several times. They live in walking distance.

'Enough!' Tash's mum yanks at Barney's lead so he is forced to stop. As her surroundings come into focus, Suzy sees a grey muzzle and cloudy eyes; he is old, smells overwhelmingly of dog.

I had a horrible dream, Suzy wants to say. *Nothing in my head makes sense... There is not an inch of me that doesn't hurt...*

'What time is it?' Her lips are dry and cracked and her throat is so sore, it pains her to speak.

'Lunchtime,' says Cynthia. 'Me know you all go out late, but me been ringing all mornin.'

'I think I passed out...' says Suzy slowly adjusting her position. She can see her legs are dreadfully cut and bruised and her feet are swollen

222

and bloodied... And, oh God. Her arm is in a sling. It hits her with such force it knocks her sideways. It was no dream.

'Me saw di news and me begin to worry,' Cynthia is saying. Of course, thinks Suzy, thoughts untangling a little. She lives in Brixton, not far away. 'You know where me daughter is?' Suzy can hear the rising panic in Cynthia's voice; she feels the same mounting dread.

'I don't know. I don't know where any of them are. I thought they'd be back by now, and they're not.'

They find Tash and Stef's bodies in the upper cabin of the boat. Along with many others, they had not got out of *The Marchioness* in time.

'Old Father Thames surrenders the dead,' says a homeless man, who, along with Suzy and Cynthia, is watching from the riverbank when they raise the wreckage. The roof of the upper deck has been torn away yet there are few other signs of damage. It looks like a plaything, a toy. It is impossible to believe so many lives were lost.

'All me keep thinking me daughter is somewhere but mi couldn't reach her,' says Cynthia, and she reaches for Suzy's hand. Suzy grips it hard, as if without it, she will be blown away. 'Now me start to believe, she did nuh coming back.' Cynthia looks up at the sky, her cheeks shiny with tears.

Days pass, but the river isn't ready to relinquish Nate, so Suzy remains at the flat, unable to change the sheets of the bed they shared, wash up the coffee cups they left that Saturday, or plump the sofa cushions where the four of them sat. Even though her father suggests she comes back, to be at home with himself and Joan, she steadfastly refuses. Their 1920s semi is too far out of the city centre, miles from the river where it happened, and Suzy has to be close. Leaving would mean leaving Nate, whereas staying, keeping things as they were, seems to keep hope alive. Who knows, they might act as a talisman and conjure her boyfriend back.

Zelda cancels everything and comes to stay, and it is not until a week

♩ ♫ ♪ ♩

later that a body matching Nate's description is found, washed up by *HMS Belfast*. Suzy finds out from his parents; as next of kin, they are called to identify him, so Suzy is spared from seeing him broken and bloated by the water. Even so, she remains haunted by the last sight she had of him; of his face floating in front of her, eyes wide with horror.

The next few weeks pass in a blur of grim formalities. The post-mortems are poorly managed and hideously distressing. Suzy is given compassionate leave from work, which only frees her to be door-stepped by the press and stared at by neighbours.

Eventually, the coroner's work is done. Stef's family decide to fly his remains home to be buried near Munich, and soon after that Nate's body is released. Suzy's parents accompany her to the funeral. 'We met him. We'd like to go,' says her father, in a tone which, for once, suggests he will not give ground. Suzy is almost certain he will have coaxed her mother, but knows he is trying his best to support her and is grateful. After the service, her parents speak to Nate's mum and dad briefly out-side the church and offer their condolences, but Suzy remains silent and spaced out, unable to think clearly, let alone feel. Later, at the flat, she rereads *The Order of Service* over and over. Pachelbel's canon, *Lord of All Hopefulness*, Psalm 23, *Perfect Day* by Lou Reed—she can recall none of it. She can only remember her father at her side keeping her upright like a cane propping a wilted flower.

A mere 48 hours and four miles of urban sprawl separate Tash's funeral from Nate's, yet it is a different world. Her invitation to the latter comes via word of mouth.

'Cynthia says it's a *Nine Night* celebration,' Suzy tells Zelda. 'Any idea what that means?' Zelda says no, and suggests she goes as Suzy's 'Plus One'. Suzy murmurs, 'I don't know if I'm allowed to bring anyone,' but Zelda is steadfast.

From the moment they step through the door of Cynthia's council flat off Coldharbour Lane, they are swept up in gossip and laughter. There are people from Cynthia's church and her allotment, Tash's school and work, and countless siblings, cousins and family friends. A woman pats her baby's bottom as she chats to a church minister about back-to-Africa revivalism, natty-dressed youths argue over dominoes and card games, fashion journalists air kiss and knock back rum punch and Barney pads around at knee-height, hoping an occasional morsel gets slipped his way.

'It's more like a rave,' says Zelda, tapping her feet to the pulsing music.

'You help yourselves to whatever you want an' have fun.' Cynthia gestures at a plate of yellow pastry beef patties. 'Mi dawta, she no dead till we bury her.'

Suzy rapidly gleans the ceremony is not about mourning loss as much as a celebration of all they lived and shared. That Tash's family and friends can do this so soon after her sudden death seems remarkable, and for a while it feels just the antidote to the tragedy that Suzy needs. After she and Zelda share a spliff with Tash's younger sister on the balcony, Suzy even manages some jerk chicken—the most she has eaten since the accident. Yet during the eulogies and the exchange of gifts, she cannot shake the feeling that she is watching from the side lines, an interloper who doesn't deserve to be taking up space at an event which Tash herself isn't there to enjoy.

'Woo, cake!' says Zelda, making a beeline to get a slice before Suzy can stop her. She is just thinking she would like to leave when Tash's father, William, grabs her wrist. He is tall, heavy set. Something in his eyes makes Suzy wary.

'You di gal who live with mi daughter?' His tone is accusing, and before she can break away, he is leaning in close. 'How ya survive then?' He stabs her chest with a finger.

'Sorry?' Suzy is dazed.

'Why was you not with her? You her friend and all?' His voice is raised, and although the music is loud, nearby guests have turned to stare.

'I... er... was on the deck...' Suzy stutters. Dimly, she recalls Tash saying that her father could be difficult, and that he and Cynthia parted ways years ago.

'You should ave look afta her! Mi baby she drowned! And here you all dress-up and party as if nuttin has happen!'

Suzy gulps, and gulps again. Wretchedly, she casts about for Zelda. I must get out, she thinks. She feels as if she will suffocate, all the chatter and bright lights and music are making her faint. But it's no use. William is standing between her and the door.

In seconds Zelda is by her side. 'What's the matter?' she says sharply.

'Mi aks ow cum mi dawta dead,' says William, briefly turning to her.

'It was an accident,' says Zelda.

But he continues staring at Suzy. 'There were four of you, how come only you rescued?'

'Fi-ive...' stammers Suzy. 'There were... there were... fi-- '

'Suzy nearly died too,' snaps Zelda. William glares at Zelda. The rims of his eyes are purple, like beetroot. Whether from drink or because he has been crying Suzy cannot be certain.

'YOU LEAVE DEM!'

'IT WAS BOILING IN THERE!' Zelda shouts. 'She needed some fresh air. Is that a crime?'

'But you girls, you stick together,' says William. Yes, thinks Suzy. We do. We did. But not then. How I wish it were otherwise, but she is too overwhelmed to speak.

By this point Zelda is squaring up to him. 'Your daughter wanted to dance!'

For a horrible moment Suzy fears they will set upon one another. Two young men slip in on either side of William and try to calm him, but it's not until Cynthia prizes him away that his muscles unclench.

'For God's sake William, is not her fault! Dis girl has suffered too. Did she tell you her boyfriend died?'

'It was no one's fault, man,' says one of the young men.

'Mi see her the next day, all battered and bruised,' Cynthia insists. 'Look at her arm—it's in sling! You blind, man?'

At once William deflates, as if all the air has gone from inside him. For a few moments Suzy stands there, unable to breathe.

'We must not let our daughter's spirit suffer,' says Cynthia. 'If we don't celebrate her passing, her shadow will haunt this community. Now you apologise and invite Suzy to dance!'

Suzy would rather do anything than dance with William at that moment, but one of young men beside him thrusts the two of them together. Suzy glances at Zelda for guidance. Zelda shrugs then smiles in encouragement.

For a few minutes Suzy hops from foot to foot, struggling to ignite her mood. Tash would want me to dance, she tells herself, as William takes her free arm and holds it aloft as if nothing has happened. Yet it's hopeless. She feels like a rag doll trying to move her limbs, too limp and lifeless to participate. She wants to slide onto a chair, be allowed to stop.

'I'm sorry...' Choked, she steps away.

William looks mystified, then he nods. 'It's OK. Mi not fi have shouted at you.'

Zelda swoops in. 'I'd better get my friend home,' she says, guarding Suzy as she leads her from the room.

Outside on the street, the shock hits her. Suzy starts to shake, and a moment later she heaves, vomiting the jerk chicken onto the pavement.

The next afternoon, Suzy's parents arrive, without warning. There they are, Joan and Ken, on her doorstep, her mother tightly wound and thin lipped, her father white with concern.

'Zelda called us. She was worried about you.' Her dad coughs, then glances at Joan. Her mother nods. 'We are worried about you.'

227

'You need to come home with us, Little Bear. It's not good, your being here all alone.'

Suzy yells in protest that she doesn't want to go, that she won't leave the flat, but in the end, it is two against one, and she is too exhausted to fight.

It is then, finally, that she collapses. She falls into bed in her old room in her parents' house and remains there. Although her father tries to tempt her with trays of food brought to her bedside, her appetite has vanished. She can only sleep in short snatches. Whenever she wakes, the pain comes back, and it's unbearable. She sees Nate's face, floating before her, hears William's voice, 'YOU LEAVE DEM!' and hates herself for still being alive. It's as if, in losing Nate and her friends, everything that has given her joy seems to have gone. She wonders constantly why she is still here, why she wasn't swept away by the dark waters. Why she, one half of a golden couple, should live, when the other half didn't. For weeks, months, she is corpse-like; lying in bed, virtually catatonic. Some days she can hear the sounds of children playing outside, a ring on the doorbell, her mother talking, voice low, on the doorstep. Once or twice she gets up, sees people retreating, not wanting to interfere, away up the garden path. But most days she is so withdrawn into her private pocket of grief that she barely breathes. Her creativity vanishes, her budding career withers and dies.

It is four months before any of the families can face dealing with the contents of the flat, but finally they agree that they cannot afford to keep paying the rental; they must let it go. Yet Suzy refuses to go back and collect her stuff from the place she was hitherto unwilling to leave, so her father does it, and for weeks her possessions remain in bin-bags in the corner of her bedroom, the person she has been in the past few years reduced to a shiny black heap of rubbish.

Eventually, it is Suzy's mother who breaks through to her. Throughout Joan has been a stoic and resigned, rarely speaking about what happened or offering solace. Then one day the following spring, Suzy wakes to the sound of brisk footsteps passing her bed and the swish of her curtains. Sun streams into the room and she sees her mum, in her pink quilted dressing gown, riffling through the black bin bags, pulling out this and that in a random frenzy.

'Here they are!' cries Joan after a while. She yanks a bag across the floor and tips the contents onto the bed as Suzy is sitting up and rubbing her eyes.

Oil paints, brushes, turps, a palette, sketch books all fall into the folds of the duvet. A couple of small blank canvases slide onto the floor.

'Come on Suzanne, paint!' Her mother orders. 'You're so damn good at it, why are you waiting? Up! Up! Get up and do it! You can't lie here forever, waiting to get better, it won't help you or anyone else.'

Suzy is still bleary. She feels bullied, a touch frightened. She opens her mouth to protest, yet Joan has not finished.

'If you won't do it for you, do it for us. Not for me, I know you won't do it for me. But do it for your father. He is dying downstairs worrying about you. Don't you see?'

Suzy is agog. She has never seen her mum so passionate about anything she even faintly agrees with or sees the point of. She had no idea her mother cared for her father—or her—in this way. And something in her opens a smidgeon, shifts, as if a gust of wind has momentarily lifted the edge of a blackout blind. Carefully, she slides out from beneath the covers, trying not to disturb her art materials. It would be all too easy for one of the tubes of paint to leak onto the sheets.

'I'll ... um... go and have a shower,' she says.

♩ ♫ ♪ ♩

42.

July 1991

I knew it would be dead, thinks Suzy. Everyone's watching the Wimbledon final, although Boris Becker is a shoo in.

The charity shop is so quiet, it seems scarcely worth being open. The day is blazing hot, which is always bad for sales. She shuffles the hangers on the rotating display, half-heartedly sorting the clothes into colour groups. Everything is clean, but an odour permeates the garments regardless. This no carefully curated collection offering vintage enthusiasts the chance to snaffle an original designer suit at price only the elite can afford. Nor can the stock compete with the stalls of Afflex Palace or Kensington Market, magnet to students seeking second-hand cool. These are the leftovers of teenage fast fashion and elderly folk downsizing: cheap viscose dresses, shirts with huge collars and itchy woollens that have been thrust to the back of a wardrobe for years before they are scrunched into carrier bags and dumped on the doorstep. Which only makes the silver lurex shift more eye-catching when Suzy flicks past it. She pulls it free and checks the tag. It looks as if it might fit, and she cannot resist holding it up against herself before the mirror.

Hmm. She cocks her head. Fluffs her hair.

Then she stops. What is *she* doing? When would *she* ever wear a dress like this? Whenever she looks at her reflection, she sees it: the sparkle that was once in her eyes is not there anymore. She hates how she looks these days. She hates herself.

'That looks nice,' says a deep voice close by. 'Suits you.'

She jumps, startled. There is a man right behind her. He must have come in while her back was turned. Hurriedly she thrusts the dress aside and smooths her top.

'Sorry. I didn't mean to alarm you.' He glances at her *Cancer Research Assistant* badge.

'You didn't,' Suzy lies and forces a smile. 'Can I help you?'

As she moves to the cash desk, she makes a swift appraisal, concerned he has been ogling her, but there are no overt signs of lasciviousness. He is considerably older than she is, about forty, and stocky, and wearing a navy polo shirt and baggy jeans. His beard is neatly clipped, and his hair is close-cut—presumably an attempt to lessen the impact of his baldness. Men like him are two a penny round here and tend to be married with young children. The leafy suburb where Suzy grew up has long attracted families. Suzy, 29 and single, is the exception. It only enhances the sense that she doesn't belong, but since the accident Suzy has grown used to feeling cut off from everyone. Pat and Colin are still over the road, but when she has seen them, she ducked and nodded, said 'Hello', and hurried on her way. She avoids talking to most people; it's simpler that way, less awkward. Sometimes she thinks it might be better, easier, living somewhere else, but it all seems so much effort. Whereas at least she knows this area well, and most of her peers have moved on—people like Johnny and Flo, who probably both hate her—so it's not that hard keeping a low profile.

'I wanted to ask about that painting.' The man points. 'I was thinking about it for a new place I've bought. Do you know anything about it?' He steps closer to the wall where it is hanging. 'It looks like an original.'

'Er...' Suzy feels herself blush.

He peers at the label. '*S.H.*' He stands back, taking it in. 'I've no idea what it's of,' he admits. He sounds like he lives in Chelsea or Fulham, and normally this would tap into her prejudices but, clearly, he's into painting—*her* painting—which pleases her.

'Nor have I, 'she admits. Since the accident, she seems only able to paint in abstract. To be tethered to reality and paint figuratively would be too painful. She isn't ready.

He nods. 'It's interesting. There is an energy to those brushstrokes... I've had my eye out for something to go above the fireplace, but I find it hard to put my finger on what, exactly. And oils... they're my favourite medium. If one's allowed such a thing.'

He says *one*, Suzy notices. How old school.

'Twenty quid is nothing.' He reaches for his wallet.

Suzy bites her lip. Should she tell him?

'Actually, it's mine,' she says, in a rush.

He raises his eyebrows. They are thick and dark. 'You mean you donated it?'

'No.' Oh lord, thinks Suzy, immediately doubting herself. I should have kept shtum.

'*You* painted it?' His brows rise further.

'Mm.' She averts her gaze, embarrassed. 'Please, don't feel obligated or anything.'

When she looks back, he is holding out a £20 note. 'It seems awfully meagre. Won't you take 40?'

'It's fine, honestly.'

'I insist,' he urges, and gets out a second note. 'What does *S.H.* stand for?'

'Suzanne Hope,' she says, hesitating before taking the notes. 'Though everyone calls me Suzy.'

'If you'll permit me to say so, you shouldn't be shy about your talent, Suzy. You should have this on sale in a proper shop. Or gallery, rather. Did you train professionally?'

'Art School,' Suzy mumbles.

'I thought so!' He rocks on his heels. 'Can't paint myself, but my dad was an illustrator—a political cartoonist, to be exact, worked for *The Times*. He tried to make sure I knew good art from bad. Not that it's always easy to tell.'

'No.'

'What are you doing keeping your work sequestered away here?'

If only he knew the full story, thinks Suzy. She is at a loss for an appropriate answer.

'I—I didn't mean...' He flounders, seeming to realize this might sound as if he thinks they are in a dull backwater, and adds, 'It's a very pleasant part of London.' He glances out of the door to Sheen high street beyond.

I suppose it looks OK bathed in sunshine, thinks Suzy. If Edwardian architecture is your thing.

'You local?'

'Er, yes...' *I live with my parents,* she has an urge to confess. How pathetic is that? There is a beat of silence, and he is still standing there, hands now thrust into his Chino pockets. What he is waiting for, she isn't sure. Curiosity gets the better of her and she asks, 'Are you moving round here?'

'No. I'm moving from here. Or from Fulham, rather. I'm joining a new firm, in Bath.' His face lights up at the words. He must like his job, Suzy decides. His enthusiasm far exceeds hers for her role raising funds for charity. 'I've found a place in a village not far from there.'

I, thinks Suzy. Not *we.* Perhaps he's divorced. Or maybe he's gay. Although the way he initiated conversation suggests not.

She doesn't have to wonder long. She feels his eyes boring into her as she is wrapping the painting, then he says, 'If you're up for it, maybe we could go to an exhibition sometime?'

You're moving miles away, she thinks. How would we manage that?

'Um... maybe.' She is struggling to process the unspoken thread running through their exchange. It has been a while since anyone has flirted with her, however casually. She knows she gives off an energy that warns people to keep away—not just prospective suitors, but potential friends, colleagues, everyone. And that's fine, she reasons. It's what I want. Suddenly she is reminded of something Zelda had said the last time they saw one another.

'What you need is a shag,' she had stated baldly. Then, misreading Suzy's shocked expression, had elaborated. 'Ha! Not with *me*. Still, it's been a while, hasn't it?'

Typical Zelda, Suzy had thought, irked. Seeing sex as a cure for everything.

Yet Zelda had pressed on. 'The longer you leave it the harder it will be.'

'Don't confuse me with yourself,' Suzy had snapped, which was uncalled for. She had muttered, 'Sorry,' in the next breath. She was loath to admit the idea of being intimate with anyone again terrified her. There would be inevitable comparisons, echoes.

The man coughs, and Suzy realizes he is awaiting a response.

'We haven't exchanged contracts yet. Perhaps we could see something here, in London. *The Summer Exhibition* might be fun, don't you think? There is usually such a mix of work to talk about. Some of it's dire, but that's always interesting. One man's meat is another man's poison.'

Suzy looks at him again. There is something about this man that she is warming to. Lord knows why. His clothes are very conventional, but she can tell they're well cut, and he has said nothing to indicate they have anything in common other than an interest in art. Yet maybe, just maybe, Zelda has a point. It has been two years. Zelda is often right, and lately Suzy has been niggled that if she doesn't make some changes, soon, she will be stuck here forever, her *Cancer Research Assistant* badge replaced with one saying *Sheen's Only Spinster*. Plus, he is so utterly different from Nate—indeed anyone Suzy has ever been involved with—it underlines her sense it might be OK. He has lost his hair and has it cropped close to his scalp for one thing, which couldn't be further from Nate's tousled curls. Plus, he looks Italian, with his dark skin and eyes, which Nate most certainly didn't, so she won't be tempted to make direct comparisons, and if he is moving to Bath, she should be able to extricate herself with ease.

'That would be nice,' she says, before she can change her mind. 'I didn't catch your name?'

He holds out a hand. Suzy takes it, suppressing a smile at his formality. His grip is firm, as she suspected it would be.

'I'm Leo,' he says.

43.

April 2018

Cam looks up at his mother as she steps back into the waiting room.

'How was it?' he asks.

Suzy shrugs. 'OK, I guess.'

Once they are out of earshot of the medical centre, he probes further. 'What did he say?'

'*She,*' Suzy corrects. 'Dr Anand. She said she'd refer me to a trauma specialist.'

'How long will that take?'

'Up to six months.' Suzy sighs, then laughs. 'Or I could go online and do a course in CBT.'

Cam grimaces. 'No offence Mum, but I reckon you need something more hardcore.'

'None taken.' Suzy squeezes his shoulder. 'Thanks for coming with me.' Without Cam's support she doubts she would have made it to the surgery. The journey there and back is the most she has walked in ages, and her legs feel as if they might fold beneath her any second. It is hard to focus too. After so long in the dark interior of her cottage she has to scrunch up her eyes to cope with the light, and the air crackles with unexpected noises, the beep-peep of a delivery van reversing, the buzz of hedge trimmers, the caw of squabbling crows. She is jumpy, easily startled.

She feels so unlike her normal self that when Cam asks, 'Did meeting Dad help you get over what happened?' it takes several seconds to absorb the question.

'Yes,' she replies, automatically. Though the truth is much more complicated. She casts her mind back. It wasn't meeting Leo which was the biggest shift, although there is no denying it helped a lot. To have someone who treated her well, who had his own practice and showered her with gifts did make a difference. That he constantly said how lucky he was to have landed a 'younger woman' and laughed at their age gap—he declared punk was a foreign country to him—this lightened her mood, also. Then there was moving to Wiltshire, that was significant, too. She hates to think what it would have been like if she and Leo had stayed South West London. To have had the river with its endless stream of memories running through the heart of her life... Suzy shudders.

No, Suzy is certain. If being with Leo had not offered her the chance to move many miles from the source of her pain, she never would have countenanced marrying him.

'Mum, so did he?' Cam is repeating. 'You said he is good at looking after people. Um...' He scuffs his shoes on the pavement, sheepish. 'Like me.'

She stops in her tracks. She had not seen what a gaping hole she had created until this moment, and she is incredulous, then horrified by the ramifications. She feels the blood drain from her face. The panic rising.

'I... Er... never told him.' She closes her eyes, unable to bear Cam's reaction. Nevertheless, she hears him gasp.

'What do you mean?'

'Leo doesn't know,' Suzy says quietly.

'Sorry?'

'Obviously, he must have been aware of the accident...' She turns away. She cannot bear to witness how aghast Cam is. She feels giddy again, spaced out, but still, it is a relief to resume walking. This, all this, is what she finds so impossible to talk about. '*Everyone* was, who lived in London. It was headline news.'

'Huh?' Cam jerks back his head, flummoxed. 'I don't get it. Dad doesn't know you were on board?'

'No.'

For a while neither of them says a word. Their footsteps sound eerily loud on the pavement, the slow clap of an audience applauding Suzy's shortcomings. She has been a poor mother in many ways, and this is surely the worst.

Eventually Cam says, 'Why didn't you tell him?'

'Oh darling, I don't know...' She flails, desperately trying to find appropriate words.

'But such a big thing! Your friends died!'

Not just my friends, but my *boyfriend*, thinks Suzy. Who knows, were it not for *The Marchioness,* I might have married Nate, not Leo... Though if Nate were alive, I would not have Cam, and I could *never* regret having him. But what must it be like, learning this about me, now? I've lied, she thinks, loathing herself. By omission if nothing else. But back then it wasn't about Cam. It was a question of her own sanity. She was hopelessly adrift, haunted by *The Marchioness*, desperate to forget about it. And Leo threw her a lifeline.

'I see...' says Cam, slowly. 'So, Dad didn't help you get over it, then, did he?' He sounds cross. Suzy hates it when he's angry with her. It reminds her of William, yelling at her. Her mother, too. Of how, internally, she shouts at herself.

'Well, um... yes... he did... He...' Suzy swallows. 'Leo was great. And moving here, you know, it made such a difference.'

I'm still not being honest, she thinks, cringing.

Because despite all of that, I continued having conversations in my head with Nate for a long while after I married Leo. It wasn't *Leo* who made the difference.

It was Cam.

44.

May 1992

All night, she lies awake, looking in wonder at her baby boy. The birth had been so fast, so fraught and frightening, and this is their first time alone together, mother and new-born. He had been in distress during birth, his heart rate had dropped alarmingly, and no sooner was he slapped onto her chest, eel slippery and blue, than he was whisked to intensive care. There it had been established that he had breathed in a mixture of meconium and amniotic fluid, and it had to be suctioned out. Suzy had been losing so much blood, she was separated from him. Leo, exhausted by the stress of charging between the two of them, had finally gone home to rest.

Three hours later, here in the maternity ward, all is calm. Her baby has been on a breathing machine, given antibiotics, and is by her side in a plastic cot, remarkably, beautifully, live and well. Suzy no longer feels the pressure and pain of giving birth. There is another mother and baby only feet away, but Suzy is barely aware of them, her focus is on no one other than Cam.

'Hello Cameron,' she whispers to him, leaning over the cot. These are the first words she says to him, directly, now he is out in the world. 'Cam-er-on...' She rolls it round her tongue. It is the name they had chosen, should their baby be a boy. 'Yes,' she tells him. 'It suits you.'

She looks at his tiny scrunched up face in wonder. It is as if he has been in a fight; his eyes, cheeks and lips are swollen in the way almost all new-born babies are, but his head is perfectly shaped, his sandy hair so soft and downy. And his hands! They are so very tiny, each with its own exquisite fingers and nails. He is a miracle. Her love for him is immediate, visceral. It overshadows everything she has ever felt before.

She leans into the cot, stares at him, full of wonder that this beautiful creature should belong to her—although of course she knows that he doesn't 'belong' to her, or Leo—he belongs to himself. Somehow that is apparent in his features; he is not her, made male, or Leo, made miniature. He is *Cam*. A new soul. The world falls away, and it is just Suzy and Cam, in a state of suspended animation. It doesn't seem real.

He is asleep, hands curled beneath his chin and in that instant, it seems crazy that he is in a cot, a *plastic* cot, so far from her. She clambers out of the high bed, heedless of her stitches, and lifts him into her arms. Sensing movement, a nurse glances over from the desk at the far end of the ward, then gives a nod. The gesture is barely perceptible, but it says that the nurse does not judge her, or fear for Cam; she trusts Suzy to do this. A second later, the nurse lowers her head again and resumes her paperwork. And then, gently, tenderly, Suzy edges herself up onto the bed again, still holding her baby, and carefully places him on the pillow next to her, easing herself inch by inch under the covers, until they are face to face, parallel, his forehead almost touching hers. He is so near to her that her eyes can't focus on him fully, but she can smell him, feel his skin, and stroke him, almost taste him.

It is an arrow straight to her heart. She knows at once that the love is new, different, totally unlike anything she has experienced before. It eclipses her love for any man. Johnny, Glenn, Leo, Nate. Suzy has loved them all, and Zelda, too... Part of her always will. But with Cam, it is different. With her love comes an enormous sense of responsibility. It is terrifying and exhilarating, both at once. Later, Suzy comes to realise that other mothers feel it too. Some take longer to bond than she has; some bond earlier, when the baby is placed on their breast, only seconds from the womb.

Her baby stirs. He reaches out an arm. She holds up her little finger and Cam reaches out and grabs it, causing Suzy to gasp. Even though the logical part of her brain tells her that it is a reflex, like a monkey reaching for a branch, it feels like magic.

Suzy does not sleep at all that night. She lies there, staring at him, as if he might disappear should she slumber. It isn't fear that keeps her alert—it is acknowledgement. It is the sense that a small miracle has occurred which can just as easily be undone, as if this time were needed for Cam to arrive, for his soul to land on the planet.

By morning Suzy has shifted. A new dawn has come.

45.

April 2018

'Online CBT?' Debs snorts when Cam and Suzy get back to the cottage. 'I could probably do more for you myself. Honestly, pet, what use to you is that?'

Suzy laughs, but to hear her GP's recommendations ridiculed does little to reassure her. It can't be a coincidence that both Cam and Debs seem to think her only hope of getting better is with hardcore psychiatric treatment. She pictures herself strait-jacketed and strapped to a gurney and shudders.

Suzy picks at a loose thread on the arm of the sofa, unease mounting. Debs couldn't be my therapist, Suzy is aware. She is my friend, and there is no way I want to change our relationship. Plus, I'd never be able to afford the fees.

A knock at the door causes them to start.

'You're not expecting anyone, are you?' asks Debs.

'No.' Instantly Suzy tenses. I can't face anyone else today, she thinks. Not in this state.

'It'll only be Doreen or someone dropping by.' Debs reassures her.

'I can get rid of them,' offers Cam.

Suzy's shoulders slump in relief. 'Would you?' Immediately she worries it takes little to become a source of village gossip—if she isn't already. Amhurst is a close-knit community; that she has darted in and out of the shop several times without speaking to anyone is bound not to have gone unnoticed. 'What are you going to say?'

'I'll think of something.' Cam is confident. 'Don't worry, I won't be rude.' He closes the door and although she strains to hear the conversation, all Suzy can make out is a faint murmuring of people talking.

'What else did the doctor suggest?' asks Debs.

'She gave me a prescription.'

'Oh?'

Suzy casts about for her handbag before realising it is next to her on the sofa. She retrieves the note. 'Pro-pan-o-lol,' she reads, enunciating each syllable.

'I believe that's a beta blocker,' says Debs.

'Mm... Dr Anand said. Apparently, they should help reduce the physical symptoms of panic. The racing heart and stuff.'

'Sounds a good idea. Was that it?'

Suzy can sense panic rising again. There is so much to think about, how on earth can she remember it all? Again, she tugs at the thread on the sofa. Then she notices how much her hands are shaking and stops, self-conscious. 'Seriously though, Debs, I can't go on like this.' Her voice wobbles. 'I'm losing my mind.'

'Suzy.' Debs swivels to face her. 'You are *not* losing your mind. Trust me, I've seen enough people go totally, well, *mental* in my line of work.' She grins. 'Sorry, not very PC of me.' She rubs the crease between her brows. 'Trauma is a weird one. The way it manifests itself can be so bloody random.' She reaches for another biscuit, chomping as she speaks. 'I had to work with this guy not long ago, Martin. Nice fella. Senior manager in a company that made costume-jewellery.' She takes a mouthful of tea and dusts *Digestive* crumbs off her top. 'I got involved because he kept losing his temper with his colleagues.' She shakes her head and inhales. 'I mean losing it, *big style*. Not just swearing at his peers, he called the MD a "Fat Cunt", he'd rage at clients, smashed his computer keyboard, all sorts.'

'Blimey.'

'So, after several warnings, the MD sacked him. But then Martin claimed unfair dismissal, said he had mental health problems, which freaked the MD out. She over-reacted, there was a tribunal, everything got very nasty. Hence my involvement.' She takes another bite of biscuit, and continues, cheeks full. 'My point is, when I talked to Martin alone, it emerged that his anger was nothing to do with his workplace or his colleagues.'

'What was it do with?'

'Childhood abuse.' Debs swallows the biscuit and sits back, arms folded.

But I wasn't abused as a kid, thinks Suzy. My mother wasn't *that* bad.

'The anger was a default reaction you see. Whenever Martin felt threatened by someone, it would emerge as rage.'

There is a silence. Oh dear, thinks Suzy. She feels obtuse for being so slow.

Debs leans forward, rubs Suzy's knee. 'You get me?'

'Not really...'

'I recall your nightmares in the hospital. I've seen your panic attacks, don't forget.'

Suzy blanches at the thought of vomiting all over Debs' concrete floor.

'Rage, panic, lapses of memory—they're all extremely common with trauma, but it wasn't until you told me about *The Marchioness* that it occurred to me.'

'You think *everything* happening to me now is because of that?'

'Pretty much.' Debs nods sagely.

'Even though it was thirty years ago?'

'That's why they call it *Post* Traumatic Stress Disorder.' Debs pats herself on the chest. 'Psychology degree, remember?'

'But I've been fine most of the time.'

'Hmm... You haven't really, have you? You said not five minutes ago you feel you're losing your mind.'

Suzy watches as Debs weighs up whether it would be rude to have another *Digestive*. She seems to have eaten over half of the packet.

'Go on,' she urges, and Debs, relieved, snatches it up.

Suzy stifles a yawn. She is terribly tired. Yet just as she feels her eyelids drooping, Cam returns to the room. Again, he pushes the door to behind him.

'Sorry, I was so long,' he says.

Suzy shakes herself awake. 'Who was it?'

Cam's expression is awkward. 'Some old friend of yours, Mum. Says he knows you from years ago? He has been trying to get hold of you, but you've not responded.'

'Argh!' Debs smacks her own forehead. 'I completely forgot!'

'What?'

'I was supposed to call him.'

'Who?' asks Cam.

'Glenn.' Debs leaps from the sofa. 'I'll talk to him.'

Yet Cam shifts, still uneasy. 'Mum, do you think you could manage a quick word? It sounds like he's come along way...' He runs a hand through his sandy mop of hair. 'I'm afraid I said you're not feeling well, so he knows you're in. I think otherwise it looks like we are fobbing him off. He seems a nice guy. Very friendly.'

Suzy is surprised to hear Cam describe Glenn this way, but he has hit on something. She has been ghosting Glenn. His shouting her all those weeks ago scared her. Still, she thinks. It's unkind to drop someone without explanation. She takes a deep breath and pushes herself up from the sofa.

'You're alright,' she says to Debs. 'I'll go.'

She makes her way slowly from the room, legs still dreadfully shaky. Catching a glimpse of herself in the hall mirror only confirms that she is bedraggled and drawn. Her face reflects her many weeks of strain, but there is no opportunity to fluff her hair or put on make-up. He'll have to deal with her au naturel.

He is leaning against the frame of the door, gazing upwards abstractedly, his profile silhouetted against the brightness of the sky.

At once Suzy is confused; instead of a motorbike, in one hand he is holding the handlebar of a racing bicycle, twisting it to and fro, like a prop in a Hollywood musical. As her eyes adjust to the light, she thinks how odd it is to see Glenn in cycling shorts rather than motorbike leathers. He looks taller than she recalls Glenn being, too.

For several moments Suzy is convinced her brain must be deceiving her. It is such a shock that she reaches out and touches him. Just his hand, as he spins that handlebar. And yes, his skin is warm.

He stops spinning at once, shocked as she is.

Of course, thinks Suzy. Her heart starts to race. She feels giddy, disorientated, unable to speak. Immediately she wishes she could unwind reaching out like that. It was reckless, inappropriate. Yet it is so strange to see him here on the threshold, without warning. His cheeks are flushed from exercise, and although his hair has been flattened by wearing his cycle helmet, nonetheless she can see his he still has the same floppy brown fringe. There is a slight upturn to his lips that suggests it won't take much to make him laugh, and she is struck not so much by the lines around his eyes or the loss of smoothness to his skin, but by the fact that he seems to have grown into himself, to be even more like the person he was destined to be.

Suzy's hands fly to her cheeks. I look *dreadful,* she thinks. My hair is filthy. I've not got on a scrap of make-up...

She leans against the wall of the hall, struggling to take it in and remain upright. Nonetheless, she can feel herself slipping. Her legs are failing her. She is falling into the abyss again. And when he exclaims, 'Suze!' she is gone, folding like a rag doll onto the carpet.

46.

Suzy is vaguely aware of a shout 'Help!' and of someone catching her.

'She seems to have fainted,' says a familiar male voice.

'Mum!'

Already she is coming to, giddy. Cam is standing over her; she is on the floor, in the hall. Suzy squints, rolls her head to one side. The light is so bright, it hurts her eyeballs. Slowly a figure comes into focus. Floppy hair, brown eyes... It can't be...It *is*. It's Johnny. Why is everything being thrown at her so fast?

'Come on, Mum,' says Cam. 'Let's get you back into the living room.'

Suzy sees her son glance warily at Johnny, notices the faint hint of a frown. Gently, Cam and Johnny help Suzy to her feet. How surreal, she thinks. My son on one side, Johnny on the other. Slowly, the three of them edge into the living room.

'I think you should sit on the sofa,' says Cam.

'Head between your knees,' Debs orders.

Suzy's heart is racing, she is breathless. She reaches out a hand to grab Cam's for reassurance. She grips his fingers tight and stares at the floor, unable to believe this is happening to her again.

'And breathe...' says Debs. 'And breathe...'

This helps. Then Johnny—oh my God, it's Johnny, here, in Amhurst—passes her a glass of water. She takes a sip and the liquid slops as she places the glass on the carpet, fingers trembling, but eventually she is no longer hyperventilating and can begin to absorb the situation.

Johnny is in the living room of her little cottage, in cycling shorts and a Lycra top. She hasn't seen him in years. When was the last time? It might have been when Cam was little... Yes, her memory sharpens. She recalls saying, 'Hi,' when they both emerged from their parents' houses in Park Road at the same time. She had Cam propped on her hip and was waiting for Leo to say his goodbyes to her parents. He seemed to be taking forever, so in the meantime, she had watched Johnny get into his car with his wife. They had two children, she had observed. Twins. Both girls. They had looked roughly the same age as Cam. She and Johnny had exchanged awkward smiles; that was all.

Cam is 26... making it close to over two decades ago. And now Johnny is here, standing tall and awkward before her.

This is someone I loved so intensely, thinks Suzy. Someone I thought I would never see again. She wants to cry. She *is* crying. Through tears, she says, 'Er Cam, this is Johnny, Johnny, this is my son Cam. And er...'

Debs interrupts her. 'Debs.' She sticks out a hand.

Until that letter, I thought I would never see him again, thinks Suzy.

'I'm sorry.' Johnny falters. He appears embarrassed. 'Is this a bad time?'

Immediately Suzy's heart goes out to him. What a scenario to walk in on! To have her faint into his arms. For her head to be such a mess.

Debs swoops in protectively. 'I'm afraid it is. Suzy isn't feeling well. We... er... weren't going to answer the door, but we thought you were someone else.'

Johnny looks even more uncomfortable. 'Oh dear.' His appraises the three of them, takes a step backwards. 'Should I go?'

'NO!' barks Suzy, suddenly terrified he will vanish.

Johnny stiffens.

Suzy tries to calm her racing mind. I sent that letter to Pat *months* ago, she calculates. I could swear I put my phone number in it. Why didn't he call or message first?

'I'm sorry you're not feeling well,' says Johnny.

Suzy realises she must apologise for alarming them. Either that or she is going truly mad, and hallucinating.

'I'm so sorry. It was a shock, that's all. What brings you here?' She forces a smile.

'Actually, my mum has died.' Johnny's voice catches.

'Oh!' At once Suzy's head is full of memories. Pat and Rita cackling with laughter, Pat chain-smoking at the breakfast table, Pat clasping hands with Colin the day John Lennon died...

Momentarily she longs to reach out for Johnny. *I mustn't,* she reminds herself. That *would* be mad.

'I'm so sorry.' Poor Johnny, she thinks. He loved his mum so much. I loved Pat, too. Her eyes brim with tears yet again. 'Er... and your dad?'

'He's OK.' Johnny stares down at his empty hands. 'I mean, OK as you'd expect him to be.'

At the mention of Colin, Suzy cannot stop herself. The floodgates open. 'I... er... my mum died, too...' She sniffs.

'I know,' says Johnny. He half sways, half hops from foot to foot.

Of course, he does, thinks Suzy. That's why he wrote, originally. She thinks of Colin: he will be devastated. She is tempted to say, '*Your mum was the mum I always wanted,*' but stops herself in the nick of time. It would be insensitive: her mother was Cam's grandmother. Joan was far softer in her treatment of him than she was with Suzy. They were fond of one another.

It strikes Suzy that Johnny is alone. Where is his wife? Maybe she doesn't like cycling. Johnny appears kitted out to ride fast, plus he is sweating, perhaps he likes to spend time alone.

She hears Zelda saying. '*Things are always happening to you...*' and has a crazed urge to laugh.

Johnny says, 'I did try calling, yesterday. There was no answer.'

Of course. Cam and Debs could not reach her either.

'We're in Bath and I realised it wasn't that far from here...' Johnny's voice trails off.

We. He must be talking about his wife and girls.

'I thought I'd let you know.' Johnny glances nervously at Cam and Debs. 'Though please, don't let me interrupt your afternoon.'

'No, it's fine,' says Suzy, still trying to take it all in.

'That's a long way to cycle,' says Cam, visibly impressed. 'Must be about sixty miles, round trip.'

Johnny always was sporty, thinks Suzy. And look at me! I'm a wreck. Not like when I met Glenn... She shoves the thought away. She cannot make room in her head for Glenn right now.

'I know you cared about Mum... So... I thought you'd like to know.'

'Thanks.' Suzy flushes. 'I'm glad you told me.'

I ought to introduce Cam and Debs properly, thinks Suzy. She is poised to do so when Johnny says, 'Look, I won't stay.'

'But—' Suzy is about to say, *'Don't you want a glass of water, at least let us get you that?'* but Johnny holds up a hand.

'No, honestly. I've intruded long enough. Let me... um... write down where the funeral is...'

Before Suzy can come to his aid, Debs is handing Johnny a pen. She shoves the pile of post on the coffee table in his direction. 'You may as well use the back of one of these envelopes.' She raises an eyebrow at Suzy and Suzy gives a small nod. Debs passes Suzy a tissue so she can dab her eyes, though she is focusing far more on Johnny than Suzy. She is staring so blatantly Suzy fears it will make Johnny feel uncomfortable.

He bends over to write, then stops and looks up at Suzy. 'Of course. It's at *Holy Trinity.* You know where that is. This is my number.' He notes it down. 'The service is unlikely to be for a while...' His voice catches. 'There has to be a post-mortem.'

Suzy would like to ask, *'Why?'* but that would be prying. She's been through her own hell when it comes to post-mortems. She is not about to be prurient about someone else's. Especially Pat's, for goodness' sake. She seemed immortal, at the time.

'We are hoping, it'll be in about a month...' Again that "we". Johnny lays down the pen and stands upright. 'If you'd like to come, give me a call or... er... message me.' He looks at her directly, seeming to want reassurance.

Suzy says, 'I'll do that.'

'Great.' He hovers for a few seconds, tapping a hand agitatedly against his thigh. 'If you're sure you are OK, Suzy, I'll get off... Call me, yeah, if you'd like to come?' And before Suzy can answer, Johnny has turned, retreated from the living room and is outside, mounting his bicycle and has gone.

Suzy falls back onto the sofa cushions.

'Wow.' Debs can barely contain a smirk.

'What?' says Cam.

Debs swivels to face Suzy. 'That was *Johnny*?'

Suzy opens her eyes wide in a bid to communicate Debs should shut up.

'Who's Johnny?' asks Cam.

'Oh, er... One of your mum's ex boyfriends.'

Cam narrows his eyes. 'How do *you* know about him?'

'I don't really. I've never met him before. It's only...' Debs fumbles for an explanation. 'Your mum and I sometimes chat about old friends, that's all.'

'But not my dad,' says Cam pointedly.

'We've talked about about Leo,' Suzy protests. 'Haven't we?'

'Yes.' Debs nods vigorously.

Thankfully, now that Johnny has gone, Cam does not seem too perturbed. 'Can't imagine *Dad* cycling sixty miles,' he scoffs.

Nor can I, thinks Suzy. Nonetheless she feels obligated to defend Leo. 'He's a fair bit older than Johnny.'

'You were telling me what Dr Anand was saying.' Deftly Debs moves the subject on. 'Did she mention antidepressants at all?'

Cam frowns. 'Mum doesn't seem depressed to me. More panicky.'

'I agree.' Debs nods. 'But there are antidepressants which can help people who feel anxious.'

'I thought you said I had post traumatic ... something...' says Suzy, confused.

'PTSD. Yes. I did. It's a form of anxiety, related to trauma. They're all just labels. We can call how you're feeling whatever we like.'

'Bonkers?' suggests Suzy, and laughs.

'What about counselling?' interjects Cam.

'That would be good too. But your mum said there is a wait. In the meantime, I was thinking medication might help. To be honest, pet, I'm not sure those beta blockers—' Debs breaks off. 'Well... they might not be enough.'

'I'm that bad?'

'It's not a question of being *bad*,' says Debs. 'Christ alive, pet. It is a question of helping you feel better.'

'Dr Anand did say something about them, yes, but I'd prefer to try the other tablets first.'

'Sure, you can always play it that way.'

'But you're advising Mum not to?' Cam asks her.

'Of course, it's down to your mum,' says Debs.

'What do you think, Mum?'

'I don't know.' It's too much for Suzy to take in. She is so tired.

'Let me try to explain,' says Debs, again rubbing Suzy's knee. 'If you think of therapy as like digging out the foundations of a house...' She checks Suzy is following, and Suzy nods. '...sometimes, before you dig out the foundations, you've got to put up some scaffolding, haven't you?'

'Ye-es?'

'My concern is if you dig into the trauma you've experienced, it could trigger more anxiety.'

'You mean I'll still stay mad?'

'Not *mad,* no! But you have had a *hell* of a lot going on, Suzy. You've lost your mum, you broke your ankle, you have the insurance claim still going through, then you met... er—' Debs shakes out her auburn hair to avoid being more specific, '—you know.'

'Mm.'

'Seriously, I think it is worth talking to Dr Anand about your options,' Debs continues. 'Medication could give you more of a buffer, so you could look at the trauma you experienced and deal with everything else more easily.' She pauses. 'Does that make sense?'

'It does.' The house is me, thinks Suzy. Only Debs is being kind. I've already fallen down. 'You think I should go back to the doctor.'

'What harm can it do?'

'Sounds a good idea to me,' says Cam.

'You're amazing, Debs. Thanks.'

Debs beams, chuffed. 'Thanks. I read up a lot on post-traumatic stress 'cos of Martin's case.' She pulls her handbag to her lap. 'I'm going to leave you. You two OK for tonight?'

'Mum?' Cam looks at Suzy. 'I am if you are.'

'You sure you don't mind staying over?' Suzy would love him to be here with her. Her boy, her sweet, understanding boy.

'I said I was already.'

Suzy follows Debs out to the hall to bid her farewell.

'So that was *Johnny,*' says Debs, sotto voce, on the doorstep. He seems nice.' She beams. 'He's good looking. You've got excellent taste.'

'You think?'

'I do.'

'First Glenn, now Johnny.'

Debs gives Suzy's shoulder a squeeze. 'I'm amazed you're still standing, after all you've been through. It's a lot for *me* to get my head round. Never mind you. What a day! I'll check in on the pair of you tomorrow.'

And with a backwards wave, she heads down the drive.

47.

May 2018

Suzy is in her garden. It's chilly, but sunny, and it feels good to be in the fresh air, tidying the pots around her front door. She is clearing space around some tulips to add some pansies. I love this time of year, she thinks, with a small burst of pleasure.

The roar of a motorcycle engine interrupts the peace and quiet. Suzy checks her watch. It's almost 11am, the time he messaged he would drop round. She watches while he parks up next to her hatchback. Then he takes off his helmet, dismounts and walks up the path towards her, loosening the fingers of his leather gloves as he strides.

'Thanks for your text,' he says curtly.

Suzy sighs as she lays down her trowel. 'I'm sorry. I should have been in touch much sooner.'

'What happened?' asks Glenn. 'Are you OK?'

'Mm.' Tears prick behind her eyes.

Glenn looks perturbed. 'I'm sorry I got so angry. I just couldn't understand why you left. I thought... well, we'd had such a nice evening.'

Where should she begin? The prospect of explaining why she took off has been filling her with dread ever since it happened. But she sees him blanche and realises he is misreading her. 'No, no,' she clarifies. 'Sorry, I didn't mean you to think I didn't want to... That bit... er... was fine.'

His expression relaxes.

This is so hard to put into words. The sex was *great*, she wants to say, but fears if she does, it will lead him to believe she wants more, which isn't true. He did scare her. Somewhere in her gut, she knows Glenn is a bad match for her. He always was.

I mustn't go too fast, she tells herself. *It's when I start to panic.*

'Be prepared for it to take four to six weeks for the tablets to work,' the doctor had said, handing over the prescription. 'Until then, try not to take on too much. You've been talking ever so quickly—did you know?'

Suzy had shaken her head.

'You're manic, it seems to me,' the doctor had observed. 'In a state of heightened anxiety. Have you been worrying about lots of different things?'

Suzy had been tempted to retort, 'There isn't anything *doesn't* worry me.' Dr Anand had peered over the top of her glasses and Suzy had reminded herself how sympathetic she had been when Joan had died. Once again, her face is full of concern, not judgement.

'Is there anything you like to do, crafts, handiwork, that sort of thing?' she had asked.

'I'm a painter,' Suzy had responded.

'Painting can be wonderful therapy.' Dr Anand had smiled. 'Though I meant more for relaxation. Anything else, that's not a professional interest?'

'Like gardening?'

Dr Anand's smile had broadened. 'Exactly!'

Since then, Suzy has focused on her cottage garden for hours at a time. Being spring, there is plenty to occupy her, and her anxiety attacks seem to be easing.

Nonetheless, she remains shaky. She has been aware she and Glenn have unfinished business, but it has taken her weeks before has been confident enough to see him face to face. She's texted a couple of times, just to check in. Otherwise, nothing.

'It was more connected to what you *said*, rather than the shouting. Though I don't like being yelled at either.'

'Oh dear,' Glenn grimaces. 'I'm sorry. I fly off the handle too easily. I know.'

'You do.' Suzy sighs. 'Still, I owe you an explanation.' She takes off her gardening gloves. 'Thanks for coming over. Do you want a cup of tea? Or we could go for a walk?'

'Don't mind.' Glenn shrugs. 'What do you want?'

'Oh. Er...' The latter seems most likely to dispel their tension. 'A walk, maybe?'

He nods. In the bright light of day, she can see his face has changed markedly from the man she sketched all those years ago. The crevice between his brows is deep, and there are dark circles beneath his eyes.

'Let's go up to the church,' she decides. 'There's a path that leads from there around the back of the village to here. I'll show you.'

They stroll in silence, up the same narrow lane where she walked all those months ago in the darkness and the rain, carrying crockery after her mother's funeral. She shudders, thankful it is daylight and dry and she is in little danger of slipping. She frets that she should open the conversation but cannot fathom where to start.

Eventually Glenn says, 'I'm trying to remember what we were talking about that night... I told you about the Falklands. Did it upset you?'

Upset me, thinks Suzy. That's an understatement. 'Um, yes.'

'Why?'

'It brought back some horrible memories,' says Suzy.

'Ah.' Glenn's frowns. He is staring down at the tarmac, but she is sure he is trying to work out what happened, to piece her behaviour together. She wishes he would talk, share it with her, not keep it all to himself.

He raises his head and gazes into the distance. 'I thought so.'

'It reminded me of... um...' But before she can finish her sentence,

Suzy feels a rush of overwhelm. Here it comes, she thinks. The black hole. She is right on the edge of it. She is so close to falling into it, she can sense how deep it is. It seems to have no bottom. She starts to shake.

Glenn is still gazing ahead. 'It was the only explanation I could come up with...' Fleetingly, Suzy wishes Debs was there with them. She is so good with Suzy when she is panicky. With Glenn it's too complicated, there is so much history.

They carry on walking, again fall silent. Then Glenn coughs. 'Maybe I had better make it clear... um... that I'm not expecting you to... er... leap back into bed with me or anything like that.' The end of the sentence comes out in a rush. 'I can tell that you're not in a great place,' he adds, glancing at her again.

'I'm not.' Merely admitting this is a relief.

They stand aside and wait for a van to pass them on the narrow lane.

When it has gone, again, Glenn looks away. He seems about to say something, then falls silent, face scrunched up so awkwardly it is as if he is in pain. I wish he would just come out with it, thinks Suzy. But when did Glenn ever do that? He has always been reticent. And she sees it; they are both so awkward, both on the verge of saying something, yet unable to articulate it.

She laughs, a tad hysterical.

'What?' Glenn appears surprised she is laughing.

'Nothing.' She hesitates. 'Only... I've just realised... How similar we are.' She laughs again. Having seen it, it is obvious.

'Do you think so? No.' Glenn shakes his head, disbelieving. He turns to her. 'I disagree. It's what I love about you Suzy. You're much more open than me. You're always so upfront and say what you mean.' He looks so hopeful in that moment, so admiring of her, she can hardly bear to disappoint him. Yet his intensity scares her. She wants to flee. Instead, she forces herself to continue walking on up the hill to the church.

He's *wrong*, thinks Suzy. He still doesn't know what happened. If he did, he would understand I *have* been hiding things. I've been hiding them from him and Debs and Cam and Leo and almost everyone. Most of all, myself. She cannot withhold it any longer, she *has* to tell him. Even if it propels her over the precipice, she cannot lie. She takes a deep breath.

'What you told me about *The Sheffield*, it, um... upset me, because I went through something similar.'

He looks at her quizzically.

She bites her lip. 'I was on *The Marchioness*,' she says.

Glenn stops dead in his tracks, so she stops, too. It takes him a few moments. 'Seriously?'

She nods. 'Yes.'

Then he grabs her hands, turns her to face him. 'Why didn't you tell me?' He is almost shaking her, he is so ardent, so keen to understand, but it feels too much, almost scary. He peers into her face, puzzled, desperate.

'There are lots of people I didn't tell,' she says.

And now he drops her hands and claps a palm to his forehead and gives a hoot of laughter. Yet, it is not happy laughter. It is the laughter of comprehension, of understanding the irony.

Briefly, Suzy tells Glenn what happened. Glenn nods, assimilating.

'I'm sorry,' she murmurs. Again, she feels tears prick behind her eyes. This time she makes no attempt to stop them. She turns and continues walking in spite of crying and he carries on walking beside her, and she has the sense he is wondering if he can take her hand, but she very deliberately keeps her distance.

'Don't be sorry,' he says. 'There is nothing for you to be sorry for.'

Suzy wants to yell. '*YES, THERE IS! How can there not be, when I left my friends to dance, and went up onto the deck of the boat alone? How can there not be, when Nate and Tash and Stef died? How can there not be, when all those people drowned and I, me, Suzy, survived?'*

Through the blur of her tears, Suzy is aware they have come to the church. She only half sees it, nonetheless she can feel its large, familiar presence beside her, sitting squat and heavy like a resting giant, with its grey stone frontage and tower-porch, surrounded by the green, green grass of the cemetery. Glenn pushes open the gate. There is a bench, close to the path.

'Would you like to sit down?' he asks.

Normally Suzy likes the sense the graveyard gives her of souls resting at one with nature; the solidity of the yew trees offset by the daffodils in the breeze would give her solace. Yet today it seems ghoulish.

'I prefer walking,' she declares, and soon is at the gate on the far side of the churchyard. Briskly she manoeuvres round it and on she strides, high hedges on either side as the path weaves back down the hill. She is conscious that Glenn is having to run to keep pace with her.

'Suzy—' he says, as the path opens out onto the village playing field and catching her arm. 'Slow down.'

'Sorry,' she says again, and reduces her pace.

'I'm happy to keep walking,' says Glenn. 'But please, we don't need to race.'

He is right. Suzy is breathless. Walking across the grass allows them both to get their breath back. At the far side of the playing field Suzy stops so they can take in their surroundings. From this distance it is possible to see the general lie of the village; the church, atop the hill to their left, the estate, straight ahead, of social housing, to its right, hidden behind a copse, is her cottage, and to the right of that is the village shop and the pub where she and Glenn met a few months earlier. They are more exposed here and buffeted by wind. Suzy's fine blonde hair catches in her mouth, and she sweeps tendrils from her eyes.

'You know what I told you that night?'

Suzy's stomach lurches but he carries on before she can stop him.

'I only got so I was able to talk because I went through something similar to you, only a while ago.' He inhales and then out it comes, along with his exhalation. 'Some people would call it a breakdown. Basically, my whole life fell apart. It was different for me than it sounds for you... I felt full of rage for some reason and started fucking up... You know me, you can imagine, I'd get so furious, I had to put it somewhere, otherwise I'd have lashed out at Pippa, or the kids, physically. I'd go off on my bike...' He squints into the distance and for moment Suzy could swear she catches a glimpse of the biker Glenn speeding through the trees on the far side of the playing field. 'It drove Pippa mad, because our kids were small. "I can't have you dying on me," she'd say, but I felt so stifled, it was the only time I felt fully alive. Then, I don't even really know why, I had an affair.'

He glances at her. It is hardly a surprise. Glenn always seemed the type who would have affairs. It's another thing about him that makes her wary.

'Who with?'

'Oh, a woman I met.' He breaks off. 'It's not important who she was. It was a long time ago. Nearly 20 years. God, doesn't time fly?' He looks up at the sky, then sighs. 'Eventually Pippa found out—maybe I wanted her to—I dunno. Anyway, she insisted I end it.'

'Did you?'

'I did. I tried keeping busy but whatever, I couldn't settle down. I started drinking. It wasn't Pippa didn't try, she did. She insisted we go for couple's counselling, make a go of it for the kids so we went, but I guess I wasn't in the right place or maybe I didn't love her enough. I found those sessions hard. I remember sitting there thinking, they want me to talk. Yet talking won't help. Talking won't cure anger or anything, will it? There I was, with two people encouraging me to talk about my feelings....'

Suzy can picture herself in the situation, in Pippa's role. To be in a

♩ ♫ ♪ ♩   260

mess like that with Glenn, she thinks. At least when Leo and I parted, we communicated well. They were determined not to let acrimony get the better of them, for Cameron's sake. And Leo was a lawyer, used to negotiating with reason. They agreed to adopt a non-confrontational approach when they separated. If anyone was confounded by all the elements they had to sort out, it was her. In comparison to Glenn and Pippa, she can imagine it was a picnic. Glenn's silence leaves people nowhere to go.

He continues. 'The problem is talking about my feelings was something I'd been taught not to do. By my dad, by my school, as a naval officer. Everywhere, it was all about manning up. Courage. Bravery. Not *feelings*.' He says the word with heavy sarcasm. 'So, I carried on drinking and not being around much, you know?'

I do know, thinks Suzy. It's spookily like what you did to me. One night saying he loved her; next morning running away.

'In the end Pippa and I realised, because Pippa told me, that we weren't going to be able to make it work, but that even so, I had to do something.'

'Really?' Suzy finds herself sympathising not with Glenn, but with Pippa. It explains the lonely life he leads, the cabin in the woods, the lack of space to be with his children.

'Yeah. It was the couple's counsellor who noticed it—I mentioned something in passing about serving in the Falklands and she pressed me about it. I flew off the handle, told her to mind her own business. Anyway, when we stopped seeing her, she gave us some numbers.' Glenn's fists are clenched, then he seems to realise and releases them. 'So, one night, when I was at a very low ebb, I rang *Combat Stress*—it's an organisation for veterans—and the guy on the phone suggested I go along to this support group. Which I did, and I found it helped.'

'Gosh,' says Suzy. *Glenn, in a support group?* It's hard to picture. Then she reconsiders. Isn't this where exactly where Glenn would have had to have headed? She casts her mind back to that night when she first spotted his profile online. *Glenn was so hard drinking, so reckless, so prone to burning the candle,* she had thought. *I wouldn't have been surprised to learn he was dead.* Of course, she realises. Glenn must have sought help. It clearly wasn't marriage and fatherhood that had tamed him.

He looks serious again. 'In that group, I began to acknowledge what I was really feeling. Other emotions like pain and guilt and grief and fear.'

'About *The Sheffield?*'

'Yes, which is why I'm glad you told me about *The Marchioness.* I know how hard it is at first, to start talking about it. Whatever *it* is.'

Suzy gulps. 'There's a lot I've missed out.'

'I'm sure.' He clears his throat again and stares at the ground. 'You don't have to tell me everything, Suzy. Really, you don't. I'm probably not the right person for you to talk to. All I know is talking helped me, and I've seen it help others.'

'Mm.' They are still standing side by side, a foot or two apart. The wind is making Suzy's ears cold.

'I run a group myself, these days, for others in the forces.'

Suzy isn't sure she has heard correctly. 'Sorry?'

'Nothing in an office, mind,' Glenn adds hastily. 'God no, hopefully won't ever have to do that. It's a drop-in thing, at the barracks near Wroughton, couple of evenings a month.'

'You never mentioned that before.'

'I didn't really get the chance.'

Suzy squirms. 'Yeah, I suppose I did run off...'

He raises his hand. 'My fault. I get I scared you. Though it's one of the reasons I moved here.'

'Not for the Forestry Manager job?'

'No,' says Glenn. 'The job came afterwards.'

'Aren't you a dark horse,' Suzy murmurs.

Glenn harrumphs. 'Pippa used to call me that.'

How funny that Pippa and I echo each other, thinks Suzy. She senses that the traits she found hard to handle in Glenn as a young man, Pippa found hard too. And although Glenn seems to have changed, she finds it hard to believe he has changed *that* much. She can see it in the way he is standing. Muscles taut, limbs rigid. He was hot tempered that night of the election. And the anger is still there.

I *was* right to run away, she thinks. I might have done it for the wrong reasons, but we aren't suited. We wouldn't be good for each other. He's too wounded. In some ways, we mirror each other too closely. She recalls Rich had called her 'a dark horse' too. The realisation makes her terribly sad.

'Sorry,' she says and reaches in her pocket and retrieves a bedraggled tissue.

'You OK?'

'Mm.' She sniffs and wipes her eyes. Her head is beginning to throb, all the walking and talking has tired her out. In the distance she hears the church clock strike noon.

'I need to go,' she says, slipping the tissue back into her pocket and giving Glenn a half smile. 'It's Cam's birthday.'

'Cam, your son?'

'Yes.'

'Sure.' Glenn nods.

'He's gone to the supermarket, but he'll worry if I'm not there.'

Cam is the one who matters more than anyone, thinks Suzy, and slowly, they pick their way back across the playing field.

48.

'You've been referred to psychological services by your GP,' says the woman, checking the sheet on her clipboard. Her hair is tightly braided into dozens of plaits which fall like beaded curtains on either side of face. When she moves, the beads make a soft clicking noise.

'Yes.' Suzy gulps. She is ever so nervous. The room is big enough for two armchairs, a low coffee table and no more. A tiny candle flickers on the window ledge and through the gaps in the blind, Suzy can see her ancient hatchback, parked directly outside. She has to fight the urge to run down the stairs and jump back into it, away from this modern brick house as fast as possible.

'And I gather you've had one session already.'

'Mm. An assessment.'

'Well, Suzy,' the woman looks up. Her expression is serious. 'I'm Cassandra. Your sessions with me won't be limited to this, so I suggest we take some time discussing what has brought you here.'

Suzy eyes Cassandra's notes. 'You've got lots of it down there.'

Cassandra looks at her again. 'I've only the very basic details,' she says.

I wonder how old she is, thinks Suzy. It's hard to tell. Forty, maybe? 'My friend says I'm suffering from PTSD. But um... can you explain what that is?'

After a couple of beats, Cassandra lays down her clipboard and again, her braids click softly. 'Why not? It's a perfectly reasonable place to start. Though please, interrupt me whenever you wish.'

Suzy has been bracing herself on the edge of her seat. She makes herself ease back into her chair. As she does so, she gets a waft of scent from the candle.

'I'm not a massive fan of labelling people and conditions, but sometimes it can be helpful. So "post-traumatic stress disorder,"' Cassandra makes quote marks in the air, 'is the term often used to diagnose those who have been through a trauma and are still experiencing its effects after the event.'

'Ah.' Suzy squirms, humiliated to be seen so clearly by others, when she can't make sense of much herself.

'Does that resonate with you?' asks Cassandra gently.

'Mm.' Suzy bites her lip. She tries to recall when the flashbacks started. It's hard to work out precisely but certainly they ramped up exponentially when she had the accident the previous year.

After a while, Cassandra says, 'It's very normal to get flashbacks you know. They feel extremely scary, but it's often better to talk about the experiences that may cause them, rather than keep the memories shut away.' The therapist raises her brows and smiles.

Suzy's mouth is horribly dry; she could do with a drink. She wonders if it would be rude to ask, then sees a carafe of water before her on the coffee table, and a glass. 'Is this for me?'

'Help yourself.'

Relieved, Suzy pours herself a glass and gulps it down.

'I avoid things all the time,' she blurts. 'After um... what happened, the big thing I mean, I hid myself away in my room, all those years ago. I guess I've avoided going to London ever since. But lots of things make me anxious. More panicky than anything.'

Cassandra nods. 'Anxiety and panic are a common response to trauma.'

Suzy frowns. 'Why?'

♪ ♫ ♪ ♩

'Imagine that we are sitting here in our armchairs having a nice chat and a man rushed in brandishing a knife.'

Compared to Suzy's worries, this seems a very tangible. 'Ye-es...'

'We'd have to switch to a different state to protect ourselves. Fundamentally, we are either going to run because we are frightened, or we might freeze, or we're going to fight.'

'I've heard of fight or flight,' Suzy assimilates. 'But I never thought of my own reactions in that way.' She is reminded of Glenn. 'Is anger like fighting?'

'They are often connected.'

'I know someone who responds like that when he can't cope,' says Suzy.

'Of course, threats come in many shapes and sizes. They don't have to physically threaten our safety. We displace feelings onto other people and situations.'

I ran from Glenn, thinks Suzy. She is struck by another parallel. 'I wonder if my dad was anxious.'

'Oh?'

'He would walk away from arguments all the time.'

'It could be a way of coping you picked up from him.'

'Maybe.' Suzy reflects. 'Though my mother was the more angry one. She used to shout at both of us. Or at me, anyway...'

'I'm sorry that happened to you,' says Cassandra.

'Though my parents did give me a place to stay when I desperately needed one, after the... um...' She glances out of the window. That it is a grey, nothingy sort of day seems to underline the sense she is alone. 'I have wondered if losing my mum somehow brought all this to a head.'

'Losing a parent is a big transition,' observes Cassandra.

'Even though we weren't that close?'

'Sometimes even more so,' says Cassandra. She is quiet for a few seconds. It seems she is allowing the notion to settle. 'Would you say you were managing well before your mother's passing?'

'I was managing better,' Suzy retorts. Then a small voice inside her says, '*Were you doing that well?*' 'I did find looking after mum very hard,' she confides a few beats later. 'About six years ago, after my father died. My son went to university, and Mum moved in. Her memory was going so it seemed for the best.'

'With him away, you must have had your hands full.'

I did, thinks Suzy. My head was always full too.

'Did you have any other help? Carers? It sounds a very intense situation, being only you and your mother, for so many years.'

'It was...'

'Did you have breaks? Any respite care?'

Suzy considers. 'It was very claustrophobic. Sometimes I felt as if I was prisoner in my own home. It was hard to go shopping...' She casts her mind back. Every day there was another loss, yet more responsibility. 'Not really, no.'

'I imagine that was tough,' Cassandra nods. 'Especially if you didn't get on.'

'Yes.' Both of us had memories full of holes, she thinks.

'Do you believe your mother's death might be connected to your anxiety?'

'Maybe... Partly.' Maybe I focused on Mum to stop myself feeling so bad, thinks Suzy. It's an alarming notion. 'I remember hearing once, it's not necessarily good to let everything out. Only now I can't seem to put the genie back in the bottle.'

'And you'd like to do that?'

'Ignore everything so it will go away?' She looks at Cassandra hopefully.

Cassandra pauses, reflecting. 'Do *you* think you can?'

'No...' Suzy's voice cracks. 'But I can't bear all this remembering.'

'We can go at your pace, Suzy. I'm not going to force you. This is your time, OK?'

Suzy nods. It's good to be reminded. She ventures, 'I thought I had recalled all the events around *The M-M-Marchioness*, but over the last few months there seem to be pieces of that night that keep thrusting themselves at me when I least expect it. It doesn't seem to make much sense.' As she says this, she feels anxiety rise in her chest once more, her throat tightens. 'What can I do?'

'That's what we're here to work out,' says Cassandra gently. 'How can you learn to live with the tragedy you went through? You can't undo what happened, unfortunately, but hopefully, over time, I can help you process it better.'

'How do you mean?'

'We'll try to stop it being a traumatic memory that reaches up and grabs you by the throat. That sense of everything being so out of control, so frightening—'

'The panic, you mean?'

'Exactly.'

'Sometimes it's like I'm on the edge of a precipice. I'm completely overwhelmed.'

'Ah.' Cassandra furrows her brows. 'That sounds very distressing. Have there been other occasions when you've felt similarly?'

Suzy pauses. 'Sorry?'

'On the edge of a precipice.'

The answer hits her unexpected force. 'I suppose it was how I felt that night...'

'Are you able to tell me about that?'

'I was on the prow and—and I didn't know—' Suzy can sense her breath coming in short gasps, but can't seem to stop it from happening '—what to do—whether to go back inside—and-and look f-f-for my friends or t-t-to jump with the people wh-who were next to me...'

There is a silence. It fills with black. A huge, dark hole.

'I felt it then,' Suzy whispers. 'But now I don't seem able to m-m-move from it...' Her teeth chatter. She can barely get the words out. 'Even though I d-did at the time. I jumped, into the w-w-water... I swam...'

'It must have been an awful moment. Feeling terror for yourself, and such panic about your friends. I imagine you felt pulled both ways...'

'I'm not sure I thought it through that clearly.'

'No, in the moment we seldom do. But it might help you understand why you keep experiencing such anxiety. It sounds like part of you is stuck there, on the edge of that moment... Ever since, you've been living in a heightened sense of hyper-vigilance and fear to the point that even having a conversation about it makes you panic.'

'Y-y-yes.'

Cassandra's face softens. Her smile feels warm and understanding, as if Suzy is being bathed in kindness. 'I am glad you came to me. I think we can work together very well.'

'Do you?' Suzy feels a thousand miles from being healed.

Cassandra leans forward so her eyes connect directly with Suzy's. Her expression is sincere, assured. 'I do. I can help you find a way through so that you are not so randomly triggered.'

'That would be g-good.'

'It was perfectly natural and normal what you did that night. It was your survival instinct kicking in. For what it's worth, I believe you're very brave to come here and talk about it. Now, I'd like you to pause a moment. Do you see how, even though you find it difficult to speak about, you are in fact OK?'

'Oh.' Suzy is taken by surprise that Cassandra sees her this way. She looks down at her body to check. It is as if hitherto she had been unaware this rest of her was there. But yes, her knees are there, in the brown leggings she pulled on that morning. Her legs are crossed, so she can see her left foot encased in its trainer. Her arms too, they are there, and her breasts, her tummy. Indeed, as Cassandra says, she does seem to be fine. 'It's like I said to my friend Debs,' she recalls slowly. 'When the fear subsides, I realise I can handle it.'

Cassandra nods. 'You're more resilient than perhaps you give yourself credit for.'

'Mm.'

'The brain is an amazing organ, and there is a lot about it that we don't know. One thing we *do* know is that trauma memories are located in one area of the limbic system. It's called the *amygdala*. It's a very ancient part of the brain and we share it with other mammals. It's where the fight or flight response resides, which we discussed earlier.'

'So, I'm like my cat?' Suzy pictures Pushkin scooting up the stairs, alarmed, when guests arrive.

'Exactly.'

'But by talking we will be helping to move those memories from a trauma storage area to an autobiographical storage area.'

'I see.'

'In so doing, we're going to make your experience of *The Marchioness* a memory that is part of your life story, a painful part, but part that is in the past and that you can live with, rather than something that feels continually present.'

'It all sounds very neat.' Suzy can almost hear the clunk of filing cabinet drawers opening and closing as Cassandra talks.

Cassandra chuckles. 'Trust me, it won't be. Processing loss isn't all about having a tidy outcome at the end. It is OK to have some messiness. Personally, I don't mind a bit of mess.'

I can see that, thinks Suzy. Cassandra is wearing a purple top and harem pants, splashed in bright splotches of clashing colours. It's not an outfit Suzy would wear, but it suggests Cassandra is comfortable with disarray.

'Nor do I,' says Suzy. 'My house isn't that tidy.'

'And that's OK for you?'

'I think so...' Suzy pictures her parents' house. All those pristine surfaces, all those continually hoovered carpets and the smell of bleach. 'I don't like everything too tidy. I don't do tidy paintings, either.'

'Interesting,' says Cassandra. 'Maybe we can pick up on this next week.'

Sensing her time is up, Suzy gets to her feet.

'Thank you. I didn't think it would make a difference, so quickly, talking to you.'

'I'm glad,' says Cassandra. 'Though remember if you feel sad or upset before we see each other again, it's quite normal, too. If you can, allow yourself to *feel* those things, but see if you can find a way of separating from them a bit. Take a step away, if you can, rather than standing continually on the edge of that precipice.'

'I'll try,' says Suzy.

Back at her cottage later that afternoon, Suzy snips open the cellophane and rolls out the lining paper the entire length of the kitchen table.

This is for *me*, she says to herself as she secures each corner with masking tape to stop the paper from pinging back into shape. I don't have to show anyone.

She works at speed and without stopping. If her charcoal snaps, she carries on, using the bit that is left. Occasionally sees a line isn't right and scrubs it out with an eraser, more often she sweeps across it with the side of her hand or blends it with her fingers until it's less obtrusive, then continues, amending and adapting as she goes. Charcoal is perfect for this, it's so pliable, so freeing. She sketches some elements with a line so fine it is almost ghostly, other parts she scribbles with a ferocious intensity, darkening shadows until they are almost black. She moves along the paper at a frenetic pace, from left to right, trying not to smudge what she has already drawn, determined to get it all down while she has the urge. Occasionally she will drag her sleeve across an area she meant not to or blow away charcoal dust and find herself spraying saliva. She can see the grain of the wooden tabletop in the shaded areas, but she doesn't care.

A while later, she stands back, astonished at what she's done. Right along the surface is that night in its entirety, a frieze of flashbacks, reminiscent of Picasso's *Guernica*. There are the trees of Battersea Park and the four of them together on the steps, then there is Oliver's flat, the cab along embankment, the party, the boat, the views of London. Then there is huge black shape of *The Bowbelle* coming in close, too close, the jagged scrawl of the colliding vessels, the hospital, the funerals. And finally, there is Suzy, cowed into a ball, alone and withdrawn.

It is the first drawing Suzy has done in decades where she can pinpoint what it represents. Looking at it is appalling. It is grim and distressing and filled with sadness and rage. Yet it is also a relief, as if she has got some of the terror out of her head at last and vomited it up onto the paper, like a giant, toxic furball.

49.

June 2018

'A few months ago, I'd never have imagined myself doing this,' says Debs, stepping out of her front door in her running shorts and trainers to join Suzy. 'Still, it'll be good for me. I'm too chubby.'

'You are not chubby! You're curvy.'

'Whatever. We're not going to go fast, are we?'

'We're certainly not.' Suzy shakes her head. 'I can't. I have to be careful 'cos of my ankle. We're supposed to stretch first.'

'Good.' Debs clips up her hair. 'I don't mind that bit—we do it in Pilates. It's the getting out of breath I cannot stand.'

Suzy laughs. 'OK. Foot up on the gate?' She hoists her leg up to rest it at right angles against the top bar.

'Sure.' Debs follows her lead, 'Anyone would think I do this all the time!'

'I won't tell if you won't,' Suzy looks from right to left to check for passers-by.

It's high summer, so already warm despite the early hour and there is no one about. The dawn chorus is still in full throttle. The coo of woodpigeons, the flute-like *ee-oh-lay* of a thrush. As she switches to stretch her left leg, Suzy thinks of Glenn, and wonders for a moment if he is listening too, alone in his home on the edge of the woods.

'Ready?'

Debs reaches an arm up beside her head, pushes on her elbow to stretch her tricep.

'Ready as I'll ever be,' she nods, and slowly they start to jog down the lane. 'Tell me about this thing you heard about running being good for PTSD?'

'It was on the radio,' says Suzy. 'A woman was talking about how her husband took his own life and she was the one to find him.'

'Oh my Lord. That must have been so traumatic.'

'I know. She was talking about how she was already suffering from PTSD, and by the time she got into running, she had withdrawn and lost all her confidence. Her story struck a chord. I thought I'd give it a go. I started a few weeks ago with a local group and it's been helping me feel better. Initially, I said I couldn't go with the group because I needed to be on my own, but they said, "You can, you absolutely can." The sense of achievement I get from being able to be able to run further than I thought is brilliant.'

'You seem to be doing much better,' Debs observes. 'And you're sure you did the right thing with Glenn?'

'I'm sure.'

'Shame. He was hot.'

Suzy laughs. 'I know.'

'Though a good call, lass, by the sound of it. He sounds like hard work.'

'Mm.' Suzy pictures Glenn's home in the woods, his solitary existence. 'Maybe I'm too conventional for him.'

'Pah! You're not conventional!'

'It's relative.' Suzy smiles. 'Compared to you, I'm downright weird.' I can't imagine myself ever living like Glenn, thinks Suzy. I'm sociable, I need friends.

'You're not *weird*,' Debs assures her. 'I love your artistic energy.'

'Seriously, Glenn helped me see a lot of stuff, but there's something about him, that anger... It freaked me out, the way he shouted at me.'

'I'd hazard a guess that being with someone who shares a similar history wouldn't be a good for you, or for him either. He reacts with anger, you're anxious; his anger makes you more anxious. Hey ho. Learning curve, my friend. Are you OK about it?'

'I guess so.' Suzy remembers the day in early spring when she'd put on the lipstick which made her want to kiss the world, and the floaty blue dress had seemed to tumble from its hanger. How, feeling pretty for the first time in years, she had driven to Marlborough then onto his place in the woods so spontaneously.

For a brief while, I really believed Glenn and I might work as a couple, thinks Suzy. To have let him go makes her sad. Then she laughs. 'The sex was *great* though. Jesus, and we only had it once!'

'Good to get back in the saddle, I reckon,' says Debs. 'And you're looking fantastic!'

'Now you're being silly. I probably look the same as last summer before I unravelled.'

'Not sure about that,' says Debs. 'I think your mother exhausted you. I'm glad she died when she did, truth be told. But I'm not allowed to say that.' She checks from side to side, to make sure none of their neighbours can hear them. 'She was always flipping rude to me.'

'Dementia means we lose people bit by bit, but with my mum, she didn't entirely lose her character,' Suzy muses. 'I reckon some of the most difficult bits remained, right up until she died.'

'Didn't you say she threw a plate at you once?'

'I did!' Suzy exclaims. 'I had to duck out of the way of flying peas and gravy and shepherd's pie. Poor Pushkin was terrified!

'No wonder she's such a jumpy little cat,' says Debs.

'She's calmer with my mother gone.'

They fall into silence. All Suzy can hear is the sound of the birds and the slow patter of their feet on the tarmac. The rhythm lulls her.

Over Mum's last few days, her anger seemed to ease, somehow, Suzy remembers. I had to call the local surgery and wait at mum's bedside. Then, when Dr Anand arrived, I had to concentrate whilst finding it hard to grasp what I was being told; something about Mum having pneumonia and although Dr Anand could arrange for her to be taken to hospital, the likelihood was that in her condition she would end up worse, even if she did get through the infection. 'It could mean that your mum's memory gets worse,' Dr Anand had said. Suzy had pictured her mother becoming even more dependent and difficult, unable to feed herself, finding it hard to swallow. Cam had been there, too, and the three of them had agreed *not* to call an ambulance, but instead to make Joan comfortable at home, in the space she had known for many, many years, and soon Dr Anand had departed.

Not long after that Pushkin settled at Mum's feet, Suzy recalls, as if even she knew my mother was ready to rest. And that's how we spent the remains of the day, Cam and Pushkin and me, listening to Mum's breathing grow increasingly shallow and tenuous, until eventually, quietly, with no drama or sudden crying out, the blankets over her chest stopped rising and falling, and she slipped away.

50.

May 2018

Perhaps it's the smell of musty books and dusty shelves mingled with cooking, maybe it's the scent of the house itself, but the memories come flooding back the moment Suzy steps over the threshold of number 32. Then, with a pang, she realizes: one element is missing. Cigarettes. They have been stubbed out along with Pat. Extinguished.

'Suzy!' Colin lurches towards her, unsteady despite two walking sticks. His cheeks are pink, presumably due to the heat. 'Good of you to come.' He raises a stick to direct her into the living room and then says, 'Lerrus have a look you,' edging back to admire her. 'It's good to see you!' He leans on one stick and pokes her gently with the other. Colin's face is more lined, as if he's a newspaper that's been crumpled into a ball, and his voice is hoarse compared to how she remembers it, but the essence—the Scouse sing-song—is the same.

'It's good to see you too.'

Suzy is delighted to see the print she sent months ago propped on the mantelpiece amongst the *With Sympathy* cards.

'Pat was very touched by that.' Colin nods. 'We were glad to see you're still painting.'

'Oh yes,' says Suzy. On impulse she adds, 'I'm sorry I didn't say much to you both when I came back to Park Road, after... you know.'

Colin picks up her inference at once. 'It must have been hard for

♩ ♫ ♪ ♩

you. Pat was worried—we both were. We could see your curtains were often closed.'

'Yeah, it was a bad time.' A lump rises in Suzy's throat. There is a parallel between our situations, she thinks. I had lost a partner then; Colin has lost one now. Colin has had to wait a long time before the funeral too. Post-mortems can prolong the agony of grief, drawing out the rituals of death, making everything happen painfully slowly. This is what happened to Suzy. It was awful.

'Your ma told Pat you weren't up to visitors.'

Suzy starts. 'Mum never told me she called round.'

'Pat was really bothered. "I feel so helpless," she said.'

'I thought she was upset with me for splitting up with Johnny.'

'Pat?' Colin does a double take. 'No, luv. She weren't one to hold grudges. Certainly not after everything you went through. She thought you had it tough. What with the press and everything, the way the papers made out you were Lords and Ladies and the like—' He stops, aghast. 'Ach, listen to me, being so tactless. I shouldn't bring it up.'

'It's fine,' says Suzy. She is surprised, but her desire to forge a connection with Colin outstrips any anxiety she feels talking about the past. I seem less wobbly, she observes. What a relief. I was dreading this funeral, but at the same time, I so wanted to come.

'I'm sorry I didn't get to see Pat again,' she tells Colin. 'She had more of an impact on me than she'll ever know.' So many missed opportunities, thinks Suzy. Though what's done is done. She has learnt the hard way. 'Would you mind if I looked round the house?'

'Help yourself.'

Flo is chatting to an elderly couple nearby and catches her arm as she passes. 'You after my brother?'

'Er—'

'He's upstairs with Billie,' says Flo. 'She's a bit, um, you can imagine, upset.'

Who is Billie? wonders Suzy. The last thing she wants is to intrude. She can take a moment if she nips into the loo on the landing. She tries the door, but it's locked, so she waits outside for whoever it is to finish. After a couple of minutes, she hears the chain flush, someone blowing their nose and the bolt being pulled aside. A tall, slender young woman edges past, cheeks blotchy from crying.

'Sorry. I didn't realise there was someone waiting.' She glances at Suzy. The big cow eyes are a giveaway. She must be one of Johnny's daughters.

Inside the bathroom, Suzy checks her reflection. All black didn't feel right for a woman as unconventional as Pat, so when Suzy had planned her outfit the night before, she had opted for a bottle green velvet jacket over a wrap dress covered in giant red and pink roses. In the coolness of the church, she had felt comfortable, but the summer day has proved very warm, so she'd handed Flo her jacket when she arrived. Standing before the mirror to fluff her hair, she worries the dress with nothing over it looks awfully lurid and exposes too much cleavage.

I've gauged it badly, Suzy berates herself. Though at least I look better than when Johnny rocked up on his push bike.

She carries on up the stairs to the first floor, past the master bedroom where Pat and Colin used to sleep. It doesn't seem right to snoop in there, so she steps softly towards the room which used to be Flo's. From the doorway she can see the bed is in the same place it always was, but the rest of the furniture has been replaced by storage units that bear the hallmark of IKEA. There are two open suitcases on the floor. A pair of trainers and some rather glamorous sandals lie discarded close by. If this is where Johnny is staying, he seems very definitely half of a couple.

At that moment, there is a creak of floorboards overhead. Someone is in the attic. Suzy has a rush of apprehension, and is sorely tempted to flee downstairs, but stops herself. Really, truly, where has it got her, all this running and evasion?

In the downstairs hall and on the first floor the William Morris wallpaper has been painted over, but the peacocks and dragons remain on the narrow staircase to the attic. They are scuffed and faded, and once more she has the sense time has stood still, and she is her teenage self again, sneaking over to see Johnny while her parents' backs are turned. She can hear *London Calling* crackling on his record player, and she can almost feel her school bag bouncing on her hip.

At the top of the house, the door is ajar. She taps gently. A familiar voice responds, 'It's fine, come in,' and she steps inside.

51.

Johnny is sitting on the floor in a pool of sunlight surrounded by record sleeves and vinyl. *The Clash* is playing on the turntable, and at first glance, it seems he is wearing his school shirt and trousers. He has undone his collar and loosened his tie just as he used to, and his hair is sticking up at odd angles in the way Suzy remembers so well. Even how he is seated, with one leg folded and the other straight, is familiar. Suzy is disarmed, then sees a discarded jacket on a nearby armchair. Of course, he must have been hot. It is even warmer under the eaves than downstairs, and the guests have been feeling the heat as it is. Fleetingly she pities men their limited options of formalwear. How constricting a suit must be.

'Hi,' she says.

He beams. 'Suze!' He sounds genuinely pleased to see her. 'I thought I saw you in the church but wasn't sure. How nice you came.' He half rises to greet her, but one of the albums catches her eye and she crouches next to him, so he folds himself back down.

Suzy picks up the dog-eared sleeve.

'*Ziggy Stardust.* Spooky. I was telling my neighbour not so long ago how we went to that gig. She couldn't believe it.' She smiles at the recollection. 'Thank you again, by the way. For the CD you sent—'

'Yes?' He looks eager.

'I listen to it all the time.'

'Really?'

'Yes. I love it. *Starman...* I guess I'd have expected you to choose that, if I'd thought about it. It's probably on a thousand Spotify playlists. But some of the others?'

'Like what?'

'The Sex Pistols and the Shangri-Las?' She shakes her head. 'All wedged together. It's so eclectic, it's genius.'

'I enjoyed making it,' he says. There is a click as *London Calling* comes to an end and the needle lifts from the single.

'I can't believe you've still got the same turntable.'

'I wouldn't let my dad throw it out.'

'Wise move.'

Johnny picks up the *Ziggy Stardust* album sleeve and sighs. 'I think the boy in me died a little, too, when Bowie died.'

Suzy nods. 'He was such an inspiration. Those punk bands owed him a lot.'

'He was like no other rock star. Such a showman, so experimental.'

'His outfits, remember? They were so outrageous.'

'And his songs were so good. As he grew older, he grew no less cool.'

'He had a really duff period in the middle,' Suzy points out. She laughs. 'Bit like me.'

They both fall silent. Oh dear, thinks Suzy. For goodness' sake! She is crying. 'I'm sorry.' *I* shouldn't be weeping, she thinks. Not today.

'Hey,' he says. 'Suze. Please. I didn't mean to make you cry...' His words remind her of the Lennon song, *Jealous Guy*.

'I got it all wrong...' she whispers.

'How do you mean?'

'Johnny?' She bites her lip, looks up at him. It feels so exposing to say all this when she is still so unsure about his life. It's *years* since she has seen him, other than the afternoon when she felt so wobbly. Is he still married? There's the suitcase downstairs... She doesn't even know what job he does. 'Can I ask what you do?'

'For a living, you mean?'

'Yeah.'

'I'm a music teacher,' says Johnny. 'You know, I go into places. Prisons, care homes, stuff like that... I try to encourage them to forget about being good or bad, and to get it out there, put on a concert, that sort of thing.' His voice trails off.

Suzy nods. It figures.

'I felt dreadful for intruding when I did.'

'It was a bit of shock.' How awful he saw me then, she thinks. At least today I've been able to pull myself together.

He lets out a hoot. 'It's not every day a woman faints into my arms.'

She feels herself blush, then glances up. Johnny's lip is curled into a wry smile. His eyes are shining with mischief. *He's teasing me,* she realises. Like he always used to. She is still crying, but she laughs. She doesn't mind being teased, not if it's done with genuine affection. Zelda does it too. She can hear Zelda saying, '*Come here short arse. 'Gis a hug.*'

'Bit damsel in distress.' She winces, and Johnny laughs again. Suzy had forgotten how much she loves his laugh. Hearing it once more, it's so familiar, so redolent with memories.

'Do you often cycle so far on your own?'

'Yeah. I don't have much choice. Billie's idea of exercise is YouTube videos. Her sister's into weightlifting and going to the gym.'

No mention of Alison, Suzy notes.

'I saw one of the twins on the stairs. She looks like you. She's very beautiful.' At once Suzy realises how this sounds. She is making a total hash of this. 'Are you... er... all staying here then?'

'The twins are going back to their mum's. I'm staying on for a bit, yes. To be with Dad.'

Suzy's heart lifts. *Back to their mum's...* That sounds as if they are in separate dwellings. Although who is to say he doesn't have a girlfriend? The way Flo spoke about him at the funeral, explaining how Johnny had been with their mum right to the end, it sounded so caring, so brave, it's hard to believe he is single.

'I want to keep an eye on him,' Johnny elaborates. 'Flo's done a lot over the last few months.' He stops abruptly. 'You in a hurry?'

Suzy is taken aback. 'Not desperately... Why?'

'Do you fancy a drink?' He glances at her sideways.

She is taken aback. She hadn't expected things to take this turn. 'Yeah, why not?'

'OK.' He jumps up. He is limber for a 55-year-old. She feels a faint stirring between her legs, watching him, like she always used to. 'What d'ya fancy—wine? It's what Dad is serving.'

'Wine would be fine.'

From the thuds, she can tell he is taking the stairs two at a time. She smiles. There never were any sides to Johnny. When he is keen, he doesn't hide it. While he is gone, she takes stock. There are two pillows in the middle of the double bed, not four, and they are in the middle. He has a right to privacy, she scolds herself. Probably one of the girls is sleeping in here.

She looks around. It's astonishing how well she remembers the room. Johnny and I used to play games here when we little, she thinks. Over there we used to draw together, scribbling on the wall. Pat didn't seem bothered. She'd leave us to it. And in this room, so many years ago, we both lost our virginity. She is still smiling to herself and thinking, *If walls could talk*, when, with a *whoosh!* Johnny returns. In one bound he sits down next to her. 'Hold these,' he orders, and hands her two glasses. He pours wine from a bottle and sits back against the bed.

'Won't they be expecting you downstairs?' asks Suzy. She feels for Colin, and Flo.

'Probably.' Johnny shrugs then takes a gulp of wine. 'I'll go down soon, but it's great to catch up. Mum would certainly say it was fine that I was here. She always liked you.'

Suzy feels emotions rise in her throat again. 'The feeling was mutual.'

'To my mum.' She hears his voice crack as he clinks her glass. 'Cheers.'

'Cheers.' She looks at him, straight in the eyes, those big cow eyes, are filling with tears. She finds herself welling up again, too. 'Oh dear.' She grimaces. 'Look at us! She was a one-off, your mum. You must miss her very much.'

'I do.' Johnny nods.

Suzy frowns, aware she must tread softly. 'Can I ask what she died of?'

'One guess.' Johnny sighs.

'Cancer?'

'Bingo.' He grimaces. 'Lung. The only good thing is it was mercifully quick.' She can tell he is struggling to steady his voice. She longs to reach out and clutch his hand, comfort him. 'It's why I didn't reply to your card. I came back from the States—I'd gone for work, they wanted to set up something similar to what I do in one of the prisons there— and everything unravelled while I was gone. Mum was hospitalised with breathing problems. Lots of tests were done and they found shadows on the scans. She was called in for a consultation meeting—Dad and Flo went with her. In a nutshell—some nutshell—' he laughs bitterly '—the oncologist told them it was lung cancer and there was no cure and when she pushed for a prognosis, she was told she had six months if she was lucky. By the time I got back from the States, it was pretty much a done deal.'

'What a lot for you to take in.'

'It was.'

And to imagine Johnny was going through that while I was unravelling too, thinks Suzy. How strange.

Johnny runs a finger round the rim of his glass and makes it ring. Then he drops his hand. 'I think Mum knew ages before that. She'd had a cough for months, chose to ignore it. Stubborn old bird. And she would have made a lousy invalid.'

'We can be too focused on prolonging life, these days.'

'I know.' Johnny takes another gulp of wine. 'All the same, it's been tough on Dad. And Flo, too. She had to move in to help. '

'Imagine what dealing with *my* elderly mother was like.' Suzy blows out her cheeks.

'I'd rather not,' quips Johnny.

Suzy laughs. 'Mum had dementia, ended up living with me for ages.'

'Sounds a *nightmare.*'

'That pretty much describes it.'

'She was not easy woman,' says Johnny. 'No disrespect, obviously.'

'You can disrespect her all you like!' Suzy laughs. 'Though it's complicated. I felt I owed her. She and Dad, they looked after me...' She shakes her head. Of course, Johnny will recall. 'In many ways it was a relief when she died.'

'I get that.' Johnny nods.

'Enough about my mum. I'm more interested in *yours.* I've such fond memories of Pat. I thought that was a lovely funeral. Your song was so special, Johnny. All those images of your mum projected huge on that screen as we arrived, too. Did you put that together?'

'With Flo,' says Johnny.

'The article your daughter read... Pat was a great columnist, wasn't she? It was such a celebration of her life.'

'There are some advantages to having had to wait for the post-mortem. We had a while to prepare. I'm glad you thought so.'

Suzy senses he is about to reveal more when there is a call from downstairs.

'JOHNNY?' It's Flo. Funny how voices change so little, even after years and years.

'I knew she'd be after me soon.' Johnny groans. 'I did promise to hand round the food.'

'You'd should go,' says Suzy.

'I'd rather stay and talk to you.' Johnny hesitates. 'But I better had. The wrath of my big sis is best avoided.'

'I'll come down with you,' says Suzy and they both uncurl themselves from the carpet. As they do so, Suzy catches a whiff of his scent.

She reels. He still smells of *her* Johnny.

'Stay here,' he urges. 'I'll help Flo and Dad for bit, then come back.'

Suzy hesitates. If he has got a partner, why doesn't Johnny want to be with her? Then she remembers her own mother's funeral. How much she had appreciated Debs lending a hand. Flo will need Johnny, and their mother's funeral is significant for her, too. Suzy checks her watch. It's not far off the time when she will have to leave anyway.

'I'm due at Cameron's at half four,' she tells him.

'Shame,' says Johnny, as he bounces ahead down the stairs.

'Ah, *there* you are,' says Flo. Suzy notices her raise an eyebrow at seeing them together. 'Here.' She thrusts a tray of canapes at her brother. 'Hand these around. Living room. There are loads more in the kitchen.'

Johnny takes the tray and pulls a face at Suzy that communicates, '*Oops, been told off*.' She can read his expressions as easily as she ever could. 'Best get to it.'

'Your jacket's upstairs on my bed,' says Flo.

'It was really good to see you,' says Johnny. As Suzy turns to mount the stairs again, he calls, 'Hey, Suze!' and she stops. 'Can I call you? I've got your number, remember?'

She does not hesitate. 'Please, do. Yes.'

'Excellent.' He grins as Flo gives his backside a gentle kick to propel him into action.

Suzy finds her jacket amongst those of other guests. It's not snooping if they know I'm in here, she justifies, and goes to the window to check out her parents' old house. The driveway and path leading to the front door are so familiar she half expects to see her dad's Austin Allegro parked outside. Yet the proportions of her childhood home look different, and on closer inspection she sees that an extension has been added onto the garage to create an extra storey. Escape from what was her bedroom onto the garage roof would no longer be possible, although hopefully whoever lives there has less need to risk life and limb.

With a sudden flash, she recalls it happening in reverse, when Johnny came to visit *her*. It was only once, and she was so distraught, it's hard to make sense of the disparate memories, but gradually, as she gazes over at the house where it happened, the elements come into sharper focus...

Suzy sits down with a thump on Flo's bed, confounded, as realisations tumble like dominos. She rests her head in her hands and closes her eyes so she can concentrate.

Crikey. Those big cow eyes... Of course. Of *course*.

Cam's colouring was so like Ken's, she'd always known that's where he'd got his sandy hair. The brown eyes, he'd assumed were from Leo. But Cam is tall and lanky. Beautiful.

Like Billie.

Could it be that Johnny is his father?

52.

August 1991

It is two years exactly since the sinking of *The Marchioness* and no matter how hard she tries, Suzy cannot get up, not today. She rings the shop first thing, tells her colleagues that she won't be in. Then she shuts the door, locks it, and climbs back under the duvet. Her parents seem to understand that nothing can make this anniversary easier and leave her alone. It is just Suzy and her grief and self-loathing, in a darkened pit of her own making.

She has no idea where the time has gone but she can tell from the pink glow around the curtains, it's sunset. She is about to drift off again when she hears a tap, followed by another, on the windowpane. She must be imagining it, but no, there it is again. A soft wrap of knuckles. She turns her head, befuddled.

'Suze!'

It can't be.

Blearily, she pushes back the duvet, gets to her feet, pads to the window, yawning. Trepidatious, she peeks between the curtains. Even though she knows who it is, she jumps. She is easily startled these days. Her life was turned upside down in seconds. There are no rules to say it can't happen again.

'Sorry. I didn't mean to scare you.'

She opens the curtains fully and sure enough, there is Johnny, face mere inches away. He is standing on the garage roof. Climbing up is the

289

sort of thing he'd have done as a kid, but for him to be here, at this moment is a shock. Her head is such a tangle of memories. So much has happened since...

She can hardly leave him outside. Carefully, she opens the sash, and, with the agility of a cat burglar, he lifts his legs, one, two, and slides through the window.

At once she is concerned, she looks a mess, her face must be blotchy from crying, she isn't properly dressed. Yet standing in the middle of her bedroom he is equally self-conscious, dusting himself down, uncertain.

'I... er...' He lifts arms, then drops them. 'I know what night it is,' he says simply.

Suzy bites her upper lip, blinks away tears.

'Suze, I'm so sorry,' he says.

'Thanks.' She gulps.

'I thought you might um...' He glances at the door. Sees it is bolted. His shoulders slump in relief. 'Want to talk. To someone, I mean. I've wanted to check, for so long... that you're ok.'

'Really?'

'Of course!'

'Even after I...?' She wants to add, *sent that letter*, but can't finish. It's yet another reason to beat herself up. She can feel him looking at her, but all she can do is avoid his gaze, focus on his hands, in his lap. How strange, she thinks. His fingers are so familiar, and his nails are short on the left, he must still be playing the guitar. She wonders if he is in a band.

'I don't mean to pry. You don't have to say anything. I only thought you might want some company...'

Oh, that is so kind! She wipes her eyes with the back of her fist in a fruitless attempt to stop her tears. She sits down heavily on the edge of her bed. How can she tell Johnny—how can she tell anyone? She still feels Nate's presence, every day. She talks to him, sometimes out loud.

Occasionally it is mundanities that have happened at work, grumbles about her parents. More often, Suzy re-treads the same ground. Begs forgiveness. Apologises again and again to her golden boy.

Then she hears herself say in a small voice, 'Sometimes, on good nights, I dream of my friends. They are still alive, you know... They move the same, behave the same, their voices haven't changed at all.' The tears flow faster. 'Sorry,' she mumbles.

Johnny reaches for a tissue from the box beside her bed so she can wipe her eyes properly. 'Don't be sorry,' he says gently. By now he is sitting beside her, and slowly, tentatively, he reaches an arm around her shoulders and tenderly pulls her towards him.

He tells Suzy that he has split up with Alison, his girlfriend, and that he still loves her, Suzy. It's nice to hear him say this, but Suzy is not sure what to do with the information; her head is so full of Nate, especially today... She leans into Johnny, just like she might have leant into Nate, or Johnny himself, come to that, many years earlier. And then she inhales the familiar, gorgeous smell of him, of *her* Johnny, and she lets go and allows herself to be comforted, almost wordlessly, in the best way they know how. Johnny holds her tight and for a few hours, the years melt away and it is only the two of them. They listen to Sade; her voice is soulful and mellow, and *Your Love is King* takes her away from memories of *The Marchioness* and back to 1984, before the incident happened. At sun-up, Johnny leaves the way that he came, a reverse Romeo, and Suzy drifts into slumber, feeling warmer inside, and loved, and when she wakes fully, the encounter seems so beautiful and other worldly, she finds it hard to believe it was real.

53.

May 2018

But it *was* real, thinks Suzy. It suited me to forget. Or if not forget completely, then push to the very recesses of my mind.

She walks to the train station in a daze. Past the familiar Victorian terraces, with their pale brick facades and white stucco. Homes which in her childhood housed actors and authors now belong to bankers and brokers and their ilk; she can see grand chandeliers and giant flatscreen TVs through the bay windows, where once there would have been paper lampshades and Habitat furnishings.

I'd been on several dates with Leo, Suzy recalls. I am certain. I felt safe with him; he was generous and kind. That he was so totally physically *not* my type meant he couldn't get under my skin... But we'd had sex, and it been good, considering.

Gradually it is coming back to her. 1991... Leo had moved to his place in Devizes, and she had been to stay. He'd bought a beautiful house, centuries old, not far from Amhurst, where Suzy lives now; she liked both the market town and the house at once, and Bath too, of course, with its classical crescents and streets lined with elegant golden buildings. She recalls telling Leo she couldn't see him that weekend and he had seemed to sense intuitively he needed to tread softly if he was to woo her.

But why did it suit me so, she wonders, to forget that night, when I still had feelings for Johnny? Yes, there was Nate, but there is something else, something missing. Suzy can feel a memory eluding her... Infuriating, confusing. She slaps her forehead, hard. Why, oh why, is her mind so full of holes?

And then she hears it. A woman's cry, reaching down through the decades. It is a wail, a howl of pain. Coming from Alison. *Alison*, on Johnny's doorstep.

Yes, she can see it, almost filmic in its abstraction. A young woman with long brown hair in a red dress, walking towards her on Park Road. Brow furrowed. Resolute. Then, just before she and Suzy drew parallel, she had crossed the road, to head directly to the front door of number 32.

I was on my way to *work*, thinks Suzy. If it was not the very next morning, then it was soon, very soon, afterwards. And I paused, because I recognised Alison from Johnny's description of her the night we were together, and thought it strange she should visit, when she and Johnny had parted ways. But there had been something in Alison's expression, an intensity, a sense of purpose, and Suzy remembers watching, transfixed, unable not to. And she had seen Johnny open his front door and look puzzled and Alison had said something, and he had gone very pale. Her heart had gone out to him, but it was then, at that moment, that Alison had wailed. And her cry of anguish was awful, so raw and piercing, that it had sent Suzy spinning back, back, to the agony of *The Marchioness* and all she had lost. The cries for help from the river as the boat went down, Cynthia clutching her hand as they watched her hauled from the water. And now she and Alison were both in such distress, whatever her own feelings, Suzy had felt like an eavesdropper, and hurried on her way. Intuitively, Suzy had known that whatever was happening between them, she could have no part in it, and had to let it go.

'Well,' says Zelda. 'This had better be good.'

'It's not good,' says Suzy. 'But it is big, or I wouldn't call you at work. How long have you got?'

'Long as you need,' says Zelda. 'I'll take you for a walk round Victoria Park so we can speak in private. My colleagues won't know you're not a client.'

'I'm on Clapham Common,' says Suzy.

'Crikey, the woman's in London? Headline news!'

'I came for Johnny's mum's funeral. I'm due at Cameron's any minute. But I got off early. Bought myself a coffee. I can't see him without talking to someone.'

'Ah.'

'I need to get my head straight.'

'Nothing new there.'

'Seriously Zelda, this is a headfuck.' It's still warm and sunny, but with the vast open space comes a breeze. All about are mums with pushchairs, people strolling and chatting, joggers and cyclists. To think this flat stretch of green used to be her stomping ground, too. If memory serves, she can cut straight across to the north side, past the bandstand and the model boating pond, and up Cedars Road to Battersea. Luckily she has a reasonable sense of direction.

'OK, your time starts now.'

Suzy can't recall ever downloading news so fast. What was it Dr Anand had said about hyper? The caffeine doesn't help.

'Woah!' says Zelda when she gets to the end. 'You're telling me Johnny is Cam's father?'

'I'm pretty sure he is,' says Suzy. 'I know it sounds bonkers. But the timings add up.'

'But that just means it could be either man, doesn't it?'

'Yes! And for years I believed Leo must be Cam's dad. Johnny and I spent one night together, that was all; Leo and I were fast becoming an item.'

'It's not just that. It's not obvious, as in so many ways Cam looks like me, and my father too, and I always assumed he got his dark eyes from Leo. But seeing Billie, Johnny's daughter, I sensed it straight away. It was probably being back there at the house... And Cam is tall, which Leo isn't. He and Johnny even have similar jobs. They both teach. It's eerie.'

'And Alison?'

'Was pregnant. That was what she came to tell him.'

'With twins,' Zelda confirms.

'Yup. Though I don't think she'll have known that then.'

'God, I can imagine your mum *loved* that.' Zelda gives a hoot of laughter.

'It's not funny!'

'No, sorry, it isn't.'

'But you're right about my mum, of course. It played right into all her prejudices about Johnny. She was *gleeful.* I remember my dad was more circumspect, told her to hush until she knew for sure, but Mum said she *did* know, as Rita had told her, and anyway, Alison's bump was hard to miss.'

'And you didn't know you were up the duff until later?'

'Up the duff?' cries Suzy. 'I hope you don't use expressions like that at work.'

'Course I don't. But it's a good excuse to haul out the cliches. It's like a blooming soap opera. Crikey Suzy, how is it things are always happening to you?'

'I don't know. I wish they didn't!'

'I'm sorry.' Zelda tone becomes more serious. 'I can see this puts you in a tricky situation. But if you didn't know before, do you need to spill the beans now? Maybe some things are best left unsaid.'

'That's what I've been thinking,' Suzy hurls her take-away coffee cup in the direction of a bin and misses. I can't even dispose of a coffee cup properly, she thinks, bending to pick it up.

'Of course,' Zelda continues. 'Some of this depends on whether you plan on seeing Johnny again. If you don't, I'd say keep schtum. If you do, I'm less certain. But whatever you do, tread very, *very* carefully. No letters, no emails. Face to face and one person at a time. I deal with this sort of shit at work a lot, and believe me, it can rip families apart.'

'You don't have to tell me that.' Suzy is laughing, but largely because she doesn't know how else to react. It is all so overwhelming.

'And don't forget the person who stands to be most hurt by this.'

'Cameron?'

'Well, yes, there's Cameron. Although I was thinking of Leo.'

Of course. Without Leo, there would have been no lifeline. He was her saviour, and Suzy would be forever grateful. Because—and here her memory is clear and sharp as a bright summer's day—within next to no time—a matter of days—she had packed up and gone to join him.

Leaving not just Park Road, not just Johnny, but London with all its heinous, heart-breaking memories.

54.

Suzy has given herself permission to wear the same blue dress she wore when she dropped in on Glenn so impulsively all those months earlier. She is adjusting her chair to catch the last of the afternoon sun, when she sees Johnny standing at the top of the steps, scanning the riverside terrace. Her heart skips a beat at the sight of him. She experiences a tingle of anticipation at the afternoon ahead. She waves and as he heads to join her, she makes a rapid appraisal. He clearly takes care of his appearance yet remains dishevelled in a way that's arguably more attractive in middle-age than youth: he is in an olive-green shirt which is half untucked from his jeans, he has a rucksack slung lazily over one shoulder. Yes, his hair is thinning, *but he is 55*, Suzy reminds herself.

'You texted saying you wanted to see me,' he says, eyes scrunched against the bright sunlight.

'And you WhatsApped saying you wanted to see *me*,' she says.

'So here we are.' Johnny grins and she senses him take in her outfit. 'Nice dress. What can I get you?'

'Tea, thanks. Nothing fancy. Though can't imagine they do builders, bit too posh here. English Breakfast is fine.'

Johnny gives a nod to the waitress, and a young woman comes over with a pad. She is pretty, probably a student, but Suzy finds herself far more interested in Johnny's forearms which are tanned from cycling, and hands, which are so familiar from all those years and years she has known him. His nails are longer on the right-hand side, as they always were, for strumming. Normally she'd be comparing herself to the young woman, feeling she falls short. Not today.

'Well, well, both in Bath,' she declares the moment waitress has departed. 'Funny, isn't it? All this time, we were so near each other!'

They both look around. Close by, small waves are shimmering and sparkling in the sunlight. Downstream, the river is parted into a V-shaped weir. Is it just me, Suzy wonders, or does the whole world look especially beautiful today?

'Very strange,' Johnny shakes his head in disbelief. 'There I was, searching on the internet, and you were only 30 miles away.'

'I looked for you too.'

'You did?'

'Oh yeah. Here's a tip. Next time you have a kid, don't call them John Brown.' *Next time you have a kid...* thinks Suzy. Why did I have to use that expression? And she feels her palms grow sticky with nerves. For the last fortnight she has been wondering and worrying, trying to work out the right thing to do. Then she'd got Johnny's message and decided to let fate play its part.

'I live near here,' he says.

'Really? Where?'

'Do you know Monmouth Street?'

'That's over there, isn't it?' Suzy gestures across the river.

'That's right.'

'Nice,' says Suzy. 'Really central.'

'We've got a flat there, you know, on the corner, looks down to the park.'

'That is so weird! I come to Bath such a lot.' She looks at his face, eager to pinpoint what has changed. Again, it strikes her: it is as if he has ripened, gained understanding. Then she looks away, not wishing to stare. Luckily there is plenty to distract her: to her right are the distinctive Palladian arches of Pulteney Bridge. Built in the late 18th century, it has shops and cafes across its entire span on both sides. They're in a great spot for people watching, and catching the afternoon sun.

'I s'pose you would. It must be your nearest city, yeah?'

'Sure is,' Suzy nods. 'I moved to Amhurst, ooh, more than 25 years ago, must be. With my husband—' she corrects herself '—*ex*-husband, Leo.' She points to a grand Georgian building on the other side of Pulteney Bridge. 'I was there a few months ago, with Cam. We came to show my paintings.'

'That gallery?'

'Yup.'

'That *is* weird. Were you exhibiting there?'

Suzy shakes her head. 'The guy who runs it turned me down.'

'Julian something?'

'Yes, him.'

'He's a wanker,' says Johnny.

Suzy splutters as she sips her tea. 'That's what Cam and I thought. Anyway, tell me. We didn't get the chance to catch up. Not properly, at the funeral. You're separated from your kids' mum?'

Johnny nods. 'Alison. Yes. Divorced. And you?'

'Leo and I divorced a while ago.' Johnny needn't know specifics, not at this juncture. 'Since then, nothing serious. You?'

'Ali and I split up, ooh, ten years ago... I had a girlfriend for a few years, didn't work out. That's it.'

Interesting, thinks Suzy. She is as certain as she can be without asking him outright: '*Are you single?*' that he is. She hopes to draw it out of him without making herself too vulnerable. His body language—he is leaning in close to her, his brown eyes fixed on her face. He is laughing a lot. Has said he likes her dress. It all points towards ongoing attraction. Nonetheless, this is such a delicate situation. Their future turns on a knife edge.

'Johnny?' She looks into his eyes. 'There's something I need to say.'

'Oh?' He doesn't flinch, so she continues.

'I'm sorry.'

'Sorry for what?'

'For how I've been. To you. I don't just mean around the accident. I mean before, and after. I got my priorities all wrong.'

'Oh?'

'I behaved badly when we finished. I was a coward. Writing you a letter. Zelda was adamant I should tell you in person.'

'Yeah?'

Suzy nods.

'If I remember Zelda correctly, she never did have a problem saying what she thought.'

Suzy chuckles. 'She's still like that. But all the same. It's been a pattern. Me, running. Avoiding.'

'We both avoided the difficult stuff, eh? We're not the first people to do that. I'm sure we won't be the last.'

'Weird, isn't it? That it's all coming back now, after both our mums have died.'

Johnny hoots. 'That's an understatement.' He too looks out over the water, following her gaze. 'As for that letter, yeah, it was a shitty thing to do. I was hurt. But it was *decades* ago. We were young. And I've made a bodge of ending things myself. perhaps there's no such thing as a good way of ending things.' He reaches up and stretches, and his elbows click. 'Ugh, listen to that! These days I feel so ancient.'

'You don't look it.' The words are out before she can stop them.

Abruptly, he reaches across the table. Takes her hand in his. 'You know recently...' She sees him gulp, senses he is nervous. 'I thought I'd start dating again.'

She smiles. 'Really? That's a coincidence, 'cos I thought that too.'

'Oh?' He raises his eyebrows. It's a look that's so familiar; flirtatious, playful. 'And?'

'It started with you actually.'

♩ ♫ ♪ ♩   300

'Hang on a minute, did I miss something?'

'No.' She laughs. 'I mean with you sending the CD. I tried to find you. But you know this as I got in touch with your mum.'

'Yes, and I explained why I didn't reply. So did you go on any dates?'

'Mm. A couple.' She is deliberately casual.

'And...?'

'It felt too much like hard work. The older I get the less I want to be messed around.'

'Sounds sensible. What's your dating status now?' Johnny leans back in his chair. She can sense him drinking her in, appreciative, curious. She is aware of her hair blowing in the breeze, her dress skimming the curves of her body.

'Free as a bird!' Impulsively she waves her arms as if they are wings.

'Would you ever... Um... Go out on a date... Er, with me?' Johnny is sheepish, yet nonetheless is smiling.

'Is that why you wanted to see me?'

'Yes. I guess so. It's just...' Johnny looks over at the river, then back at her. 'Well, you were always on my mind.'

'Like *The Petshop Boys* song.' Suzy smiles.

'Yes. Though I can't stand *The Petshop Boys*.'

'Me neither.' They both laugh.

'Willie Nelson's version is much better.'

'Not sure I know that one.'

'Maybe I'll play it to you sometime.'

Suzy coughs to clear her throat. 'I'd love to go out with you Johnny. I promise, there's nothing I'd like more. But before we go any further...' This is the moment, thinks Suzy. It's not fair or right to keep it from him. 'I thought this would be impossible to tell you... A terrible idea. But now I'm here, I can't carry on and not be honest.'

'Oh?' Suzy can see a line form between Johnny's brows. He might be bracing himself for hurt. She mustn't prolong this.

'You remember that night, the anniversary?' A mere mention, and

Suzy is back in her darkened bedroom in Park Road on that warm August night in 1991.

Johnny's face clouds, and then he seems to recall.

'You came to see me,' she reminds him.

'I did.' He blushes.

'What a Romeo and Juliet we were.'

He is watching her face, clearly wondering what's coming next.

'We had sex that night, didn't we?'

He looks abashed. 'Er... Yes. I'm sorry, I didn't set out for that to happen.'

She shakes her head. 'I know you didn't. Nor did I! Actually, I remember it as lovely.'

'Me too.' Johnny smiles: a shy, intimate smile, full of gentleness.

Suzy continues. 'Back then, I'd just started seeing Leo...'

'The guy you married?'

'Yes.'

'And we'd slept together, several times.'

'Oh,' says Johnny. 'I didn't know that.'

'Of course, you didn't. And then I saw you... with Ali... the next morning, I couldn't cope—' Suzy's voice fails her.

Johnny runs his hands through his hair. 'God the timing! She came to tell me she was pregnant. The next day!'

'I know. My darling mother told me.' Suzy's lips are quivering. 'So, I left. London, I mean. To be with him.' Her voice is a whisper. 'And then, a few weeks later, I found out I was pregnant, um, too.'

Johnny stretches out his arms over the table. Puts his head down, hiding his face, assimilating. After what feels like forever, he raises it again, looks at her. His cheeks are aflame. 'Are you saying what I think you are?'

Suzy gulps. This is it. Now or never. 'Yes.'

'Jesus,' says Johnny.

'I'm not sure,' she explains. 'If we really wanted to know, we'd have to take a paternity test. And that could have all sorts of ramifications – for your girls, for Leo, for Cam...'

Slowly, Johnny sits upright again. 'I must admit, I thought I'd had my share of surprise pregnancies. Though if anyone was going to surprise me... I'm glad it was you.

I wonder... if Alison hadn't come knocking...'

'I've wondered that too. But, well, she did.'

'And your mum would probably have sent me away. From how you describe, it sounds like she was protecting you.'

Suzy likes this notion. 'Could be.'

Johnny scrunches up his face. 'I can't remember that clearly what Cam looks like.'

Suzy reminds herself to tread softly. 'If you like, I can show you his picture...'

'Sure.'

She reaches for her phone. Flicks through her photographs. She doesn't have to go back far. She has so many shots of Cam.

Johnny scoots through them with his thumb. 'He's much fairer than me.'

Suzy fluffs her hair. 'Gets that from me. Well, and my dad. Cam is more sandy, it's got some red in it, which is just like my father. Cam's eyes though, I can see a similarity there.'

Johnny expands the shot on screen and nods. 'Mm.' I do see what you mean. Then he says, 'I guess we all fucked up in different ways.'

'I suppose.' Suzy's mouth twists. 'And I don't regret leaving. It would have been awful if I had hung around.'

They fall silent, imagining for those moments the mess that could have ensued.

'All these memories returning. What was wrong when I turned up unannounced? Flashbacks?'

'How did you know that?'

Johnny shrugs.

♩ ♫ ♪ ♩

He was always so intuitive, thinks Suzy. So bright. And in tune with me. 'Yeah. They came bubbling up when Mum died. Or exploded rather, like a fucking volcano.'

'That's a good metaphor.'

'I'm beginning to see why. I shifted my focus to caring for others. Only I went too far the other way. Lost myself, somehow.' Suzy exhales. 'I blanked all sorts of things, forgot masses. Anyway, there you have it. I'm so sorry to have shocked you.'

'Yeah, you have done that.' Again, he looks out over the water. 'Does he know?'

'Who?'

'Cam.'

'No,' says Suzy.

'Are you going to tell him?'

'That, um... sort of depends a bit on you. There seems little point if we're not sure.'

Johnny nods. 'And Leo?'

'God, no! I mean I will if that's what I... um... we... decide. But no. I wanted to talk to you. First.'

'Thanks,' says Johnny.

'You know Cam teaches? Kids?'

'Really? Wow. It's a lot to get my head round...'

'I know. Like I said, I'm sorry.'

'A son... Good God...'

'I... er... can go if you like. I understand you probably need some time...' She pushes back her chair and stands.

'NO!' Johnny grabs her hand. 'I've only just found you again.'

She feels others in the café turn to stare. She sits back down and pulls her chair closer, so they won't be overheard. 'I honestly think you should take some time to digest it.'

'I don't need time to digest it. I mean I do, but it won't change how I feel. I love you, Suze. I always have and I always will. That we may well have a child together doesn't change that. If anything, it makes it stronger.'

'Well, yes, but...What about your girls?'

'I love my girls. And I did what was right. All those years. Alison, too, come to that. Our pregnancy wasn't what she wanted, either. But it happened and we dealt with it. We were good, in some ways, parenting together. I can never regret that we made that decision. But as a couple...?' Johnny shakes his head. 'We weren't so good.'

'Oh?'

'No.'

Fleetingly, Suzy thinks of Leo. *We weren't so good either,* she has a yen to admit.

'I'm so, so sorry for everything. That's what I was trying to express, in my letter... Although Alison getting pregnant, my divorce, losing my mum... All of it seems to pale into insignificance, compared to what you went through, Suze.'

Suzy catches her breath. She had not expected this, too. Not so directly, so fast. It is so terrible, even now, her voice fails her. She can only nod.

Once again Johnny reaches out and takes her hand. 'What a fool I am, I didn't mean to upset you.' She allows her palm to rest in his. The physical connection feels tender, exactly what she needs.

'There's no need to apologise.' She whispers. 'It's good for me to talk about it. I'm beginning to understand there is lots of stuff I never worked through.'

'Some things are so big maybe it's the only way we can cope. I avoided stuff too, like I said.'

'You know, losing Nate—he was my boyfriend—on *The Marchioness,* it tore out my heart.'

The words hang in the air, leaden. *I've never stated it so baldly,* Suzy realises.

Johnny falls silent and stares at the table. 'Were you and he... er... very serious?' He looks at her quickly, then away.

Suzy does not want to minimise her feelings for Nate, nor does she want it to sound as if he was the only love of her life. The truth is complicated. She has been in love several times. Each time was different, nuanced.

'Yes, I guess so. We were living together. But it wasn't just him. It was my friends too.' Friends have *always* been important to me, she thinks. She pictures Tash and Stef. Their lives were curtailed when they were so young. She wonders where they would be now.

'I never got the full story,' says Johnny quietly. 'That anniversary night, you didn't say much.'

'No. Though I remember we listened to Sade.' Suzy smiles. 'Is that why you put it on the CD?'

'Yeah,' says Johnny. 'That whole album has stood the test of time.'

'Mm, I'll bet.' For a few moments, Suzy can hear Sade singing once more. Her voice, so cool, yet full of yearning. She takes a deep breath. Exhales. 'So, *The Marchioness*. Do you want to know?'

'Only if you're happy to tell me.'

'Long as you don't mind if I get a bit teary.'

''Course I don't. Jeez, Suze, what kind of person do you think I am? I've seen you cry a million times!'

Suzy takes a deep breath, lets out a long exhalation and begins. 'There were four us.' She licks her index finger and draws a square on the metal table. 'Me and Nate and Tash and Stef. We shared a flat. We were all very close.' Then she dips her finger in the dregs of her tea and redraws the square, so it lingers a while on the surface. 'No, that doesn't explain it right. It wasn't like we were great philosophers or anything. We were out a lot. Party animals. Had a laugh. You know me. I love all that. We went to raves. Listened to *Soul II Soul*...You know that track was playing on the boat that night?'

'On *The Marchioness*?'

'Yes.'

'Gosh, I'm sorry. I'd never have included it on the compilation if I'd realised.'

'It doesn't matter. In some ways it's good to have it there. It would be weird not to have a track that marked it.'

'I just thought... it's a great song.'

'Yeah, well, they were from Brixton, their club nights were at *The Fridge*, and we lived near there... It's Tash it reminds me of most,' says Suzy. 'She used to swoosh her hair round and round when she danced to it like they do in the video. It has a great beat...'

'Yeah, and the strings, and the vocals on top. I can see you dancing, too.' Johnny's eyes mist over. 'I always liked the way you dance. Can I ask—and you don't have to answer this—did you talk to anyone at the time?'

Suzy shakes her head. 'I couldn't speak to the friends I normally would; they had died. There was Oliver—he was this guy who invited us to the party, but I didn't really know him—we only met that night—and he didn't really seem my sort of person...'

'What about the other people on board?'

'I think most of those who survived were just as messed up as me. There didn't seem any point in meeting up with a bunch of strangers going through the same thing.'

'Oh? I heard a many of the survivors helped support each other.'

'Where did you hear that?'

'I can't remember,' he says.

'I had Zelda.' Suzy nods. 'She was great. She still is great...' She hears her voice crack, and swallows to regain her composure. 'God knows why, but I lost touch with her for years...'

'Sometimes it's hard to face people who've seen us at our lowest.'

'Maybe...'

'Everyone deals with grief differently. The journey we make is a singular one. I've seen that over the last few months with Mum. Billie and Jodie seem much more able to express how they feel about their grandmother dying than Flo or Dad or me.' He blinks several times and once more looks away across the river.

Suzy steels herself to continue. 'The four of us were creative people with budding careers. Except Steff. He worked in the city. But I was a painter, doing well then...' She glances in the direction of the gallery, feels the stab of Julian's rejection once more. 'I lost my creativity after the accident. I turned in a very dark direction, had suicidal thoughts. My life was no longer recognisable. My parents had to support me financially.' She smiles at him wanly. 'Having Cam, it... um... changed that. Helped me find a way through.'

'I'm glad.'

'It means a lot that you're not mad at me. I can't tell you how much... And to think he may have been conceived on the anniversary...'

'Oh, er, yes...' Johnny runs his hands through his hair. 'I hadn't thought.'

'It sort of feels nice, a life for a life. But, you know, we have to be careful... There are a lot of people's feelings to consider.'

'Of course. Show me the photos again...'

She hands him the phone.

'He's a nice-looking lad.'

Suzy feels a burst of pride and joy. 'Of course, I think so.'

'It doesn't surprise me. He looks like much more like you than me. And I still think you're beautiful.'

Suzy blushes. 'Really?'

He shakes his head. 'Doh! I'm kidding. Yes, really.'

'And from what I remember, he seemed sensible enough.'

Suzy hoots. 'You mean he could deal with his mad mother?'

'That's not what I meant, no. Though come to think of it... It comes in handy.'

She gives him a playful slap, and he catches her hand, and then reaches towards her, and she leans in and slowly, tenderly, they kiss. At once Suzy remembers what it was like to kiss him, all those years ago. How it started on the day of the Silver Jubilee and how much she liked

♩ ♫ ♪ ♩

kissing him then and again and again, for years and years, whenever they were together.

'Shall we get the bill?' Johnny suggests. 'Bit unseemly, snogging in a café.'

'Specially at our age.' She laughs. 'Tell you what, it's getting chilly. Why don't we go inside?'

'Great idea,' says Johnny. 'There are those little alcoves with velvet seating. We can have a drink!'

'Ooh, yes,' says Suzy. 'A cocktail!'

They decamp to the interior, where the lighting is dim, and no one will give a hoot how old they are.

'I'm going to have a Margarita,' says Suzy, clapping her hands.

'You used to have them at Camden Palace.'

'I know,' she squeals. 'Gotta be done.'

Again, the pretty waitress takes their order and minutes later she returns with a tray.

'Perfect,' Suzy beams at her. It looks so elegant, with salt around the rim.

Johnny has a bottle of exotic beer, which the waitress opens and pours into a tilted glass.

'Cheers,' says Suzy when she has gone.

'Cheers,' says Johnny. They chink glasses.

I'm happy, thinks Suzy, two hours later, as they wend their way back to Johnny's flat.

'We're in luck,' Johnny had said. 'The girls are with their mother.' They turn a corner and the vast gothic exterior of Bath Abbey is upon them, stretching up, up into the dusky blue sky. It's lovely being with Johnny again. It feels OK. No, more than OK. It feels *right*.

Sure, there are enormous obstacles to overcome. But what can they do but take it one day at a time, being mindful of those they love and who love them? There is no great rush. A while back she received some money from the driver's insurance at long last, which has eased her situation. And the truth of what happened all those years ago doesn't have to come out in nightmare flashbacks or great big punches of information that will send everyone reeling. It can be managed carefully, considerately, slowly, with appreciation for what they have, and what they—and others—have lost.

With Johnny I don't have to worry or tiptoe or play games or run away, thinks Suzy. We are friends. Best friends.

I know he loves me.

Of this she is certain.

He always did.

55.

One Year Later, August 2019

Daisy moves carefully around the table, pouring four glasses of wine.

Zelda is poised to slide into her chair. 'Shall I serve?'

'If you don't mind.' Her girlfriend nods, and Zelda lifts the lid of the casserole. Steam billows from the pot, the waft of garlic is unmistakable.

'Smells lovely,' says Johnny. He looks up at Zelda. 'What are we having?'

'Chilli,' says Zelda. 'Tell us, then. Daisy's been on at me to explain. How *did* you two get back together?'

'Zelda says it all started with a CD,' Daisy urges. 'Really?'

Suzy nods. 'Yes, if you want to say it started anywhere, then that's probably fair.'

'How intriguing. What was on it?'

'Music,' says Johnny, simply.

'Yeah, but not just any old music. It was a mix tape,' says Suzy. 'Johnny had made it for me years ago and came across it again. Didn't you?'

'Yep,' says Johnny. 'I found it at my parents.'

'Only it was a cassette. And he burned it onto a CD. We can listen to it if you like,' offers Suzy. 'I've got the playlist on my phone.'

'Ooh do let's!' Daisy claps her hands.

'You might not like all of it,' warns Johnny. 'They're not exactly tracks picked for eating supper...'

But Suzy has already flicked and found it. And to sit there with another couple listening to the songs flow from the opening crackle of *Starman* through the frenzy of *God Save the Queen* to the soulful sax and vocals of Sade, it seems to make sense of Suzy's relationship to Johnny in a way that nothing else can. Beats change, vocals shift, moods alter, years pass, and yet the two of them are together, sitting opposite one another, smiling in Zelda and Daisy's flat in East London. As they listen, Suzy picks up the story.

'Then, at Johnny's mum's funeral we talked a fair bit, didn't we?' Suzy puts down her fork and reaches for Johnny's hand to give it a squeeze.

'Mm.'

'I guess it was, I dunno, a few weeks after that...'

'In that café, wasn't it Suze? In Bath.'

'That's when we kissed,' admits Suzy.

'I still really fancied her,' confesses Johnny.

'Aw,' says Daisy.

It was in the way he touched my arm, the way he concentrated on me as I spoke. I had all his attention, Suzy remembers. We were both waiting for something to happen. He held me surprisingly tightly, as we walked back to his place. It felt so nice. I kissed him once we got into the flat, she recalls, with the kind of fierceness I had forgotten existed. A light had turned on inside me. One which had been off for months, nay, *years*. Other than that brief interlude with Glenn.

'Well, thank fuck for that,' says Zelda. She turns to Daisy. 'Suzy had me really worried when she said she'd been in touch with Glenn.'

'Who's Glenn?' asks Daisy.

'Oh, no one important,' says Zelda.

That night Suzy and Johnny hunker down on Zelda and Daisy's sofa bed together. Suzy tucks herself into Johnny's armpit, the way she always does when they're sharing a bed together. She'd like to touch him everywhere, yet she's conscious Zelda and Daisy are right next door, in earshot. Plus, it's a big day tomorrow. They make do with whispering.

'Shall we listen to your song again?' suggests Johnny. 'We can each have one earphone.'

'Let's.'

Johnny's fumbles with her phone, passes her the earpiece and in seconds Suzy is being transported by the gentle guitar and deep, melancholy voice of Leonard Cohen. And as he sings again of how a woman with her name lures him to her place by the river for tea and oranges, and how he's touched her perfect body with his mind, Suzy listens and is lulled. That the song is about water and sailors and drowning is part of its beauty, as are the heroes in the seaweed who are leaning out for love and the sun that pours like honey. And gradually slumber carries her away on the wings of its backing vocals, and the garbage and flowers in the lyrics enter her dreams.

When she wakes, the earpiece is still in her ear, and the other earpiece is still in Johnny's, so they are connected by a thread of white wire, and sunlight is streaming between the gaps in the blinds, beckoning them to surface to make the most of what lies ahead. As if by intuition, Johnny wakes simultaneously, and looks down at her as she looks up.

'Morning Suze.'

And she smiles at his beautiful familiar face, with his big cow eyes and still floppy brown hair.

'Morning,' she says.

'How are you feeling?' Zelda is on the doorstep.

'Shit scared,' admits Suzy. She clenches her jaw to prevent her teeth from chattering.

Zelda takes both her hands. 'You'll be okay,' she declares firmly, bouncing Suzy's arms up and down. 'You're an old hand at this surviving malarkey. You got through a night alone in Newbury jail. You'll breeze through this.'

'You can always leave,' says Daisy. 'The most important thing is to take care of yourself.'

'No, she can't,' says Zelda.

Suzy suppresses a smile. She can't imagine Zelda in a relationship without this sort of dynamic. She was born to take charge.

'I won't leave,' Suzy promises. 'Though Daisy's right. The most important thing is to look after myself.'

'I'll keep an eye on her,' says Johnny.

'You do that,' says Zelda sternly. 'And you're meeting this elderly lady there?'

'Yup. We're going to walk over the bridge together.'

'I think it's a really good idea of yours to go,' says Daisy.

'It was Johnny's suggestion,' says Suzy.

'I've always been aware of the anniversary,' he says. 'I thought if we were going to do it, then this year should be the one.'

'Good luck.' Zelda drops Suzy's hands and opens her arms to give her a hug. 'Still a short arse,' she says over Suzy's head. They step apart. 'We'll be thinking of you.'

'Thanks,' says Suzy. 'And thanks for letting us stay.'

'It's really nice that you two got back together,' says Zelda.

'You old softie.' Daisy leans her head on Zelda's shoulder.

'Trust me. Johnny is by far the best of her exes. You should have seen some of the others. Well dodgy.' Zelda flashes Suzy a knowing smile. 'But when did she ever listen to me?'

Suzy blushes. Some things are best kept between me and Zelda, she thinks, appreciating that Zelda feels the same. Greenham is ancient history. Neither of them wants to hurt they people they love.

'We're glad we got back together too.' Johnny pulls Suzy in close. 'Aren't we?'

'We are,' says Suzy.

'And it's cool you're taking it slow about Cam,' says Zelda. 'I think you're right to give pause to finding out for sure.'

'Mm,' says Suzy. 'He's very close to Leo.'

'That's a good thing,' says Zelda. 'You're seeing him later?'

'And his girlfriend,' says Johnny. 'We're going to their flat.'

'Keep up the painting,' says Daisy. 'Your new stuff looks great.'

'Thanks,' says Suzy. Daisy's enthusiasm means a lot to her. Currently Suzy is experimenting, feeling her way into a new style.

'I hate to say it,' says Zelda, checking her watch. 'But you really do need to go. It'll take you half an hour, minimum, from here.'

'C'mon,' Johnny urges. 'Don't want to be late.'

They hurry up the escalator and through the barriers, but she is already waiting by the ticket machines. In a bright turquoise dress, she is white-haired and much smaller than Suzy remembers, so that the bunch of flowers she is carrying appears nearly as big as she is.

'Cynthia?'

'Oh me dear girl!' Cynthia peers closely into Suzy's face and Suzy assumes her eyesight must be poor, but then she reaches a bony hand and pinches both Suzy's cheeks. 'IT IS GOOD TO SEE YOU,' she declares, voice echoey due to the tiled surround of the underground station. 'What took you so long?'

'I don't live in London these days,' says Suzy.

'You're not dat far,' says Cynthia. 'Near Bath, your email said?'

'Yes.'

'You don't ever come back for da theatre, da shoppin'?'

'Not much. I found it hard to return, to be honest. Only recently managed it. Now we tend to head to Battersea, mainly, where my son lives.'

'But look what you've been missin!' Cynthia waves with a flourish and starts walking, and as Suzy takes in their surroundings, she can see what Cynthia means. There is still the classical dome of St Paul's Cathedral, but it is dwarfed by a dizzying array of alien shapes that thrust upward to the sky. 'Dat is the Gherkin,' Cynthia tells her. 'And they call dat the Walkie Talkie.'

'I recognise that one.' Suzy points at a building with so many ducts and lifts on the exterior it appears inside-out.

'I should hope so, girl. Dat is the Lloyd's building.'

'And the Shard, right?' Suzy points straight ahead.

Johnny laughs and nudges Cynthia. 'You know she's an artist?'

'You needs to do your 'omework!'

'I do,' Suzy admits.

All around are gleaming steel structures and great expanses of glass. The entire silhouette of the city appears to have altered so much it looks more like New York or Tokyo than the London she remembers. It is easier to find it so changed; that it is daylight helps, too. Nonetheless when she sees the river stretched before her, grey and churning, Suzy closes her eyes for a moment to steady herself.

Cynthia thrusts out an arm. 'Gimme your hand.' She reaches for her.

Suzy is grateful. 'Let's give these to Johnny,' she says, and he takes the flowers.

As they venture onto the bridge, Suzy can feel her palm is clammy in contrast to Cynthia's dry, cold skin, but the slow click of Cynthia's heels propels her forwards, and half-way across, she feels able to look around tentatively to get her bearings.

'I think it was there.' She points eastwards, upriver to show Johnny.

Seeing it now, she can't quite believe she is back where it happened. Little waves twinkle in the sunlight. There are seagulls, boats on the water, tourists on walkway to the south. Nevertheless, the north bank is a long way. *I swam across to the other side,* she thinks. She can sense the pull of the current, the rush of the tide.

Johnny comes to stand behind her and wraps his arms around her. She leans back into him and exhales slowly. She realises she had tensed every muscle. *It's OK,* she tells herself. *I am safe.*

'You 'er 'usband?' Cynthia asks Johnny, as they set off walking again.

Suzy shakes her head. 'Johnny's my boyfriend.'

'*Boyfriend* eh? I wants one of those.' Cynthia guffaws.

Suzy is tentative. 'Is... um... William not coming?'

'William dead,' says Cynthia bluntly. 'And good riddance.' This time her laughter is protracted and wicked; she knows she is breaking a taboo.

'Suzy?' A deep voice calls from behind them, and Suzy turns to see a man of about her own age, dressed in a blazer and jeans, running with difficulty to catch them up. 'It's Oliver.'

'Oh!' Of course. She recognises him now. Those ruddy cheeks, the striped shirt. These days he has a sizeable paunch.

'Cynthia said she hoped you were coming.' He is panting.

'You know each other?'

'We met at the public enquiry,' says Oliver.

'We come 'ere every year,' says Cynthia. 'Those of us who survived are left, still wondering why, still missing our loved ones. Yet this is a good thing. Considering. We is all suffering the same.'

Suzy is humbled. 'I had no idea so many people would be here. And, I admit, I—I thought you would be angry with me.'

'Me? Whatever gave you dat idea?'

Suzy casts her mind back. 'Maybe I assumed it,' she says eventually. 'I imagined it, because I survived, and your daughter didn't.'

'Yuh silly girl!' says Cynthia. 'Why mi want two dead, not one?'

Put that way, it does seem entirely irrational.

'Sometimes di hardest person to forgive is yourself.'

On the south bank, a crowd is beginning to gather. A trio of middle-aged women go to the railing and throw petals into the water. An elderly couple, about Cynthia's age, cling to each other, their faces etched with pain. A group of friends whisper together, others stand alone and solemn, shielding their candles from the wind.

The Bishop of Southwark says a few words. It has been thirty years, he tells them, to the day. Three decades since the dark waters of the Thames swept so many away.

There are tears, the boats on the river sound their horns.

Cynthia goes to the railing with her giant bouquet. She tucks it under her arm and one by one plucks each bloom to hurl with deliberate intent over the side. Some flowers fall at speed as if they are diving, others are lifted by the wind and break apart, petals fluttering before they slowly give way to gravity.

Suzy and Johnny watch a while until Oliver, who remains close by, clears his throat. 'I, um, brought you something,' he says gruffly to Suzy, out of Cynthia's earshot.

Suzy is immediately on her guard. This is not what she expected. She is eager to avoid a fuss.

He rummages in his blazer pocket, retrieves a small box then checks over his shoulder, wary he might be jostled. 'You need to be careful. Open it this way.' He demonstrates how to release the lid. His fingers are beefy, a contrast to the tiny button. He passes the box to her.

Wondering what on earth it can be, Suzy opens it and gasps.

'A four leafed clover,' she says.

'What is it?' asks Johnny, coming to look.

He leans in. 'Wow, so it is.'

She looks up at Oliver. His cheeks are bright pink.

'It's the original one,' he says, sheepish.

Suzy is at a loss for words. There is even a loop and a chain, so she can wear it as a necklace. 'I can't believe you kept it all this time!' She manages to say, eventually. 'It still looks so green.'

'It dried. Then I got it set pretty much straight away.'

'Nate found it in Battersea Park,' she tells Johnny. 'That night. I left it at your flat, didn't I?' she says to Oliver.

'You did,' says Oliver. 'I thought you might come to the service when Princess Diana laid the memorial.'

'I'm so sorry,' says Suzy. She cannot even remember when that was, but it feels like a lifetime ago.

'Do you like it? I wasn't sure about the setting.'

'I think it's lovely,' says Suzy. She lifts it from the box. 'Can you put it on me?' she asks Johnny.

'Sure,' says Johnny.

As Johnny fumbles with the catch, she says, 'Thank you, Oliver. Thank you so much. It means more than I can say. I will wear it often, I promise.'

Oliver's face is aflame with embarrassment and relief. She senses he has been holding his breath throughout the whole conversation.

'You're done,' says Johnny, so she reaches for Oliver.

'I'm glad we made it,' she says, and they embrace, each inhaling the unfamiliar scent of the other. 'Better two left than none of us, eh?' Her voice cracks.

Then they break apart and they move to the railing, alongside Cynthia.

And then, in a rush, Suzy is on that precipice again, staring into the yawning deep with the black waters swirling and the boat sinking beneath her feet. She blinks furiously, jerks her head up, and she is gazing into the sky. She is atop the Rice Krispies' climbing frame in the garden of number 32, balancing on the highest rung, and it's a rocket, and Johnny is bellowing *Starman* next to her while she watches the clouds and tries to get her head around the notion that higher and much further away there are stars, which are not visible because of the sunlight. Time speeds up and she is watching a Red Admiral open and close its dappled wings and her lips are tingling from her first kiss, and with a whoosh she is thrust forward again, as if she is aboard HG Wells' *Time Machine*. And she is at The Hacienda, hypnotised by the pulsing lights as she dances to *Blue Monday*; next second she is clinging to Glenn with the road only inches from her feet and air beating like a drum against her new leather jacket. No sooner that, than she is feeling the chill of the wind on top of the silo, whooping in victory with Zelda and Yoshi and believing they might change the world. And now time is slowing...

She is with Tash and Stef watching football on their tiny telly, and Zelda is shouting at the linesman, and Suzy is sneaking glances at the friend of Stef's who has just arrived. With a lurch she is back on the precipice, but it is as if Johnny has felt her body stiffen, for he tightens his grip around her with one arm and lifts the other to stroke her hair, and she realises she is here, in the sunshine, in 2019, and 1989 is part, but not all, of her story.

'You OK?' murmurs Johnny.

She nods because it is hard to find any words, yet she wants to communicate she is getting through this, just as she got through all those other days and nights that led to this one. She will get through more days and nights, and some are bound to be hard, because life can be cruel as well as beautiful, and she is getting older, and so is he, and the world seems to be spinning faster and bringing their end nearer.

But we are not done yet, she wants to say, we have children and people we love and more to give. If we were flowers, like the ones the mourners have been throwing, we would be petals that catch on a breeze and fly thither and whither as if dancing, or butterflies opening and closing their wings in gentle rhythm, or two starmen atop a climbing frame, laughing.

THE END

Author's Note

The characters in this novel are fictitious, but the major events described are not.

In August 2019, the 30th anniversary of *The Marchioness* disaster was remembered in a vigil next to the Thames. Survivors and families of the victims joined a procession from Southwark Cathedral to Bankside, where a short service was held. The names of those who had died were read out and petals thrown into the water. Boats from the Royal National Lifeboat Institute (RNLI) and the fire and rescue service and Port of London Authority gathered on the river for the crews to pay respects.

When the tragedy happened in 1989, London did not have a coastguard or lifeboats on the Thames. In 2002, as part of recommendations to improve safety on the river, the RNLI set up four lifeboat stations at Gravesend, Tower Pier, Chiswick Pier, and Teddington. Since then, they have been the busiest lifeboat stations in the RNLI network. Lessons learned from the tragedy mean dredgers now move in and out of the Thames and are more aware of other ships and craft due to improved navigation and lookouts.

I started this book in 2019, just before the pandemic hit. As I finish, over four years later, global events continue to impact the world beyond our worst imaginings. I pray these times will pass and, although they are certain to leave us changed, they serve to encourage us to be compassionate.

Meanwhile, in London, not far from the site of *The Marchioness* disaster, a memorial to the victims can be found in the nave of Southwark Cathedral. Every year a service of remembrance is held for the 51 people who lost their lives.

Their average age was 22.

This book is dedicated to them.

The Playlist

Thank you for reading this novel. Should you like to listen to Johnny's compilation, it can be found on Spotify, under *Searching for Mr Yesterday*. I hope you enjoy it as much as I enjoyed compiling it. It's the soundtrack of a generation.

David Bowie: Starman 1972
David Bowie: Rock 'n' Roll Suicide 1972
The Sex Pistols: God Save the Queen 1977
Blondie: Hanging on the Telephone 1979
The Beatles: Come Together 1969
Leonard Cohen: Suzanne 1967
Siouxsie & The Banshees: Spellbound 1981
The Shangri-Las: Leader of the Pack 1964
The New Order: Blue Monday 1983
Frankie Goes to Hollywood: Two Tribes 1984
Soul II Soul: Back to Life 1989
Sade: Your Love is King 1984

A Letter from the Author

Dear Reader

That you are reading this letter suggests that you may have finished *Searching for Mr. Yesterday,* and I'd like to take this opportunity to thank you so much for joining me on this journey. Whether you're reading on your phone or tablet, or are flicking the pages of a printed book, I hope the novel has entertained and moved you.

It's the first novel I've published in a few years, because recently I've been focusing on my non-fiction series, and it takes me considerably longer to write and edit a novel of 100,000 words than it does to write a non-fiction guide that's only half as long. For these reasons, I'd hugely appreciate your feedback. I would be grateful if you could leave a review on Amazon or GoodReads, or on your blog or preferred choice of social media. Share wherever you think it most helpful to other readers. I often put my reviews of other author's books on Facebook and perhaps you like to do that too. And if I like a book jacket, I'll photograph it for Instagram. But we're all different, so I leave it with you.

If you'd like to join my mailing list, you can sign up via my author website below. I only send about half a dozen newsletters a year, so you won't be inundated with messages, and your email address will never be shared. Plus, you can unsubscribe at any time.

www.sarahrayner.com

Warm regards

Sarah

♩ ♫ ♪ ♩

P.S. I've already started the follow-up to *Searching for Mr Yesterday*, so you can rest assured the gap between this book and my seventh novel will not be as long. I love hearing from readers and the best way to get touch is via my newsletter, or via

Instagram @thecreativepumpkin
Facebook www.facebook.com/creativepumpkin

Acknowledgements

People often ask if my novels are drawn from experience, and the honest answer is 'Of course they are.' That doesn't mean my books are autobiographical: they're not. My husband didn't die on a train like Simon in *One Moment, One Morning*, I've never been through IVF like Lou and Cath in *The Two Week Wait* and the experiences of Suzy in *Searching for Mr Yesterday* are not my own.

I do, however, have first hand experience of anxiety and depression and feel passionately that the problems of mental illness are very real and immensely painful. I believe mental health should be taken as seriously as physical health, yet still, in 2023, it often isn't. This is partly because the symptoms are often not visible, and it's also because these topics are hard for many of us to talk about. If reading about Suzy's PTSD helps others understand what flashbacks are like, and how scary reliving trauma on repeat can be, then the four years I've spent writing this book will have been worthwhile.

Many people have helped me develop and hone this novel, and I'd like to thank my agent Gaia Banks and her assistant Alba Arnau at Sheil Land Associates, family members Polly Rayner and Emma Hall, and dear friends Laura Wilkinson, Niccy Lowit, Rosalind Georgeson,Dave Cuff, Becky Faith and many more, who read drafts of the novel and buoyed my spirits as I wrote. My friend and page designer Leigh Forbes has worked closely with me over recent months to produce this beautiful edition, and Jonathan Roberts has designed the stunning cover.

My poppet of an audio producer, Pete Stannard produced the audiobook with me.

Last but by no means least, a huge thank you must go to my darling husband, Tom. He has had the year from hell in 2022, experiencing his own trauma in a cycling accident. Still, he has remained grounded and funny, kind-hearted and physically determined. There is a great deal of Tom in Johnny – they both love cycling, music and are good with women whose names begin with S for a start.

Alongside this novel, I have also recently revised and updated my popular *Making Friends* series of non-fiction books – *Making Friends with Anxiety, Making Friends with the Menopause* and *Making Peace with Depression* – and you can read about them on the following pages. I dearly hope new readers find these books supportive too.

Making Friends with Anxiety:
A warm, supportive little book to help ease worry and panic
by Sarah Rayner

Does anxiety have a hold on you and your life? Do panic and worry tend to dominate every moment? In this friendly and supportive little book, bestselling author Sarah Rayner draws on her own experience of living with an anxiety disorder and shares the life-changing coping techniques that have helped her manage her anxiety and panic at home, at work and in all areas of life.

'Simple, lucid advice on how to accept anxiety.'
    —Matt Haig, *Sunday Times* bestselling author of *Reasons to Stay Alive*

'Reassuring, informative and written in a kind, inclusive tone, I cannot recommend this book highly enough.'   —Josie Lloyd,
    Sunday Times bestselling author of *The Cancer Women's Running Club*

'I am not a reader, but I ended up loving reading this book!!
100% recommended!!!'   —Amazon reviewer, 5 stars

'Provided lots of comfort during one of the worst periods of anxiety in my life.'   —Amazon reviewer, 5 stars

'A very helpful book... Everyone should own a copy.'
                    —Amazon reviewer, 5 stars

**Available in all formats (eBook, audio and paperback)
on Amazon worldwide from only $2.99.**

Making Peace with Depression:
A warm, supportive little book to lift low mood and ease despair
by Sarah Rayner, Kate Harrison, Dr Patrick Fitzgerald

Is depression or low mood stopping you from living life to its fullest? Are you feeling alone, struggling to find a waythrough? *Making Peace with Depression* is here to help.

In this comforting and supportive little book, bestselling authors Sarah Rayner and Kate Harrison, with Dr Patrick Fitzgerald, draw on their own experiences of living with depression and share their life-changing coping techniques that have helped them manage low mood and depressive episodes.

They explain that actively trying to fight your depression can actually prolong your suffering – instead, making peace with difficult emotions and compassionately accepting them can restore mental health and happiness.

'I ABSOLUTELY loved this... so practical, so down to earth, so non-preachy and so relatable.'   —Amazon reviewer, 5 stars

'Amazing read!!!!!... I laughed and I cried as I can relate to almost something in every page.'   —Amazon reviewer, 5 stars

'A gem. Full of compassion, understanding, humour and practical advice... Read this book and you feel you've found a friend. A real lifeline for those living with depression.'   —Amazon reviewer, 5 stars

Available in all formats (eBook, audio and paperback)
on Amazon worldwide from only $3.99

Making Friends with the Menopause:
A clear and comforting guide to support you as your body changes
by Sarah Rayner, Dr Patrick Fitzgerald

Night sweats, mood swings, weight gain – the menopause can be a challenging time, leaving us feeling isolated and as if we're losing touch with ourselves. But you are not alone – *Making Friends with the Menopause* is here to help.

'Brilliant and makes you feel like you are not alone!... like talking to a friend. I felt so much better after reading it, and keep dipping into it when I need a reminder.'   —Amazon reviewer, 5 stars

'Superb... can't praise it enough. Made me realise I am normal, thank goodness!'   —Amazon reviewer, 5 stars

'Incredibly helpful and informative... so helpful I can't recommend it enough.'   —Amazon reviewer, 5 stars

'Comforting words and real-life examples, I felt much better simply having read this.'   —Amazon reviewer, 5 stars

**Available in all formats (eBook, audio and paperback)
on Amazon worldwide from only $3.99.**

Threads of Life

A unique collection of sewing advice, memories, mantras and more, from TV's favourite fashion guru

by John Scott (author) and Sarah Rayner (editor)

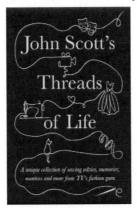

'John's book is jam packed with energy and intrigue, a page-turner from the first to the last page!' —**Bonnie Langford**, Actor and singer

'Gorgeous John! He always does everything with such style and such grace. I love him!' —The late, great author, **Jackie Collins**

'We need John Scott running the world. Until he does, thankfully, we have this book.' —**Sarah Greene**, TV presenter

ABOUT THIS BOOK

John Scott has lived a varied life, but whether it's behind the scenes of a regional theatre, working on costumes for Hollywood movies such as *Interview with a Vampire* or *Four Weddings and a Funeral* or presenting TV shows like *This Morning* with Richard and Judy, his love of sewing and the humble needle and thread has run, like a rich seam, through everything he does.

As a costume supervisor, stylist, fashion guru and lead expert on sewing TV, John has gained a catalogue of unrivalled expertise and here he weaves together his knowledge of sewing, quilting and fashion with eclectic stories from his extraordinary career.

Available on Amazon worldwide (paperback and audio), starting at $2.99.

♩ ♫ ♪ ♩

Made in United States
North Haven, CT
26 March 2024

50419961R10205